THE BOATMAN

SARAH BETH HUNT

GRASSY WATERS PUBLICATIONS

FOR MY PARENTS,

who told me I could follow my dreams...

Copyright © 2018 by Sarah Beth Hunt

All rights reserved.

No part of this book may be reproduced in any form or by any electronic or mechanical means, including information storage and retrieval systems, without written permission from the author, except for the use of brief quotations in a book review.

PREFACE

For many years, Petro had imagined that he would die by swallowing a diamond. His death would be glorious, he thought. It would really be remembered. A glamorous death fitting of his important and unique life. He would wear his favourite black wool jacket with the bright blue stitching sent for during his age of maps and tales of adventure. It had been bought from the market on the isle of Joon, and Petro was certain it would reveal how, despite appearances, he had actually been a worldly man.

He would sit in front of the map, crumbling with decades of misuse and spreading out with its wild lands across the dining table, and then he would swallow the diamond. He wanted his last meditation on life to be of this map that charted the secret contours of his lost dreams. Then slowly the blood would pour red and boiling across the age-stained map like a river of new hope or final absolution. Later when they found him they would all wonder at this great man, this sage whom they had known all their lives but never truly understood, whose face they recognised but had so obviously failed to grasp.

And yet, when death finally came to Petro, it was not the glorious ending for which he had always believed he was destined. It came not from the spectacular edges of a rough cut diamond, but from the poison of an old fish, kept too long in the heat, which led to days where Petro clung to the edges of the toilet, drowning in the stench of sickness. And silently, it crept up on him one afternoon as he sat in a heap in his armchair, too sick to contemplate the meaning of his life, too weak even to conjure up the prophetic sequence of his most significant moments which should have flashed before his eyes revealing the ultimate meaning of his small existence.

Death happened like this—one moment he was breathing, his chest labouring away, his eyes glassy as he stared at the nearby window but not to the sea beyond it, and the next minute he wasn't breathing. And that was that.

If he had been lucid in those final moments, Petro might have wondered at the great gulf that had widened over the years between his small secluded life, which stretched out as grey and flat as an old winter's sky, and the life of inflated colours that he had always meant to live. If he had been lucid, Petro might have wondered where it had gone, the elusive, irretrievable life he had dreamed of. Instead, Petro took his last step to join the decomposing remains of his neglected dreams and left these larger, heavier questions behind, leaning against the doorstep, waiting at the threshold of a long forgotten house for another who would return to find them.

PART 1: THE ISLAND

1

The day the boatman arrived on the island, he caught everyone except Isla by surprise. At the exact moment that he crossed the horizon, Isla was sitting as usual on the stone wall that overlooked the pale sand dunes, watching the fishermen paddle their small boats back to the island and haul them up to rest on the folds of sand. Her wild dark hair danced languidly in the breeze as she swung her legs in the numbing silence of some daydream and her silver eyes peered across the blinding glassy sea contemplating magic and places far away.

Over and over the waves rolled peacefully against the sandy shore, the endless whispering that was the backdrop of island life. For as long as she could remember, Isla had whispered back, willing these waves to reveal the secrets of their long voyage, what wonders they had seen, what magical lands they had brushed past before reaching the shores of her island. But the language of waves is not the language of little girls, and Isla could not make out the mysteries they might have revealed to her. And so instead Isla simply sat, twirling the stem of a red hibiscus she had picked from the front porch of her house between her two fingers and thinking of all the things she might do if only she could cross the sea.

The island where Isla had been born was surrounded by a wide stretch of sea which rocked and crashed in on itself and was silent for a journey of three days by boat before it reached the shores of the mainland. And because the islanders could not see the mainland from where they stood, and the mainlanders could not see the island even on the clearest day, both believed that they were separate, independent. Just as people had for generations.

As for the island, local fishermen often called it the Great Pearl because when they were far out at sea, the island shimmered an incandescent shade from the rows of blooming losa and gave them hope. But Isla had never been far enough away from the island to know it from this view, as a thing apart from herself. To her it was the island, and nothing more.

It had all begun one day during the rains of that eternal blue year that her mother had died. They had stood together amongst the rows of losa, and Isla had reached up to grasp her father's hand and had pointed out to sea.

"What's there?" she had asked.

"The sea, of course," Petro had replied.

But Isla had shaken her head, "then what?"

Petro, startled from some dismal reverie of his late wife and his own empty bed, had sighed and then told his first lie to this young daughter, knowing it would not be his last.

"Nothing," he said, "nothing lies beyond the sea."

So perhaps the seed of this yearning to know the world beyond the sea had not begun with Isla at all, but was born out of the great lie that her father told, because Petro had wanted the island — which also meant he himself — to be the border of Isla's world. And to be enough.

But Isla had not believed the lie, and so as time passed the questions came, again and again welling up unbidden from that empty place in her heart.

"What does the world look like?"

"What's beyond the sea?"

So that even when Petro began to tell her, "the mainland is there, a treacherous and barbaric place," these fool answers could not stem the flood. Isla learned from her friend Lucas, a trader's son, that it was the mainland kingdom that lay beyond the sea, and that long ago it had controlled all the lands of the known world and all the islands in the sea. The mainland had given the islanders their language, she was told, but it had been unable to dislodge the deep knowledge islanders held of themselves.

Hearing these things, the first tangible evidence of life beyond her island, was like hearing a clear bell ringing out through silence, and she had run to Tomas, as she always did when a new idea had raised a spark in her mind. "What do you think is out there, beyond the sea?" she had asked this boy she loved most of all. But Tomas had simply shrugged. To him it was an unanswerable question — who could say what was beyond the sea? Even his father did not know such things.

Over the years, when a certain blue mood fell upon her, Isla would ask this question again and again, "What is there beyond the sea?"

But the people around her would simply reply, "*Anshallo*, Isla." Leave it alone. Be satisfied.

If her mood was truly dark, she would protest, "There must be something else out there!" Then their faces would pinch and they would say, "What are you, a trader that you must know these things? We are here and that is that. Why does there have to be anything out there, beyond the sea?"

Why she asked these questions? Even Isla didn't know. For how could a child know when even her father did not, that these questions of life beyond the sea were not really questions of the island and the mainland, nor of the difference between a familiar and an uncommon life, but were in fact the first stirrings of a young soul who had not yet lost the desire to know why it had come to this life, why it breathed in and out with such passion, and where its place was in this vast universe.

For Isla's part, she only knew that she felt a great emptiness, and because she had not yet lived long enough to fill this emptiness with the quest for wealth or status or love, Isla could only gaze along the edge of the island as the shoreline wound out to her left and to her right and disappeared into the shifting waters of the sea and repeat again and again — "There must be more than this."

They began to call her *ubash*. When she had asked Dari up at the café what that meant he had laughed in his low, bellowing way and told her, "It means you are discontent, Isla-ja. It means you aren't happy being like everyone else." And Isla had wondered why anyone would be happy being the same as everyone else.

At home, Isla had interrupted the warm indigo scent of the evening and asked her father what it meant to be *ubash*. "Well," Petro said, looking up curiously from the boiling pot of losa tea. "It means you are like Ubash who was the first son of Tali and was always dissatisfied with what life offered him. It means," he nodded at her meaningfully, "that you aren't happy with what life has given you."

He paused and the cicadas had filled the silence between them with a comforting cacophony and the boiling of the tea had diverted this great weight of words. "Perhaps it means you are too selfish to appreciate what the world has given you," Petro spoke and fell silent again, and his brow creased with sharp, uneven lines as he ruminated on some present disappointment or past regret. And because Isla could not discern which it was, she was also silent in that sinking night and drummed out an old tune with her fingers on the broad wooden dining table.

Here on the island of her birth Isla knew all the answers to her life. She knew the steady roots of the banyan trees and the habits of the bands of monkeys who lived in its lofty branches. She knew the secret fresh water springs, the migration of the black-faced gulls, the salty taste of the wind before a storm. She knew which of her friends would become fishermen, which harvesters, which losa growers, which traders and tillers. She could not remember a time when she hadn't known where a path would lead, what might be around the corner of a cliff, or whose voice was calling out after her in the dusk.

And yet it felt to Isla as if she was always wearing someone else's clothes. Or as if she was stepping in another's footsteps pressed firmly into the sand, the way she had once skipped after her father along the shore of the sea. The life stretching out before her felt used and smelled suspiciously familiar — but of someone else — and it seemed to Isla, even at the age of ten, as if she knew how each step on the path of her life would feel before she took it, where each contour lay, and how it would inevitably end.

Then, in that white morning light, the boatman arrived.

As Isla stood, balancing for a moment along the stone wall, worn smooth by generations of islanders who had also sat in that same place over uncountable years watching the sea, awaiting loved ones' return, meeting lovers after dark, escaping arguments and telling stories about the stars, his boat crossed the horizon.

For a brief moment, Isla glanced back and saw the bright red bags of the losa harvesters on her own land, weaving at an imperceptible pace along the rows that flushed a familiar purple hue and sent the soft fragrance of losa wafting through the humid sea air. And then she looked again out to sea, and she saw his boat rise up clear on the horizon, sails full of the winds of destiny, and it was a boat unlike any the islanders had seen. Fishermen turned from their glistening lines to point and call, "Look, look. What's that on the horizon?" and islanders began to gather at the stone wall, peering out into the glistening mirror of the sea.

Yet despite her leaden feet which had swung lethargically like pendulums keeping time, and despite the hundreds of days she had sat on that very spot staring into the empty sea and counting over and over the seventeen small boats floating in the distance, Isla was entirely unsurprised to see this new boat, larger than any other, gliding towards the island. While crowds gathered on the sandy shores and pressed against her on the stone wall, a wide smile spread across Isla's face and she could only whisper, "At last."

2

"Did you see him?" Isla asked Jaro as he knelt pulling weeds in his garden in the shade of the lighthouse. Looking up at her, Isla could see from his smile that he was thinking many things which he would never say to her. "I have not. Tomas said you were both at the shore when he arrived." He turned back to the earth, working slowly, gently, as if he were tending to something that required more than work. "Well, are you going to tell me about him?" Jaro asked, and although Isla knew he asked because he loved her and not because he was interested in this stranger, she began again with her tale of the strange man, the fire colour of his hair, the strange way he clapped his hands as he spoke.

Above them both near the edge of the cliff, Tomas stood in the evening light, his hands held high as he signalled to the gulls he was training. They swarmed above him like a living cloud, diving as he called to them to catch pieces of fish. It was a beautiful sight and even with this exciting tale to tell, Isla was brought several times to silence as she watched the gulls draw daring arcs in the orange sky.

"It's time, Isla." Jaro's voice was soft and deep, as it always was.

"I know," she said, but still her hands dug into the soil of the small garden as if she were clutching at the earth itself. Clutching at her story. And at the one who cared enough to listen. Jaro's hand rested against her back, "Your da will worry if you're not back before dark."

"I don't know why," Isla muttered, but she stood up, brushing her hands across her bare, soil-stained knees.

"Bye, Isla. See you tomorrow," Tomas called to her.

"Bye," she called back, feeling her voice waver, as it always did at this treacherous hour. Then she stepped out alone into the twilight air and down the narrow path through the underbrush that had been laid by a thousand footsteps and led unmistakably to her house.

After a time, she turned and looked back up the hill to where the lighthouse stood like a white one-eyed watchman, and it seemed to Isla that the lighthouse was staring not out to sea as it should, but directly at her instead, and it made her feel strange and safe and part of a greater mystery that had no name. At the top of the hill she could see Tomas calling to his gulls, and she listened to them call back to him. And then Isla saw Jaro, also standing at the brow of the hill, watching her, and she raised one hand slowly, as slow as the twilight creeps towards darkness, and she saw his broad hand rise up as if to say, "I see you, Isla-ja." Then she turned back to the path before her and began to walk home.

The dusk brought many memories to Isla as she walked, for this was its special gift, and she thought of the boatman, the look of his red, uncommon face, the things he would have seen of the world, and the stories he could tell her if only she could find the courage to ask.

Isla walked without seeing. This was her island, and she

knew it as she knew her own body, for she had already laid many memories upon its face. Passing the banyan grove, she thought of the fort she, Eva and Lucas had made among its great root pillars the week Tomas had been so ill. Then, as she traced the outer edge of a valley on a tract of Lott's land, another memory came to her from some unknown place, and Isla remembered the day she and Tomas had tried to dig a hole through the centre of the world. Although it had been only a few years ago, to Isla it seemed like an age, and she remembered the day, which had been so full of hope, with a sadness that she did not understand.

It had been hot, as summer days were, and a day with no school to bind them indoors or chores to occupy them. The idea had come to her that morning as she sat on the wide flat rock outside her bedroom window, absentmindedly breaking apart fallen leaves and searching vaguely for some sign of adventure on the horizon of the jaded sea. Disappointment clouded her sight, as the day was much like every other—sunny and hot, the shallow sky swaying with the possibility of rain and the sea stretching out as blue and vast and empty and impassable as ever. And that was when Isla had decided to take adventure into her own hands by digging a hole through the centre of the world and climbing through to the other side.

"I think we should walk down to that valley near Lott's place and start there," Tomas had said. "The ground in that valley is so low we won't waste time digging through a mountain first." And Isla had been relieved Tomas knew where to begin. After all, it wasn't going to be easy, tunnelling through the earth.

In her mind now, Isla saw them walking together over this same overgrown path across the hills and scrubland, her pace quickening but never feeling quick enough. Her long dark hair had blown wild in the thick humid breezes, and Tomas had caught her hand, swinging it in time to match their childish stride.

"What'll it be like, do you think, on the other side of the world?" Tomas had asked her.

"Probably it'll be more like the mainland." Isla reasoned, as if either of them knew what the mainland was like. "They'll have really tall houses, tall as that banyan tree. I bet if you get to the top of them, you can see forever."

"Yes, probably forever," she repeated, nodding at him to make it seem more real.

"You can see really far from the top of that tree." Tomas replied. "Or from the lighthouse actually."

"But you can't see anything interesting, Tomas," Isla replied. "Just more trees, more fields, more losa. Over there we'll be able to see all kinds of things that we've never seen before."

"Like what?"

"Who knows? That's what I want to find out."

"You'll go with me, right?" she added suddenly, and for a moment, the idea of going without Tomas made her voice waver like a spider's web in the wind.

"Of course I will," he said. "We're going together, like adventurers, just like you always say." Then, Tomas had looked up into the wide expanse of blue sky where a single gull circled, dipping and rising idly in the invisible currents.

Isla remembered the look of Tomas's face, his brown skin bleached gold in the fervid light, and it struck her that if she was like the sun, always staring out to the horizon, then Tomas was like the moon, for he was always looking either up to the sky, the sun filling and reflecting against his smooth almond face, or his face was turned towards the island earth, broad features hidden in the shade of a gentle, private midnight. Isla poked him in the ribs, and they both laughed.

For awhile, the two had fallen into the loud silence of the island morning. Islanders called it *drune*, when time stretches out so far that it almost disappears, when the edges of a time-bound life lift away and one feels surrounded by space and sunlight streams into one's very soul. After a time, Tomas began to hum a song that they both knew from an unknowable time, passed on through the blood from their great-great-grandparents' generation, about the beauty of the island, the green of its trees, the magic of its purple hills, the coolness of its waters, the safety of its isolation. Then, he sang another song about a foolish man who tried to walk on his hands and talk backwards and got himself into all sorts of trouble, and Isla had laughed at all the funny parts and squeezed his hand absently when he had finished.

Strange, the slippages of time. Isla stood on the path she had been following. She stood there, and yet she was not there, for her mind had fled into the past and her eyes stared blindly down into the empty valley seeing nothing while her mind's eye saw many things.

No longer could she detect the exact place where she had cleared away the leaves and underbrush, raking her small hands against the earth while her hair flew like a banshee, collecting bits of twigs and leaves that fell like rain in the air. "How about there?" Tomas had picked up a spade, suddenly strong and grown up and drove it into the earth with determination. Isla had followed his lead, straining as she lifted the spade over the mouth of the hole. In her mind, she could already see the pathway they were creating to distant lands, filled with unfamiliar foods, indecipherable speech, bizarre sounding music, new ideas and unexplored terrain...how they would be famous adventurers, perhaps discover real treasure, make their fortunes, be together forever.

Isla remembered how she had looked up the hills to where her father's land rose above the tops of the trees, and noticed as if for the first time how the purple losa flowers sparkled like fireflies in the afternoon sun, how the rows of losa dipped and swirled on the hillside like a flock of birds. Tomas had worked beside her, pulling at the earth quietly and steadily, loosening the larger stones and cutting through roots when Isla got stuck, and it had seemed to her then in that lengthening day that she and Tomas were on their way to freedom. Overhead in the piercing blue of the sky above the trees a lone gull had let out a sharp cry, and Isla had thought, *gulls are also free to fly wherever they want,* and she had taken it as a sign.

But she had not made it to the other side of the world. She had not laid eyes on those magical foreign lands. And her heart had fallen into despair that nothing would ever change in this changeless, isolated place. The island had stood before her eyes like a sleeping sea monster that had raised its head and opened its fiery eyes to note the passage of a great explorer, but then had simply closed them again and sunk back into its own silent, unchangeable meditation.

But now the boatman too had come and perhaps the Great Event of her life had only just begun.

Isla turned from the grasslands onto the sandy path that would lead her home, scuffing her shoes and dragging her feet. Yet as she walked Isla felt something shift beneath her feet, as if the island itself were emerging from the cocoon of her childhood where it had rested docile and half-asleep for ten years. Now it seemed to stir with a new possibilities.

An evening mosquito hummed in her ear, and Isla

swatted at it in the still, heavy dusk. Many evenings she had walked this way, humming some lazy tune, breathing in the warm smoky smells that wafted out from the homes she passed and out down the street. Now she wondered what the boatman would see in this place, what his eyes would perceive. And what they would miss as well.

Isla glanced down at the white stones on the path to her house and, for the first time, noticed that they seemed rough and unstable, and the house ahead began to feel poor, diminished. In Isla's mind, the boatman's wild hair glinted red and grey in the chicanerous sunlight. She saw his burnt skin, his blue open eyes, and she found herself wondering yet again where exactly he was from and what it was like there and what else he had seen in his long life of adventure and freedom. Did all people on the mainland look like this? Walk and smile and speak like this stranger?

Isla had never imagined that anyone could sit so unreproachfully in their clothes or could speak so easily to strangers, as a flowing stream which expects to rest each night on different shores. She peered out into the hazy distance beyond the sea, searching for the place the boatman might have come from, the shape of his home, his family, his life on the other side. By the time Isla noticed that she had stopped walking, the mist had descended into the valleys and crevasses between the hills of the island.

"Get home child. It's almost dark." A warm hand fell gently on her shoulder.

Isla nodded and the woman moved out into the distance, the red cloth bag of the losa harvesters hung full across her back with vegetables from Isla's father's garden. Darkness was almost upon her, and yet Isla still dragged her feet, turning to watch the red bag until it faded into the green and purple shadows. Then she began to walk again, past warm yellow windows where riotous laughter and clattering dinner dishes brightened thick patches of the night, and for no reason at all, Isla thought of her father. Not this way. Not the creased lines of his face, not the quiet man of the present, but the young father she had once known. And seeing his face before her, Isla remembered that she had not always dragged her feet when the path before her had swung towards home. Once, she had followed her father like a shadow, listening as he instructed the harvesters in the losa rows. Once she had run eagerly back and forth from the fire-warmed kitchen to their blue evening garden at every request her father had made for more herbs, lettuce, squash, peppers. Was it he who had changed? Or she?

Hens clucked and chattered behind wooden fences and crickets sang earnestly as the last streaks of blue faded into the night sky. Far off, Isla could hear a dog barking. Overhead a seagull called out in its free and lonely voice, turning Isla's young mind away from such thoughts that stole the colour from her heart. She would keep her mind on the boatman, she decided. On adventure.

And it was at that moment that Isla decided that she would follow the boatman, track him as she and Tomas did island creatures, watching for prints mislaid in the sand, clues of the path he had taken. The boatman, perhaps without even knowing it, had thrown a line of hope off the end of his boat, and it trailed in the water before Isla's hungry gaze like a string of pearls.

3

The boatman's face was like a map of ancient lands, full of faded lines, illustrated dragons, shimmering oases—a meeting of the promise of treasure and assurance of deepest peril. While his calm, almost lazy gaze spoke of wide expanses, wind-swept grasslands and hot sunsets, the fierce sea air had sanded away any discernible marker of age, so that those most interested in the boatman, namely the island traders and hoards of school children who roamed the island after the predictable rains each afternoon, could not be certain whether he had passed through the storms of four decades or eight.

There were certainly enough contradictions in his complexion to facilitate heated arguments on the subject, for his eyes were so clear and blue, someone would say, but they were held up by a spider's web of creases, and his thick hair which grew wild like jungle undergrowth was flecked with more grey than red. And yet something in his smile, half-hidden in the vine-swept treachery of his beard, also seemed to grow younger and more carefree with every passing day the islanders watched him.

Let alone his age, no one on the island could even agree whether the boatman was a rich, eccentric adventurer, in which case he should be embraced and quickly coaxed into the bosom of island life so that the traders and single women could have their way with him, or whether he was in fact a homeless vagabond, in which case most agreed he should be encouraged to push back to sea as soon as possible. His boat, the island's most experienced fishermen assured, was finely crafted, carefully painted with the three red bars which was the symbol of the mainland kingdom and skilfully sealed against the battery of salt air and sea water. But the mothers and grandmothers were quick to point out among themselves his cracked, dirty fingernails and his suspicious lack of any baggage.

So, without a firm consensus on the degree of shadiness in his character, the boatman was put up in the Palm Losa, the sprawling home of the last remaining member of the Prenai family, a family which had made its fortune during the great losa boom in the last century but had declined in both glory and lineage since the death of the family patriarch, Manel Prenai. Sylvia Prenai, the last of that great house, had found herself towards the end of her life, a woman with no husband and no children, but with an ingrained and unshakeable sense of style and propriety that marked her status. With the last vestiges of her family home crumbling around her like a carcase picked clean by the wild things of the world and left to shift slowly into the sand, Sylvia put on every piece of antique jewellery still remaining in her family, which included twelve rings (some of which dated back even before the Losa Boom) and seven pearl necklaces, and greeted this strange visitor to the island with a soft drawling voice she imagined to be the height of traditional island sophistication.

When the boatman walked up the three whitewashed steps of the Palm Losa and was welcomed into the fading grand house by the trembling of a bejewelled, bony hand with skin like the finest paper, he tried to smile approvingly. Out of a strong sense of both politeness and wonder, he ignored the veil of dust that covered every square inch of the furniture and shifted quietly with each footstep making the exact moment of his every step traceable by the tracks he left across the wooden floorboards. He pretended, also, not to hear the anxious creaking of the staircase, the deep grooves of generations of steps hidden underneath a carpet of bright red flowers and green parakeets, and he did not allow the shout of dismay to escape his lips when the water pipes shuddered and the tap spat out a bit of mud and two dead flies but would not release any water.

"Where can I find a good meal?" the boatman asked Sylvia Prenai on his way out an hour later, and the old woman raised one pale hand with effort due to the sheer weight of her jewellery and said, "Darling, there is only Dari's."

When the boatman found Dari's, the clouds were already moving in, a slow fading of the distant views, and it seemed to him that the island was drawing into itself like a great secret, sinking into some reflection that made everyone suddenly aware of the tension in their chests. The air outside was green and cool and silent, so different from this morning's scorching sun and glimmering purple backdrop of the island hills at midday. He stepped gratefully into the warm yellow noise of the cafe and sat down at a corner table and did not wonder where he was going to go next.

Time felt different here—there seemed so much of it. He fingered the knot in the rough wooden table and looked over at a group of fishermen who had just sat down around the large centre table. They spoke loudly, as if still fighting the whipping sea winds and stretched out distances between their boats, and their voices crashed over each others' so the boatman had to strain to understand what they were saying.

Slowly, the boatman became aware of a large man looming over him. The boatman looked up and met the stranger's eye.

"What would you like?" The man's thick moustache moved confidently on his broad face.

"What are they drinking?" The boatman pointed to the glass bowls of steaming purple liquid that the fishermen cradled close to their faces so delicately as they yelled at each other across the table.

"Losa."

"I'll have that," the boatman nodded, but the large man didn't move.

"You arrived this morning." His voice was soft and deep like the echo of slow giant waves booming against the rocks, and because the boatman knew it was not a question, the he simply smiled.

"Hmmm." The man nodded, but he did not ask where the boatman was from. "I'm Dari. If you want some food, just let me know."

Later, long after the fishermen had gone, the rain fell, shrouding the hills in a mist of white silence. A great sigh emanated from the old men who sat with frail dark hands playing cards in the corner of the cafe, and then from the older woman who sat gazing out of the wide pane-less window drinking steaming tea with her grandson balanced in her lap, and then even from the group of teenagers who laughed erratically and filled the air with the whispers of their adolescent woes. And the boatman joined them, releasing the breath of air he had unknowingly held clenched inside his chest since early that morning, or perhaps much longer, letting the cool damp mist wash over his face.

For that moment, he forgot about the rough seas, the scorching stinging tendrils of the sun, the hours he had spent on so many days tossing, rowing, straining naked between the open sea and the empty sky. In a state of grateful amnesia, the boatman leaned back into the warm room of the café, fragranced with its strange smelling tea and smoky fire and listened to the voices of these strangers that sounded like wind blowing through dense forest trees.

Everything around him felt new and he was grateful for the escape. The cascade of tiny purple flowers that covered the island in carefully tended rows, now seemed to rise up and hover like wisps of cloud and their strange thick fragrance hung in the damp air like a muse, inspiring the imagination. He let his gaze wander down the dusty street, past the shops, the tailor's stall, the fish market, until it curved around behind the purple hills, and he decided that later, after the sun returned, he would follow that road and see where it led. For now, the boatman was happy to sit amongst the blue afternoon breezes that lingered on his eyelids like a good omen. The place was so new, seemed so untouched—and so to him, it seemed perfect.

The boatman was rarely alone in those first days on the island. Every morning he stepped off the front steps of the Palm Losa to find a new companion who would walk the white sandy paths to town, past the three tracts of lands where people working in the losa hills paused to watch him stroll by, faces indecipherable in the shade of their wide-brim hats, hands brushing without pause against the losa bushes feeling for the soft purple buds. His companion was usually some trader, on his way to town to open his shop. First it was Jon from the fish shop, the next day Lott who owned the cheese shop in town, then Silse the tailor, a small thin man who drummed his fingertips together when he spoke and didn't seem to do much of anything. Each day no matter the time he rose and dressed and stepped from the sighing house that was called the Palm Losa, someone would be standing outside at the edge of the veranda, armed with gossip about the island's more prominent inhabitants or tales of the island's history.

The boatman listened carefully during these walks, searching with a finely tuned ear for the old language that rode beneath the current of each tale. For his part, the boatman understood his place on this island. He understood that he was not to become a local, and these walks into town were not a sign of assimilation or even of acceptance. He was a foreigner, a man apart, and his role was to remain a good audience, a silver mirror for the islanders to present their best versions of themselves. So the boatman listened thoughtfully to the islanders' tales of when they were at their bravest facing the storms at sea, tales of skill and craftsmanship in their trade with the mainlanders, tales of their good fortune and blessed luck as they caught sight of mermen and gentle sea giants, tales of the beauty and good judgement of their women and of the magic of their purple island.

The boatman did not tire of these tales because he spoke the old language of the world and so understood their true meaning. In many words, each said to him — "This island is the best of all places because it is where I am. I love this island because I know it. It has always been this way, and this is the way it will always be." It was the eternal tale all humanity tells itself in order to feel important in a vast unknowable world, and in order to feel safe. Once upon a time the boatman had told himself this same tale.

But the boatman knew as he stepped off the wide sagging veranda of the Palm Losa and into the brilliance of the morning sunlight that he no longer wanted to tell this story himself. Nor was he planning to stay on the island very long. He treasured most these early days in a place when no one knew who he was, when everyone told him their best stories and each island path still led him across an odyssey of purple hills that stunned him into a humble silence. But eventually, if he stayed on too long, all this magic would fade, his mind would become devoured by local arguments and petty matters that crawled on their bellies like iguanas and entered every home.

Worse still was the undeniable fact that his past would eventually arrive on this island as well, and this beautiful place where he was both unknown and known in the truest sense as simply a human being, would be blotted with the spreading stain of his past, his work, his family, his social place. And who he truly was would be lost—again. No, the boatman was determined he would stand free, relying on the winged grace of living life without a past. He would soon move on. The boatman was a worldly man. He had seen many things, and he knew that there were many islands like this in the sea, many isolated places which smelled like cardamom or gardenias or losa and reminded him of home.

These were the boatman's thoughts as he headed down the rocky path towards the docks. The wind had been up the night before, knocking palm fronds against the side of the house and blowing like a hellion through the windows, flinging the white cotton sheet off his feet which hung off the end of the bed and stirring up all kinds of noises in the old Prenai house.

He wasn't worried. After all, his little boat had seen much worse nights in the ports scattered like stars across the wide sea. It had *algave*, his boat, old and worn out, but it had a value that went beyond such things. *Algave*, an island word. The boatman felt the word roll between his teeth. It meant quality, a quality that comes from memories, from emotions and experiences that had woven into the thing and given it greater value.

Yet, quality or not, the need to check on his boat gave him a sense of purpose, something he had been lacking for days. So the boatman set off down the white dusty road with long, careful strides, his sandals kicking up clouds of sand in their wake.

The lane that wound down from the homes of the fishermen to the port was steep, and the boatman stepped carefully amongst the grey cobbled stones and white gravel still glistening treacherously from the previous night's rain. Along the lane, the wooden houses stood shoulder to shoulder like gulls on the sea wall, bracing themselves against the unpredictable sea winds. Nets and lines with shining metal lures hung across porch railings, and the boatman noted as he passed that most of the houses had been recently painted an optimistic blue and that their front porches did not sag and warp like the wide imposing veranda of the Palm Losa, but were replaced often with straight wooden planks.

The men and women who walked and jostled and swayed along this lane had large dark eyes and spoke in loud but gentle voices, as if they had lived all their lives accustomed to speaking above the roar of the sea. Many nodded and smiled as the boatman passed by, but they were busy people and had seen many stranger sights out on the water than this foreign red-bearded man. The boatman liked these people who lived, as he did, amongst the many moods of the sea. They smelled warm and rubbed the fine layer of salt between their fingers and knew many songs that he recognised from other places and perhaps also other times.

As the boatman approached the turn in the lane, he saw Jon the fishmonger climbing towards him, and in that moment the boatman was suddenly hit with that strange sense of foreboding that always accompanies déjà vu. Hoping to avoid conversation, the boatman turned instead down a narrow alley where a series of stairs cut down the steep hill and led directly to the docks. It was a perilous climb down unsteady rocks which formed the stairs, and so was usually deserted apart from the lines of dripping laundry and the occasional straggling child.

The boatman slipped around the corner of the alley, expecting solitude and shade and the murmur of waves rising from the docks. Instead he collided headlong with two children who were running nimbly and without faltering up the unreliable steps. The girl staggered back two steps and clutched the stone wall for support. Even before she had steadied herself, she was staring up at him with a look of both terror and elation, and her eyes shone silver even in the shadowed alleyway and pierced his soul with their resolute curiosity. For a moment they stared at each other, and in that single instant, the boatman knew two things—first, that the eyes of this girl were not those of an islander, and second, that this girl would eventually leave the island of her birth.

"Why don't you have any of your things with you?" The

girl reached instinctively for the boy's hand, clasping it tightly even as she spoke with a bold voice.

The boatman hesitated, as one always does in the fierce face of destiny. "I'm just going down to check on my boat," he began. "I don't need anything to do that."

"No, I mean, on this island. You didn't bring any of your things with you to Madame Prenai's house and you don't keep anything on your boat."

"Isla…" the boy pulled at the girl's hand and she fell silent, but her eyes did not waver from the boatman's face, and the boatman remembered something, a face from long ago which had held this same look.

"How do you know that?" The boatman asked the girl, but he was looking now at the young boy who stood beside her, and he saw that the boy's eyes were a warm brown and that the boy thought many things which he did not speak aloud and that his silence was not cowardice but something else that the boatman also recognised in himself.

"How do you know that I don't keep things on the boat," the boatman said again, and this time he must have seemed more threatening because the boy stepped forward, shielding the girl from view, but still he said nothing.

The boatman laughed. "I don't need many things, you know," he said more easily now. "Just clothes on my back and food in my stomach. The rest I keep up here…" and he tapped his finger against his temple.

"Well, what are you doing here?" The girl asked, stepping out from behind the boy.

"I'm a traveller," was his reply.

"I knew it!" The girl whispered. Ahead the boatman could see the choppy grey waters of the sea. Before him the boy was pulling at the girl's arm, whispering something which the boatman didn't catch.

The boatman had taken precisely seven steps down the alley stairs when the silver-eyed girl called back to him, "Sir, excuse me, sir...Have you ever been to the mainland?"

The boatman turned and nodded. "Many times." And then the boy grabbed her hand and both children disappeared around the corner onto the winding lane.

4

Petro did not like the stories he heard about the stranger from the mainland, who smoked one rolled leaf on the stroke of every hour and sat from mid-morning until late afternoon drinking cup after cup of losa tea and listening to stories of the island. *No foreigner should be able to drink that much losa!* Petro thought to himself, as he sat with several friends on the porch of his house.

"What does he do?" He grumbled aloud. "And more importantly, what does he want here?"

But since all the boatman did was smoke and drink tea and nod his head as people passing by the café stopped to talk, no one could really say. In truth, no one had actually bothered to ask.

"Perhaps he doesn't want anything," said Jayan, tapping a pipe that he filled but never lit against the weathered wooden rail of Petro's front porch.

"Everyone wants something," said Petro confidently, leaning back in his wicker chair and rubbing his thumb for a moment thoughtfully against the reeds in the armchair. Perhaps it was the man's greying red hair or the way he turned his head at a slight angle to show he was listening. Whatever the case, this boatman had an unusual aura about him that drew people like moths to a flame. They hovered about his table at the café — fishermen on their way back from the beach would forget their usual morning hunger and take the long detour into town to tell the boatman about the day they saw a mermaid in the ocean, a city from another world in the clouds, a fish the size of a mountain. Mothers on their way back from walking their children to school would relate the long histories of their families, would clarify who on the island had true clairvoyant powers, who made the best losa tea (and the worst), what songs islanders sang at births and which ones were sung at funerals. Children, once released from school would eagerly compete to tell the boatman the names of the trees and fruit, where the best swimming spots were located and which of the wandering dogs belonged to which family. And the men at the café, Petro heard from Fazza and Jayan, narrated pieces from the history of the island.

"Hmmm," Petro thought, because he knew these histories were the most dangerous of all, not because they were any great secret but because they would lead the boatman eventually to him, and if it was one thing Petro hated, it was reminders of the mainland.

"Who cares what he wants?" Fazza said, blowing blue smoke into the air with each word. Then, thinking again, he tapped his thick forefinger against the wooden table, clattering glasses and sending chaotic ripples through the surface of the men's cooling tea. "As long as he keeps himself to himself and there isn't any more of them coming over. He's a mainlander alright, but then," he sighed and leaned back, and his wicker chair creaked, "so was Myrium after all."

Petro grunted but said nothing.

"Wonder if he's planning to stay on," Jayan said, eyeing Petro carefully.

Petro's dark eyes snapped back from the distance. "I'm telling you he won't stay. Mark my words. I've seen the look in that man's eyes. He's a wanderer and no mistake. Flitting here, flitting there." Petro waved his hand in the air, spilling dried leaf from his pipe. He dusted several strands off his knee before he continued. "He'll soon get bored with this place, and he'll move on."

"Hmmm," Fazza nodded, and Petro noticed how he glanced conspiratorially sideways toward Jayan and clicked his tongue softly. And then, the next moment, Petro noticed how old Fazza looked, that grey had seeped slowly into his face, staining a few patches of his clipped beard and wild eyebrows with the unmistakable marks of declining age.

And then, Petro wondered if he was only noticing this because he had started to feel so old himself. He felt tired and confused, searching for a wisdom and sense of peace, which had been promised to the ageing but had thus far failed to materialise in his own life. Instead, in these early days of his autumn, where he had expected sun and an increasing clarity of high cloudless skies, a fog had settled instead, frightening him with a premature winter chill.

In earlier days, the land and losa hills had run well, and Isla had traipsed eagerly alongside him, peeling insects from the delicate losa leaves and listening to him tell her about the crop with wide, serious eyes. He had known what to do with her then — point out colourful beetles that he was collecting when, in the early days after her mother's death, he had determined to catalogue the island's flora and fauna down to the last insect. And if that failed to interest Isla, he would swing her by her arms until her tiny skirt was a blur of red or blue and she screamed happily and he would laugh loud and long into the sea air.

But every day, in these new times, his daughter seemed to grow farther away from him. She no longer walked the terraced hills with him after school, but stayed out playing with her friends until darkness forced her return to his company. When he asked her about school, or tried to help her with her school work, which he knew he could explain far more clearly than that fishmonger's daughter who now taught up at the schoolhouse, Isla would push him away and shield her papers with tiny hands insisting that she didn't need his help, that it was easy.

Petro winced when he recalled how Isla had rolled her eyes at his suggestion that she take singing lessons — rolled her eyes at him, her father, who had brought her into this world, had been there with his heart in his throat until he heard her first cries, had been the one to feed her and clothe her since Myrium had died. This little slip of a girl had rolled her wide silver Myrium-eyes at him and turned away. As if he was no one to her.

So Petro had showed her who he was, that he was her father, and she was going to those singing lessons now whether she liked it or not. Myrium had always loved learning to sing the old island songs. Now, sitting in the shade of the porch, Petro stared out at the sea and wondered why this daughter wasn't more like her mother and why he felt such a distinct foreboding that things in his life were only getting more uncertain, fractured, like a mirror slowly losing its reflective qualities in the ancient breezes of generations and fading and staining itself black.

And now there was this new danger to deal with, for Petro was not blind to the way Isla's eyes darted excitedly when she recounted the latest news of the boatman — how he had been seen yesterday at the docks making repairs to his boat, how he always carried with him a string of wooden beads which he fingered one after another in the quiet moments of deep afternoon, and how Silse the tailor, Jon the fishmonger and Lott the cheese-maker competed over who among them would accompany the boatman into town each day and were now arguing amongst themselves about which days were theirs by right and who would reveal which bit of news, and which piece of island legend to the boatman's attentive ears.

No, Petro was not blind. He too had once had dreams, and he knew how this mysterious boatman must seem to Isla and what such reckless ideas of adventure might do to one's soul. But how could he protect her from this new element? How could he prevent it from mixing dangerously with her imagination? The answers eluded him, and so instead he glanced up to the sky and remarked, "It's going to rain again soon," and felt a bewildering sort of relief when both Fazza and Jayan nodded, "indeed" and went back to sipping their tea.

5

The coming of the boatman ruptured the placid flow of Isla's childhood like the trembling of an earthquake on glassy water. Without meaning to, his wild hair and the strange lilt in his voice brought Isla's fantasies out of the realm of night-time dreams and into the unmistakable heat of the day. It was not entirely unexpected. After all, when a person's world is small, a grain of sand can seem like a mountain, a single word can become a hurricane that blows the traveller off course, and the meeting of a stranger from another land not so far away can tap dangerously against the fragile glass of a familiar world.

Each day, Isla found a reason to wander by Dari's, looking in the cafe that was full of shade and voices and the smells of losa. Sometimes she sat on the steps waiting for his voice to spill out the wide windows. And when he wasn't there, she would interrogate those who sat at the tables — What did he say? Where was he from? What is it like there? Who did he talk to?

It was only in the face of this young girl's flashing eyes and persistent voice that the islanders realised they still didn't know the first thing about the boatman, and so all they could say was — "No telling child. He's a stranger."

When, after several days, Isla's voice hit a note of desperation, a fisherman called Jove assured her that the boatman was a wealthy mainlander escaping from the burden of duty. But then Ida who worked in the bakery said, no, she was sure he had been looking for news of a lost love. As the stories grew more intricate, building their roots on the flimsiest of sideways looks and half-remembered comments the boatman had made during his stay, Isla turned to Dari, who stood leaning his massive frame against the back wall and drawing long and deliberate puffs on his pipe.

"Have you talked to him, Dari?" Isla asked.

"Not much." Dari answered without looking down. "He isn't a talker."

"Hmm." Isla thought for a moment, and her brow furrowed as she thought. "Dari?"

"Yeah."

"How do people get to the mainland?"

Dari's thick eyebrows rose like a jungle above his dark eyes and he looked down, scrutinising something deep in Isla's face as if he were looking for something he had overlooked before. "Ahhh," he said at last. "Hardly anyone goes to the mainland these days, Isla. But if one wanted to go..." Dari paused and his black eyes held her, "they would take the trader's boat that leaves for Joon island at the end of the harvest. From there many boats leave for the mainland."

Isla looked down at her hands and began picking at an invisible spot on her finger. Then she took a deep breath. "How do you know whether you should go or not?"

Dari drew a long last puff on his pipe and the end burned red in the heat of the tropical afternoon. "That's a different question altogether," he said at last. "For that kind of question, you need the oracle."

Isla turned towards the front steps of the café, scuffing her feet as she trudged out into the blinding sunlight, a sudden solitude rising up inside of her. People like her didn't go see the old woman called the oracle anymore.

And then, just when Isla had managed to gather her courage to seek out the boatman herself, she heard that he had gone. "Just this morning, child," Sylvia Prenai said from the wide verandah where the sea breezes blew soft against her face. "He was a traveller, that man." And Isla felt anguish tear at her heart that she had not seized the chance to learn the truths about the world, as she was certain the boatman would have been able to impart.

For days Isla wandered about, unable to lift her eyes from the sandy ground of the island. Her father, lost in his own eternally shifting moods and committed to the detailed distractions of his office papers and his land, did not notice, and it was only when Tomas took her hand and pulled her up into the thick wide arms of their banyan tree that Isla began to breathe again.

"Look out there," Tomas pointed to a large boat of traders that was just setting sail for Joon island under the care of several seafaring fishermen. "Do you see that?"

"I see it," Isla said, looking down to pick at one of her fingernails.

"No you don't! Look!" And when Isla looked up again and saw the white sails rise up full of sunlight, Tomas began to tell Isla her own story. "One day you'll be on that boat, Isla. Imagine what it will be like when you see that sail rise up and you feel the winds begin to pull you out to sea. Imagine, the island will begin to look small and will glimmer like the fishermen say, and you'll finally see it as they do. That's when you'll know — you are on your own adventure."

"Do you really think we will?" Isla said, knowing Tomas would hear the way her voice trembled slightly as she spoke.

Tomas looked back at her. "We can't leave the island yet anyway, silly. We're only kids!"

"But one day?"

"Of course one day," he said with a courage that rose from the roots of the great banyan. "It's already decided." And Isla smiled because Tomas was the only one who never told her she couldn't follow her wild dreams.

Whatever Isla's fears might have predicted, the boatman's first visit to the island was not to be his last, and after several years his visits became as foreseen as the migration of the gulls or the harvest of losa. He was always put up in the same decrepit room at the Palm Losa where Sylvia Prenai would let him leave a neatly folded stack of clothes, a toothbrush and a black comb. And each time he came, he brought nothing but a pocket full of money and new stories of adventures beyond the horizon — although never of his own part in them.

The stories that the boatman told were full of colour, magnificent as a red sail filled by the winds of the high seas. There were stories of wise men, crazed lovers, heroes and demons of other lands. Favoured especially by the islanders were the stories of families he had met on his travels whose lineage stretched back to the dark ages before time and whose secrets and deceptions were balanced by great moments of compassion.

Only on the rare occasion would the boatman speak of the mainland, for he knew well enough that the islanders had little patience for the people and only as much interest as would keep these mainlanders off their island. Thus, it was unusual that one afternoon he looked up from his third cup of losa tea and suddenly said, "The mainlanders' greatest wish is that they might live forever."

The boatman sat back in one of Dari's creakiest chairs. He had spoken quite casually, as if commenting on the direction of some mild breeze, so there were few amongst the crowd of islanders at Dari's that day that took any notice. "They want power too," he continued after a time, "make no mistake — they are powerful enough to reshape the land to their needs. They command rivers to change their course, draw up mountains to protect them and flatten land to make wide plains where rolling hills once lay."

"Let them try such things on the sea!" one fisherman replied dismissively over his shoulder.

"You are right," the boatman nodded. "The sea bows to no man."

"But," he added, "I no longer underestimate the will of mainlanders, for it comes not from greed for power — although they wish to be powerful. And it does not come from their steadfast faith that the mainland rests at the centre of the world..."

At this, a few islanders grumbled, muttering under their breath at the audacity of such people when it was well-known that it was their island which stood at the earth's centre and was the origin of all life.

Without acknowledging these fierce looks the boatman continued, "The mainlanders are a desperate people, and their will never wavers because what they seek does not end with power or status, which are easy enough to acquire. Each of them is raised with this wish for eternal life burning in their hearts and so they brand the earth with the mark of their heavy footprints, and they reshape the flow of nature to confirm the immortality of their life through their work, since this is the best they can manage."

Some of the islanders who had grown accustomed to the boatman's expansive tales waited for the story to continue, but it did not. Instead, the boatman took a noisy sip of losa tea and was silent for a long time.

Over these years that lapped at the island like waves upon the shore, Isla grew to depend on the boatman's visits for news of the world. "On the mainland there are adventurers who conquer whole regions of land by the shape of their shoes and the golden bands on their arms," the boatman would say, and Isla would sit on the front step of Dari's listening enraptured. She would listen for hours to the boatman describe these adventurers who had wandered through the jungles to the east or the mountains of the north, conquering lands with only their silver steps.

Adventurers! True adventurers! Isla whispered these words to herself, and she was so blinded by the unexpected joy of it, that she didn't hear the boatman say, "The people these adventurers conquer believe them to be gods, but they are simply men who longed to see the world and were swayed to act against their conscience by the seductive sensation of power."

Thus it was through the boatman's stories that Isla learned about the plague of insomnia that had swept across the mainland and the technological advances and great learning that had been its result. How statues has been erected to celebrate the cult of innovation called the Philosophy of the Rising Sun, and how losa from the island was used on the mainland not to make tea but was pressed into an expensive dye that families used to colour cloth robes and the paper flowers that anointed the gravestones of their ancestors.

"The mainlanders' great strength," the boatman relayed another afternoon, "comes from the plague of insomnia that has swept through the region. They drink a magical liquid that looks as thick as mud and makes the heart race as if one had run across this island full of hills. Their eyes go wide and their tongues move fast, and they work and work and work, writing papers, making targets and grand plans and complex predictions, and when at long last their work is done, they create more targets to meet and plans to fulfil so that they are not caught resting. It is seen as a great strength, this inability, this refusal to sleep," the boatman continued, looking out into the wide stretch of day, and what he was thinking to himself, the islanders could not have guessed.

"Nonsense," said one islander sitting at the next table. "What can anyone achieve in the middle of the night?"

"Sleeping is a waste of time, they say. Nothing is achieved by sleeping," the boatman replied with a strange smile upon his face. "These mainlanders believe they are doing important things. They believe they are changing the world. But," he added, sighing to himself, "the world has been changing on its own much longer than they can imagine."

Isla, perhaps quite unconsciously, used these visits from beyond the horizon to mark time more consistently on the island, so that Isla would later remember her early childhood before the boatman's arrival in a vague way, as one long drawn out summer of torrential rain and hot nights lying under the stars waiting for the blue evening breezes. But after the boatman's arrival her time keeping became much more exact.

She remembered, for instance, that it was after the boatman's fourth visit that Eva had first kissed a boy under the dome of the willow tree behind their school and then quickly relayed the slightly sickening feel of a desperate lapping tongue in one's mouth. Isla, for her part, had tried not to die with jealousy. Then several weeks later she had woken from a nap to find the soft skin between her thighs smeared with black blood and had run silently through the sleep-filled afternoon to Eva's mother who had given her clean clothes and had explained this monthly fate of women while she rolled dough back and forth on the kitchen table with a wooden rolling pin.

It was during the boatman's ninth visit Isla remembered that she had been caught studying the folded map buried underneath her father's papers in the wooden cabinet in the main room which had started the cyclic warfare between father and daughter over Isla's mother and her unexplained relationship to the mainland. And it was preceding the boatman's seventh visit that she was haunted by nightmares of drowning.

But the discovery of the underwater cave, that came earlier, after the boatman's fifth visit, when Isla and her friends still precariously straddled the wide gulf between childhood and the vast unmarked territory that lay beyond, when signs would suddenly come to mean several things, where paths would become vague and eventually fade into the grasslands, and no matter how often one gazed back in longing at earlier, clearer days, there was irrefutably no return.

6

It was in that year of declining magic that Tomas discovered the hidden sanctuary of the sea pool which lay sheltered from harsh sea blasts by a certain uncommon curvature of rock. High summer was fast approaching and although change was in the air, none of them perceived it. The world spun on its axis in the universe vast and starlit, but the children still felt large, masters of their world, and did not contemplate the serpentine paths of destiny.

In those days there seemed nothing more enticing than missing school in order to see for themselves this mysterious pool Tomas claimed to have found, a pool that somehow, in all their endless wanderings, had evaded their sight. After an hour's walk through a heat that stood out in the air like a wall and made time waver unsteadily before their eyes, Tomas announced, "There it is."

Isla, Eva, Marco and Lucas stared down the edge of the cliff into its bottomless depths surging green in a morning shade that fell like silk around their shoulders and were unable to fathom that after all these years, they had really never seen this place before and that the island of their birth might still be unknown to them. The idea made their young barefaced hearts pound and even Isla danced lightly on her toes with the yellow intuition of adventure.

"I was out there diving, and I saw it from the sea," Tomas said, pointing to some place out in the glassy water, and with that he jumped off the edge onto a large rock several feet below, placing first his left foot, then his right as he picked his way carefully between the reptiles that lay comatose with heat and the dragonflies that flitted from the weedy blossoms that grew stubbornly out of the rocky scree until finally he joined them to skim the water of the salty sea pool with the earth-stained sole of his foot.

After him, Marco and Lucas hopped recklessly from one stone to another, and Isla laughed because for all their loud, fiery ways, they looked very much like the awkward, long-legged insects that crawled over the decaying logs and invasive vines of the forest. She was about to climb down after them when Eva's pale fingers grasped her shoulder. "Isla, wait. I have to talk to you about something."

She paused and crouched down into her skirt that billowed out around her, fluttering lazily in the breeze. Isla crouched down next to her, watching Eva's eyes that shifted with an uncommon worry. "I don't think Joal likes me after all, Isla. I don't know what to do."

"What are you worrying about?" Isla tried to keep herself still so that she wouldn't reveal her own insecurities. The boys always chased after Eva. They didn't chase after her. *Not that I want them to*, Isla told herself sternly. *I've got more important things to think about.*

"He didn't meet me yesterday after school. He just walked off. And then I saw him talking to Rosa."

"Try not to worry," Isla searched for the right words. "I'm sure he likes you. Everyone likes you, Eva."

"Not Joal, I'm sure of it!" Eva said, her eyes filling with a rim of tears that she quickly brushed away.

"Well then he's a fool!" Isla spat against the ground behind her, and made a face.

Eva laughed. "Okay, well, let's go on. I don't want the boys to suspect anything." And with that she set off down the sandy hill and disappeared down the rocks.

For a moment, Isla remained where she was, for it seemed to her as if in that moment they had all suddenly grown up. Below her the boys splashed in the water, their voices deeper than they had once been, and Isla suddenly realised that her hands were clenched into fists and when she released them, two small piles of sandy earth blew off into the air and over the edge of the cliff.

Isla looked down at her hands for a moment, and it seemed as if the course of her life was written there like a map, only she couldn't read it, had no way to decipher its coded lines. Standing up, she made her way down among the rocks, trying to shake the feeling that had suddenly come upon her, that things were getting more serious now and that one day time would have run out and she and her friends would find themselves grown.

When Isla reached the lapping waters of the pool, she came face to face with the green reflection of her own confusion and also a tingling bitterness of inadequacy. At the water's edge, she hesitated, suddenly aware of her own body. She wondered how Eva was able to remain so unselfconscious as she flung off her top shirt and cotton skirt and hit the water with a falsetto shriek that the boys mimicked again and again until they were hoarse and their mouths filled with sea water.

For the first time, it occurred to Isla to wonder whether she was beautiful, whether her stomach was fat or her hair too wild. Slipping beneath the surface, she hid from herself, shaking her head in the slow muffled silence of the sea. She felt too full, bloated with too many unanswered hopes and impossible dreams that were stagnating, rotting inside her because she felt sure now that she was older and knew the ways of the world, that they were never going to come true. She had been born on an island that sat isolated in the wide sea, and girls from such places married boys from such places and had babies and cooked food for their families and stayed friends, for better or worse, with the same people all their lives.

Thinking of her inevitable future, Isla lay still for many breaths, suspended in the water and wishing away those dreams that tortured her, wishing for the first time that she could be more like Eva. *You're an island girl.* She thought. *An island girl. This is your life. One day you'll have to marry one of these island boys too. Or be like Madame Prenai, alone forever.*

A swift yank on her foot startled Isla from her thoughts, and she rose to the surface coughing.

"Hey!"

"You're acting weird all of a sudden." Tomas said, eyeing her.

"I'm not."

"Did Eva say something to you?"

Isla shook her head. Then she blew at the surface of the water, scattering droplets into Tomas's face, and they both smiled.

"Hey, what are you drawing now?" She asked.

Tomas shook his head and his dark hair threw drops of water like rain into Isla's face. "I've finished with lizards.

Now I'm trying to draw birds, but..." he paused, frowning, "they move too fast. With lizards, I had ages if I was quiet enough. But you can't get a bird to stay still for more than a couple seconds."

Then he added, "Kind of like you."

"So what are you going to do then?" Isla asked, ignoring his comment.

"I don't know. Keep trying I guess."

Tomas paused and he looked over at Eva stretched out in the sun. "She looks like one of my lizards." Tomas said slyly, and Isla laughed and felt suddenly free.

"Wanna see something else?" Tomas asked, and without waiting he disappeared again.

Isla dove after him and as she pushed deeper into the pool, she felt a force pushing inward as all colour and sound and smell receded from her world. Kicking with all her might to keep up with Tomas below the surface, she saw him go deeper and deeper and fear began to flow through her veins. She was losing sight of him in the vague current.

Isla kicked harder against the cacophony of her heart, and suddenly, Tomas's hand grabbed her wrist, pulling her through a wide opening in the rock and they rose like rockets, breaking the surface of another world that curled gently beneath their island and gasping for breath. It was an underwater cave.

The cave wall swayed above them with the tide and Isla breathed in an ancient smell, recognising something in the rhythmic silence and indigo light, although she was sure she had never been in this place before. It reminded her of the moon. A place where even memory lost its meaning.

For many breaths they treaded water, gazing upward until they had found the small cracks where pale stray rays of light seeped into the cavern. "This is a secret place," Isla whispered, and Tomas nodded, "I found it last week. I was waiting to tell you. Look here..." and he swam over to a ridge that jutted out from the cave wall. "I want to show you something. But careful, it's slippery here. That's how I got this."

He held out his arm, but in the dim light, Isla couldn't make out the scratches. She waited while Tomas stepped carefully across the flat ridge and stuck his hand into a hole in the rock. He returned with a small box carved from driftwood and handed it to Isla. Hanging on to the ledge, she took it and saw that it held three iridescent pearls.

"I'm collecting them," Tomas said, crouching down to where she held on to the ledge with one arm.

"It's amazing Tomas. They're so pretty."

"I can dive pretty deep now you know." Tomas said.

Isla nodded. She reached out and swirled her index finger in the box, listening to the soft rustling sound the pearls made. Something about them made Isla feel happy, as if somehow there was still hope that things might work out alright in the end. That maybe it wasn't too late and she would still have adventures after all.

"Here, take it. I'm going to drop it." Isla reached out.

"You're not going to drop it," Tomas said, but he took the box and replaced it at the back of the wall and slipped back into the water.

Isla could feel the warmth of his body so close to hers, the motion of the waves he made as he treaded water. Time fell away, and in the pale indigo light Tomas's face seemed at once more familiar, as the boy who was her truest friend, and at the same time almost unrecognisable as one she did not know. She felt his eyes watching her through the darkness, and some shyness gripped her and made her look away.

It was quiet again as the sea rocked them back and forth against the rock ledge. And then, Tomas reached out and cradled Isla's sunburnt cheek for a moment in his warm damp hand, and in the blue uncertain light of the cave, Isla met his gaze and did not pull away.

7
———

All the signs were there—Tomas's stormy eyes, the faltering cadence of his voice, the ominous moments when, thinking his father wasn't looking, he gazed out at the sea and seemed to shrink into himself. This is it, Jaro thought, but still he hesitated, filled with a sudden and unexpected paternal longing to clasp his son to his chest and whisper — you came from me, you are a part of me, you are mine. But his son was no longer small, and so Jaro bit his lip and contemplated the inevitability of life.

It had begun the day Tomas returned home in the uncertain blazing hour of evening and stood before Jaro bathed in the first hints of declining light and announced, "I didn't go to school today."

Jaro had looked up from the long row of yellow tomatoes. Propping an elbow on one earth-stained knee, and with a handful of weeds wilting in his left hand, he waited, watching his son.

"Well," Tomas had said at last. "Aren't you going to say something?"

"What would you like me to say?"

"Don't you want to know where I was?"

"Okay, where were you?" Jaro was listening not so much to his son's words, but to the way his skin hummed beneath his flat sandpaper voice, the way each word fell off his lips like great despair.

"I took everyone to a new swimming hole I found on the other side of the island."

"Mmmm..." And when Jaro didn't say anything else, Tomas had stomped off. Later, he had seen his son sneak around the corner of the cliff down to the small stretch of sand below that opened out like a sliver of moon into the arms of the sea, and even with his back turned he saw Tomas's right arm moving in such a way that he knew he could wait no longer. His son was becoming a man with or without him. Jaro knew then that he would have to send word to the oracle.

In the last moments of day, as the blue sun merged into the sea, Jaro opened out his palms and, in the indigo silence that stretched out between him and the universe, cradled his last moments as the father of this boy before he became a man. He sighed. And then, laughing at his own foolishness, Jaro picked up the pile of sweet tomatoes that lay at his feet and walked into the house.

Several nights later, when Tomas's mood had shifted, Jaro stood up from the dinner table, filled two small glasses of spiced liquor and set one on the table in front of his son, gripping the other in his wide dark hand.

"Da, what..." Tomas looked up at his father and his expression reminded Jaro of when he had been a small child and had been afraid to climb up the dark stairs of the lighthouse alone.

"Go ahead, drink it." A deep nostalgia filled Jaro's heart

when his son tipped the amber liquid into his throat and coughed until his eyes streamed.

"Tomas, what do you want from your life?"

"What do you mean?"

"Well, you are growing up. You all are. I hear Marco is leaving school after this year to start fishing full-time with the rest of the family. Lucas will almost certainly learn the trading business from his uncle. What do you want to do with your life?"

"Is this about me missing school the other day?" Tomas tried to frown, but in the warm light his face softened, and he simply looked at his father.

"No." Jaro shook his head, and the candles flickered in the warm, familiar room where the smell of losa tea had permanently stained the air. "It's got nothing to do with that. But, everyone grows up Tomas. Some people realise this and learn how to choose their own path rather than letting others choose it for them. I hope you'll learn how to be one of these people, how to take your own path in life." He paused. "It's time for you to see the oracle." And he noticed Tomas's skin prickle even in the warm night air.

What had it been like in those early days of fatherhood when he hadn't known what to do with a crying baby. "He's old enough now," Tomas's mother had said. "You must take care of him now." And Jaro had been afraid. He remembered that he had been afraid, although now, for the life of him, he could not think why.

Two days later, Jaro left his son at the oracle's small cottage built up against the side of a rocky hill at the far western point of the island. He watched as Tomas stood tall and still in the slanting light, hands clenched against his thighs. Then he walked back to the lighthouse, and for the next seven days, Jaro knew that — at this moment the oracle would be telling his son the old stories of the island that contained the secret ebbs and flows of the universe, just as her mother had told them to Jaro. And at this moment, she would cover the fire with dry herbs and that strange bitter smoke would fill his lungs. Jaro breathed in and remembered the smell that had clung to him, taken him away from the world he had always known, shaken his body and revealed to him his unspoken desires, his impossible love for Althea, his destiny to watch over the lighthouse, and the uncommon life that awaited him.

Jaro's mind returned to his own past and those days before Tomas, when there had just been him alone with himself in the world. Slowly the day grew dark and the lightning bugs flared randomly in the black night. He did not taste the food he placed in his mouth, and he wondered what strange transformation he himself was undergoing and whether all fathers felt such a pain while their sons sat inside the oracle's cave. Jaro folded his hands and prayed that his son would find peace.

Seven days later Tomas strode over the hill. His shirt was in his hands and across his back the oracle had inscribed three rippling blue lines of the sea.

8

That first night after his return Tomas couldn't sleep. His familiar cot that he had helped his father drag outside to escape the stifling heat of the lighthouse felt strange, sagged in the wrong places as if it did not recognise his body. Tomas turned onto his side and the cot creaked under his weight.

"You okay?" His father's voice was muffled and drowsy.

"Uh hm."

"Try to sleep." Jaro sighed deeply, and Tomas could hear his long, slow breath as the night's first dreams flooded his father's mind.

Tomas closed his eyes, but quickly opened them again. He could hear every creaking cricket, every mosquito whining in his ear, every howl from the band of monkeys in the trees, every crashing wave rolling at high tide against the rocky cliff below. His back burned where the oracle had inscribed the dark paste into his tender skin.

"It is the mark of the sea," she had told him, her voice soft and serious. "It is the water, which both separates and connects us to others, the sea that divides but is also the great bridge between worlds." Tomas had tried to listen as he gripped the stone table and squeezed his eyes shut to vanquish the scream that rose like a fire in his throat. The more he thought about it now, even in the cool nocturnal breezes of this new night, the more his back throbbed despite the oil his father had smeared across it just an hour before.

There was something about the balmy night, riotous with chirping insects, but also immensely tranquil with the far-off stars illuminating the dark vast canopy above, which inspired a certain intimacy with his own thoughts. Tomas's mind wandered over the events of the past week, wondering what his father had seen in him that had let him know it was time. Time for him to walk through the dark hall and breathe at the oracle's fires and come out again. Time for him to learn to be a man.

Tomas turned onto his other side. He could feel the ache of his back, but each throbbing sensation brought the memory of the past week. It raised a fierce knot of pride to clutch at his heart, and he caught himself smiling back into the night where no one else could see.

Turning his head to look up at the wide black night, Tomas thought about the oracle and about what his week with her had meant. The oracle had looked different than Tomas had expected. Or rather, what had surprised Tomas was that she had not looked different at all. Her eyes were a warm brown and her long dark hair was streaked with wisps of white. Yet apart from the dark spiralling bands tattooed across her wrists, she looked rather ordinary, like anyone's mother might look.

But the oracle did not speak like a mother. In a voice that sounded like rain against the trees, the oracle had told him many things. She had told him stories about the island that he had never heard before — stories of where it had come from, where it was going. Stories that reminded him of himself.

She had said, "This island is one of many islands in the sea. In some small way, I am its keeper because it is the oracle's providence to remember that this island was once part of the mainland in the times before it drifted out to sea. And that one day, many days from now, it will dissolve into the sea and will be no more."

Perhaps the oracle had known that this would frighten Tomas, so she had waited, sipping her tea at the wooden table and listening to the hollow melody of the wooden wind chimes from the porch. For a moment she had stood to light two more candles, banishing the last of the shadows from the room. Then she had looked straight into Tomas's eyes. "This is the way of the world, Tomas. Everything changes. Everything. Nothing is forever."

And then she had said, "Now eat your supper."

Tomas had been taught many stories about the island's past. Histories of the days when the island had been ruled by the mainland, of times when it had been forgotten as the mainland kingdoms waned. He knew that recent trade with the mainland had begun again two hundred years ago. He knew the history of Manel Prenai and the Losa Boom, and he knew of the founding of the losa co-operative.

There were other stories too. Stories islanders told to their children and to each other when the day's light waned. Myths and legends of the island's sacred importance as the foundation stone of the earth. In all these stories, the island was eternal, unchanging, full of magic. All islanders believed it was here that life had first taken form when lightning struck the sea, and Isa joined with Tor.

Tomas had always loved these stories that told him his

island was a magical place, the foundation of all things. The idea of his island as just another piece of the land, drifting about in the vast sea before it dissolved unceremoniously and without hesitation into the water frightened him, made him suddenly aware of the shifting sands beneath his own feet, made his bones creak. But something about the way the blood jumped in his veins when these words were spoken told him that it was the truth.

Tomas closed his eyes and remembered. While he had been with the oracle, time had floated and shimmered and eased past. The oracle had said, "You must discover who you are, Tomas, and also who you are not." Kneeling over the smouldering fire he breathed deeply, and then his thoughts had fallen backwards and Tomas felt that he was floating in the sea. Above him the moon had shone full and so low in the sky it was like a glowing orb, the third eye of his mind. And yet, although he knew he was alone in that place, that there was no land and that the sea spread out to infinity on all sides, he had not felt afraid. Instead he had rocked with the tide and knew that this was peace.

Tomas remembered that there had been many times over the course of the week when he had sat at the oracle's smooth wooden table eating stew from a bowl and listening to the silence that filled her home. He had known only from the slant of the light from the window how much time had passed, and he had lost track of the days when he slept in his blankets in the small grove of trees outside the oracle's gate. Day after day he had wandered back into the cave, carved like a womb in the mountain, and he had breathed at the fire. Day after day he had done little but sleep, eat, and search his mind for the wisdom that would make him a man.

The oracle had said, "We must let go of all false paths,

for grasping at things which are not to be is where our suffering begins," and in his mind, Tomas had seen Isla on the day they had dug the great hole that was meant to carry them to the other side of the world. "Let's dig a hole through the centre of the world!" She had come to him breathless and full of the force of her childhood imagination. "We can climb through to the other side. See what's there! Have a great adventure!" Following their young naivety, they had found a place and begun to dig, and Tomas had helped Isla lift the sandy earth out of the hole that she perceived to be her salvation from a life of boredom.

It had not been exhaustion or simply inevitability that had ended their adventure. It had been the sea that had welled up from the earth itself, and Isla had looked up at Tomas as if the sky was a gigantic grey wave rolling down upon her, crushing and tearing at her dreams. Tomas, then and now and forever after would remember that moment for the look on Isla's face as she stared up at him from the depths of her beloved hole, tears cutting rivulets through the fine layer of sandy earth on her young face. Tomas could not have known how many times he would recall this image of Isla's face over the coming years, but in his darkest hours, when he would wake in the middle of the night, his heart trembling with solitude, it would be the look of her face at this particular moment of despair that would remind him of destiny and restore his sense of peace.

Yet all these years later, the smoke of the oracle's fire had changed Tomas's memory. It had showed him a different vision than he remembered, that he stood alone in the hole of dark earth, sinking, sinking, and that the sky was fleeing from the crown of his head, and it occurred to him, as it had not then, that he was moving towards a place he did not want to go.

Laying on his cot Tomas listened to the cicadas sing, and he wondered what Isla would think of him now. The moment in the underwater cave had sent him into a maelstrom of confusion, and he struggled against the vast web of feelings that bound him to this girl who had always been his best friend. What was happening between them? This yearning to be near her, to hold her hand and touch the wildness of her hair. And at the same time, this new shyness that felt like a disease under his skin and held him back from doing these things he had once thought nothing of. Did it feel the same for her? Lost in the labyrinthian world of these thoughts, Tomas shifted and immediately gasped as he rolled too far and scratched his back against the woven hammock of the cot. Pain shot through him, burning a trail into his throat and sending tendrils of fire up the back of his neck.

It's Isla, Tomas told himself with a sudden sternness. *You know how she is. She isn't thinking about you like that. You should stop this all now, before you do something stupid.*

Tomas turned again trying to find a comfortable way to lie. From his cot, he peered over at his father's sleeping face, and he noticed for the first time that the creases from all his father's years of smiling and squinting into the sun and peering into the darkness from atop the lighthouse no longer faded with the peaceful countenance of sleep. His father was growing old.

Perhaps it was the look of his father's face, or perhaps it was simply the next step his wandering mind was meant to take, but in that single moment Tomas remembered something else from the oracle's cave. A vision. And with it the terrifying feeling that he was no longer a part of his father as he had once believed. It had not occurred to Tomas before his visit to the oracle that his father would not always be with him.

"All the world is changing," the oracle had said. "Bodies wither and die, mountains slowly crumble into plains, even the water of the sea shifts and ebbs and changes its form. You must find what you are, Tomas, and also what you are not." Perhaps the oracle had said more, but Tomas no longer saw the walls of the cave, for his mind's eye had brought a vision of his father laying in a white cloth hammock — and Tomas realised that his father was dead. In the vision, the wind had risen up to shake the trees. It had screamed over the cliff of the lighthouse so loudly that it had engulfed Tomas by its piercing sound. In the face of this great wind, everything fell away and Tomas had realised he was alone. And he had been afraid.

Tomas looked now at his father lying asleep beside him on his cot. Jaro's breath was low and steady. Tomas gasped with the power of the vision that had come to him, and his face burned hot with tears that no one could see. Again and again he whispered into the night, "What will I do? What will I do?"

What could he possibly do without his father? How could he ever learn to live alone? Was this what it meant to become a man? If so, Tomas was certain he did not want it. His da had taught him everything he knew — how to train the gulls with bits of fish, how to assemble a slingshot from a branch of the willow tree, how to tell when an approaching storm would be a welcome end to drought or a dangerous cyclone. Just last month, his da had taught him how to shave, and while he had stood practicing with shaking, sweating hands, Jaro had also revealed in the most casual way the secret of what happens between men and women during the heat of love. His father was the constant presence in Tomas's life, his answer to all questions.

But in the fear of this night, Tomas heard the oracle's voice — "You must learn who you are, Tomas. Then you will never be afraid to take the path that is marked out for you, and you will walk your own way amongst the beings of the world."

9

The year Isla turned sixteen she began to dream about her mother. At first she was able to shake her head in the morning and the vague visions fell away like so much dust, but as the dreams persisted, they began to follow Isla also in her waking hours. Slowly, she began to remember the features of her mother's face that had become vague and inconstant from the passing years. She began to hear again the soft voice and the comforting laughter that followed at her back when she ran through the losa hills of her dreams. And gradually, Isla began to remember something else — that her mother was not from the island.

Standing at the east end of the sagging veranda of her house in the light of the afternoon sun, Isla began to wonder for the first time in many years what had brought her mother to this island. What had drawn her to such a remote and stagnating place? Had she been searching for something which she had finally found on this island? Or had she been fleeing a troubled past of her own? Isla looked across the losa hills of her island out to the sea her mother had crossed and felt the great empty expanse also in her own heart that was so wide no bridge could cross it.

"Isla, are you ready to go?"

Isla followed her father's voice back into the depths of her house. She stood alone in the main room, gazing across the thick wooden table that had warped and cracked in its own way, and watching the way the white bands of light marked out the space of this room. Noticing how dark the house was, Isla found herself wondering if it had always been this way, back in her deepest memories, even in the bright days when her mother had been alive. In that moment, it felt to Isla as if the house had filled with the shadows of despair, as if the darkness was not so much a protection from the sweltering afternoons, but rather a reflection of the sombre voices that echoed there, a palpable remoteness which had crept between her and her father over the years of her life.

"Not yet. I'm not ready yet!" It was a soft voice that stole into her mind from the fertile depths of her dreams, and Isla's blood ran cold as this other memory washed over her. Her skin had looked so pale surrounded by the mass of tangled black hair, which had clung to her neck and forehead in thin, damp wisps as she lay without desire or thought against the white sheets. "Mama." Isla had sat next to her on the bed and tugged at her arm. "Mama." But her mother had not moved, only lay there breathing a ragged unhealthy breath that sounded like wind through a hole in the roof.

Isla clutched the edge of the wooden table and sat with all her weight against the seat of the chair. How could she remember this? Why was she remembering it now? "Go lie down, your mother is still sick." It was in her mind that she heard Petro's voice. And then she saw him, like a ghost before her, hurrying from room to room, boiling water, bringing clean blankets, his shaking hands fluttering through the air as if he believed he might hold death off at the threshold by his sheer commitment to movement.

Then, suddenly, her mother had moved, grasping the crumpled sheets in her fists. "No," she had whispered. "No, not yet. I'm not ready yet." In these moments between fever and death, Myrium had looked at her young daughter's face, the child she was being forced to abandon unprotected in a world that had shown itself to be treacherous and full of shadows.

"Not yet. I'm not ready." Isla heard her mother's voice echo in her memory as her mother lay wasted and consumed by sickness. These were the words Isla remembered and she took them as her mother's truth, spoken as they were in Isla's unexpected memory of the hour of her death. Her father had wanted her to leave, but she had not. Had her mother held her small hand and prevented him? Had Isla simply refused to leave? Why couldn't she remember?

The vision fell again and again through her mind, but Isla could not recall the moment her mother had let go of the pain in her heart and found peace. So instead, Isla had to imagine the moment of heavy stillness that must have followed her mother's last breath. She was alone in this imagined moment, alone in that still room where no one breathed, and Isla too held her breath. Would her life be like this too? Reduced to a footprint in the sand that would wash away in the tides of time, so that one day it would be as if she had never lived at all. The years would fly by and she would eat and sleep and talk about island things that didn't matter. She would mark her age by the lack of smoothness in her skin and the number of children that she had borne. *If that's all that ever happens to me, what is the point of me even being on this earth?* Isla muttered to the room and to the memory she prayed would leave her, although she knew with an unquestionable certainty that it would not.

"Isla, we're going to be late." Her father strode into the kitchen.

"I'm ready," Isla whispered, still caught in the web of her dream.

As they walked, Isla tried to shake the cold, sad feeling from her skin. She focused on the warmth of the evening sun at her back and then on the faint but growing sound of the drums that were calling all islanders to the great fire for the Binding Celebrations. Perhaps it would be a good night after all. Everyone was always full and happy on this night, even her father!

Isla and Petro found a place on a long, dried-out log. Behind the shouts of a thousand conversations, Isla could hear music — the steady thump of a drum and the high sweet notes of a flute — and she found her fingers tapping out the rhythm which she knew by heart against the side of her knee. Petro too began to tap his foot in the bare earth. He was clean shaven. He sat with his back straight and his hands folded and still in his lap. And yet there was something in his eyes that told Isla he was happy.

From across the fire-circle, Eva waved. Her lips were stained red, and as she pushed one of her younger sisters from her lap, Isla noticed her discretely smooth her hair and glance toward the tiller's son Jacob as she crossed her ankles imitating her mother. Isla scanned the crowd of faces looking for the others. Marco would certainly be with his family, lost amongst the crowd that had come up from the harbour colony. Her gaze rippled like a wave over familiar faces, looking for Lucas and for Tomas, but she could not see them.

The bonfire was lit at the precise moment the fiery belly of the sun skimmed the living waters of the horizon. Everyone was there — the fishermen and their families, the losa growers and harvesters, the tillers and traders, shop owners, and craftsmen. Infants suckled new mothers' proudly swollen breasts. Children screamed with laughter as they ran faster and faster between the legs of the adults in their chaotic circumambulation of the fire. Parents, in their turn, waved to friends and scolded their adolescent children for slumping in their seats.

Slowly, the crowd fell quiet, and Isla looked up to see Sylvia Prenai step up onto the small platform at the eastern edge of the fire. Despite her many eccentricities, Sylvia Prenai held a reputation that was unrivalled on the island. She stepped with elegance in satin shoes entirely unsuited to the tropical climate, and the coiffure of white hair which few could remember ever being black was always immaculately maintained with its intricate twists and tied securely against the nape of her neck. And yet, the great reverence with which she was always received by the islanders flowed not from a recognition of her exemplary spirit or even from the antique wealth which had collected at her feet over so many generations of Prenai landowners and entrepreneurs. It surfaced instead from an undercurrent of narcissism that had gradually infiltrated island life, for most islanders saw Sylvia Prenai's sophistication as evidence of their island's high culture, her wealth the result of their island's great natural riches, her faded memories the shreds of their island's glorious past. So it seemed self-evident at the time of the annual Binding Celebrations that it should be Sylvia Prenai who would inaugurate the festivities by tying the first band, as she had done for the last seventeen years since her father, the great Manel Prenai, had died.

Sylvia Prenai stood as a seagull on the stage, regal because of her stance and stature rather than her actual features, for up close, she looked windblown and tattered as if she had spent long days atop the mast of a sail far out at sea. Her most prominent feature, seen even from the back rows of the crowd and of utmost importance to her position was her nose, which was long and slightly hooked and was the mark of her family's inheritance — including a great many more things, though not as many as most people on the island supposed. When she spoke, she gestured widely with one hand and her words carried in the still evening breezes.

"I have lived on this island for many years," she began. "My father, Manel Prenai, may the oceans preserve his memory, oversaw the founding of the Iosa co-operative which guards our livelihoods to this day. And in my own time, I have seen many a thing. I have seen most of you born...and I remember you all as children. It is the privilege of the old to understand the depths that we islanders are all bound to each other."

The fire crackled as two large men heaved on more logs. Sylvia Prenai continued, "Today we remember that who we are has much to do with who we are bound to in our lives — bound by love, by years spent together, by this land and sea. As Isa and Tor first emerged from the sea and joined themselves on this land that is now our own, so too these Binding Celebrations renew ties, not only to each other but to the land itself, this island, the most sacred of all places, where we were born, where we have lived, and where we will all end our days..."

Isla's mind began to drift. The flames of the fire danced,

licking the edges of the declining light, and it began also to suggest to Isla all the vague unspoken things that also bound people to the island — fear, love, idleness, familiarity. Through the entrancing whispers of the fire, Isla saw that the people she knew, all those who sat before her and beside her, all of them were playing the roles they were born to fulfil, following those roles because they could not imagine what else they might do or who else they might be.

Is that all that we are? Isla thought. *People defined by those we are bound to? Are we not something more than that? Something that is just ourselves?*

Isla looked at Sylvia Prenai alone on the stage, gesturing with her frail, trembling hands and speaking of the glory of her forefathers long dead and sent to the sea. And although this was the day set aside by all island calendars as the Binding Celebrations, Isla thought instead of all the people on the island who were unbound and alone — Sylvia Prenai who lived as an apparition in her draft-ridden crumbling house, the old woman called the oracle who lived alone on a cliff far from town where she kept her knowledge of restorative herbs and remedial concoctions and whose only daughter had gone away and had never returned. There was Jaro, Tomas's father, who was alone in his lighthouse, who had raised Tomas on his own after Tomas's mother, who had not been Jaro's wife, had come and slipped away again by the sea, abandoning them both. Sylvia Prenai, the oracle, Jaro...and Isla's own mother who had not come from the island but had spent her days as a foreigner here.

How many more were alone on this island? Isla wondered. *Alone with their secrets?*

Isla's gaze rose from the fire to Sylvia Prenai's face, and it seemed to her that despite the tremor in her voice and the awkward waving of her hand, she was the strongest woman

Isla knew. Despite years of pressure from her family, she had never married. Of course there had been rumours, rumours of her deformed breasts, rumours that as a girl she had twice been found unclothed beneath the twisted roots of the banyan tree with a harvester's daughter. Why had she remained here? Was it simply fear, the seeming impossibility of making one's way alone in the world? Had it seemed better to stay on the island where one was known and recognised, even if that meant being alone, rather than venturing out into a world unknown and strange with only the irrational hope that one might be known again, loved again, bound again to other better things? Had this other possible destiny ever occurred to her?

As she studied Sylvia Prenai's face, a familiar panic rose in Isla's throat and she felt as if she must know, must understand what had kept such a woman bound here, trapped on this island. Through the heat of the fire, Sylvia Prenai's features swayed unsteadily on her face, aspects so particular to her distorted, wandered far from their usual places, and for an instant, it seemed to Isla as if Sylvia Prenai's features were being slowly replaced by her own, and the meaning of this terrible prophesy shook her with a thunder.

It was only then that she heard the old bejewelled woman calling out her name and felt her father patting her back in congratulations.

"Such a blessing it is for me to see in this younger generation, children brought up in our island ways," Sylvia Prenai announced. "I am sure Petro is quite proud of his daughter, and I know it gives us all immense hope to know our island will be in such hands after we ourselves have passed to the sea."

Before Isla knew what was happening, she was pushed to her feet. Petro grasped his daughter's face and kissed both cheeks with such extravagant gusto that Isla immediately went red. A moment later, she was standing on the small platform at the eastern edge of the fire, and Sylvia Prenai's cold bony hands were on her wrist knotting the first band, ostentatious with its gold-coloured threading, around her arm. Up close, Isla noticed Sylvia Prenai's skin looked paper thin and, in the white light of the fire, it seemed as if she were truly fading away. And then Sylvia Prenai wrapped her arms around Isla's shoulders and whispered in her ear, "You remind me of myself, my dear. And of your mother too. One day, you too will be a great woman of the island." Isla shivered as handfuls of flower petals flew through the air.

Isla returned, as she knew she ought, to her father's side. Drawing from her pocket a thick band that was the dark blue of the sky in mourning, Isla knotted the band around her father's wrist. She kissed him three times on each cheek as custom required, and tried to stop herself from wondering how it was possible that after all these years living together, eating together, working the hills and garden together... after so many hours of lessons in which Petro had taught her the names of the insects he had collected, then the crickets and cicadas, then the stars... after all the many days she had practiced her music lessons to the metronome of his attentive ear, how after such enduring physical proximity, it still felt so awkward to kiss her own father. For his turn, Petro tied a delicate purple band around Isla's brown wrist which he explained was to remind her of their losa fields. Then he had kissed each cheek sentimentally, looked into her eyes and pronounced, "You still look like your mother after all."

"Thank you father," she had replied because she had not known what else to say. Then, she slipped past him into the crowd. Every step she took, her father's friends and families and young children and school friends caught hold of her arms, put sweets into her mouth and tied bands around her wrists until both arms were stained with the fresh dye of a thousand shades of colour.

Finally, on a low branch of a banyan tree, she found Tomas and his father sitting quietly and surveying the crowd. Jaro puffed at a slender wooden pipe and whispered something that made Tomas laugh. Many years later, Isla would remember them on that night as the way they both had looked when they were happy.

As she approached the great twisting roots of the tree, she called up, "Hello Jaro-da. I have a band for you."

"And I for you, Isla-ja," Jaro said affectionately. "I have quite a view from up here. Always have liked heights — you can see a great many things from up high. But it would be difficult to come down. Tomas will tie mine as well."

Isla didn't hear what Jaro said to Tomas. The words came from the corner of his mouth as he drew on the long pipe, and they spilled out in trickles of blue smoke. Then, Jaro patted his son on the knee, and Tomas jumped to the ground.

"Seriously Tomas, I've got to get away from here. These people are making me crazy." From the tree, Jaro laughed. "If it were me, I'd go find out what Lucas has done with that bottle of spiced liquor I saw him swipe earlier. I'm sure he'll be looking for company to get into trouble." Isla looked up and above them, the banyan tree spread out like another kind of sky, and as Jaro shifted to lean against the central trunk, Isla lost sight of him in the cool shadows.

10

Lucas was indeed waiting for his friends next to a small scraggly tree that clung close to the cliff not far from the lighthouse. The night was still and the light from the small fire cast his face into silhouette. His latest girlfriend, Flava, leaned against his legs smoking a rolled leaf, which she twirled slowly back and forth between her thumb and forefinger.

Tomas and Lucas clasped hands in their way, and Lucas smiled at Isla. "Hey it's the First Band!" he teased. "You must be so proud!"

Isla glared at him and shook her head, irritated that she could no longer feel her hair sway loose at the back of her neck. She was older now and had to tie her hair tight against the wild winds of the sea.

"Don't."

"I'm only joking. Relax," Lucas shrugged, taking a drink and rolling his eyes at Flava.

Isla sat down, and only when she had removed every last band from around her wrists and shoved them into her pocket did she turn towards the fire. Seeing the bottle of spirits resting upright in the soft earth, she grabbed it by the neck and pressed it to her lips. The spirits scorched her throat and raised the tears which had been buried behind her eyes. She drank again, finding a strange relief in the pain that spread through her throat and into her belly and seemed to fill some great chasm of solitude. She could not end up like Madame Prenai, wasted and alone. She could not end up like her mother, filled with regret. Isla looked out towards the wide sea that taunted her with its uncrossable vastness. Then she pulled the bottle to her lips and let the liquid fire burn through her.

"Gods Isla!" Lucas said.

"Go drown yourself Lucas, you drink this all the time," Isla cursed. Out of the corner of her eye she saw Tomas hold up his hands when Lucas caught his eye.

She took another gulp, and this time Isla felt a hand rest on her wrist. "Slow down, Isla." Tomas's voice was low, and when he spoke, Isla felt a long breath leave her body.

"Sometimes I really hate it here," she whispered to no one in particular. Her head was beginning to swim and thoughts she had always kept sealed tight inside her began to climb into her throat and spill out with her words.

"I like it here," said Flava, flicking smoke into the sky with her tongue.

"How do you know?" Isla challenged. "You've never been anywhere else."

"I just know. I like it here," Flava replied unperturbed.

"Well, you're crazy," Isla said. "People just rot away here. No one does anything with their lives. All anyone on this island cares about is themselves and their little patch of earth. How can I be the only one who sees it? Well, I'm going to do something with my life. My life is going to mean something."

Before her eyes, Isla saw her mother's face, pale and grey with the certain light of death, and she could not look away. Tomas took the bottle from her and handed it back to Lucas.

"Sylvia Prenai has been alone forever, you know," Isla said. "Her whole life she has lived in that house and she has been alone. I can't end up like that, trapped here, never understanding anything, always alone."

"What are you raving about Isla? There's life, there's the sun, there's this bottle." Lucas raised his arm triumphantly. "You'll never be alone. It's not possible to be alone on this island!"

He looked over at Isla but something in her face made him suddenly hesitate and even Isla heard his voice shift. "You're not going to be alone, Isla." Lucas looked over at Tomas, but Tomas was staring into the fire and was silent.

"How do you know I won't be alone? Maybe I will be alone. Maybe I will be trapped here. Maybe I'll never get out and nothing will ever happen to me." Isla could feel the force of these thoughts spilling out ahead of her. They were things she shouldn't say. But she couldn't remember why. Her head felt heavy and her vision swam.

"It's sea, sea, sea. Everywhere you look. Outside my window, here, sea, sea. You dig down deep — sea. It's surrounding us and we'll never escape it, never cross it. One day it will take us too and it will be too late for anything else, too late to make a mark on this earth. It will be like we never existed..." She paused, but the words were coming as if pulled by a thread that held to the rest —"Just like my mother."

"Everyone remembers your mother, Isla. That's the important thing. Everyone remembers her."

Isla sighed. "Being remembered isn't the same thing as living."

"No," Lucas said suddenly, staring away from the group, his face falling into shadow. "No it's not."

They were all quiet for a moment, and Isla took the rolled leaf out of Tomas's hand and relit it in the embers at the edge of the fire. She leaned back against Tomas's shoulder and smoked and was silent. Her mind closed like a shell, and Isla saw that it was the eyes that had betrayed her in her dream, and that it was not in fact her mother but she herself who lay on the death bed, those same silver eyes dulled to grey, calling out the names of all the things she hadn't done, finding names for all her dark dreams and lost hopes, knowing with the unshakeable, inescapable certainty of final regret that it was too late, too late to go back.

Sometime in the indiscernible hours of night, Isla opened her eyes and found herself staring sideways at the fire. For a long time, she lay there, remembering the evening, wondering how long she had been asleep. There was a sour taste in her mouth, and she knew she had been sick, although she couldn't remember it. Off to her left she heard Lucas snoring. Then, it occurred to her that someone must still be keeping the fire alive and at that same moment, she noticed that she was lying on something soft. Isla stirred, buried her face into the shirt. It smelled like him.

Tomas was sitting at the edge of the cliff. The light from the fire warmed his back, and Isla noticed again the three dark rippling lines that spread across his shoulder blades and were unmistakably the mark of the sea. He turned his face to look at her when she approached, and the momentum of his silence was such that everything around him seemed to fall still — the breeze, the sea, even the birds suspended in the high dawn air. From all the years Isla had spent sitting next to Tomas and looking out to sea, she knew with certainty that he was thinking of the future, perceiving something in his mind's eyes which lay ahead of him in inescapable time, and so she simply sat down next to him and waited. Together they sat in that *drune*, looking out towards the sea and seeing such different things in it.

"I didn't mean it," she said at last, and Tomas looked over at her, his eyes still filled with a faraway look.

"About being alone..."

"You meant some of it," Tomas said, though his voice was calm and relaxed as someone who has accepted what is before him, and Isla strained to remember what she had said and what he might mean.

"I've been dreaming of my mother," she said, looking away from him out into the empty space before her. "And it's made me think of all the things I'll never know about her..." Isla watched as her voice drifted gently out over the cliff and rose into the air. The world around them was still and even the light tiptoed over the land at this hour and with such a tenderness that it seemed to Isla as if she and Tomas were the only two people awake and that she could reveal things and they would be kept secret.

Tomas looked over at her, waiting for her to say more, but she couldn't bear to speak of things that would return her to that terrible deathbed and that terrifying vision of her mother's voice, and when he saw in her eyes the things she could not say, Tomas put his arm around her for a moment and squeezed her shoulder.

"Can I ask you something?"

"Sure."

"Can you tell me about the oracle? I never asked you and..." she paused and leaning back she traced the lines of blue that crossed his bare back. "Did she tell you what this means?"

"Well... yes and no," Tomas replied, bringing a hand

over his shoulder and across the blue lines he could never see. "I think it's up to me to find that out." Then he began to speak of the oracle, for despite appearances, she was often on his mind. He told Isla what he could remember of the house that sat above the silver mangroves and leaned against a cavernous ridge, of the bitter smell from the smoke of her fire, of the tattooed bands that crossed the oracle's wrists, and of the mercurial passage of time.

"She said this is just one island in the sea. One of thousands. It's not special. But, I don't know why…it still feels special to me. Even though I believe her. Even though I see now that it won't last forever and that it wasn't there at the beginning of all things like we were told. Still, there is something about it — something I belong to. Or something that belongs to me. Maybe that's enough."

"Why now?" He turned to her, his brown eyes filling with the dawn light. "You never asked me about it before."

"I don't know," Isla shrugged. "I guess maybe I was afraid."

Tomas laughed. "Afraid? You?"

Isla smiled, and then her face fell and she looked away from him again. "Sometimes it feels as if I am always afraid," she said quietly. Then she sat in the unexpected truth of these words, and in her mind, she wondered how Tomas could feel so peaceful here, so connected, while she felt at odds with everything. And she wondered how not knowing what else was out there in the world could ever feel like enough.

11

"Tell me the real story," Lucas said. They sat on the veranda that overlooked the sea to the right and the purple losa hills to the left. Petro was smoking, and the humidity from the recent rain held the blue smoke in the shelter of the wide porch, and it spilled over Lucas's head like the cloud of men.

"We were all young when the Losa Co-operative was formed," Jayan replied, and he tapped his pipe against his knee as was his habit during these kinds of discussions.

"It was the greatest single act in the island's modern history," Petro affirmed. "They had foresight, our grandfathers. And Manel Prenai was the greatest among them because he saw it first, what no one else had noticed."

"They started picking us off, one-by-one," said Jayan. "No sense of Enough those mainlanders. More, more, they always want more. But More comes with sacrifices of its own, Lucas. Never forget. In order to get More of something, you always have to give something else up."

Jayan leaned forward in his wicker chair and its joints creaked in the damp afternoon air like an angry voice of the gods whispering enigmatic wisdoms in a house of plain wood and plain words. Jayan pointed with thick knuckled fingers into Lucas's young face, and Lucas nodded solemnly even though he didn't understand. They had learned about the co-operative in school. He knew about the founding members and evil mainland traders and the current laws that governed the co-operative. But he had no idea why it had been necessary to form the co-operative in the first place. What Lucas did know was that when the old men on the island talked about those days during the great Losa Boom, their eyes danced with new life.

Now, sitting on that blue, smokey porch, Lucas wished it was his father who was telling these stories, his father who stared intently off into the distance like Petro, or passionately into his eyes now like Jayan, and remembered their small part in the great history of the island. Lucas's own father had been a trader, like his uncles. He had not been a part of the early co-operative, and he had died young, when Lucas was still a small child. *Before he had had a chance to do anything important,* Lucas thought to himself. Lucas promised himself that he would not fall to his father's fate, a life that was too quiet, too simple, and therefore easily lost. His father hadn't made a name for himself, and so he had been easy to replace, and it hadn't been long before his mother had remarried his father's older brother who had also lost his own wife several years before. Now Lucas's younger sisters called their uncle, 'da', because they had forgotten they had once had a da of their own.

Erased. That was how Lucas thought of his father. Yet when he heard stories about the men who had founded the co-operative, Lucas understood that if you did a great deed in the world, if you made a name for yourself like these men had done, you would not be forgotten. These men, men like

Manel Prenai, would not be forgotten. Even after they had died, a part of them still lived on, immortalised in the reverence of their name.

"You have to start at the beginning, Jayan," Petro shook his head. His wide brimmed hat shifting unsteadily with his movement and his moustache that was carefully clipped each morning at sunrise, gave him a certain authority that equalled the seriousness of his scholarship on matters of island history. "The losa we grow on this island is purified by the sea air, nourished by the slant of the sun against the hills and imbued with the qualities of the island soil. It is valuable to the mainlanders because the leaves and buds are used to make a high quality dye. During the age of our grandfathers, the mainlanders started to use losa to dye cloth. They began to need more and more losa, so several mainland traders broke with custom and instead of heading to Joon, they sailed directly to the island to try to convince the islanders to grow more losa."

Petro paused and looked out into the fields where Isla was walking with Tomas, and for a moment he was filled with regret that he was not telling this story to his daughter, that it was not his own daughter who had asked this question about their island's past. Why couldn't Isla see how much he had sacrificed for her? How he had given up his dreams of travel, even his wife. Isla had brought fever into the house, but it was his wife who had been sacrificed in the end. And still, Isla never gave back to him, never humoured him with questions which he had spent decades trying to research and record in full and meticulous detail with the scratchings of his black pen. Isla always did what was expected of her, but no more. She wasn't like her mother. Myrium had come to the island and had given him everything. Six short years, they had gone like the flash of a shooting star, tearing a beauty across the sky, and then gone forever.

The rain started again, and Petro saw Isla and Tomas standing under a wide banana leaf pulled down like a curving green roof over their heads. Isla's back was to Petro, and he gazed at this daughter that had grown into a woman with her hair tied back in the usual knotted ring at her neck. She stood at the edge of the mango trees in her thin dress, one hand on her right hip, and Petro thought to himself that she looked as Myrium would have looked — as Myrium once had looked when they had been the ones to hide from the rain together under such great leaves that stretched as long as a man's height and half as wide and were as green as the youngest losa leaves.

Perhaps, he *thought, I am worrying for nothing. She is an island girl, after all, and island girls stay near their fathers. It has been a good many moons since she has mentioned that boatman and the mainland. Perhaps these are all just childish dreams after all. Yes, perhaps I will arrange for her to marry Tomas, and they will move into this house and give me grandchildren and a bit of joy after all my years and it will be alright in the end.*

He gazed out into his land, looking at his daughter and thinking of his wife. As she turned, he raised one hand from where it rested on the arm of his damp chair. But his daughter did not wave back, and he remembered again that it was not Myrium but Isla that stood before him, and that Isla was not like her mother.

Lucas sat on the highest step of the porch watching Petro gaze into the distance of the island's past glories. He knew it was not his place to interrupt, but he was anxious with the dreams of men and great destinies. "Petro-da, what happened when the mainlanders came to the island."

Petro blinked and withdrew his gaze. "I'm telling you

Lucas. This is what I'm telling. They came here with big boats. Expecting to take something back, they were. Spoke straight to the growers themselves, spoke to any islander who had a bit of land. It was always the same. They stood tall, spoke with big voices as if they were important people. But the mainland had declined by then, it was small—hardly bigger than the island itself."

"It had more people though," Jayan cut in, shaking his pipe again at Lucas and speaking louder than he needed to to make himself heard over the rain, and perhaps over Petro as well.

"That's true," Petro said. "So they tried to convince everyone on the island to grow more losa. Said it would be in the island's interest too. Said with all the mainlanders wanting to buy our losa, we could all become rich. But then they talked to Manel Prenai — even then, his family had many hills of land and most grew losa, but the mainlanders had missed him because they are dull witted people. And, of course, the Prenai land is far from the port and our hills. The Prenai family had already made much of their wealth by this point because they were already growing and selling the most losa to the mainland when the losa boom hit. But Manel Prenai didn't like the look of those mainlanders. He saw immediately that they were scoundrels, targeting one losa grower at a time, creating divisions among us. So he called all the growers together and any islander with land."

"They met at the great fire circle, and Manel Prenai challenged those mainlanders. He came with his stick that he always carried with him when he walked in his losa hills and he said — 'You have made many promises, mainlanders. But tell us, if everyone here with land to their name grows losa, then who will grow our food?' And the mainlanders smiled as if they had caught Manel Prenai in a net and said, 'You can easily buy food from the mainland with all the money you will earn by trading your losa.' And Manel Prenai asked, 'You make many promises, mainlanders, but is it not true that the more of us grow losa the more common it will become and the less people on the mainland will want to pay for it?' The mainlanders tried to smile but their faces twitched and twisted and their eyes darted nervously because a whispering had started softly amongst the growers.

"The mainland traders tried to argue their case," Petro continued, as if he had recounted this story many times to himself and knew the words by heart. "But they were no match for Manel Prenai and his walking stick. 'What happens if you mainlanders raise the price of food?' Manel Prenai challenged. And then he turned to his fellow islanders and said, 'We have something here that is special. The losa grown on this island is purified by the sea air. It is nourished by the slant of the sun against the hills. It is imbued with the qualities of the island soil. It is irreplaceable, irreplicable, and we must guard it against such men as these. After all, we are people of the island. Our island stands strong in the vast sea. It does not lean against the mainland. And neither do we.'

And then Manel Prenai said, 'We should establish a council among us. Let islanders decide together who should grow losa and how much and who should grow wheat instead and who vegetables.' And then Manel Prenai stamped his walking stick against the ground, and he said to the island growers, 'Men, for my part, I shall give up growing losa in half of my hills so that all may be equal among us and no single grower be unfairly advantaged against another in the matter of losa.'"

The rain had stopped again, and Petro saw that Isla had

picked up her basket and had returned to collecting the ripened mangos from the branches in the grove. He saw her mouth move as if she were singing or perhaps chanting some rhyme again and again, but Petro could not hear her voice. Then he turned his gaze back to Lucas whose face was wide and flushed with the humid heat. "That is how the co-operative was formed. And that is why there is a single group at harvest time that collects and weighs each grower's losa according to each's allotted amount. It was decided by the first council that losa growing rights would be passed from father to son. My grandfather was one of the first councilmen and from then until now, the losa council has protected the rights of the losa growers. So, when the mainlanders conned other regions into growing losa which was not as high quality, the council created the seal which is still put on every sack of losa we trade with the mainland and which insures we can still sell it at a high price because of its high quality."

Petro's attention had started to waver. He was thinking about his father. There had been a time, a day, when his own father had sat on this very porch, telling him the story of the co-operative, which he had lived through but had been too young to bother understanding. Petro thought of the time of music and play and great expanses of days when they had all lived together in this house, his mother with her black satin hair, and his father with his straight unwavering frame, his indomitable grandfather who smoked a pipe and sank into his belly when he fell asleep in his favourite chair, and his grandmother who always smiled when he had misbehaved and told him bedtime stories about monsters at sea and fairies that lived among the losa. Later, he had wanted to leave to travel to the mainland, to see snake charmers and wandering sadhus, to hear strange tongues ring softly in his ear and feel new foods burn ferocious in his mouth. He had wanted to leave this home and his family. But now he couldn't remember why.

Petro thought of his grandfather, how he had married off two daughters and watched his son grow into a man, and then sat while his grandchildren played at his feet. Petro imagined his grandfather reclining into his favourite wicker chair that sat warped and arthritic in the left corner of the porch, imagined him blowing smoke into the air with a sigh of satisfaction, surrounded by a family he had created and protected and nurtured into fullness. Petro blew smoke into the air and leaned back in his chair and waited for peace to come upon him.

12

It was just after the yearly rains when Jaro felt a deep cough shake his chest. When he looked up he could see through his streaming tears that the moon hung ominously low in the sky. A week later the fever broke long enough for a sudden lucidity to come upon him, and Jaro commanded Tomas and Lucas with a momentary strength of purpose to drag his frail body which lay against the woven grasses of his wooden cot out into the openness of the night.

"Go home," Tomas said to Lucas when it was done. "The fever has broken. Everything is going to be okay now."

Tomas watched as the shape of Lucas's body fell into shadow and grew faint as he made his way along the road, and Tomas thought there was something in the way he walked that had changed. *We're grown now*, he realised. *He walks like a man. Are we old enough for what that might bring?*

The night stretched on and the heat was unrelenting, even in the deep black hours, but Jaro shivered again in the cot and his skin was dry and flushed with an internal fire that would not be quenched. "Check the lighthouse," Jaro mumbled, and Tomas sat by his side and reassured him that the light was already ablaze. "Light the fire," Jaro whispered. And Tomas held water to his father's lips and told him that the light shone bright and would certainly be seen even far out at sea.

At last sweat broke out on Jaro's arms, his neck dripped with water from the sea, and he took a long deep breath. Peace fell upon him, his eyes cleared and Jaro knew that this was the moment he had foreseen. He held his son's hand, or perhaps his son held his, and Jaro was overcome with amazement at this man by his side who had once been so small. He wanted to tell his son so many things. He wanted to say, 'Tomas, you will be strong. Don't be afraid." But he could not speak.

Jaro fell again into a dream and remembered the day Althea had handed him this infant boy, and in the midst of his great fear at the prospect of fatherhood, the boy had gripped his thumb with such ferocity that Jaro had felt comforted and had known that life would be true to them both. "Tomas," he tried again to say, "don't be afraid. You will go on after I am gone." But Tomas could not hear the voiceless words, and his hands shook because his father's fever had come on again and he could not bring it down. He was afraid, and he could not make his hands still.

Jaro tried to hold Tomas in his eyes. He wanted to tell his son, "These things are not decided by you or me, but by a force much greater than us both." But instead his body was seized by a fit of coughing and he gasped and struggled for breath.

And then, Tomas was never certain whether the beam from the lighthouse fell upon them in their hour of need or whether it was his father's eyes themselves that filled with light. Jaro found his voice. It was light and sounded as fleeting and ephemeral as the wind. "I have loved you so greatly, Tomas," Jaro said. He gasped. "But my time as your father is over. I have another path to take now." Then, he closed his eyes, and Tomas knew he would never open them again. When Jaro's breath finally stopped, it was not with a poignant sigh to mark his passing on the earth, but as the wind when it simply does not stir. And still his face was bright.

"Do not disturb him," a voice whispered from behind. It was the oracle and tears were in her eyes. "He has entered the clear light between worlds." She sat down next to Tomas, putting her hands with their strange spiralling tattoos into her lap and did not reach out to comfort him. Yet because tears flowed from both their eyes in the same unstoppable way, Tomas felt that he was not alone.

Moments stretched on without time. Then, without warning, Jaro's hand fell from his side and his face turned to ash like the dark side of the moon. "He has left us," the oracle pronounced softly and rose to leave. Tomas blinked and noticed that the sun had begun to rise. He watched as the oracle gently touched her thumb to his father's forehead. He wanted to ask her how she had known to come. Instead he said, "What am I going to do now?"

The oracle glanced over at him, her hair whiter than he remembered from the caves, and her eyes flashed with an inexplicable irritation. "You will live your life, Tomas," she said. Then, seeing the anguish in his brown eyes she paused and laid a hand on his shoulder. "Being parted from one you love is always difficult. But if you are wise, you will see that it is inevitable and so pointless to resist. As the wise have often said, death is the greatest teacher, Tomas, for it reminds us that nothing lasts forever, not even ourselves."

She turned to go and then, the oracle hesitated and in the pale untainted light of dawn her finely draped clothes lost their enigmatic appearance, her face abandoned its impenetrable stoicism and she smiled at him with a new gentleness. "I remember when you were born," she said. "Your father loved you greatly." Tomas did not speak, but the oracle could see the questions that were burrowing into his mind, so she said, "You will understand all of this one day when you meet my daughter. She has gone to the mountains beyond the mainland, to the land of snow to learn her vocation. When she returns she will know many things that even I do not understand, things that have become lost to us here on the island. One day she will come back to this island, and on that day many things will become clear."

The day of Jaro's funeral the birds fled to the trees so that not a single gull marked the earth with its shadow or cried out with its typical cacophony of petty complaints, and the startling silence this brought to the skies was so disconcerting that it made the mourners hurry on their feet as they carried the wooden raft down to the shoreline, anxious for the loud crashing sounds of the sea. Within the hour, the men had assembled the raft by weaving the logs with a kind of twine rolled from sea grasses and arranging with ritualistic care the pile of wood and cloth soaked in bitter scented oil.

It was only then that the procession began, and the women took the lead in the mourning hymns —

We will miss you,
We will miss you,
Our Jaro,
Son of the island,
Man amongst us.
All life begins and all life passes away.
And so too Jaro, so too our Jaro.

Clear his path,
Clear his path, as he goes forth to the sea,
He is taking the journey beyond this life.

Again and again the mourners sang this song, the white mourning clothes they wore fluttering in the languid breeze. And Tomas also sang. Deep came his voice as he stepped carefully down the rocky slope carrying his father's bier upon his shoulder like a soldier at peace. To his left stood Lucas, matching his slow pace and when his steps faltered, Lucas's steps fell too into an inconstant stride. Behind them walked the café owner Dari and Lohan the trader, two of Jaro's childhood friends. The whole island was there, standing behind him, and even the oracle and the boatman, who stood a man apart, watched this son carrying his father to the sea.

Tomas felt the rhythm of the song lift his feet — *we will miss you, we will miss, our Jaro, my father.* He felt Isla's hand brush against his side as she walked next to him, dressed in a delicate white robe, the white cloth encircling her crown revealing only a few strands of dark hair where it kissed her forehead. In her hands she clasped a bouquet of red hibiscus, which she would leave to rest on his father's body after she had kissed his face, and allowed the tears to stream down her throat.

She also sang, her voice gentle even through her sobs as they approached the sea — *all life begins and all life passes away, so too Jaro, so too our Jaro. Clear his path, clear his path, as he goes forth to the sea...* As he walked, Tomas felt a strange calm come over him, and it was then that an unexpected thought came to him for the first time. "I am a man," Tomas said to himself. He looked at his father's ashen face, his eyes held closed with two polished white stones that gleamed in the slanting sunlight, and he thought again without conviction. "I guess now I am a man."

So later, when at last his turn came, Tomas removed the band his father had tied upon his wrist only a few months before. He laid it on top of the pile of bands others had also returned to show his father that he too was strong enough to let go, and that he would be okay. Then he took the torch that was handed to him and although his hand trembled, he did not hesitate in touching it against the oiled cloth, and when the fire had spread to engulf the body, he nodded to Lucas and together they waded out and pushed the raft out to sea.

When Tomas finally reached the shore again, and because he was now a man, he allowed the tears to flow down his cheeks until it seemed they might never stop. So while one-by-one the mourners moved away, they stood waiting, Isla and Lucas, Marco and Eva, and at last when he came to them and took their hands, they watched together as the fire glowed wild and bright against the darkening sky as Tomas's da drifted out to sea.

13

There had been the feast, toasts and memories and tributes. The women had cried, and some men too, and Dari had embraced Tomas and whispered, "My home was always your father's home. My home is your home." But as the dark hours of that sleepless night dwindled with the dying fires, Isla couldn't find Tomas. She walked over the winding stony path to the lighthouse, and when she saw that it was lit, she expected to find Tomas there. But Tomas was not sitting in his room, nor did she find him at the top of the lighthouse leaning against the whitewashed wooden railing.

She found Jaro's cot in pieces leaning against the side of the house as island tradition dictated it should, but an empty silence was there, as if Tomas had not been in the house for many hours. Then, Isla noticed the missing paddle of Jaro's small boat that always hung against the wall, and she knew without a doubt that Tomas was in the sea.

Isla turned immediately toward the path that led along the coast, her eyes searching the moonlit water for the shape of his boat. As she walked she remembered all the times she and Tomas had walked this path together. It was as if a sail had been tied to this weight of memory, and in its wake Isla felt a hurricane of great wind and rain tear into the sail until it was ragged and all she could feel was Tomas's pain and all she could remember was how she loved him.

What did it mean, this ferocious love that had come upon her earlier that day as she had watched Tomas shoulder the weight of his father and face this new life without him? Isla thought of the moment in the underwater cave when Tomas had shown her the three pearls he had plucked from the iridescent oyster shells. He had touched her face, and Isla had known then that he loved her, but it had not occurred to her then that this was anything significant. Of course he loved her. Tomas had always been with her on the island, and he had been an unquestioned part of her thirst for other worlds.

Now, Isla thought, *there is no reason for us to stay*.

He could go with her, as he always said he would. He had promised the day she had decided to dig through the centre of the earth and climb through to adventure on the other side of the world. And now that Jaro-da had died, what was left for Tomas here? Perhaps that was what this love meant. All of it had led her to this moment, to help Tomas survive this moment, so that they could leave together and make a greater life for themselves beyond the shrinking boundaries of this island.

On the high cliff, Isla finally made out the shadow of a small boat rocking gently in the rolling black waters. She took the path down towards the shore and waded in like a blind woman walking into her future. The water was unusually warm, and it swirled around her with an inky blackness as she held onto her courage and swam out into its depths. Yet when she arrived the boat was empty, and for many minutes Isla pulled herself onto the bow and then sat hugging her arms around her, water dripping down her ankles, her mind racing with the drumbeat of her heart.

Surely she was not mistaken. Tomas loved her and he would leave with her. That was what she wanted, wasn't it? Then why was she afraid? The moon bent its head low in the sky, watching her like a silver eye in the night that had grown old. Soon it would be morning.

When Tomas's head broke the surface, it was as if he suddenly peeled away the inky mirror that had reflected so many of Isla's hopes, and Isla was met with a face that she did not know. Tomas's mouth was flat with despair, and his eyes held a hollow look in the pale light as if he could not see what was in front of him, but rather was captivated by something beyond sight. But there was something else, a determination in his body as he treaded water.

"Tomas," she said. "Why did you leave without finding me?"

Tomas heaved himself over the side of the boat and lay like a stone in the hull. "I wanted to be alone. Out here in the sea." Isla noticed that he didn't look at her when he spoke. Reaching out, she lay a hand on his shoulder but he shook her off. "I can't talk to you now, Isla," Tomas said. "You shouldn't have come."

"Of course I've come." It was so hard speaking to him like this, to this face indiscernible with shadow and to this voice of a stranger.

He rowed them both back to shore, and when they had dragged the small hull onto the sand, Isla tried again. "You're not alone, Tomas."

"Yes I am!" He shouted this at her. At the night. At the world. And then he blinked and he stepped back away from her. "Go home, Isla." There was a warning in his voice that she had never heard, a fierceness like a growl of a wild animal, and she knew it was pouring out of him now, his great despair.

What could she do? Isla had already taken the step toward a future from which she could not turn away. A steady momentum propelled her forward with the hope she had built up over so many years of living on an island where no one dreamed her kind of dreams. sla had held those unacknowledged dreams through the flat days filled with questions but no answers, through long summers of hope without possibility, through years of her father who wavered between strict rules and absolute indifference, through centuries of island tradition whose meaning had long been forgotten.

Tomas stood on the sand, and Isla understood that he had been her beacon of hope through all of these dark days. And now, he was paralysed with his own sorrow. But Isla could still see him and she knew she could bring him back to himself. So when Tomas disappeared into the impenetrable water of the hidden pool they had discovered when they were still young and unburdened by life, Isla held her breath and followed him anyway.

In the sea of ink and mist, Isla felt her way along the barnacle-covered rock and pushed through the opening into the cave that sat beneath both the island and the sea. Dawn was just creeping into the cavernous hollow and a pale light spilled through the fissures in the rock when the crown of Isla's head split the surface. The purple light flowed into the space mixing with the salty scent of the sea.

Tomas sat crouched on the smooth rock ledge staring into his own reflection. But when he saw Isla, his own desperation overwhelmed him, and Tomas reached for her outstretched hand and pulled her body against his on the flat ledge and at last tasted the sea in her mouth. His hands searched her body for the hidden places where he did not know her, and she guided his hands there and felt at last safe and held and known and loved. She felt him lift her, move inside her, and Isla fell into the blinding light of love which penetrates the darkest places of the soul and only began to think again when she heard Tomas cry out in final fulfilment of an unspoken hope and she felt her own cry echo against the cold rock.

14

When they resurfaced a new sun was rising above the sea. Isla and Tomas stepped out of the water together and climbed the steep cliff to the path above. When they reached the top Isla paused, but Tomas took her hand. "Go home, Isla, before your da wakes and misses you. I still have things to do here." He gestured down to his boat.

Isla nodded, but some uncertainty must have flooded her eyes because Tomas reached out then and held her face in one hand, wrapping his fingers into her wild dark hair and stroking the line of her brow with his thumb. "I'll come for you later this morning, Isla-ja."

Isla-ja. Isla-love, an island phrase used so often between family and friends, but Tomas spoke it with a new tenderness, and Isla smiled. "Okay," she nodded and turned away to walk the winding dusty path home. When she reached the bend in the path she glanced back. Tomas was still standing there where she had left him. The smooth lines of his bare shoulders shone in the morning light, but his face was in shadow, and Isla could not read his expression as he watched her from a distance.

He came for her later that morning looking like a different man. His hair was washed and combed and his face was clear, as if whatever demons had haunted him the night before had also been washed away by the sea. Isla had been sorting the dried losa buds into jars to store and glancing up to the path on the hill from the corner of her eye when she saw him walking towards her. For a moment she paused watching him make his way down the steps that led to her father's house, and she wondered if his heart was also beating like a fervid drum in his chest. He raised his hand, and she was startled to hear her father's voice from behind her.

"Hello there, Tomas."

"Hello Petro-da," Tomas returned.

"How are you holding up, son?"

"As well as I can, sir. Thank you."

Isla stood, brushing bits of losa from her skirt. "Father, I'm going for a walk with Tomas, okay?" She was sure her face flushed, and Isla was suddenly overwhelmed by an awareness of her body, the brush of her skirt against her shins, the awkward hurried steps she took off the porch. But her father only nodded. "Be well, Tomas. Make sure you ask if you need anything."

"I will." Tomas folding his hands to Isla's father, and then waited with a careful, quiet look as Isla made her way towards him.

They walked together in silence up the hill, but as soon as they were out of sight of the house, Tomas stopped walking and took Isla's hand. "Isla, are you okay?"

"I should be asking you that." She looked at him then, his smooth neat clothes and his carefully combed hair, and an urge took hold of her and she reached out. "You don't look yourself," she said, and then she buried her hands in his hair and ruffled it until it stood up this way and that. They both laughed, and Isla felt at home again.

"I was trying to look presentable," Tomas explained.

"Well don't." Isla looked at him for a moment as if she was trying to decide something important. "Come on," she said at last. "I know a place."

They lay under a tree far from town for most of the afternoon, talking and watching the sun pass in its arc overhead. The tall grass hid their presence and opened the sky to their view, and they lay in each others' arms watching the clouds float by. "Look a school of dolphins," Isla pointed into the sky where a group of clouds soared silently overhead. "Look a cricket jumping."

Isla drew her imagination in the wide blue of the sky above their heads and stroked Tomas's dark hair back from his forehead and wrapped him into her arms. She did all the things she had wanted to do for days to take care of him since his father had died, and for the first time he closed his eyes and let her.

"Are you okay?" She whispered after a time, and he sat up on his elbow in the flattened circle of grass and held his hand up to his eyes to shade the glare of the sun.

For a moment he just looked at her, his brown eyes searching her face as if he were reading the map of his future. "What about you?" He replied at last.

"What about me?"

"Well, this wasn't exactly what we planned..." he began. "Last night, I wasn't... I mean, I would never..."

Isla could feel a distance suddenly rise up between them, and the memory of the previous night brought a heat to her cheeks. He was right, as often as she had imagined travelling with Tomas away from the island, she had never imagined the things that had passed between them in the underwater cave. She had never imagined herself that way at all. These moments of beauty and love were things that happened to Eva, not to her. She was serious. Determined. Not beautiful. Not desirable in the ways that women were to men.

"Are you really okay, Isla?" Tomas asked her again.

"Why do you keep asking me that?"Isla's gaze shot up at him.

"Because this is new, what's happened between us..."

"But..." Isla twirled a bit of grass around her forefinger, feeling the emotions in her spilling to the surface. "It's good...right?"

She felt a hand against the side of her face, and when she looked up at him, she saw he was smiling and there was a new joy in his eyes that mingled with the grief that had settled there. "Yes," he nodded, and this time she heard the relief in his voice and she realised he had been as nervous as she. "It is good."

Then he had brought her face to his and had kissed her mouth and she felt the places of fire where the sun had burnt into his skin. Tomas pulled gently at the knot of hair she had tied in the island way and her long hair fell wild into the wind as if it had been longing to escape. He wrapped his fingers around and through its streaming waves.

"Tomas! You know I'm not supposed to wear my hair down anymore. I'm too old. Father will have a fit!"

Tomas made a sound in the back of his throat and shook his head. "Your hair is the most beautiful thing I've ever seen. It belongs in the wind."

Isla rolled over into the crook of his arm and let out a sigh that made Tomas tremble, and together they watched their hopes sail up to meet the clouds.

15

It was the news of Eva's secret engagement, the deceptively sensuous scent of the gardenia blossoms Eva had woven through her hair, and the blinding glare of a life rooted forever to this small isolated piece of earth that reminded Isla of her future destiny.

"Don't tell," Eva had whispered.

"Who would I tell?" Isla had replied, not because she wasn't happy for Eva, but because a bitter sickness had welled up in the back of her throat like the season of the red tide at the thought of settling down on this island.

Eva clasped Isla's arm with her almond fingers. "Are you so surprised?" She asked after a moment as they walked between the rows of losa. They were far from the house and the hills were quiet after the recent harvest. Isla ran a hand over the tops of the pruned green bushes and thought that maybe this wasn't the worst thing in the world. It certainly wasn't a surprise. They were eighteen, and Eva had been with Jacob for over a year — his family owned several fields although they did not have the right to grow losa — and after all, he was always very nice to Eva. They had decided to tell their families within the next few weeks, Eva explained. Her mother had married at eighteen, so her parents couldn't object.

Isla stood for a moment among the losa rows after Eva had gone, remembering that Eva had once seemed so confident, so proud. Today her voice had wavered, and Isla thought that maybe everyone felt afraid for their future and worried that their dreams might not come true. Eva no longer seemed the untouchable vixen of their childhood. She was now simply doing what most young women expected they would do — marry and settle into a dependable life. After all, so many girls on the island got married at eighteen. *Some people's paths are already well-trodden,* Isla thought to herself, *so it is easy for them to see where to go. But for other people, all they have are dreams to guide their steps.*

She remembered the first day the boatman had appeared on the island, his hair wild and red and his voice so strange. Isla had always thought of that day as the tremor in her earth, something that had shaken her from her old thoughts. But now, standing in her father's losa hills, she realised that she had dreamed of leaving the island long before the boatman's arrival, and she wondered where this dream had come from and why it had chosen her.

Whatever the case, she had never, through all these years, been able to shake the conviction that a more meaningful life waited for her beyond this place. Some sense that her life mattered and that she was of value.

Apart from the boatman, every person she knew had been born and raised on this island. Most had followed their parents, gone to school, learned their trade, worked to build a house and feed themselves. They had families, and year after year they grew older and older until finally they lay flat against the wooden raft wrapped in white.

"That can't be all there is!" Isla's voice startled her in the empty afternoon. She blinked and saw again the rows of losa swirling along the curves in the land before her.

Isla began to walk back down the hill to the house thinking that even her mother had left the place where she had been raised and had come to this island alone. Was it really so foolish to dream of doing the same? Isla was no longer the naïve young child who had believed she could dig a hole through the earth. She had met the boatman and she knew the mainland was no magical place.

But still — it was a different place. A place more exciting than here!

Tomorrow, she told herself. *Tomorrow I will talk to Tomas. He will understand.*

But it did not go well. When she met Tomas at their banyan tree that next afternoon, her mind full of Eva's news and the depressing vision of her future on the island and a vague plan to set sail across the seas, she found herself looking not into the face of her best friend who had promised at the age of seven to join her in a life of adventure, but into the face of an island man who had sunk his feet deep into the earth below him and stood tall and unshakeable as the banyan tree.

"We can't leave the island," Tomas said, looking at her for the first time as all the others had done — as if she were crazy. "Where would we go? Everything is here!"

"What do you mean?" Isla's voice rose with her anger. "There is nothing is here!"

"I can't leave, Isla," Tomas reached out for her arm, trying to calm her. "Who would look after the lighthouse? It's my responsibility now that my da is gone."

He gave her other reasons, and Isla knew they sounded sensible, but she felt them as a great betrayal, and in the end she stormed away from him, her fists clenched tightly against this new and unexpected obstacle that stood in the way of her dream.

"I can't stay here!" She kept repeating to herself. "I can't stay here for you!" She spat the words like a curse into the sea air, although she didn't know whether they were meant for Tomas, or her father, or simply all the islanders who had called her *ubash* and had made her feel like a foreigner in her own home simply because she longed for something they did not.

Isla spent many days after this fight hiding among the rows of losa in the furthest hill of their land where Tomas would not know to look for her. She avoided all her favourite places. When they needed food in the house, she ran to the market and back through the hours of brightest sunlight when few were on the streets, and she spent her time at home with ears straining for the sound of his voice.

Somewhere deep inside, Isla could feel the bonds tightening around her feet. There had always been her father, who had hidden away his map of the world forbidding her to dream of travel, forbidding her to speak of the mainland, of her mother's home. But now Tomas too seemed to be holding her down with his long looks and questions that she dared not answer. "Why isn't this island enough for you, Isla?" And she knew he meant himself.

16

How could either of them have known what lay ahead? Whether destiny is a continuous path or a series of poignant moments, whether it is fulfilment or experience, pain or love, they each walked blindly, as all must, into their future.

Then one evening Isla met Eva in the field as she was walking home. Reaching her, Eva grabbed Isla's wrist and pulled her down between the rows of losa and kneeling in the dusty earth, Eva whispered, "I'm pregnant!" A silence engulfed them that was louder than sound. "Aren't you happy for me?" Eva asked after awhile. "Aren't you going to say anything?" But Isla wasn't thinking of Eva. Panic had stricken her dumb as she wondered how many weeks it had been since the blood had come between her own legs, and instead of Eva's changing face, she watched as the future she had fought so long to avoid spread out before her like a spreading stain. Marriage, babies, island life forever.

I must go now, Isla thought. *I must go anyway. I must go whatever the cost.*

When she finally arrived home, she knew that he had

been there, waiting for her. On her bed, she found a single pearl that was the only trace of him, a pearl of the most unusual shade Isla had ever seen. But she could not see the hope that shone from its iridescent skin. Instead Isla could only count again and again on her fingers the number of days, number of weeks since Jaro's funeral. Why was it so impossible to keep track of time on this island? Had it been two weeks or three? Why couldn't she remember? Was this her only choice — to stay and surrender and be with Tomas or to leave him forever and follow her dreams?

Before her, Isla felt a nightmare growing like a shadow when one's back is turned to the sun, and she saw the babies that would come to tie her down, heard her father's grey voice repeating the same warnings of her impending future. A huge void swelled inside her chest until her eyes filled with images of her mother and a frail voice echoing "Not yet, I'm not ready yet." Isla picked up the pearl and lay down on her bed, because she could not bear to imagine what she knew she must do.

Isla knew that by the time the fishermen were pulling back to shore in the rising heat of midmorning, the boatman would be at Dari's. She found him there, sipping tea, the small cup buried in his wide calloused hands. He had just finished his first cup of losa.

Isla had planned what she wanted to say, and so when she reached the boatman's table set against the wide open window of the café, she did not hesitate. "I need to ask you something," she said to the boatman, "because you are the only person I've ever known who doesn't want to stay in one place. You leave. Again and again. You leave and I want to know where you go. And I want to know why! Why you don't want to stay here."

The boatman leaned back in his chair and looked at Isla

as if he were weighing something about her up in his mind. Then, he caught Dari's eye and gestured for another cup to be brought to the table.

"Sit down, Isla," the boatman said, "and tell me what you really want to know." So Isla held her tea and told the boatman about her dreams of drowning, of the sadness that trailed in her wake wherever she stepped, of the empty future she felt herself walking into like a ghost. She told him how she had been born here, that she knew no other place but this island, and yet somehow felt as if she didn't know her place in this world. There were things she wanted to know, things she wondered about — and these questions divided her from her father and her friends who did not wonder such things.

She told him too how she couldn't imagine leaving the island. What would happen to her? She asked him. How could she be sure that she would be okay? That she could survive such a journey. How could she leave everyone she loved? And if she left, would it have to be forever?

And then Isla told the boatman a thing she had never before spoken aloud, of her mother's dying words which had been ones of regret, of her mother who had died without having fulfilled her destiny or having understood the meaning of her life.

"Without knowing what this life means," Isla said, "all the things you gain in this life, all the things you love and everything you have can just be taken away from you in the blink of an eye. Once you die, you can't go back. You don't get any more chances to do things over. And then you have nothing. No losa fields, no home and family, no future and no answers. Life has to be about more than this!" Isla's cup sloshed with dark tea that had grown cold, and she grabbed the boatman's weathered hand like a woman lost in a dark room. "Life has to mean more than this…more than nothing!"

The boatman had been silent while Isla's voice had poured out of her, but as she at last fell quiet herself the boatman knew what he must say. "Everyone deserves to find happiness," the boatman said. "But not everyone finds the source of happiness, Isla. You see, there are some things we can know because others have discovered them before us — things like which specific roots cure headaches, or that the mainland is there beyond the sea in that direction, or that the world is round like the finest pearl.

"But there are some things, Isla," he paused and sipped his losa as an islander might have done. "There are some kinds of knowledge that cannot be passed on from one person to another. Each person has to learn such things for themselves…things like what it means to love someone, what it is to lose or leave behind one's family, what it is to be at peace, what one's life means in the end. It is up to each of us to find the source of happiness. This search for the root of lasting peace is a journey each person must make on their own."

"So you see," the boatman said, setting down his empty cup, "these questions of meaning and of life, they are important questions, perhaps the most important, and the journey to find the answers is arduous and filled with diversions. But…" the boatman leaned forward until Isla could feel his salty breath against her face. Then he looked her in the eye. "Never doubt that there are answers to such questions, Isla. They may not be the answers you expect, but there are answers to such questions if you want to find them."

17

Where in this vine-twisted jungle, where among the currents of this wide shimmering ocean, was the path that would show her the way? How could she take that first step off the island and deep into the world when it meant leaving behind everyone she had ever loved? Everyone who recognised her face? All these people who had taught her every sound and song that now fell off her lips as if they had been part of her all along?

If she left, who would ever care for her like her father? Who would ever know her like Tomas? Who would ever listen to the nonsense stirred up by the moths in her throat if not Eva? And if she did not go, who would fill this empty place in her soul that longed for answers no islander knew? Who would comfort her in those last moments when she whispered, "I'm not ready" and her heart was still full of regret from the things she had never done.

Isla fell, headlong, into this deep pit of nocturnal fears where the souls of all humanity collapse from time to time, united by their most secret terrors and blinded in their conviction of utter solitude. But while such fears brought on in many, including her father, a permanent paralysis that started in the soles of the feet and spread like venom until the heart itself succumbed to its power and lay frozen and cracking in a pool of its own stifled dreams, Isla's feet kept moving.

Almost against her will, they walked, down the rocky pathway and through the grey dawn until she saw the boatman's sail bobbing in the shallow sea. He was there, waiting to take her across the sea to the mainland. Just as he had promised.

Isla stood between these two worlds, one familiar and one frighteningly unknown. For one long eternal moment she looked back up the indigo island hills and the along the shore to where Tomas's lighthouse stood. Its white light shone out like a pearl in the shadowy dawn of that morning, and without warning, the tip of its clear beam struck Isla just below her right eye and the fire pain that tore across her cheek was the only tear she shed for the love and the life that might have been hers.

"I can't leave the island now, Isla." She heard Tomas's voice in her head. "There is the lighthouse and the garden and our friends and the sea and…Everything. We aren't children anymore. We have responsibilities. I have responsibilities to what da has left to me."

Standing face-to-face with the island, Isla heard herself whisper — "What will father do? Who will help him manage the harvest? What about Eva? What will happen to Tomas if I leave?"

And then in her mind, she heard her own voice as she had answered Tomas only a few days before. "I can't stay here, Tomas. Maybe you feel you can't leave, but I can't stay here for you." And hearing these words, she knew again that they were true.

Isla grasped the leather bag that her mother had first brought to this island in her trembling hands. Its soft wide shoulder strap and black stitches still held firm. Before her eyes was the image of her mother, years before her birth, stepping off the trader's boat that ran frequently in those days back and forth to Joon, looking out upon the wide world with Isla's own silvery eyes, with Isla's same sense of hope, and with an unshakeable courage. And if nothing else, it was this imagined memory of her mother flowing through her blood which gave her courage. *If she can do it,* Isla said to herself, *then so can I. I might be young and small and only an island girl, but I can still follow my own path.*

Isla took one last look up towards the rotating light emanating from the lighthouse like a deadly hope, and she wondered whether Tomas was awake on this greyest of grey mornings. How could she have known, so close to the shore and the hull of the boatman's ferry that would soon cut the first grooves into the new path she had chosen for her life, that Tomas had sat sleepless for three days and three nights at the top of his father's lighthouse, staring out into what was still for him an endless and eternal sea, peering into a despair so profound that time stopped and hovered there like a firefly in the darkness of his watchtower and each rotation of the wide blinding light was the same, single rotation.

His sense of dark, eternal stillness was only broken when he felt his heart jump, and he looked out and caught a glimpse of a small, slender figure in flowing blue descending steadily from her home, along the paths of the island towards the boat that was destined to carry her away. Her long dark curls streamed out behind her in the wind and twisted with every movement of her body. Watching her, something inside Tomas broke open, but still he could not bring himself to abandon the lighthouse that was his only home and the only place the memory of his father still felt alive. And so he found himself caught in an unresolvable nightmare where everything was lost and there seemed to be nothing he could do.

He watched her as she walked. And then he saw her pause, turn back and a sudden hope shot out like a ray of fire and shone like a pearl that had almost been buried in the sands beneath the ocean currents, and struck her face with a force unknown. But as he watched her, he felt his heart shift, and his despair returned, because he knew that if she stayed, he would face a lifetime of those far-off looks that had always characterised her face, a lifetime of sideways glances, looks of regret, and that this would pull at them both like quicksand burying them no matter how each of them struggled to reach solid ground.

And against every yearning of his heart, his hands fell to the switch and Tomas extinguished the light of his watchtower and collapsed into his bed where he dreamed the fitful dreams of things that were never destined to be.

PART 2: THE MAINLAND

18

Isla stood before the Great Fountain that marked the centre of power and purpose on the mainland and stared at the pearl that lay peacefully in the palm of her hand. It was not white, as most of the pearls in Tomas's wooden box had been, but was the colour of the horizon at sunrise or sunset, a colour that spoke of change and felt as if it should fade quickly with time. But it had not.

The pearl rolled calmly in her hand with the eternal tides of the sea still left somewhere beneath its iridescent skin, and Isla wondered why she had kept it through all these abrupt and unrelenting years. What it now meant, she did not know. Whether she missed her indigo island, she couldn't say. That she missed Tomas, she couldn't bear to say. But all these years, she had put one foot in front of another. And she had made it, hadn't she? Across the ocean that everyone told her she would never cross, into a world she thought she could never enter. What she did know as she stood in front of the Great Fountain on the day that marked both the seventh year of her arrival on the mainland and her first day of work in the mainland's Central Administration was that it was time to forget her past.

The pearl slid over her tongue and down her throat like a snail to the pit of her stomach. Its faint silvery trail left the scent of the changeable sea in her mouth, but then Isla breathed in and the fragrance of roses filled the air and took the place of unwanted memory. In her mind, Isla pushed back against the lingering taste of the island, and rather than follow the eternal path of misplaced nostalgia, tried to remember her first day of freedom, and in this way, measure how far she had come.

It had been cold the day she had first arrived on the mainland docks carrying nothing but her mother's small leather bag across her left shoulder and wearing her mother's old brown coat that smelled damp and abandoned like a forgotten corner of her house. Isla had taken seven steps onto the mainland dock before she had looked up. What she had seen then was a land soaked in crystal white light so cold and pure, Isla had been certain she had finally reached the magical place of her dreams.

"It will all be worth it," she had whispered to herself to quiet the pounding beat of her heart, and she had repeated these words again and again because the first time hadn't felt convincing. The wooden planks on the dock had been treacherous and slippery from the salty spray, and the boatman had held her elbow to keep her from tumbling into the waves. She remembered the way his hand had felt, rough and warm against her jacket. Then he moved on with only a silent wave, and she had felt suddenly unsteady and alone as this last hand that had accompanied her from the island was gone.

As she stood on the dock, waiting for the ferocity of her childhood courage to catch up with her, a woman had brushed past. Isla remembered her too, the unfamiliar click of wooden heels ringing in her ears, the warm black robe sewn with strange intricate patterns of colour that had forced Isla to look down at her own brown coat and finger the hole mice had chewed in the upper right sleeve. Standing on the dock, the mainland of her future was suddenly so real that Isla felt ambushed by the uncertain fog of doubt, and in her mind, a voice had cried out — *What am I doing here? What if this was a huge mistake...*

From the edge of the dock, the mainland rose before her as slopes of blue tiled roofs stretching as far as the eye could see, latticed wooden windows with paper shutters that kept out the furtive draughts with images of the dragon, streets that wound ever upward towards the Central Administration District at the base of the mountains. The temperate winds of the mainland city blew along these streets, never hot or humid, yet never quite cold enough to bring snow down from the northern mountains, and without knowing what she was looking at, Isla watched the mainland spread out like an ominous goddess across the rolling foothills. North to the crown where the wealthy land-owning families who could trace their ancestry back to the first mainland kingdom had built up mansions which extended far beyond the contours of their original family bungalows. East and West to the districts where officials of the Central Administration inhabited immodest homes, gilded with the fading golden trim and wide windows of the third kingdom. Down to the docks by the sea where the goddess dipped her delicate toes into the turbulent waters of timeless transience and poverty.

On that first day, filled as it was with the tremors of terror and what seemed like impossible dreams, Isla had not had an answer to that feverish voice in her mind that told her to turn back. Nor did she know what to do with the sobering possibility that perhaps her father had been right after all. Maybe she didn't know what she was doing. Maybe this would be her biggest and most irreparable mistake.

But then she had taken another seven steps off the slippery dock anyway, holding her bag without confidence, and had put one foot in front of the other in the direction of one grey cobbled street until she found herself standing breathlessly in the front hall of the women's boarding house set along the side of the southern city road.

Isla stood before the Great Fountain, dissolved in the memory of that first day of her new mainland life. The women's boarding house had sheltered the ageing faces of white-haired widows, the battered hatchling faces of teenaged orphans, and other faces with wide city-struck eyes and lips that never opened as they nodded 'yes' and shook their heads 'no'. Isla had felt the dead silence of that house, heard it beneath the floorboards of the flat halls, sensed it in the thin, wavering walls and immediately had known two things—first, that she alone was here as a traveller, meaning here in this forgotten house by choice, and second, that she must leave this place as soon as humanly possible.

On the second floor, the landlady pulled a key from her dress pocket. "This will be your room," the woman said, and Isla remembered that she had smiled then, kindly, as if to say that she knew Isla was not so lost as she seemed and that things would be alright.

But then she had gone, and Isla heard the vast silence swallow up the banging sound of the closing door, and it was at that precise moment that Isla realised it was done—her dream to leave the island, her long unrequited desire to see the mainland had finally come true. She was here. And it was not what she had expected.

"It will be okay," Isla whispered aloud to break the dominating silence, but the silence roared back with a great voice, and Isla could not find the courage to speak again. Putting down her mother's bag, she had surveyed the room, hoping to find some element of hope.

Isla had never before seen a room like this one with its flat bare walls, slate fireplace and limp sheet that covered the sleeping mat, reminding her of the many bodies that had lain exactly where she now stretched out her own body. Underneath her, Isla felt sure she could sense the impressions lent by heavy hips, bony shoulders, and the dry damp of forlorn tears. The rooms she had known on the island had always belonged to someone, had been draped in shawls and work sandals, had walls covered with drawings of island flowers and shelves lined with figurines carved from discarded pieces of wood. They were rooms that had smelled like the people that slept and argued and sought shelter from the torrential rains within their walls.

This room was different, detached from any sense of belonging, used and forgotten as the faces of the orphans she had passed on the street. The imperceptible warping of the floorboards in the middle of the room served as the only evidence of the vast human passage it had witnessed in its belly, and Isla lay on her side staring back at it without moving, as if she were looking into her own reflection and felt the empty space inside her where Tomas had always been.

19

After several weeks of long walks together which Isla had used to map the mainland streets, the family who owned the women's boarding house had deduced that Isla was well-brought-up and from a land-owning family, even if she was an islander. Through their connections, they introduced Isla to Madame Rohal, a widow with long grey hair that reached down to her narrow waist and who happened to be looking for a lodger and a bit of company in her waning years.

Madame Rohal lived in a large unrepentant home in the coffee district where she had spent all the days of her married life. She knew the mainland city as one knows their mother's face, although there were lesser lanes that she would never have admitted to having traipsed through during the years of her ingenuous youth. Who knew whether it was the world finally reaching out a hand to Isla, a reward for her desperate faith, or whether it was simply the inevitable destiny of this restless girl to meet Madame Rohal who took it upon herself to initiate Isla into the inner world of mainland culture.

It was Madame Rohal who taught Isla the fine art of conversational hand-clapping all mainlanders used at precise moments to punctuate their speech. It was Madame Rohal who educated Isla in the vast and undulating history of the three mainland kingdoms and their relationship with the surrounding regions. It was Madame Rohal who escorted Isla to the first interview for prospective students at the Central Institute of Culture and Higher Learning. And when Isla fell into moments of panic that she was too unrefined, too stupid, too inadequate to be one of the prestigious mainland scribes, it was Madame Rohal that said, "Pfff pfff, now get on with it girl. You got yourself here didn't you?" And though they weren't the words Isla wished for, they felt a strange warmth of comfort in the great emptiness of this foreign place. If this grand mainland woman believed in her, Isla would think to herself, perhaps everything would be okay after all, and her heart would give a little jump in her chest with excitement for the future.

Isla had been living with Madame Rohal for exactly three weeks when one day the woman appeared in the doorway of her room, dressed in an embroidered black robe and said, "Come along Isla, we are going for coffee."

It was only once they were seated under a pergola of winding yellow roses with delicate cups of dark black coffee in their hands that Madame Rohal spoke again. "Isla." Her sharp brown eyes stared into Isla's silver ones. "You have been raised well, by a good family. I can see that about you. But in order to make something of yourself here in the city, a good family background from a peripheral island is not enough. You must understand the place you've come to, and to do that you must understand the Rising Sun."

"I've heard..." Isla began uncertainly, but Madame Rohal simply raised a calm, thin hand. "What you've heard or haven't heard is no matter, dear. Some who speak of the Rising Sun are fools or worse. What is important is that you understand. True understanding, Isla, this is the key."

At this Madame Rohal shook one finger up towards the sky as if the yellow roses above their heads held all the answers she would need, and said only "More is better, New is best." Then she paused and sipped her coffee, and Isla forced herself to swallow small sips of the bitter drink as well.

To her right, Isla could see the high arches of the Palace, its gold dome blazing with a power accumulated and guarded over countless generations of men, its slanting roofs flowing blue like a river or a mirror to the sky that stretched back as far as Isla could see. Before her stood the Central Bank with its monstrous arcade that never slept. And next to this cauldron of economic power was the Great Library, treasured most by the lords of the third kingdom who had covered its walls with tapestries of their moments of victory and with paintings made by emissaries to the furthest corners of the kingdom which were mostly of women with naked breasts and painted faces, and of the strange beasts that the adventurers claimed to have seen there.

Behind the library was the Boulevard of the Jewels where there stood a single row of large houses inhabited by the most powerful officials of the kingdom. And behind these, the Lane of the Treasured Ones curved elegantly with its silvery almond trees and trimmed citrus trees imported from another age where the mainland now housed the leaders of the lost regions once they returned to the mainland kingdom.

The Rising Sun. Isla turned the name over and over in her mind as she listened to Madame Rohal recount its history. It had begun with the renaming of the mainland city streets. As the cult of Newness spread, it seemed a most obvious and important step for the Central Administration to demonstrate its own efforts at progress. Districts were rearranged, given new names, and these names were displayed proudly on wooden signs and mounted on the sides of buildings and on blue poles in district squares. In the coffee district, Sahesh Street, which had originally been named after the beloved owner of the city's first coffeehouse, was renamed Prosperity Street. The winding road which had been known as Brook Lane became Progression Lane, and the Lavender Way, known by the street boxes of swaying lavender which appeared in the summer and provided a gentle demarcation between the busy street traffic and the men and women sipping their cups of coffee on warm cushions was renamed Advancement Avenue.

For a time, Madame Rohal noted wistfully, these old streets seemed to take on a new gleam. They shifted underfoot, curved in startling places, arrived at the Central Boulevard at new angles. For a time, the city seemed to swell with newness and mainlanders felt certain they were achieving something wonderful.

It had taken longer for the Administration and the Philosophy of the Rising Sun to reach the docks, but eventually there too, the Fish Market became Opportunity Square, and even the small narrow lanes in the neighbourhoods of the poor and destitute, which never used to have names at all but had been distinguished by locals according to the longest living inhabitant there — Jolen's street, or Bartam's street — were given official names as well.

"Things are changing," people said to each other on these streets, and this was only the beginning.

There were new initiatives by the Central Administration, new aims and objectives for increasing the wealth of the mainland kingdom. New technologies soon meant people on the mainland could move faster across distances. People began to speak faster, became more productive and efficient with their time. New fashions in clothing and shoes, hair-styles and jewellery, bags and watches, robes and face paint meant that the people of the mainland city were also able to continually redefine themselves, reassert new identities — or true identities, or aspiring identities — through these new consumer goods. And they felt happy. They felt more themselves.

Almost overnight the oracles and card-readers, fortune-tellers, sages and sadhus were transformed into the readers of this new complex language of fashion, for there was no longer money to be made in predicting the future or imparting old wisdoms for modern times. What the people of the mainland city were, however, desperate to know was — what would it say about me if I wore only the colour red? What if I wore a single diamond at my throat? A bracelet of jade?

Young women looking for a husband descended on the augers as locusts on the city, desperate to discover what colour robe might imply that they were an innocent virgin burning with the secret fire of repressed passion. Men who had failed to make the fortune they had dreamed of in their twentieth year begged the sibyls to reveal which black marks drawn on the forearm would communicate strength, which silk trousers or which golden ring-seal would reflect their imminent rise in society.

There grew a new language on the mainland, and this new language often overshadowed all that was spoken.

People on the mainland became busier, they accomplished more. And there was always more and more to do, for all the new technology and new procedures and new initiatives and new ordinances demanded a constant relearning, and so the mainlanders seemed to become the most educated of people.

All this movement, the rapidity of change, and the dominance of the Rising Sun resulted in a faith that rose effortlessly like a bird on a warm breeze that More was better and New was best. The perpetual newness gave people of the mainland the impression that progress was happening so fast that they had to run to keep pace with it. And this made the people of the mainland proud.

It was like an elixir, this new philosophy, a drug more potent than the great religions of the world which had once been able to wield the stars overhead and pre-ordain the future and order the world's peoples with threats of brimstone and eternal fire. Mainlanders felt as if they had spent a thousand generations asleep in the fog of unknowing and had finally awoken to the clarity of the present age — there was no god wielding their fates, no magic hidden from them by a privileged few. The meaning of life was clear and was available to all who were willing to work for it.

Suddenly, everything seemed so obvious the mainlanders shook their heads in wonderment and laughed ruefully at the blind faith of their ancestors. The answer had been right here all along. The answer was progress and the goal was More. The answer was the Rising Sun.

The Rising Sun said 'More is better, New is best' so that mainlanders could weigh their importance with scales they could see. And so mainlanders could visualise the path. With this vision before them, they strove to be the most successful people in the world and felt the confidence of accomplishment as they began to stand tall again in their high wooden-soled shoes. *At last,* they thought, *at last we can be certain of our importance, at last we will know we truly are the most important people in the world.*

As Madame Rohal spoke, Isla felt the possibility of all this change. She could do something meaningful here. She could be part of something great, something greater than herself. She could help change the world, even if her part in this progress of humanity was small. The final outcome of all her work, of her life, would mean something.

20

Yet, although Madame Rohal helped restore to Isla her long-held convictions about the greatness of the mainland and the possibility of adventure, Isla was nonetheless met by a strangling loneliness in that first year of her life on the mainland.

At first it was the silence that wove through her days like a ribbon fluttering in the wind and made her aware, for the first time in her life, how comforted she had been by the constant noise of the island, the creaking of the green and brown cicadas, the fluttering whistles of the red parrots, the immodest screaming of the monkeys islanders affectionately called *munshaw*. Then, it was the sterile damp smell of the mainland streets, void as they were to Isla of the familiar spicy draughts of home cooked meals, of perfumed smoke trailing off the wooden shrines, of the light ephemeral scent of harvested losa.

There was a solitude here which Isla had never felt on the island where everyone had known her name, her family's past, her favourite foods and all the things that she had done as a child that even she could not remember. On the island she had searched for small nooks, crevasses where she could be alone, and when she found them they were but moments, transitory treasures sure to disappear with a familiar face turning the corner or her father's voice calling long and empty from out in the distance for her to return home.

Being alone on the mainland was different — a crowded kind of loneliness, as a thousand strangers walking together on a street, unknown, unrecognised, untraceable, who sense they are alone not by the ringing silence, but by the certainty that if they were to disappear no one would note their absence.

During the many months of that first year, this sense of loneliness overwhelmed Isla like an avalanche that crashed in upon her at odd moments when she was eating breakfast or washing her feet in the pale wooden basin before bed, and seemed as if it would go on crushing her forever. At such times she would install herself at a coffeehouse, determined to force down cup after cup of the dark mainland drink until her confidence and faith returned.

And yet more often than not she would sit holding a single cup of coffee as it grew cold in the temperate air and stare unseeing at the mainland streets while her mind filled with visions of the island she had abandoned...her father with his careful, watchful eyes...Eva in a carefree dream...and Tomas, his warm sunburnt face, his wide rough hands, the slight frown that fell upon him when he was deep in thought, the mark of the sea that spread across his back. Often she was lost for hours in memories of him, and she would find, when she returned at last to herself, a faint smile touching her mouth. Other times, though, she was haunted by their final days together, by their parting words, by the wound she had inflicted when there should have been only tenderness and love. These visions choked her, drowning all her hopes, and she would hurry home to her bed and wrap herself in a mainland quilt and cry and cry as if the sea itself were leaving her.

Yet, over time, Isla learned to wear this loneliness like a cloak and also to rejoice in its freedoms. She began to love walking the city streets without the feeling of judgement trailing in her wake, to recognise the liberty such solitude gave her to try out new paths, knowing that because there was no one tracking her footsteps she could always reconsider, go back and start again.

Then, Isla met Neha. Tall, beautiful Neha, who had been born to the mainland and wore its culture like a silk cocoon. Isla had been sitting with the rest of the novices in the main hall of the Institute of Culture and Higher Learning. The room was lined with rows of blue silk cushions for the students. Tapestries woven with the sign of the dragon and newer images of the Rising Sun covered the stone walls. Above the nervous faces and anxious whispering, curved wooden beams soared to a pinnacle overhead, amplifying the echoes of each footstep.

Isla was silent. In that moment, it seemed to her as if speaking would be a kind of betrayal, as if a hallowed hall at the centre of the world was not a place for her island voice, the wrong tone of her vowels, the strange cadence of her speech. She sat with her hands folded, her back straight. Then, thinking twice, she shifted the cushion beneath her and smoothed out the thick folds of her grey robe. Isla was so consumed by her own terror in the face of this mainland grandeur that she hardly noticed the tall woman who sat down beside her.

In fact, it wasn't until the woman spoke, breaking her

nightmarish reverie of failing at this crucial moment, that Isla looked up and realised that perhaps she was not alone in her fears. "You don't look nervous..." the woman's soft voice found her below the echoes of the hall.

"Honestly?" Isla whispered back, "I'm terrified." The woman had smiled and nodded in a way that Isla understood she had found a friend.

"I'm Neha," the woman said, tapping the palms of her hands.

"I'm Isla," Isla replied, clapping twice.

Every week for the first two years of training, Isla and Neha met at their favourite coffeehouse to study. In reality, they spent these evenings after the working day was done discussing everything but the Institute — their family backgrounds, whose father was stricter than whose, the latest gossip among their friends, which of the novice scribes had married young, which would probably complete the training and which would drop out before the year was done.

But more than anything else, Isla and Neha debated the ideas of the Philosophy of the Rising Sun and their hopes for the mainland's future, which was their future as well. Why had the last kingdom really declined? What were the various merits of busyness? How could they each make their mark on the world?

"A person's work makes them who they are," Neha would say. "So it should be work with meaning. Something that will make a mark on the world." They sat sipping the bitter coffee that made the heart race and made all things seem possible. And Isla would smile because she had never known a person to speak such dreams aloud.

"After all," Neha would add, "The highest purpose of

one's life is to create something entirely unique. New ideas are what move society forward. More is better, New is best."

"Yes," Isla would reply, thinking always of her island that never changed. "Hanging onto the old brings stagnation. New is best."

After a few years of living on the mainland, Isla found that she had been restored to the position of a native, for the city had slowly become a place that she knew and which knew her. People recognised her on the streets, shop keepers kept their eye out for her favourite olives from the north, the best chillies from the west, the purple silk she loved from the south-east.

And perhaps most importantly, her visions of Tomas and of her island began to fade.

Then, on her twenty-fourth birthday, Isla discovered a small sprig of dyeing-losa in her shopping basket, and when she saw the shop owner with his wispy grey beard and long weedy eyebrows smile at her, she realised that she was no longer a stranger, for the mainland did not need traditions passed down for generations to create a sense of belonging. It did not require its inhabitants to share the same colour eyes or the same flattish noses to incite the passions of homeland. The mainland that Isla knew offered them all — Jhona the bearded shopkeeper, the widow Rohal, the administrative officials in their blue-black robes and Isla in her grey novice scribe's robe, and the optimistic woman who ran the coffeehouse on the corner — a sense of purpose, a desire for progress, an opportunity to feel important in a universe so vast it would otherwise dwarf even the greatest of men.

From a time before her memory began, Isla had searched for her place in the world, and what she discovered was that such places aren't located on a map and are never written on the palm of the hand. The place where one belongs is a shape woven like a spider's web into the fabric of the universe. It is hidden in a corner of the mind, waiting to recognise its reflection in the world of shape and form. It is a wandering path which only reveals its destination upon arrival. Simply, you know when you are there — and you know when you're not. And in these small gestures and small steps, the discovery of certain new foods she grew to love and associate with herself, the recognition of mainland streets and shops that began to fill the mental map she called Home, Isla began at last to recognise herself again.

In fact, there were so many different things to do, so much work, it seemed to Isla no longer necessary to search for the meaning of her life. It was clear she was important simply by the fact that she was so busy. Everyday the Higher Institute and Central Offices where she had trained were filled with activity, urgency, people needing things done, other people hurrying to do them. She had no time to waste pondering these vague, childish memories or to ruminate on questions of existence. She had things to do, reports to write, exams to pass, senior scribes to please, projects to survey. She had to make her contribution to the progress of humanity as the mainland expanded under the Philosophy of the Rising Sun.

And because she was so busy, Isla did not stop to wonder — if all these new procedures, new titles and new technologies were really making life easier, then why did it seem that everyone had to work harder than ever before?

She was not alone. Mainlanders were busy people and no one had time to ask whether all this innovation was really improving their lives. In truth, it would have been sacrilegious for mainlanders of this new, exhilarating age to ask such wasteful questions. Their minds were focused with unwavering clarity and attention on the Philosophy of the Rising Sun which, in all its dedication to rebuilding the kingdom to its former glory, had given them hope and invited them to feast on the banquet wealth of a new way of life.

Reduced to the oft-repeated mantra 'More is better, New is best', the Philosophy of the Rising Sun was such a satisfying answer to the questions of value and purpose. It tasted so good on the tongue, fell so easily off the lips. And mainlanders also believed because they thought they heard a whisper echoed in the words of the Rising Sun that said — More means happier, and More and More and More means happiest of all. They followed the Philosophy of the Rising Sun because they believed that More would give them a better life, an easier, worthier, happier life.

Or perhaps the people of the mainland believed simply because they didn't have any other answers themselves, and when the waters of life feel choppy and the threat of a storm looms on the horizon, it is not weakness of character that makes people feel afraid and cling to the first hope they see.

For Isla, the end to the questioning of her mind was such a relief, it was as if a huge weight had been lifted from her shoulders. As if she had been swimming through wave after wave, across miles of seemingly endless ocean and had suddenly found herself in a current, a warm jet stream that carried her effortlessly along. Once, she might have said that her life felt small. It did not feel small anymore. Isla felt important. After all, she was changing the face of the world, participating in the progress of humanity, working so that one day all people could have More. Isla knew it was not that the mainlanders were inherently better than her islanders, not that their eyes were more open to the truth or that their convictions were more sacred. It was simply and especially a matter of opportunity.

The humming in her mind stopped. The endless questions stopped. She had arrived. And so for a time, all the work, the studying, the qualifications, Isla's life itself seemed to flow peacefully with the currents of destiny.

21

Isla's accent and wide silver eyes made her an obvious candidate for the Department of the Lost Regions. Once an inhabitant of a 'lost region' herself, Isla would work in her final years of training as a novice scribe to help the mainland administration bring these peripheral areas, the desert lands to the west, the hill villages of the north, the islands scattered like stars in the southern sea, back into the mainland kingdom.

Today, Isla was one of the hundreds of faces and robes that converged at the Great Fountain of the administrative district. She had walked up the small lane past the store that sold spices in neatly labelled paper packets and turned where the mouth of the lane fed into the great River Avenue flowing with people who all hurried with certitude and purpose towards their destinies. She was a part of things now. Today, she knew who she was.

Isla paused before the Great Fountain with the stillness of one standing at the precipice of the world in the days when the world was flat and so many things were still unknown. It was said that this Great Fountain had never been turned off, never stopped flowing with the waters of hope, hope that one day it would again stand at the centre of a great kingdom. Each year, Isla left roses at the edge of the fountain to remember those she had left behind. Now, she stood still and tall as people rushed past her in clouds, and sparrows swarmed overhead in great storms of chatter and wind.

Some voice had set up a steady stream of whispering in her mind, and with all the water falling and rushing around her, at first Isla didn't hear the voice as distinct and of her own making, separate from the mad rush outside on the pavement. But when she listened more carefully, she heard the voice say *Father was wrong,* and she couldn't decide whether it was a real premonition or simply her own deepest wish. But as soon as she heard it, she also suddenly remembered the first time her father had shown her a map of the world.

The map must have been several decades old because the paper had been brown and marked like the sun-stained skin of a fisherman's hands. Her father had first used the map to point out the location of the island and the mainland. Then, to stop her constant questions, he had pointed to the mainland again, and banged a shaking forefinger against the taut paper. *People who went there never came back the same*, he had warned. *They were always different when they returned.* At the time, Isla hadn't wondered why her father kept this map when he seemed so unconcerned with the outside world. Neither had she wondered who these people were who had come back so changed, or how her father, wrapped up tight on his small island had known these adventurers. *Different how?* was the only thing she had wanted to know then, for everything she knew had seemed the same. But Petro had folded up the ageing map then and slipped it back into the drawer. *Different*, he said again in a way that Isla had understood the discussion was over. Now, standing amongst the broad streets heaving with crowds, Isla wondered what would become of her now that she too was 'different'.

Above her head, Isla felt the sky stretching up and up, and so she too stretched up through the soles of her feet and into the crown of her head and felt tall as a mainlander should. Suddenly out of the sky, a tiny brown bird landed on the crown of the fountain's southern goddess. The bird eyed Isla with its small black face, and Isla pulled her hands up into the long sleeves of her grey robe and watched the bird. *I wonder what I must look like to that bird,* she thought.

The breeze blew a dark ribbon of hair across her cheek and ruffled the feathers of the tiny bird, and it occurred to Isla that she had probably travelled much farther than this sparrow, even though the sparrow was a bird with wings, because these brown speckled birds were hatched in the stone chimneys of the mainland city, fed off the crumbs strewn between the cobbles and had never been driven from the mainland by either famine or frost, while she, Isla, had been compelled by a force beyond herself to leave her home and travel far from the place she had been born. She remembered then something else Tomas had once said about the gulls he trained when they were young — "Having wings doesn't always mean birds will want to fly very far."

Isla looked down at her grey novice scribe's robe with its blue embroidery at the wrists and on a single thick panel across the front where it wrapped into her skin like a cocoon. She might still be a novice scribe. But she was working now. The years of study were finally over. She had expected to be relieved, to taste the elusive confidence of the elders who had trained her, but instead she stood in front of the Central Fountain and still could not move. Was this what it was supposed to be like? Did she feel the sense of completion, the satisfaction she had expected? Isla shifted in her heeled shoes and the sudden movement startled the bird which took to the sky, joining the cloud of birds who were flying carelessly or perhaps carefree and without destination.

"I hope I know what I'm doing," Isla whispered to herself, and it was not for the first time.

On the other side of the fountain, people moved in streams like rivers, looking so certain of their destinations, so certain of where they wanted to go and of how they were going to get there, and their confidence made Isla wonder whether she had been born cursed with doubt like a fever that would never leave her. Her father's voice echoed in her mind, bringing all his fierce expectations and festering worries no matter how far she fled. Where did this confidence of the mainlanders come from? She wanted to know. How did they seem so certain of life while she stood frozen, waiting to know what it all meant and whether she was doing the right thing before she could move again.

Across the courtyard of the Great Fountain a bell began to toll, and Isla recognised it as the mainland itself shaking her from paralysis. The answer was to keep working. Keep busy. Keep moving towards the goal of success and progress. The sun fell golden out of the sky, reverberating against the white stone edifices of the mainland.

Here I am, Isla thought, *standing at the centre of the world. I hope I know what I'm doing!* Then, Isla turned towards the white stone building with the sign engraved in black granite, Department of the Lost Regions. The engraving was new. They had added it three years ago when Isla was still studying. Now, it was also her building, and as she joined the stream of people heading towards its tall open doors, Isla tried to imagine joy expanding inside of her like a great hope.

22

The boatman had not seen Tomas for many months. Perhaps it had been years. Time was slippery and one could never quite be sure. The last time the boatman had gazed at the island from the sea it had been harvest time and the island had glowed purple in the distance as the oasis of his unending dreams. But by then, Tomas had already deserted the island and now several harvests had come and gone, and the island was glowing green and rich with the promise of losa, but he still had yet to return.

The boatman found the island much the same. And yet, as he pulled his boat to dock and climbed the steep winding lane into town, he sensed a nervous energy, which he had begun to notice on his infrequent visits. The fishing families by the dock laughed and yelled to each other from their front porches in the usual way, so at first he thought he was mistaken, but as he came closer to the losa fields he thought he heard a frantic whispering, the haunting winds of rumours unleashed, and this dredged up so many unpleasant memories that the boatman spat against the earth and began to walk more quickly.

Where did Tomas go each time he set off to meet the horizon in that small boat which fishermen called a toy for the sea? More important than Where was Why, and it was a question uttered in kitchen doorways and on garden steps without pause. First Isla, then Tomas...why were all their young people leaving? What delusions were driving them or drawing them away from this unmistakable paradise that had always been enough for their parents and grandparents and grandparents before them?

The whispering was most frantic, the boatman found, in the upper town where older mothers told each other "that girl was always different" and "her mother wasn't an islander and it showed after all". They said these things without malice because they had loved Myrium and still kept their eye on Petro in his declining years, but with a firmness that helped them feel that the wandering disease which had infected Isla could not, would not touch their own families. This could not happen to them, their children would not abandon them for the world.

But then Tomas had begun to leave the island. For longer and longer months he fled, and after a few years of this, people stopped blaming it on grief and began to worry that perhaps things were changing and that perhaps their children would be the next to go. The boatman sensed this translucent panic that hovered in the island air and blew about in its breezes in the years after Tomas had first left the island shores. It was the fear of change. He knew it well.

At the Palm Losa, Madame Prenai nodded at him from her chair where she sat stitching the faces of her family into a wide tapestry which was her final effort at assuring their immortal place in island history. His room was the same as he had left it. The collection of shells lined the window sill, pale in the unrelenting sun. His comb lay against the water basin next to a pair of scissors and he realised he must have been gone longer than he had thought for rust from the humid tropical air had grown across both blades and had begun to eat at the sharp edge. He would have to get a new pair soon.

It was coming on afternoon, and the heat blew in on the high sea breezes that wafted between the insubstantial curtains until the boatman could not resist the torpor in his limbs. He took off his shirt that was stained with the obstacles and adventures of the world and lay back against the white sheets and imagined he was floating on a cloud into a thick silence of peace.

When he awoke the sun had shifted and the shadows fell long and lazy across the floor boards. Outside his room he saw that someone had left him a bucket of water. This he dragged into the bathroom and splashed and scrubbed until he was both clean and wide awake for his walk into town. He wanted to reach Dari's before the afternoon crowd so he could hear the news in detail.

"What can I say boatman?" Dari's voice boomed as he slid a cup of losa tea onto the table. "Everything has changed since you were here last. The fisherfolk are up in arms because those mainland boats continue to violate the boundary of our waters and our favourite kinds of fish are becoming scarce. The men who meet on full-moon nights are gambling with drams of spiced liquor now like their fathers used to do. My middle daughter has married." Dari paused to light his rolled leaf, but he did not sit down.

"Sounds like much the same," the boatman said, sipping the cup of losa.

"Depends on how you look at it," Dari replied.

Outside two young boys kicked at a ball in the dust, their brown limbs flailing wildly as they jumped and gestured and shouted. "Tomas still out at sea?" The boatman asked, not looking at Dari, and it was a long time before Dari replied, "Yes, I guess that is the same."

The boatman wanted to tell Dari not to worry, that Tomas would return when he was ready, but Dari simply grunted, "We'll see," and walked into the kitchen puffing his rolled leaf and filling the empty space behind him with fading clouds of smoke.

The boatman sat, as he always did at this hour on the island, smoking his pipe and sipping three cups of losa tea one after the other and watching the islanders wander by. It was the season for afternoon storms, but it wasn't until the boatman noticed the third islander glance nervously up at the clear sky that he himself noticed the unusual lack of clouds and cool damp air. It wasn't going to rain. Perhaps things were changing.

The boatman sighed and the smoke that left his mouth hung in the air before his eyes and clung to the fiery tendrils of his beard so that he found himself in a sudden fog of his own making. Should he tell the islanders he had seen Isla? Should he tell Dari? Would they be happy that she had looked well? So tall in her new scribal robe? So world-wise as she clapped her hands together while she spoke. Would they feel comforted to know she was making her way in the world?

The boatman tipped out the burnt remains of his pipe and tapped it against the table to dislodge the ash. Then he swallowed the last of his tea that had cooled in the long stretches of his uncertain imagination and stood up from the table. If it was not going to rain, he would take a walk down the road out from town that led towards the grove of silver mangroves.

23

When Petro heard the rickety door slam against its wooden frame he understood that Lucas had left. Such a short visit. "Just to check in," Lucas had said, trying to hide whatever it was he was thinking about Isla having left her father in this house all alone.

In the moment before Petro turned back to his friends, he caught himself wishing Isla had turned out more like Lucas. *It would have been different if Myrium had been alive,* he thought. *I don't know what I did to deserve this abandonment, but the girl had needed a mother. If Myrium were alive, she would have been able to persuade Isla that there was nothing for her to find on the mainland. That it was all a dream she was chasing, and it would come to nothing in the end.*

Petro stared into the soft darkness beyond his house. Fireflies flashed and twinkled in the young night. *What's so wrong with this island that she needed to leave? This land is good enough for Lucas. And it has always been good enough for me.* As these thoughts travelled through Petro's mind, a sharp pang leapt up in his heart, and he quickly turned back to his friends gathered in the living room.

"Petro, are you in or are you out?"

Petro returned to his chair and threw down two copper coins in response. His eyes stared at the others menacingly.

"Oh, he's bluffing for sure," Jayan laughed.

"Shut up and play your own hand you ass," Petro replied, his eyes glowing against the fire of the candles. He remembered the days he and Jayan and Fazza had had to sneak up into the woods by the ridge to play cards because their parents had forbidden gambling.

Petro looked at the faces of the men who had come to sit at his table to play cards and talk ever since his father had passed and he had become the man of this house. *We've become old* — the thought came to him suddenly, and he looked over at Jayan and realised that his thick black hair had been white for some time and that the deep scar across Fazza's forehead was now barely visible amongst the creases in his leathery skin. And then, another thought flashed in his mind — *our time is almost up.*

"That Lucas has turned out okay, for a trader's son," Jayan was saying.

"Certainly has," agree Fazza. "Remember those years after his father passed? That kid really went out to sea for awhile. And who could blame him with that uncle of his. But he's become a good trader and a good man for all that."

"Hmmmm," the men agreed.

"Leaving this island never does anyone any good, trader or no," Petro said with conviction.

"Hmmm," they murmured again sympathetically.

The men were quiet for a moment, pretending to scrutinise their cards.

"Maybe she'll come back," Jayan said, looking at Petro. But Petro did not raise his eyes. He felt a strange pull — he had been feeling this more often lately, a pull deep within, yanking his entrails, a hole deep in his chest like a damp pit, a choking hand which would not let go. And he didn't like where this feeling was taking him.

A voice inside him cried out like some long forgotten dream, but Petro busied himself worrying about the state of his cards, the lay of his land and other urgent island matters that he must attend to immediately, and in this way shook off the cold ache in his heart. As he had done before.

When had the fear taken him? Petro didn't know. When had it moved from the edges of his skin into his bloodstream, begun to flow with a regular course until it seemed to belong there like something organic, unchangeable, inevitable. Once, long ago a differently kind of fear had haunted Petro like a nightly plague, descending suddenly and without warning when the moon was full and he could see far out over the glittering water that reminded him of the soul of the world. Then, it had been the fear of his dreams, or rather the consequences of his dreams, which was the fear of the metamorphosis of the soul.

As a young man, he had dreamed of leaving this island and had sent away for several maps and marked out his route in thin black ink while he sat at the old dining table. Then he had ordered books from the Isle of Joon filled with complex illustrations of magical domed buildings, fakirs with ochre-coloured turbans and sadhus with carved walking sticks. He had memorised foreign poems that sounded like soft smoke and the welcomed grit of the road when he murmured them in the evenings to himself.

Once, when he was quite drunk at a clandestine poker game with Jayan and Fazza, he had looked up from his winning hand and declared defiantly, "You both are sons of bitches. I'm leaving this island. I'm going to travel across the mainland and even beyond." But the finality of those spoken words shook him so deeply that he never mentioned them aloud to anyone again, and instead he began to pray with an unexpected fervour that his friends had been too drunk to remember this unguarded confession.

It was his dreams that had frightened him then. Notions of leaving a life that was familiar, of walking down that unknown path and getting caught up in an unforeseen riptide that might sweep him along this way and that until he lost all sense of the direction of his life. Lost control. It brought with it a fear that this unknown path would change him, would mould his mind and shift his heart so that some day years from this moment of departure he would be unable to remember the exact curvature of the road to his home that he could now walk drunk in the middle of a starless night without stumbling once. Or that one day his best friends might begin to speak a strange indecipherable language that rung strangely in his ear. It was a fear of losing recognition, of drifting so far that neither personal vendettas nor close tragedies could inspire him to shed a tear and return for the night.

Then, just when he had begun to suspect deep in his chest that he wasn't actually planning to leave after all, Myrium had appeared on the island like a remedy to his foolish youth. Myrium with her wild dark hair and uncommon silver eyes and exotic smell to her skin. It only took one glance at this woman to inspire in Petro a passion he had never known, and he had decided instantly as he stood on the sandy crossroads of the island, that life with this woman was the illustrious, unprecedented adventure he was actually destined to take.

It was several years after his wife's sudden death when the knocking in his chest began again and Petro felt his dreams, like the scent of a distant memory, blink after their long sleep. It happened early one morning. Petro had been sitting on his favourite chair blowing noisily on his steaming tea when Isla had wandered into the living room, her curly hair still wild from sleep, her small body hidden inside the sack of one of Petro's old shirts which she had taken to wearing to bed. Petro had always loved this small daughter with a fierce riotous passion leftover from the future years he had expected to love his wife, and because Isla's small feminine gestures and silvery eyes reminded him of Myrium, she made him feel that some small part of Myrium still lived and was still his. But that morning when Isla had wandered in scuffing her bare feet again the floor boards, it struck Petro as it had not before, that Isla also greatly resembled him, that she was not only Myrium's daughter but his daughter as well. And something about this new thought reviled him, and he said something cross and frowned at the part of himself that he thought he saw in her and turned away.

After that his old decrepit dreams of the mainland returned to haunt his every waking step, and he had to fight them off with every ounce of strength, every thread of love he had for the island and the people he had not left behind. At times he left it to fate. *It's too late*, he told himself. *I wasn't meant to go or else it would have happened.* But other times, when he could not deny his own part in the neglect of his dreams, he would whisper back anxiously, *I did what I knew was right. I've led an honourable life. If I had just up and gone, what would be left of the losa hills of my grandfather?*

After Jayan and Fazza had gone, Petro sat in his house, listening the cicadas sing and it seemed to him as if he were completely alone, set adrift in the dark, silent ocean of the world. Almost before he realised what he was doing, Petro had walked over to the wooden cabinet which stood in the corner of the room and had stooped down to retrieve the old map. His knees trembled and ached as he tried to stand up, and Petro thought to himself — *this is what it feels like to be old.* The shaking in his legs terrified him to the depths of his soul, and he gripped the dining room table fiercely as if it would hold him there, in that room, and prevent this life from slipping away.

The light above the old wooden table shone brightly as Petro spread out the map. Several corners of it had begun to crumble and the map tore in some of the creases where it had been folded up for so many years. He remembered the day Isla had come home enchanted with magical notions of the mainland and he had taken out this map. That day he had used the map for the very opposite purpose for which it had been intended...to kill Isla's dreams of far off lands. Petro slumped down into a chair as the weight of some invisible burden fell upon his shoulders. This map had come to him under such different circumstances. *I was free then,* he thought. *But times are different now. The world is more dangerous. I was trying to protect her.* His dark eyes stared blearily at the map, but it lay silent and did nothing to allay his guilt.

How have I gotten here? Petro thought to himself. *How has it come to this?*

Who can say whether it was the paper map spread out in that cool darkness or whether it was some other map, inscribed onto Petro in the hidden empty spaces of his heart, but after many decades Petro noticed that the ache was not in his body after all. It was somewhere deeper, older even than the many years he had felt old. Older than he could recall. Before him he saw his wife's young face, her dark hair whipping in the island wind coming off the sea. She looked up at him with silver eyes, across the indigo land of their hills. Before his eyes, she smiled contentedly, and Petro, alone now in the deepening night, began to cry because he had not felt that content for so many years of his long life.

Enigmatic winds full of hot dusty incense and things left unspoken blew from the folds of the map calling to him in an ancient language of adventure that he hardly recognised. "I have been chained to this island," Petro cried into the winds. "I had no choice. They couldn't have done without me here. I had to stay. I had to stay." And his tears fell long and hard as the rain because he knew this wasn't true.

24

Tomas looked at the iridescent waters of the lagoon, and they seemed to him like the shimmering belly of an oyster shell. "Most oysters do not contain pearls," he reminded himself. "It was always wrong of me to hope for more."

The waters glowed with the colours of the setting sun and cast deep shadows onto the warm sandstone walls of the merchant city. This city had once seemed infinitely grand when Tomas had sailed into port for the first time in his tiny boat that was sanded smooth with the anger of unrequited love and the paralysis of indecision. Now, as he stared into the quiet lanes that rested in shadows at the edge of nightfall, Tomas could also see the cracks in the tall tower wall and the refuse that clung to the edges of the water channels below.

The Merchant City was only one of several port towns dotting the ocean and coastline. Yet it had beauty in its stone walls, the coloured glass that set the windows aglow at night, the great sundials that decorated the tall towers, the radiant bells whose voices resonated through the maze of canals and tiny lanes and over the crowns of the people like god's own breath. There was something about this Merchant City that mesmerised Tomas like a flame dancing silent in his darkness. So why was he never happy here?

Tomas turned his face away from the window and considered the woman who slept through the stillness of this late afternoon. Stripped by some unknowable dream of her frequent frowns and the grasping gaze of her eyes, she was still beautiful. But instead of going to stand next to her as he would once have done, instead of stroking her hair, heated gold in the last of the sun, Tomas sighed and ran his fingers through the small sack of pearls in his pocket. He felt their weight in his hand. Yes, they would be enough. Enough for now. Enough so that he would not have to return here again for many many months.

Tomas picked up a cup of red wine that had been abandoned earlier that afternoon. It tasted sour, like the blood of an animal he had killed. He emptied it into his throat, then counted out a pile of coins for Leventia and walked out the door.

Night had fallen and the narrow lanes were filling with people like the inevitable rising of the tide. Several street children tugged at Tomas's coat, pleading and whining and threatening in their innocent way. Tomas bought them a round of bread from one of the street stalls, and they scattered again screaming into the night. On his way to the bar to meet Muran, he passed two masked courtesans, their young pink breasts on proud display, but their faces hidden by glittering sequins and coloured feathers. One called his name, but he did not turn to see whether he recognised the eyes or the shape of the breasts. He did not know her tonight.

Muran was waiting for him when he stepped through the small dank alley and into the sour comfort of the candlelit bar. Tomas threw the small leather sack onto the table and called for a glass of wine. He was surprised by how carelessly he lived these days. But then, it seemed every year more life drained away from him and the less he could bring himself to care about anything, even his pearls.

Muran picked up the leather pouch and lifted it in her hand like the sea lifts a boat up and down in the waves. Then she poured a few out into the palm of her hand. Tomas saw the flicker of a smile. She was pleased. "I can get you a good price for these Tomas. No one has seen pearls in the market for months. I will go first to Harrodas, but if he is not willing to meet my price there will be many others."

Muran no longer wore a mask to meet him. Her dark black hair was streaked with the silver of her waning days, and she was too old to stand on the evening streets playing at love. But she had been Tomas's first, and she was loyal as was the way with courtesans, and she could get a better price in the market with the wealthy merchant men who wished they still loved her. So Tomas gave her his pearls to sell, and she always got her promised price.

"No news of her?"

"Why must you always!" Tomas looked up from his cup of wine and saw Muran staring at him as if searching for something beneath the skin. He sighed. "There is always news of her," he replied again and his voice felt suddenly hollow. "She is still on the mainland, working as a scribe for the administration. She writes," he explained.

"But not to you," Muran finished, and when Tomas looked up at her, he remembered again what had drawn him to this woman, this courtesan who had been older than all the others. Tonight her hair was streaked with grey, but only a few years ago it had still been black, black and curly and wild like the vines of a jungle. The eyes were different, and she was not as beautiful, but something about her had reminded him of Isla.

"Well, I let her go, didn't I?" Tomas said. "I let her go alone. In the end, I was the one who broke my promise to her. We had always planned to go together, on adventures..."

"Perhaps you made the decision that was right for you," Muran said, but she did not patronise him by reaching across the table to touch his arm.

"Perhaps I am just a coward," Tomas replied. But then he smiled and said more gently, "Let's talk of other things." And because of the fragile look in his eyes, Muran amused him with news of the merchant city — how a wealthy trader from the family Jolena had lost his fortune and had been banned for life from the western spice market because it was believed he had been cursed by an ill-favoured wind. The news was also of marriage and the merging of two great trading families. And there was news from the streets — the council of courtesans, which included several women who were as wealthy as any merchant trader, had determined to build an orphanage for the growing number of street children abandoned by their impoverished mothers and rejected in equal measure by their young trader fathers.

The merchant city was a world unto itself, governed by the Merchant Superior who paid tribute to the mainland in return for the city's autonomy. 'Freedom at any price' was the city's only philosophy, and trade was its only business. In fact, the merchant city was hardly a city at all, with its transient population that hovered like sea birds before moving on to sell the very goods they had just acquired to seaside villages and smaller trading islands.

The city had begun only as a group of small flat islands that rose from the depths of the sea so close together that many of the water channels between them were little more than two boat-lengths wide. Over the years the islands had been enveloped by stone buildings and covered wooden markets that stretched far over the water channels like trees on a riverbank, until the city appeared from the sea to be one single landmass, artificially divided by a series of water channels, instead of the other way around.

Perhaps it was this unique character of the Merchant City that attracted so many traders to this seeming oasis of pleasure. The traders seemed never to tire as they swarmed through the city's spice markets, its furniture markets, its carpet and textile markets on narrow black boats pushed through the shallow passageways by long wooden poles. Or perhaps it was the city's location far to the south-east of the mainland which made it a natural crossing point in the sea.

Either way, while the Merchant City was not unique in its specialisation as a point of ocean trade, it was by far the most splendid. And the wealthier its traders became, the more ostentatious the city grew, so that its stone buildings sprouted delicate spires and gleaming golden domes, its market squares were decorated with statues of all the exotic animals the merchant city lacked in reality, and silk paintings of mythic beasts that protected the city and its traders even far out at sea decorated the inner sanctums of the great houses.

Yet besides an impenetrable circle of elite trading families who were bound together by both generations of affection and intermarriage as well as by mutual distrust and rivalry, and most importantly by the unwavering defence of their elite station from the lesser transient masses, there was little else in the way of a stable community in the Merchant City. This was because the city mostly attracted single wayward young men hoping to make a quick fortune, and it kept them in the circular pattern of arduous trips between the city and other sea ports until middle age when their blood began to thin and they longed at last for their parents and their home.

Over the years, women had also gravitated to the Merchant City. Some had been cast out of their homes for the crimes of premature love. Others had fled when their bleeding had stopped and they foresaw their own condemned destiny and believed only the illicit doctors of the Merchant City could save them. And still others had simply fled the bondage of their arranged marriages and the living death of unending boredom.

These women arrived in the Merchant City, and most never left its shores again. The women of artistic taste and intellectual interests grew into a community of courtesans who decorated their bodies with paint and feathers and silk and gold. These women danced at elite functions, played stringed instruments that sounded like heaven, and because they took only one lover at a time, they were regarded as a kind of treasure and were paid handsomely for their company by the men who were driven to increasing greed by their own good fortune.

The other women who arrived haphazardly and in droves to this opulent city and found themselves without particular talent or beauty joined the band of prostitutes who littered the narrow cobbled lanes and attended to those desperate youths who had neither the money nor status to attract the rosy lipped courtesans. Whether they were happier in this precarious freedom than in their days of security and marital bondage no one could say, for even these women did not ask themselves such questions.

Muran also did not ask herself if she was happy. She looked across the table at Tomas and knew that even rich men were troubled in their hearts and that no one found peace easily.

25

That night Tomas dreamt of Isla, and when he awoke the memory of her was all around him filling the room as the dawn light. He lay still, one arm slung over the side of the tall bed, the scent of sleep holding him suspended between this bitter bedroom and the world he saw in his mind.

She had been waving to him from the other side of a ravine. Behind her a tall mountain rose from the earth and between them a river roared green and white, drowning her voice and stealing it from the air. What had she been trying to say? Had she looked happy or sad? Tomas blinked and couldn't remember.

Outside the city bells cast ripples through the merchant city, marking a new day of trade. Now he remembered. He was here, in the Merchant City. Soon he would dress and make his way to the western spice market where Muran would be waiting for him. He had made a decision the previous night as he had wandered back along the streets, wavering with drink and trying not to mistake the dark waterways that crisscrossed the city for the solid cobbled pathways. It was time to leave the Merchant City — forever. He must return to the island that he had always loved and hope it would take him back to the man he had once been.

Tomas couldn't remember now how long he had remained on the island after she had left. It had been many months of a single flat sky, a fog that even the brave beam of his lighthouse could not penetrate. During the endless days he had dived for pearls and tended the garden. At night he had fled to the top of the lighthouse where he sat, staring into the darkness, watching the white beam collide helplessly against cloud and fog.

Paralysed by the chaos of his mind, Tomas poisoned himself with guilt, struck himself again and again for his cowardice, drowned himself in an anger that knew no bounds against the woman who had chosen an unknown life over him. Doubt chained him to the lighthouse and yet, in moments of self-loathing, he knew he had been afraid to leave the island. He knew Isla hadn't loved him as he had loved her. He knew that he was weak, had always been too weak to deserve this wild, wayfaring woman. And he knew was not the man his father had tried to make him believe.

He was not the man he had hoped to be.

But there were other moments, more rare, when his mind fell quiet, when he watched the slow undulation of the tides and also knew he had stayed not simply because he had been afraid to leave, but because, unlike Isla, he had always loved the island. It was his home. It was where he belonged. And even worse than losing Isla would have been to lose this truth of himself.

Out in the open night he would doze, but when then he would wake and remember again that his father was dead and Isla had gone and there was only the white noise of silence left. The island turned cold, and though Tomas reached out for it, it would not touch him. Who could say what had changed? Why the sand turned coarse beneath his feet. Why he suddenly stumbled on the uneven ground. Why the birds no longer sat still, eyeing him while he drew, or why the lazy iguanas suddenly began to hiss and nip at his toes.

Still, it was only when Tomas looked up one idle afternoon from one of his singular ruminations and realised he no longer recognised the path he had been following, nor the vegetable fields that ran to his left, nor the flat shrub land to his right, that Tomas understood the truth. The island had become a stranger to him — he was lost in his own home. And the agony that he felt at this new loss finally convinced him that he must leave the island after all. Just for a while. Just to prove he too was man enough to stand on his own.

That was when he began to build his boat, stripping wood, soaking and stretching the planks into the smooth curve of a hull. Tomas worked with the frenzy of a man pursued by the beasts of the world, and when he had finally secured the mast and Marco's father pronounced the boat sea-worthy, he had filled the store with seventeen days worth of food and water, retrieved his box of pearls, which was the only possession he still valued, and left the island of his birth for the first time in his life.

He did not sail towards the mainland.

Instead, Tomas turned the bow south-east, and within a day, found himself in a warm current that carried him even when the wind was still and did not fill his sail. On the fourth day, the light of the sun fell from the sky like a great rain, drowning his vision, and the soft sea air came gently onto his skin, and Tomas found himself wrapped in a silence so vast and powerful that it consumed the voices of his mind and he remembered again what it was like to be at peace.

Then, Tomas thought of the boatman. He recalled the way the boatman sipped his tea when he came to Dari's, how he walked slowly but without faltering down the unfamiliar lanes of the island, how he listened to everyone's stories but was unhurried to tell his own, and Tomas realised the boatman also knew this silence of the sea, that somehow the boatman carried this vast silence within him. For the first time, Tomas saw that he had something in common with the red-haired stranger whom he had always regarded with suspicion out of the corner of his eye, and on that day at sea, he had felt glad that the boatman had come to the island after all.

The following day, Tomas had arrived in the Merchant City.

The bells of the Merchant City struck the hour, but Tomas lay still, knowing that the briefest movement would cause his body to waken and dispel the palpable feeling of her. Had he clung this tightly to Isla when they had been together? Tomas suddenly remembered the look of Isla's silver face in the underwater cave, the way the indigo shadows had played across her cheeks, the way the dark waters had clung to her hair like a veil. But he had been afraid. He had chosen the safety of the island and the memory of his dead father over Isla, and in the end, both had abandoned him. So here he was again, thrown by the sword of his own doubts into the brazen generosity of the Merchant City with its lines of inadequate lovers and the wealth from his pearls that could not buy him out of confusion and despair.

Tomas sat up on the edge of the bed and put his head in his hands, letting go at last of the lingering scent of his dream. Soon it would be time to meet Muran. In the meantime, he had many supplies to collect. There was a trader in the spice market that sold the coloured powders he wanted for his paintings in tiny wooden boxes sealed tight with blood-coloured wax. He needed shades of yellow ochre, and the heated ochre that was the colour of clarified wine. Also white lead powder. Blue he could make himself from the leaves of losa on the island. He would have to hurry if he wanted to push off by late afternoon when the tide had turned. Tomas's face turned expectantly towards the silent sun that never failed to meet him and his small boat, but he still felt lost. He had forgotten the tattoo that still marked his back with the sign of the sea.

26

If only one day I could become a senior scribe... Isla thought to herself as she stared at the wide, imposing doors of the Department of the Lost Regions. But then she paused because she honestly didn't know how this wish might end. *I would be happy,* she finished silently to herself. *I will have made it.*

It was spring, and pink blossoms fell from the branches of the trees in slow motion according to the whims of the breeze, and for several weeks, the proud statues and the soaring edifices of the great buildings of the Administrative District were covered in a utopian shade of rosy petals. Isla walked through the central square immersed in this alluring fragrance of new beginnings, and the frantic clicking of heels on cobblestones filled her with a sense of energy and progress, for mainlanders did not wait for the turn of spring but had created their own urban rhythms, their own seasons of change that made them feel the true masters of the world.

Isla's gaze followed the steady stream of men and women walking with purpose in the dark blue robes of the senior scribes and the black robes worn by banking merchants. There were the red robes of governing official and brown robes worn by the architects and engineers and the pale white robes of the scientists, astrologers and seers.

Turning the corner onto a cobbled lane, Isla walked as the mainland had taught her — straight ahead towards her goal, a steady unwavering line from her past into her future. She still remembered that there were places in the world, outlying places where things didn't move forward but simply went round and round in endless cycles of time, where the same things happened again and again like the coming and going of the seasons and where no one could progress because people believed whatever was past was bound to happen again in the future. Isla knew it was her purpose to bring such places progress, as the mainland had brought progress to her, and she pounded the pavement with the fervent faith of the newly converted.

At the precise moment her gaze fell upon him in the shifting living crowds he was standing on the pavement in a dark, tailored suit, his black hair cut into an unmistakable line at the nape of his neck in the style of banking merchants. He glanced up as he passed her on the street, and there was something there in his face, some striving look in his crystal eyes that she recognised also in herself, and also something soft and beautiful about the small dark mark that sat high on his forehead. Isla brushed by him on her way, skirt swaying in the blue winds of her footsteps, and she noticed as she passed the subtle scent of thyme — the scent of the mountains.

His name was Jackimo, and standing still on the bustling street, he revived Isla's awareness of her own breath, her beating heart, and reminded her most assuredly of love. What was it about him? Perhaps we are never meant to understand such things. But in that glance, Isla felt a new hope open inside of her like the wings of a butterfly from the rough silk of the cocoon, and for the first time she believed she really could become a new person, a person of her own choosing.

For weeks afterwards, as the cool breezes continued to blow through the winding city lanes, Isla searched for him, around corners, in the down-turned faces of tall banking merchants, amongst the crowds at the Dragon Festival that filled the streets for days with coloured paper streamers and celebratory cries and the luxurious yellow smells of freshly baked cakes. She found herself surveying the faces at the coffeehouses, one after the other, until she had studied so many faces, so many noses and eyes and eyebrows and chins that she was sure she had forgotten what he looked like altogether.

And then, standing amongst the crowd at Neha's art exhibition, she smelled the scent of thyme and he was there, standing squarely below her on the stair, staring up at her with eyes a reassuring shade of clear blue. They both smiled at each other in recognition.

"Can I get you something to drink?" he asked her, and when she replied, "yes, I'd like that", he paused and looked at her again. "Your accent... you speak like an islander. But your eyes are from the mountains."

It wasn't until much later that Isla realised it had not been the years of training, of scholarly apprenticeship, nor the hours spent practicing the mainland accent or the sudden seemingly inexplicable way mainlanders clapped their hands while they spoke, nor even had it been the wide friendships she had gained during her years on the mainland. But it was the appearance of Jackimo in her life that had inaugurated her true and final arrival on the mainland, for it had been Jackimo who had made her forget that she ever meant to return to the island, Jackimo who had made her believe there was more than one place she could call home.

In that first moment on the stairs, however, she did not know what lay ahead, and so she replied honestly, "I was born on an island in the southern sea, but my mother was not an islander after all."

At that moment, a breeze from the balcony lifted her hemline, and Isla hoped that this man would notice the sensuous red silk lining of her robe, so he would see that although she still spoke with the intonation of an islander, her sophistication flowed in natural harmony with the mainland.

Bodies wove between them on the stairs, blue silks, golden embroidered sleeves, hands floating thin glasses in the air, but Isla and Jackimo stood still, smiling awkwardly at each other as two people who realise they are about to fall in love but don't yet know why. The interior of the art studio flickered in orange candlelight, and as Isla descended the stairs ahead of Jackimo, she caught sight of Neha standing in a long blue embroidered robe surrounded by a group of suited men and bejewelled women, and Isla found herself wishing that she felt as calm.

Neha had the advantage of having been born here, on the mainland, at the centre of the world. She was not intimidated by the grace of the mainlander women that now surrounded her in their impossibly high heeled shoes, nor did she flinch at the men's rising voices as they debated the various qualities of true innovation and the intricacies of the Philosophy of the Rising Sun. Neha never shook from the intense gravity of her own nerves. She never questioned the legitimacy of her work, her authority to speak. No, Neha never needed to question herself, nor prove herself to the vast hierarchies of mainland elite. She was one of them, born from the sophisticated womb of the mainland goddess herself, and when she clapped the palms of her hands to punctuate a word, she did so softly, with the delicacy of a silver knife against crystal.

Isla gripped the thin banister as she stepped carefully down each stair on her tottering heels. *After all my years of practice*, Isla thought sternly to herself, *I will not lose my balance tonight!*

"She's going to do well tonight," Isla heard herself say as they reached the bottom of the stairs, and Jackimo nodded. "No one has expressed the power of Newness and change like Neha. Her work will be the icon of our age."

With glasses of wine in their hands, Jackimo and Isla moved to a corner of the studio, and in the cool shadows, it seemed to Isla as if she were suddenly protected from a storm she had hardly noticed whirling around her. Across the wide hall of the studio, twisted metal pipes jutted deftly from a black wooden post; further to the left, broken pieces of glass were arranged in random precision on long boards of wood. Baked bricks were stacked into sculptures that had no names but stood like sentinels along one wall of the room.

Neha's artwork was not beautiful. She was becoming famous now, not for the grace of her art, nor even for expressing some hidden meaning of life that struck the viewers off-guard and penetrated their souls. Neha's artwork had become the latest sensation of the city because no one had ever before showed such a bold commitment to the idea of what was 'new'. No one had ever before dared to create art that demonstrated nothing but innovation. Her pieces were large and careened into one's vision like an obelisk, reaching for the sky just for the sake of touching it. Looking at her artwork, Isla felt disoriented, as if she had wandered off the end of a map and was stepping slipshod into uncharted territory.

Isla remembered the morning when, sitting in her usual place in the great hall and amidst the restless voices of the innumerable novice scribes, Neha had told Isla fearlessly and without doubt, "What I want is to do something that no one has ever done before — something different, something that proves I am alive." Neha had paused and her gaze had fled over the many faces of the other novice scribes, and Isla had wondered then whether Neha was not also afraid of vanishing into these crowds of humanity, of being lost forever in the muddy waters of mediocrity.

But then she had seen Neha raise her chin as if to defy the gods and say, "My art will be different. It will be new. If nothing else, at least I will have that!" To a girl like Isla, who had felt so long buried under an island of stagnating customs and meaningless acts, Neha's convictions about innovation and the satisfaction it could give to people's lives meant everything. To feel unique in the riot of humanity...to long for proof that one's life was not without meaning — even with all her years on the island, Isla wondered if everyone didn't think such thoughts at some point or other, even if only for a moment, even if they never spoke them out loud.

"Are you here to buy one of the pieces?" Isla asked.

Jackimo smiled. "I'm here for the same reason as everyone else. To see the edge of innovation." Then he laughed, and Isla noticed that his ears stuck out foolishly from his careful haircut when he smiled and, knowing this, something in her began to relax. "Everyone who wants to be a success is committed to the Rising Sun," he continued.

"Why do you think the rich are out in such numbers tonight? They know where this artist is headed, what her work means — and what it means for them to own her work!"

"Isla!" She turned to find Neha embracing her. "You made it! It's absolutely crazy here!"

"It's amazing, Neha!" Isla returned. "I'm so proud of you! You've really done it!"

Neha squeezed her hand, "I've got to go..." and then she noticed Jackimo, standing quietly beside Isla holding his glass of wine and her eyes flickered back to Isla and her smile grew wide.

"So..." Jackimo said after Neha had glided away, "a woman from the islands with mountain eyes who is a friend of the mainland's most inspirational new artist." Emptying his glass of wine, Jackimo stuck his hands into his pockets as if he might be nervous too. "You're certainly not like anyone else I've met in this city," he said, as if to himself, and Isla felt her face flush with the spontaneous fever of pride. She could feel Jackimo's eyes watching her and even as she brought the glass of wine up to her stained lips, she prayed that the candlelight was dim enough that he wouldn't notice her burning cheeks.

It occurred to Isla then how ironic it all was — that she had spent so many years now mimicking the mainlander's speech, copying their gestures, trying to blend into the mainland city. And yet these words Jackimo had spoken, telling her that she was unique, that she stood out — they meant everything. And she wondered at the great canyon of space between feeling foreign and feeling unique, the mountain that divides the experience of safely fitting in and the security of feeling at home from the fear of being the same, of fading away without distinction.

Isla and Jackimo spent the evening exchanging stories between sips of wine, and they found the night had grown old.

"But that's what I love about the city," Isla found herself saying. "You can do something meaningful here. That's not true everywhere you go. Some places don't let you breathe."

When Jackimo looked at her, his eyes flashed with a dawn, a blue that had been other places, had opened its gaze upon other parts of the world and knew from the experience of years that what she said was true. *He is not from the mainland*, Isla thought to herself. *He speaks like a mainlander, but he is not one of them by birth. Just like me.*

The heavy skirt of Isla's robe swayed as she shifted her weight from one heeled foot to the other, and in that small movement she caught sight of herself in the candlelit reflection of the window and paused because she did not recognise the woman who stood before her with her elegant robe and hair that hung straight as silk in thick bands, like rays of a dark sun down to her waist. Her heart jumped in her chest as she remembered the small, wild girl who had stepped off the boatman's craft all those years ago. Like lightning a thought came to her — *Tomas wouldn't know me anymore* — and her heart jumped unsteadily in her chest.

Isla tried to smile comfortingly back at herself, tried to remember that this woman who stood tall in her heeled shoes, who drank coffee now and worked with great loyalty towards the progress of the deprived Lost Regions, this woman was exactly who she had always wanted to be. Someone with purpose.

In the reflection, her silver eyes stared back at her over the shimmering bodies that moved in and out of sight, back at her with this handsome mainland man at her side, and Isla remembered all the things those eyes of hers had seen, all the lands, the avenues of the great city, the villages of the surrounding regions, the people who had come and gone in her life over the seven years she had lived on the mainland.

I've changed, she thought again, and something deep inside her suddenly lifted in great relief because if there was anything her heart had always feared, it was the possibility that her life might never change at all. *At least now,* she thought, *no matter what happens, I won't have to wonder what might have happened if I hadn't left the island. Now, at least I know.* And she stood for many moments at the threshold of the studio, encircled by the heavy silk robe with the silver embroidered flowers that reflected the light from the window and shone out in the dark wide night.

27

"The northern hills are not green like this plain of the mainland," Jackimo said, and he twisted a smooth stirring stick between his fingers and looked out across the wide square as if he expected to see these dark mountains rising up from behind the blue roofs of the buildings there. He was not from the mainland — Isla had been right about this fact. She always recognised outsiders by their smell. With Jackimo, she had known by the scent of thyme.

On her left now, the slanting tiled roof of the Central Bank marked the boundary of the Administrative District, and Isla and Jackimo waded into the warm, invigorating aromas of the coffee district. At once both sweet and bitter, the dark drink cast its enticing perfume into the air of the narrowing streets, and Isla opened her lungs to the reassuring scent that always reminded her of purpose and the lofty heights of achievement.

He had come to the mainland from a small region directly north of the city that sat on the side of the great mountains, he admitted when they both held cups of dark coffee and had found their seats out in the open air where boxes of lavender separated them from the flowing crowds on the street.

"The earth is brown and the wind is dry and in the hot season the sun passes so close overhead that it singes the crowns of the trees and the whole land turns a blinding white for long stretches of the day and everyone has to hide indoors. When I was young my grandmother used to tell me that if I was caught out by the sun's eye on those days my hair would turn white as the sun!" He clapped his hands for effect and then looked at Isla and smiled in his crooked, sideways manner. "Crazy what we believe as children."

"Tell me." Isla smiled so that he would know she recognised that deep longing that came with the memory of home.

His family farmed land that grew grain and apricots and dates, he told her, hesitantly at first, though his voice grew more solid as this silver-eyed woman continued to smile.

"Our farm was seven terraces of land which lay along the southern side of the mountain."

"Facing the direction of the mainland city."

"We couldn't see the city."

"But you knew it was there," Isla commented, and Jackimo laughed. "Yes, I was always gazing out over the hills and into the distance..." He looked at her, and his eyes shifted and twinkled with mischief. "I see now I was not the only one..."

"You were not," Isla felt the corners of her mouth rise ruefully.

"My father believed all things came from the gods," Jackimo continued, "and so he went every evening to offer seeds, or pieces of the harvest, or simply his words to the face of god that some seer had carved into the side of the mountain rock. His faith never wavered. I always believed my father was a special kind of magician, for he always knew exactly when the apricots would turn sweet or when the almonds would drop or how to protect our seedlings from the hungry insects and small birds that passed by every spring. He seemed to know everything there was to know when I was young. I was still very small when I began to help with the harvest, and I held the storage bag that father heaped full of dried fruit and nuts and pushed it into the air as he hung the sack between the storehouse rafters. But I got bored," he finished simply. "I became so bored with that life."

Arriving in the mainland at the age of fourteen, Jackimo had decided that the only way to rise above his old life was to complete his schooling. But the mainland had not been the oasis he had imagined, for the older mainlander boys at the lower academy mimicked the way he held his spoon at mealtimes, stole his pen before exams and refused to speak to him until he spoke like a mainlander, like their equal. For a year, he had cried in dark corners and had practiced making the long fluid vowel sounds of the mainlanders' speech, repeating words again and again until his tongue ached and his throat felt tight as if there was a collar around his neck. But the second year, he returned to the academy with a perfected mainland accent, and because he also ran faster than any of the boys in his class, he was finally accepted, and he forgot his old rivalries and made new alliances and eventually loved these mainlander boys like brothers.

He had succeeded. He was a banking merchant now. Now he too was important in the progress of the world. Jackimo leaned back against the cushion and drew the cup of coffee to his mouth. His black robe cut squarely at his shoulders and folded against his bent knees, and Isla found it difficult to imagine him in this foreign setting, in mountain clothes, walking through a rocky terrain. His mainland robe fit him so well.

"It's so easy for me to imagine leaving that dull, arid place," Jackimo said to her, "but your island sounds like a paradise." And Isla wondered if that were true.

"Ever since I was young, I wanted to see the world," she replied. "That's all I know. The island has a particular way of thinking, and if you don't believe in the things everyone else believes in, then you can't exist there, you are like a bird flying against the wind."

Green parrots and orange sunsets, indigo hills and red losa bags moving up and down the rows — images of the island flashed through Isla's mind as if a phantom of her past had whispered gently, enticingly, in her ear. The great banyan tree, she and Tomas hiding amongst the shadows of its soaring branches listening to island gossip from the people walking below. Isla shook her head and the buzzing voices of the coffeehouse returned. Looking up, Isla's gaze fell upon the wooden pillars so common in such ancient buildings of the coffee district. The carvings of the dragons reminded her of the mainland's history of power, the rose of beauty and artistry, the large eye of the mainland's foresight and progress, and she knew that she had made the right choice.

"I wanted an unusual life," she said, facing Jackimo. "I wanted a life like no one else's, and it always seemed to me that, if I could have that, a unique life, if I could do things that no one else on the island had done before and see things that no one else had ever seen, then I would have a life worth living. The island, you see, moves like a banyan tree grows, slowly slowly slowly. Nothing ever changes there and no one ever wonders about the purpose of their life because, I suppose, the island is enough for them. But I must be more like my mother, because it was never enough for me."

"If simply keeping our stomachs full and our bodies warm in their beds were the purpose of our lives, we would all be at peace," he spoke again. "But we're not! We are not satisfied. It is in our nature to want More." He looked at her, willing her, this woman from the islands to understand this thing which mainlanders born to the city of progress and plenty could never truly know. Jackimo's face frowned, and he tapped the small coffee-stained stick against the table like a drum that forced the rhythm of his heart. "We must make our own peace by doing things worthy of our life," he concluded. "We must do things that change the world."

It was through these small stories that Isla learned the textures of Jackimo's quiet determination, for the way he had transformed his adolescent disenchantment into a renewed effort to succeed felt as familiar to her as her own skin. They stood in the same place, outsiders of the mainland that they adored and were now bound to not by birth or any accident of fate but by a common dream to make a mark on the world and to live at the centre of all things. Their pasts were different, the names they recalled, the contours of the lands they remembered, the crops they had nurtured to grow, the sounds of the people they heard in their dreams. But something in the story of Jackimo's childhood mirrored Isla's own memories of her early years on the island. These stories felt remembered, as if they had also happened to her. They felt like the lines on her palm that she was finally able to read.

Over the months and then years that followed, Jackimo told Isla many things she had not expected him to say. He told her that what he loved most in the world was the taste of fresh apricots and the scent of thyme on the hills. He told her how he missed the migrations of birds that had once marked the passing of his years with dark diamond flocks that brought life to the flat, open skies. He told her that he had fled the boredom of life in the mountains, but he had not fled from his family, and that one day he would fulfil his duty as the only son by bringing his parents here to the mainland city so that they too could enjoy the advantages of progress, of newness, and of plenty.

She in turn told him about the colour of losa that made her island glow purple. She told him of swimming in sea pools and of the school teacher who had taught them that their tiny, meagre island was the centre of the world, and of summer afternoons filled with blissful sunshine and buzzing insects. She told him things she had not even revealed to Neha, the truth about her father's silences, the way she had felt a foreigner even in her own home. And she told him how she missed the island, and how she felt like a coward because she could not bring herself to go back. The only thing she never spoke of was Tomas, for he seemed something sacred and rare, something only for her, like a pearl in her mind, a buried secret that one day she would have to face.

Around them the light was falling but the breeze that blew across their faces seemed to come only from the mainland streets, as if its energy had been borne by the city itself, and it seemed to both Isla and Jackimo as if the mainland were a world without boundaries and yet held no relationship to these foreign lands of their past.

Above them, a lattice of vines filtered the view of the evening sky and the silk cushions gradually lost their colour in the growing dark. "I should go," Isla said. "I have a busy day tomorrow." She wrapped the loose collar of her dark blue robe tighter against her skin, and Jackimo noticed how her eyes glowed silver as the embroidery of her sleeves, and it seemed to him as if she had always belonged in such sacramental attire. And then he noticed something else, a subtle strain behind her silver eyes, and a fierce set of her mouth, and he understood that she had also fallen victim to the plague of insomnia that had become the foretelling mark of success in this new age.

28

It was raining the day Isla stepped through the doors of the Department of the Lost Regions and found a senior scribe waiting for her. "You're being sent to the desert," he said. "There is a project in negotiation, which will offer people a better life." This was how Isla found herself riding across hidden sandy roads in the middle of the night.

When they arrived at the village, a fire was roaring in welcome, and they were invited to sit until food was served. Isla listened as the voices of her three colleagues travelled easily in the immense, open space. They shouted in careless, happy voices, praising the food that smelled of turmeric and chilli, shovelling it from the metal plates into their wide mouths, unresponsive or perhaps unaware of the shadow of people who waited at the edge of the firelight to eat from this pot of stew when the mainlanders were done. The bonfire leapt fiercely into the air, its erratic light falling against the sides of rustling tents and throwing stark shadows on the obscured faces of those who watched these strangers from the mainland city.

Isla stood up, wrapped the wool shawl around her

shoulders and stepped into the cool desert. She felt the sand beneath her toes. It was still warm from the day's sun and had not yet given over to the dark of night. Tomorrow she and her colleagues would talk to the chief. As the junior scribe, she was there to listen, to understand what people needed and, more importantly, what they desired and to bring that knowledge back to the centre. She was the bridge between the mainland and the region. She was the bearer of the mainland's bounty, and she understood that by tempting such outer regions with More, she was helping them on the path to the irresistible possibilities of progress.

Accompanying Isla was a senior banking merchant who would reconcile the region's financial needs with the mainland's capacity to give. If it was determined that the mainland's capacity exceeded the region's desires, the banking merchant was happy and would drink a glass of clear liquor that sent his mind into ecstasy and make passionate love to his wife. If the region's needs exceeded the mainland's capacity to give, he would curse and spit over his left shoulder and ruminate on the degraded state of humanity. Inevitably in the morning, the same solution would come to him, and he would settle on some trinket of the new age to export to the region in question, at first for free and then at some slowly increasing price that was like reeling in a great fish from the depths of the sea. Eventually they were always caught. Then, they consumed their loyalty to the mainland as an opiate of their wildest dreams.

Also accompanying Isla into the western desert was an engineer who analysed the pathways of water and could harness it through the systematic construction of modern water channels and the scientific methods of reservation and diversion. And then there was the most senior member of the team, the Chief Administrative Officer who was also specialised in trade and investments. This official had been to the desert before, and it was his responsibility to develop a political intimacy between himself and the chief of this desert tribe. Out of all the men, he laughed the loudest, plied the elder tribesmen with smoke and clear liquor, spoke corrupted phrases of their local dialect and chided the desert men on their need for the wheels of progress. More and more it seemed the desert men laughed and nodded sagely with him.

Isla stood silent now, watching her feet sink incrementally into the desert sand with each dusting stir of air. Off to her left, Isla heard voices whispering like silk ribbons fluttering in the light breeze. When she turned, she noticed two young girls crouched so low that their bony knees came up to their shoulders. Their faces were turned away from Isla, but when she looked closer, she saw that they were washing the metal plates with sand. With their left hands they held the plates almost vertical and with their right they scooped the white sand, rubbing rhythmically as if the sand were a cloth around and around in circles.

How long did she watch them, whispering and splashing the sand against the metal plates before she realised she was thinking of Eva? An unspoken longing overtook Isla. She was far from home and, in an instant, she felt the distance between her and the island by the palpable wrenching in her gut, and she realised she missed the days she had spent crouching next to Eva, their dresses ballooning up beneath them, whispering simple secrets and giggling over nothing and praying wildly for their naivety of love to end.

Of course now she had Neha. And Neha understood the way Isla spoke about the world and what she wanted from it. Neha understood Isla's questions, the desperate burning just below her skin, the flame that drove her to search for the meaning of her life. Neha knew what it was like to feel like she might die if she did not make a mark on the world. But Isla had never giggled with Neha over the foolish sleeping iguanas who occasionally fell off their branches in the middle of some unimaginable dream. She had never worried over the smallness of her budding breasts or gossiped over the flaking legs or the balding head of Sylvia Prenai with Neha. "It didn't mean anything," Isla told herself. "It doesn't mean anything now."

Eva had just had her third child. She had written last month. Her letter had seemed happy, but Isla knew there was so much you couldn't tell if you were unable to look into your friend's eyes. Was she truly happy? What had she meant when she said things on the island felt different? What could be different in a place that never changed?

Isla stared out into the desert. The ripples of the sand reflected and sparkled in the starlight. The sand radiated into the soles of her feet, and suddenly Isla felt that the sand she was standing on spread out in every direction, spread out and out until eventually it collided with the edge of the mainland city, and then with a road that led to another road and another until it wound its way to her home.

She thought of her clean blue room with its wooden ceiling beams where she had hung a thousand colours of ribbons and its traditional sliding window panels covered with the thick paper that kept out the cold. And she thought of Jackimo sitting in his own house just blocks away. The house had a grey tiled roof that glowed blue in the rain, and the picture of a winged dragon was painted on the paper shutter above the front door. He would be sitting in the pale warm light of his front room smoking his water pipe, and he would sigh unknowingly into the silence the way he always did when he finally felt his mind relax, but there would be no one there that night to hear him.

Standing in the sand of the desert, Isla felt herself pulled back into a feeling of connection with her world, and something inside her relaxed, and she crouched down and ran her hand across the wisps of white sand. Then, she lay back into the sand, stretching her arms wide, moving them up and down against her body. The warmth of this shifting earth filled her, and when she stood again and the white powder rained off her back, she smiled and saw the image in the sand that looked like a woman with wings.

The next morning Isla stood with her mainland colleagues along the wide expanse of water held by the reservoir watching the chief approach.

"What is it you people want from us?" The chief towered in the air like a tree that reached up to the sky. His neck was long, like a branch and his hair sprouted from his head in thick ropes that were held back from his face by a strip of red cloth. His eyes were so black that they fell into his pupils like a deep deep well, and there was no way of knowing what lay at the bottom in the hidden, shifting dunes of his mind. There was talk that this chief could not feel pain or fear. He looked like a tree, but there were no trees in the desert.

"What *we* want...together," the Chief Administrative Officer corrected him. "We are all part of the mainland kingdom now."

The chief shrugged but the sand-dried blackened skin on his face gave nothing away. "We have our dam now," he said. "We will repay the loan. And we will live in peace. But do not come here to my village claiming no responsibility for this dam and its consequences when it was a group of you people who brought this idea to our land in the first place."

This comment brought silence again to the desert, and the chief stared at the officer and the officer stared at the chief, and Isla tried to discern what had passed between them already and what this desert chief might mean. Behind them, the dam's reservoir spread out wide and flat like a new moon shining in the sand or a small ocean in which all shores could be seen and accounted for.

"You do understand," the officer said in a voice which held the slow confidence of the python, although there were no pythons in the desert. "You do understand," he repeated with menace. Then, without turning his gaze away from the chief's face, he addressed Isla. "Madame scribe, your presence here is unnecessary. Please continue your work with rest of the village so that you can write your report." And he did not speak again until Isla had reached the opposite shore of the reservoir.

As she walked along the precise shoreline of the reservoir, Isla heard a high whistle and without warning, the wind picked up. Sand blew like a demon against Isla's forehead, slicing across her cheeks like wayward words, reckless and violent. Isla felt her breath labouring in her chest as she shielded her eyes and mouth from the choking wind and tried to remember that she had always wanted to go to strange and foreign lands.

Then it was gone. The land was still again. Still and plain and seemingly empty as the dunes that reached out to grasp all edges of the world. Was it changing, this place? What were these small sudden shifts of sand that left everything changed and yet indistinguishable from the moment before?

Isla looked towards the tent city of the desert people and

her eyes met the clear piercing eyes of the woman who stood before her, beckoning towards the recesses of a tent the colour of the dunes which was marked with the sign of the scorpion, and she saw that she was among people who knew the delicacies of change, who saw the small shifts of wind against their moving earth and marked the metamorphosis of life in a way that she herself could not see.

29

When Isla stepped inside the scorpion tent, a darkness fell across her eyes like water across the sun. Then slowly, like a wavering mirage before her, faces broke through the darkness, faces with wide, black eyes, watching her. Silver, copper, shades of dyed cloth, she saw faces decorated unlike any women she knew on the mainland. Men wore thick shining bands on their upper arms, their hair long and woven with colour. The women too flickered like ornamental stars in the cool light, their reflections bouncing off each other as they sat along a stone channel that flowed with clear water. This water, now readily available from the reservoir, pulled the heat from the air and rose as vapour to cool the tent.

The people looked like their chief, tall, indomitable, and as she stood among them, Isla felt with a wary certainty that prickled her skin that these people, who stood so still, could move anything they wanted with the force of their stare. Above her, Isla could hear the tent roof flapping as if it was the only sound in the quiet desert.

And then, Isla began to sense something else. A smell,

soft and damp. And in this dry, foreign land, Isla found the place in her memory where this scent lay, untarnished by time, undisturbed by whirling thought, unmistakable as the sound of her own voice.

"Losa!" She gasped, and when a man handed her a bowl of steaming liquid, Isla raised it to her face and inhaled so deeply that for a moment she was lost from time and did not notice that tears fell like the sea from her eyes.

"Losa," the man said, patting her hands that held the bowl. "Made by the heat of the sun. Drink. It makes water come to the skin, cools the body."

Isla tried to speak but her throat was so tight she could only nod. It was only after she had drunk three, long sips of the losa tea that an older woman moved towards her from among the crowd. Her hair was long and filled with beads and dark blue strips of cloth were woven through in a pattern that revealed more than Isla could understand.

"She knows this losa," the woman said, waving at the bowl in Isla's hands. Then she looked at Isla, peering into her face as if she were seeing her reflection. "Ahhhh," she cried. And then, "You do know this losa. You are not a mainlander!" It was not an accusation, only a statement, and Isla found to her surprise that she smiled and without hesitating, replied, "I am an islander. We grow this losa on our land. But I haven't seen it for so many years!"

The old woman laughed with glee and her voice cut across the crowds in the tent. "Ahhh!" she said. "Drink, drink daughter. You are home!"

Isla tipped back her head and buried her face in the bowl, pouring the sun-warmed liquid into her mouth with a sudden greed that defied the strength of her thirst. Losa. How she had missed it! But when she lowered the bowl and looked out at the sea of faces, Isla found herself staring into the eyes of the desert, for not everyone in the crowd seemed as happy as this old woman at her revelation.

Suddenly the tent was buzzing with voices, and question after question fell upon Isla as the invisible insects that emerged from the desert sands after dark. "Are you truly not a mainlander?" "What are you doing here then?" "What can an islander do for us?"

From among the crowd a man stepped forward. "We would like to speak to a representative of the mainland," he said and his voice was flat and propelled towards Isla with unwavering conviction. "We were told the commission from the mainland was coming to promote further progress here. We have adopted the Philosophy of the Rising Sun. We want progress. We want to speak to a mainlander."

It was only then that Isla glanced around this foreign tent and began to notice that which was also familiar — the by-products of the Rising Sun. Many of the men standing around her wore its sign on their copper armbands. Some of the women stood on heeled shoes that seemed out of place in a world of shifting sand. But it was the unmistakable shape of mainlander waterpipes leaning against a curving wall of the stone water channel that revealed to Isla what she should have seen before — that while the losa may have called her dreams of home out from their shadows, she had also come home by another path, for like herself, these desert people had also come under the influence of the Philosophy of the Rising Sun and believed with an unshakeable faith that they too would soon reap the rewards of time and the ever expanding wealth of progress.

Like a mirage before their eyes was a tower of gold that grew and grew and grew until it split the sky. "Our children should be better off than we are," one man said and others nodded. "That is the way the world should be."

The young man who had spoken above the others was watching Isla, and so he noticed as she began to stand taller and straighter in her shoes. He noticed the way her body stiffened, the way her face hardened like a mask of power, the way she held her hands poised before her in the way other mainlanders had done before they spoke, and so he too raised his hands to the others and the tent grew quiet, for all except Isla knew that this man was the first son of the chief.

When he spoke, it was not to Isla alone, but to the crowd of those whom he considered his people, and his voice held a strength that even the spirits of the ancestors would have noticed reverberating in the air. "Our grandmothers used to tell us our lives were ruled by fate and nothing we did could improve our lot in life. But the Philosophy of the Rising Sun has shown that life is about choices and that there is no magic or mystery or gods to save us. We must rely on ourselves, on our personal strength to see us through and on the choices we make in our lives. Now, we should put aside our old beliefs in god and magic and the ways of the spirit and understand that true purpose in life lies in progress, as an individual, as a tribe, and as a kingdom. Our minds must not dwell on the past, but should look to the future so that we too will be able acquire More and to make discoveries and contribute New things to the progress of the kingdom."

For a moment, the people in the tent were so still that the flapping roof seemed a lonesome voice calling out above the wind. But then Isla stepped forward and found that she had instinctively raised her hands before her. Bringing them together with a force, she spoke out in a new voice, "I am a mainland scribe," she told these desert people, "sent as part of a commission of the Central Administration to welcome you onto the mighty path of progress and to congratulate you on your successes. This desert world is not an easy place to live, and I see that, in collaboration with the mainland, you have been able to dominate your environment and wield it to your own desires. You can use the desert to your own advantage rather than remain at its mercy. If you would tell us how the mainland can continue to support you on this journey, we would be most willing to assist your development towards a better future in which we are all one kingdom, living in ever increasing prosperity and peace."

That day, Isla learned not from her own colleagues but from the desert people that the dam had been build by engineers from the mainland who had employed all local men and women between the ages of twelve and forty-two, the age according to tribal tradition one became an elder, to work in the construction of this unprecedented project. The reservoir was dug by women who had carried sand away in metal bowls balanced on their heads and padded with cloth torn from the woven carpets that had always been spread over the sand inside their tents.

Meanwhile, in the sea of sweat and grit, the men of the village had travelled to the edges of the desert where their animals were loaded with carts of stone. They returned months later to learn of births and deaths, only to leave again, and it was two full years before work began to build the great wall around the shores of the reservoir. The whole project had taken no less than four years and seven months of labour so hard and long that no children were born during the period of the dam's construction because husbands could not lift their heads to visit their wives in the usual way and fathers stopped recognising the faces of the children they had already sired, for they continued to grow and change while these fathers moved through the desert to secure the stone reservoir wall and thought only of the future.

"But at least all this work was for us," a woman explained. "Before, we were slaves of the kingdom and our work did not benefit us but our mainland masters."

In this way, Isla also learned the hidden history of her mainland. The story of the Lost Ones.

That night, the old woman with the beaded hair told her, "No one was immune from them, daughter. They would come in raids at night and take the strongest boys for their military and the beautiful young girls were sometimes taken too, but we don't know whatever happened to them, only that sometimes we saw the sons again once their bones were too old to fight, but we never saw those daughters again once they were taken."

As the night wore on, Isla heard more and more stories of the slave-trading habits of the mainland kingdom, and she wondered as more and more voices from the crowd added their stories of an aunt who had been taken as a child, a great grandfather who had fought in one of the mainland wars, how many faces she had seen on the mainland city streets who had once been slaves or who had been born to one of those desert women who had disappeared into the night. And no words could describe the guilt which rose up in her heart that she had not known this history and might have passed by such people without seeing their faces.

When she finally arrived back in the mainland city a week later, Isla felt a profound foreboding as if she was returning to her destiny. For many minutes, she stood on the threshold of her bedroom at Madame Rohal's grand house, looking behind her through the open door that swung in the bright hallway, and it was as if she was looking upon the white wake of her past, the footprints in the sand that had led her to this random moment in time, this moment between moments when the day was over and there was only the stillness waiting for her.

She knew she shouldn't be afraid, and yet she shivered because she knew what this kind of quiet evening could do — the loneliness it could bring, the doubt, the regret. So instead she looked back across the path that had been her destiny and chose to see the strength in her stride, the straight unwavering path of purpose, this work she was doing which would make her life great.

Then Isla sat at her desk to write her report, and there was no reason for her to doubt her faith in the straight and single-minded path of the mainland kingdom, which continued without serpentine ambiguity or the smell of stagnant death into the infinite, illuminated future. She thought of the man who had said, "Our children should be better off than we are. That is the way of the world," and she knew the only way to make this dream possible was infinite and uncompromising growth. Shouldn't this man see his own sons and daughters benefit from the advantages Isla had found on the mainland? Wouldn't her own islanders be better off if they could do something meaningful with their lives rather than walking around and around on a wheel where everything was always the same and people's whole lives were wasted on frivolous concerns and petty gossip.

For this reason among many, Isla did not hesitate when she raised her pen to the paper and used clear, bold words with the confidence she had always envied in others. Yes, she wrote, these people from among the desert tribes had understood the proclamations of the Philosophy of the Rising Sun and would certainly become invaluable members of the expanding kingdom, that the tenacity with which they guarded their water supply even in the face of the arid desert sun showed not an ignorance of their environment but rather was proof of the way they had wholeheartedly accepted the kingdom's call for progress, for they were set, Isla wrote, with an unshakeable fury to conquer nature and develop themselves.

Who can say why, before she went to sleep, Isla wrote out a second copy of this report which she folded and kept amongst Eva's letters inside a box decorated with the flying dragon Jackimo had given her on their first anniversary. For the remaining years of her life, Isla kept that box on the chest next to her bed, but she rarely opened it unless it was to smell the scent of teak and coffee which always lingered there and which had the power to transport her back to those early years of her life on the mainland when everything had seemed so complicated but had actually been so simple because she had still believed back then in the linear progress of humanity through time.

Then one day, in her middle age, Isla opened the box and found this report she had written for the mainland kingdom laying folded inside, and upon reading the words she had written there, fell to her knees and cried for the part she had never meant to play in the lives of these desert people.

30

The Council of the Losa Co-operative was not at peace. Although neither the losa growers, nor the harvest workers, nor even the families of these traders could have known the reason for the traders' growing disregard for the Council, it could not be denied that something had happened on the Isle of Joon which had not happened before. And thus a mutiny had begun among some of the discordant traders, and rightly or wrongly, it had spread from the oldest growing families down to the harvesters who pulled the tender blossoms from their stalks twice a year with careful, practiced hands.

The feeling of discontent rolled across the island like noon thunder, threatening to inundate the island with irreversible change. Among those who grumbled around the tables of Dari's café and hushed their voices to a whisper in the central market, the most adamant voices were undeniably those of the island traders who had recently returned from the Isle of Joon where they had as usual sold the island's most recent harvest and had returned for the first time with desires greater than the grain and spices, soaps and fabric that they would sell on their own island in the months to come.

Only the traders themselves knew that this year, the market at Joon had expanded beyond the old town walls due to an increasing number of mainland traders. Whether this expansion of the market had begun gradually some seasons before or whether it was as sudden and dazzling as it seemed to the island traders upon their arrival, none could say. But all the island traders agreed that never before had they laid eyes on so many wonders of the world.

There were shelves lined with seventy-two different kinds of shoes, many with remarkable heels of the kind the wives of the mainlanders were said to wear. There were tables with strange foods, pickled vegetables, sweets that exuded strong, yellow fragrances. There were stalls with intricate gadgets used to see the moon, rotating charts to navigate the stars, jewels from every land of deep ocean blue and living spring green and sun-heated gold. There were tailors that sewed day and night in the depths of their shops to meet demand for their sparkling brocade robes, their blue-embroidered felt jackets, their flowing blue and red and yellow patterned cotton dresses. There were signs engraved onto cards that could tell the future, which was a world of Rising Suns, and there were medicines sought out from the four corners that claimed to cure the most desperate fevers, the most unrelenting dysentery, and various kinds of troubled pregnancies.

In the face of such splendour, the island traders looked down at their own sandalled, calloused feet, their own poor tastes in common soap and pale, monochrome fabrics, and felt not only shame but an intense heat that was the ignited blaze of desire. Wouldn't their daughters look beautiful in such patterned dresses. Wouldn't their wives stand out in such spectacular heeled shoes. Why shouldn't they too have these brilliant contraptions that would show them the stars as if they held these far off lights in the palms of their own hands? What attention they would get on the island of their rustic mediocrity if they returned wearing the gold bands engraved with the esoteric symbol of the Rising Sun! Why shouldn't they, the island traders, advance with the rest of the world?

It soon became clear, however, that the money the island traders earned from the sale of losa in a record three weeks at the markets on Joon would never be enough for all this mainland finery. A single silver armband engraved with a rising sun cost the same as seven large sacks of grain, and they could not justify it. And so, discouraged and slightly bewildered by the flash of such costs, the island traders made their way through the markets as usual, buying the staple items for their stores and the few modest articles islanders had ordered before they had sailed east to Joon.

Yet even as they folded their rough sacks that had held the sacred losa of their trade and checked the last of their supplies and packed the seventeen wooden chests that would carry the most precious of their cargo and fed the flock of chickens they had purchased to reinvigorate the island flocks, mainland traders accosted their struggling conscience with demands for more losa.

"We are overwhelmed by orders," the mainlanders had said, clapping as they spoke. "You must bring more losa next season," they commanded, and their voices were stern as they stood tall above the islanders in their sombre heeled shoes. And though the island traders tried to explain that there was the Losa Co-operative that restricted the amount of island losa grown each season, the mainlanders didn't seem to hear.

"We are helpless," the island traders explained again as they fastened the locks of the seventeen wooden chests. "Don't you think we want to earn enough to buy such beautiful linens and jewels and mechanisms as can be found in this trading market? Don't you think we would sell more if we could? There is no more to sell."

But the mainlanders shook their heads. "There is always More," they said. "Grow more and see what can be yours," and their gestures were as grand as their embroidered red trader robes. "The Co-operative is an archaic institution. These outdated organisations are beyond use. Your island should move with the times. These days, everyone is joining the movement of the Rising Sun because the Rising Sun is the path of prosperity and what people would deny that they desire greater prosperity, more wealth, unending plenty that can put an end to all suffering and hardship."

"More is better," they said as if they understood things the island traders did not. "New is best."

Then, on the way to the docks, Lucas and his brother Aimen noticed a man loading several sacs of losa into a wide wooden chest. The man's hair was black, tied in strands as thick as ropes, and his eyes were wild and deep as wells in the dry earth. And something about this man's haughty manner made them stop and stare, for he was not a mainlander as his clothes would suggest, but was one of the desert people who purchased only the losa buds and used them for tea as the islanders did.

Seeing the brothers watching him, the man waved Lucas and Aimen over and soon a crowd of island traders had surrounded him because the man did not waste time with idle chat but spoke instead of the glories of the Rising Sun. He told stories of the dam which had been built in the middle of the wide desert, turning the narrow banks of the ancient, torpid river into expanding fields of greener land that felt like an emancipation although the man could not say from what. He told how the moonlight looked as it glittered across the water that had once been the most treasured and sacred of commodities in this desiccating land. With a loan from the mainland, he explained, his people had made something of themselves. They had begun to tap into their true potential. They had become hardworking and efficient. Everyone was now working together for the progress of the community.

The man with the wide, deep eyes spoke elegantly as he stood surrounded by chests which overflowed with all the riches the island traders had coveted for themselves, and so the island traders stood listening to the man for longer than they had intended, hoping in the soundless pandemonium of their minds that the man would disclose the secret of his conspicuous wealth.

"The dam has brought us not only riches," the man said to his audience, and the island traders pricked up their ears. "It protects us from the unpredictable nature of the desert. It has put an end to all struggle and suffering, and now our children will have a better life than we have had. They will never feel the lack we have known."

And then he said, "Right now, you islanders have a small life as we desert people used to live before we committed ourselves to expansion, growth and to joining the mainland which is the centre of the changing world. You should take my advice. Follow our example and join the mainland kingdom. Then you can also give your children more than you have had — for this is the way the world should be."

"Now wait one moment," said Aimen, who was still young and quick to take offence. "Who are you to call our life small and say what we islanders should do?"

Another older trader called Lohan caught hold of Aimen's anger and added his voice to the crowd, "Why should we want more for our children?" he asked. "We have had a good island life. What is this 'more' that we should want to give them?"

To that, the man simply spread out his hands and the islanders' gaze dripped slowly over the open chests of mainland gadgets, strange wonders, opulence and finery, modern treasures that the islanders wanted to hold precisely because they had never seen such things before and so could not even imagine what these things might be like. None doubted the desert people were now rich. After all, several traders remembered that the man had also bought six bags of island losa without bargaining or twisting words — and the price, as usual, had been high.

"What would we do with shoes as these in the sands of the island?" Lucas asked, more to the entranced crowd of fellow traders than to the desert man. But something had shifted in the minds of the island traders as they looked upon these wonders and imagined that these spectacular things were their own.

At the front of the crowd, Aimen's eyes flashed with desire. "It's not just the shoes, Lucas," he said in a new voice filled with wonder. "This man says his people no longer have to struggle! Imagine that. A life without struggle!"

"Struggle is not always bad," the older island trader Lohan tried to argue, but no one was listening for the island traders were thinking now of the long journey that lay before them, how their hands and shoulders ached at sea, how they missed their families while they were away, and this imagined life without struggle shone in their minds like gold.

31

The traders returned, but their minds remained across the sea, for the dark-eyed desert man had shaken their faith in their island life like a great wave that churns up the sand in the sea and does not allow it to settle. By the light of day they fell into distraction, making mistakes in their accounts of which losa grower was owed what share of the profits from the recent trade, and handing their customers items they had not asked for at the market.

In the evenings, the traders' wives threw up their hands because they did not hear the calls to watch the children or bring wood in for the stove or grab the pot that is boiling over. And at night they tossed under their sheets and dreamed of fairytale devices that would rid them of all their worries and toil and strain, a large splendid apparatus that could bestow inexhaustible wealth and would endure and would give them pleasure and peace at last.

Finally, exhausted by their solitary daydreams, they began to talk to one another. "Perhaps the island should grow more losa," one said.

"If there is such a market for our losa, why should we limit ourselves," another agreed.

Soon, more and more of the traders stepped out of their houses and stood in the dusty street under the white heat of the sun, shifting between the brief pools of shade provided by the crooked palm trees, and watching each other's loyalties with shielded eyes. And so their talk grew until it was determined at last that Cassius and Hamen and Josa who were the traders who sat upon the Co-operative Council, should raise the issue at the next meeting and put forward the courageous request that the Council lift its restrictions on the growth of island losa.

The proposal was not well received. "Are you suggesting we go against the Charter of this Council?" said an older grower with a thick, greying moustache and watery eyes. "My grandfather helped draft that charter," added another grower. "There is no way I will agree to any act that goes against its traditions. It is the foundation of the whole Losa Co-operative."

"But the Charter was written many generations ago," argued one of the traders. "It unfairly privileges certain families and it sets limitations that no longer make sense for us in this new age of growth and advancement."

"We should review the Losa Charter," cried one of the harvest workers who sat on the Council, and the other two harvest workers who were known to take quiet naps through the monthly Council meetings nodded their heads with unusual vigour.

Frowns crossed the faces of the losa growers and angry shadows gave a fearful look to their ageing countenances. The youngest among them was Fazza's son, Fazzar, who like his fellow growers, was unused to his family's status being questioned. "We should not question the wisdom of the Founding Fathers. It was Manel Prenai who wrote this charter and we should trust in his wisdom as all of our fathers have done," and he peered out across the room into the eyes of his fellow Councilmen and did not like what he saw.

"But why," Josa the trader asked. "Why should there be limits on how much losa we can grow? Why should we tie chains to our own feet? The mainlanders are begging us to sell more losa — so if we can sell more, why should we not?" Josa's question hung in the thick humid air of the room, and suddenly the men became painfully aware of the sweat that had plastered their shirts to their backs and stuck their trousers to the backs of their knees, and the torpor of their bodies made their minds also fade, because none had an answer to this challenge except that, in their lifetime, there had always been limits to the growing of losa and that was the way it had always been.

It was hard to admit that such waning, weak-minded men were all that remained of the Council which had once shouted down the official mainland entourage and had safeguarded the value of the island's losa for more than three generations. For these growers of the Council, the authority to grow losa was not the humble honour of a long, drawn out struggle as it had been for Petro and Fazza or any number of ageing, twilight men, but felt instead a diamond right, harsh and clear and cut decisively from the rocks of the past.

For this reason, they did not worry that they could not remember the sacred words of Manel Prenai which had once been recited from memory before every Council meeting by all those present. Nor did it seem a dangerous digression that none on the present Council could recall the exact nature of the Co-operative's history and original establishment.

No, if the Council had once been filled with men of wisdom and foresight, it was no longer. From the grower families, there was Samuel, Jobe and Fazzar, three men spanning the years between 25-50. Yet all thought with one mind, as all had been raised in losa-growing families and it had occurred to neither old Samuel nor to young Fazzar nor to Jobe that this privilege might ever be taken away.

Petro and those who remembered the early days of the Council, if not from memory then certainly from the vivid stories that had passed among the islanders as common lore in those days, had long ago retired from their duties to the Council. Most had sons, as Fazza had Fazzar, to represent their families on the Losa Council and bring home news of the Council's predictable decisions and of harvest gossip to the ageing men. Petro himself had passed on his seat to Jobe, a sturdy man with land to match Petro's own glowing purple hills and then had proceeded to fade, as if deliberately, from Co-operative life. He was spoken of often, but rarely kindly, when Jobe had stepped out of the room.

Fazza's son, though he called Petro 'Petro-da' and thought of him as an uncle, was one of Petro's harshest critics, for he had never seen days of hardship and had little patience for the stumbling steps of the old. To be fair, Fazzar also did not listen to his own father, who often stopped by Fazzar's house at dusk to ask for news from the Council meetings and to drop hints by clearing his throat at certain moments or by tapping his pipe in a particular rhythm that meant to suggest he had some advice to impart. Fazzar pretended that such overtures went unnoticed, although afterwards he would complain bitterly to the air and anyone who would listen about these unwelcome intrusions, and he certainly never asked for his father's advice or paid attention to his father's winding, convoluted stories about the founding of the Losa Co-operative.

They were men of a part, and though one was young and one was old and one was as dependable as a rock, none could say why limits should be set on the production of losa. And they did not care. Such questions had always been far less interesting than the yearly register of storms which tore plants up by their roots or the remedy of root fungus that occasionally attacked the losa plants in a row and if unmanaged would spread without remorse through a grower's entire crop.

The three representatives from among the harvesters, for their part, sat upon the Council as penance for unrecorded misdeeds against their community and there, helped organise the shifting workloads throughout the year. The growers and traders might have considered the three rotating seats on the Council to be an honour for the harvest workers who filled them, but never could they have imagined the extent to which their beloved Council was derided among the harvesters as the source of endless snide jokes, nor the relief each harvester felt when his term on that dreary Council was finally at an end.

So were the men who sat, fanning themselves against the weight of that uncomfortable afternoon, and silence reigned until Samuel stood, pulling at the trailing wisps of his grey moustache to disguise the anger held in his face. "We should all consider what has been said today. Yes, I am quite sure we should consider these things carefully," he said. "Since no immediate decision on such matters is possible at present, we should simply...consider. Yes, yes. Meeting adjourned," and he laid his hand on the table more forcefully than he had intended and watched without shifting his stance until the rest of the men had filtered back out into the deceptive light of the day.

32

Another letter. At first glance, it seemed to fill the air with a tropical nostalgia that could only come from the island of her birth, but as she approached the low table on which it lay, Isla could feel her heart fill with foreboding. Lifting the letter between her fingers, Isla studied the rough, poor look of the paper, noticing the familiar languid hand, the words no doubt filled with peril. But she did not open it. Instead she dropped the letter, letting it drift in the calm, sheltered breezes of her bedroom until it landed with silent solemnity on the dark, polished surface of the low table.

Isla walked away without so much as breathing to the window where she slid open the paper shutter and looked out onto the rooftops of the coffee district and beyond to the sprawling voluptuous body of the mainland city. It had been many years since the first day she had stepped onto the docks of the mainland city, many years since she had moved into this room at the generous, upright house of Madame Rohal, and over those years the voice of doubt and fear that spoke with the sombre intonations of her father had slowly dissolved into the crevasses of time. But it had not disappeared entirely.

She had intended to go back. She had always intended to go back — after she had had her adventures. But it had never seemed the right time, and the bitter taste of saltwater that rose in her throat whenever she thought of the island stayed her footsteps time and time again. Isla could sense her father's disappointment waiting restlessly on the edges of the island, unable to reach her in this unfamiliar city, and she was reluctant to re-expose herself to his contagion of despair.

Isla, this is your father writing to you in the years of his old age. The land has been productive this year. At harvest, we were over our allotted amount and had to keep two sacs of losa back for the islanders. I have been unwell, but that is to be expected at my age and without a soul to look after me.

His letters were often short and impregnated with the melancholy which she knew so well and which only drove her to new heights of fury and never towards compassion or understanding, for these letters were not designed to inspire such natural feelings of fidelity, but were written only to fulfil his own desperate desires and never hers.

Isla, I have recovered from my latest illness so you need not worry. I know you won't. We have a new harvester working with us, Janen's daughter, who has yet to be married but her work is quick and I have no complaints. A storm that blew through after harvest pulled down six of our mango trees so I will not expect a crop this year. If only I had more help in the fields. Take care of yourself, your father.

To Isla, they were all the same.

Isla, I hope you are well and making good use of yourself and that you will think over what I have asked you before. You are a woman, Isla, but still there are responsibilities to consider. I can only hope now for your imminent return, your father.

Isla did not need to open this new letter — she knew the unrestrained melody by heart, felt it reverberating in the hermetic, waxed envelope that held her father's understated venom.

Isla, how did I raise such a selfish, cruel daughter? Tell me, do you think you are too good for this island? As your father, I can tell you that if it was good enough for me, it should be good enough for you. My health is deteriorating I am sure. I feel a hunger in the pit of my belly that is eating me alive and I am quite certain it will be the end of me. I continue in vain hope that you still remember your father and will return home as I have asked.

These letters came several times a year, and Isla skimmed them for essential pieces of news. They never included news that she wanted to hear, and so she would set the paper alight in the white stone fireplace in her room before her mind could recognise the old guilt that such letters summoned to the surface.

Isla's letters, in turn, remained a standard two pages but over the years, declined in truth, as she censored her hopes and replaced these things with the facts that her father would need to know — she was well, she was studying at an institute for scribes, she would not be returning to the island this year. She would write such letters with anger and fear and sadness filling her heart, but each time it came to sign her name Isla's hand would begin to tremble and she would drop the pen and leave the letter lying on the low desk in her room.

At night the dreams would come and she was a child again, trapped in her house, pounding against the doors for her father to let her out. Only once, and without premonition, she saw Tomas at the window in her dream, banging for her to come out, only the door had become heavy and she couldn't push it open and she knew, without having seen him, that her father was holding it shut.

At dawn the nightmares would pass and Isla would sleep, exhausted, in the pale dawn of her countless regrets, and in the morning, she would always sign the letter and send it off and cry softly in her room because despite all the distance between them, her father was still the only family she had ever had.

Now there was a new letter. The same letter. More ferocious, or perhaps less. And she did not read it.

At the coffeehouse around the corner she laid the unopened letter on the table. "Read it and tell me if he is okay," she said to Jackimo when he arrived. Her voice was flat as the eastern plains, flat and dry and covered with nothing but blowing, sunburnt grasses.

Jackimo eyed the woman sitting across from him. Her robe was silver with fine red embroidery that traced her neckline and encircled her wrists with a delicacy of an arcadian autumn. Her dark hair fell in straight, thick bands across her shoulders. She was a mainlander woman now and she sat, an embodiment of power and sophistication. He had seen this woman stand tall before the Institute Examiners who made it their practice to distinguish the great from the good through the trickery and warfare of their questions. He had seen this woman hold impassioned debates with his own banking colleagues about the nature of progress and the deep and profound and inescapable Philosophy of the Rising Sun. He had seen this woman unbowed by the fluctuating illnesses of Madame Rohal, whom she had cared for like a daughter when others he knew would certainly have fled at the first possibility of impending death.

What, he wondered as he looked from Isla's pale, silver eyes to the letter that lay silently, seemingly innocuously on the table, could possibly be in this letter that could cause such a woman as this to tremble. Jackimo tore open the letter. "It's from your father," he said before looking into her eyes and realising that she already knew. "I see," he said as his eyes scanned the letter. "I see," he said again as he came to the end. "Are they always like this?"

"If you mean that I am a horrible beast of a daughter who has abandoned her father and doesn't care whether he lives or dies..."

"Isla..."

She could feel him watching her, waiting for the gravity to lift away like a mist, but her face felt like lead and she could only cry back, "but that's what he says, isn't it? Isn't that what this letter also says?"

"But that isn't what he means, you know. He just misses you, Isla. He doesn't understand what you are doing here, how important your work is. You are his daughter and he misses you."

"I don't know why," Isla shook her head but could not raise her eyes. "I was never good enough for him. He was always complaining — why couldn't I be more like my mother, why did I have to be so difficult. And then, the one thing I do that is like my mother, travelling to see the world... Well, it's never right. Nothing I did was right."

"He just doesn't understand you."

"He doesn't want to understand me, Jackimo. All he cares about is himself, don't you see! But still after all these years, part of me still wonders — is it okay that I made a life for myself here and left him on the island all alone? Do I have a responsibility to go back?"

Finally Isla's eyes rose from the table and fell upon the face of this man with a drowning, desolate look. "He is my father after all, no matter what happened when I was young. He wasn't a bad father. And maybe I do owe it to him to go back and take care of him."

"He's not alone, Isla. He's got the whole island there," Jackimo told her, laying a hand across her thin, pale fingers. "That friend of yours, you said she looks in on him…"

"Eva? Yes, she does…"

The shadows of the evening drew long across Isla's face, and he could feel her faith wavering, as if the tide itself were drawing her away from the shore and out into the dark, watery space. But Jackimo saw something in the letter that Isla did not, a lost voice hidden between the angry words, and with this flash of intuition, he spoke.

"Maybe it is possible," Jackimo said, "that your father loves you and that he only cares about himself. And maybe it is also possible that you love him and that you don't want to see him. This is your life, Isla. He had the freedom to choose what he did with his life, and now you get to decide what you will do with yours. This is the way the world should be."

33

Over the next year, Isla made six more trips to the desert. She became used to the wide, lonely skies where solitary birds soared as they followed the river, and she began to look forward, in some unexpected way, to the fierce arid winds, the way the sand moulded beneath her body as she lay on sleepless nights working over the day's events in her mind. Though she rarely met the chief, she heard his concerns, his dreams for his desert people's future in the deep steady voice of his son who met Isla each morning while the clear coolness of the previous night still hung like gauze in the air.

The desert people needed More. They needed more cloth fashioned in the way of the mainlanders' robes, more silver moulded into thick bracelets, flowing necklaces and rings engraved with the mark of the Rising Sun. They needed more coffee, which the chief and his wife had taken to drinking throughout the day to ward off the afternoon torpor brought on by the sweltering desert heat and which they now knew for certain they could not live without.

"Do you drink coffee now?" Isla had asked the chief's

son, and he had shifted his expression so that she could not tell what he was thinking.

"I am trying," he said at last, "we must all make an effort to improve our tastes…"

"But it is hard to give up losa," Isla replied, and the chief's son, discerning something in her silver eyes and perhaps remembering the day so long ago now when this straight mainland woman had cried into a bowl of losa tea, finally released his serious expression and his face fell into a smile that cracked open the desert mask of his people. "Yes, it is," he agreed.

The truth was, few of his people had been able to stomach the harsh, black liquid that made the heart race and the hands shake like they had done during the days of exhaustion when they had all worked day and night for the reservoir of their future. But the chief's son did not speak of trivialities. "My people need More," he told Isla. "The more we have, the better off we will be. My people have seen new things from the mainland, and so what we have is no longer enough to satisfy us. But to have More, we must increase our income." He paused, waiting for Isla to show she understood. "The chief has plans to expand the reservoir," he continued, "so we will be able to expand our production of sisilus for the mainland markets, but we will need your help."

When she had returned to the mainland city, Isla spent several nights at her desk, sitting in the refreshing breezes until she had revived from the heat of the desert and the inconsistent noise of the flapping tent. And then she sat longer still, waiting for the words to come. She must write reports to the Offices of Mainland Trade, to the Integration Officials from her own department. She must find funding from the Central Bank to expand the project.

This could be her chance to move into a senior position on a project.

Senior scribe — the words rolled over her tongue, smooth and light as a pearl. They tasted like destiny. If she could become a senior scribe, she would finally have what she had always dreamed of — a place of importance in the world. For no one could doubt the importance of a senior scribe of the Mainland Administration which was the source of all progress and a seat at the centre of the world. She had no regrets. Wasn't that what she always said?

And yet, on certain nights such as these when she smelled smoke drifting through the silence, Isla thought of her father and the small house surrounded by its terraced purple hills. It had been so easy to leave the unrelenting gravity of the man, who was always serious, who looked at her and always saw someone else who she had failed to emulate or to remember. It had been so easy to stay away, all those spring years when her life had seemed full of new possibilities.

In her memory, the house was small and narrow and full of too many unspoken expectations which she was now certain she could never fulfil, while before her eyes the mainland laughed without restraint and dreamed of a better future for itself and its inhabitants and seemed to have all the time in the world for an island girl like Isla.

So the choice between the island and the mainland had come to her like this, a choice between confinement and freedom, between the stunted sapling and the towering tree, between a life of regret and a life of purpose. It had seemed no decision at all.

But these nights when the insomnia plagued her, Isla would open the balcony window and lean out into the city night and breathe in the vague fragrance of smoke as it drifted through the air from some other life that had nothing to do with her. On these nights she would pull at her oiled wrapped hair or the sleeve of her night-robe and tell herself that it was the noise of the city streets or the busyness of her mind that kept her from sleep. She did not miss home.

But still her mind would wander back over the years of her past, and Isla would feel compelled all the same to enact an uncertain penance for her disloyalty to her father, to Tomas, and to the island of her birth.

Over the streets of the mainland that only slept between the hours of three and five am, out from the docks where the fishermen and poor wanderers lay in their tilted sea-swept shacks, out from the wide wide sea that lay beyond, the questions came, and Isla did not try to halt their passage into the very heart of her.

Was she doing enough? Had she done enough yet? Was her work important enough to justify leaving him all alone in that house? Why had she really come — was it for herself or had she unknowingly chosen to follow the spirit of her imagined mainlander mother over the living reality of her island father? Did she deserve this life? Or did she have a responsibility to the man who was the only family she would ever have? Was Jackimo right? Was it really possible to love someone and be unable to bear them? Was it possible to love someone and still abandon them to the unpredictable winds of the world? And why why why, when she felt so close to her dream, did it still seem as if nothing was certain?

On some melancholy midnights when the moon was full, Isla would look up and hope without any assurances that her father lay well and asleep under this same full moon, and that perhaps Tomas or Eva or someone was looking after him, protecting his world from the onslaught of despair.

Other times, when the moon was covered with shadow, she would look down to watch the groups of youths trawling the lamp-lit streets and anger would fill her heart and she would wonder why she had had to fight so hard for so little, and why she was condemned to spend such infinite nights of her future wrapped in guilt and sadness for a thing mainlander children were handed without a thought. These nights it seemed to her as if the shifting silt of her past carried down river, and so Isla did not cry. She only stood looking out over the city and surrendered to the deep solitude that opened up like a chasm in the earth and swallowed her again and again.

34

The boatman sat in the oracle's kitchen eating torn handfuls of island flatbread that the oracle made so well. He closed his eyes, savouring the warm faint sweetness in his mouth. It had become so familiar to him over the years of his visits that it was like a door to his home, and he missed it when he was gone. The morning sun fell through the open window, and even with his eyes closed the boatman could feel its fragrant heat which filled the room with the smells of hope and peace. "I may push off soon," the boatman told her, his eyes still closed.

The oracle put a cup on the thick wooden table in front of the boatman and said only, "drink your tea while you're here then." When the boatman opened his eyes at last, he saw that the oracle had sat down at the table across from him, her hair fell loose like a cascade over her shoulders and so the boatman understood that she had not yet been outside in the waves of wind as was her habit on days when the sun rose early.

Taking the cup of tea into his hands, he rolled it back

and forth, watching her. The oracle gazed towards the door thinking over something she could not say. She held her own cup of losa tea balanced on the palm of her hand, and its colour in the sunlight was a clean purple because the oracle only dipped the small losa buds into the boiling water for a moment and did not let them seep into a dark purple brown as many islanders did.

Feeling his eyes on her, the oracle shifted slowly in her chair, until her warm brown eyes met his clear blue ones. Then she sat back in her chair and began to hum one of the old island songs that even the dust of the earth and the spiders in their corners and the long-necked birds in the silver mangroves at the bottom of the cliffs also knew, for it was a song sung by all islanders through all ages of the island's past. And when this song was on her lips, it reminded the boatman that, however separate the oracle might seem from the rest of this small community, living alone at the edge of the island, she was still an islander nonetheless.

Another song followed, filling up the morning, and just when the boatman felt certain the oracle did not worry about anything because, perhaps she could see all there was to see, the oracle began to speak of Petro, and the boatman saw that the oracle watched so carefully precisely because no one can see all ends.

Many months ago, perhaps it had been years, for who could say such things, the oracle had begun to hear strange rumours of Petro's mounting eccentricities. Since Myrium's death, there had always been such talk — of his uncontrollable habit of capturing and cataloguing all the insects on the island, his uncommon obsession with the island's past, his increasing silence which was most unconventional for his age.

The oracle hadn't placed much importance on such talk. She knew the power of loss and the strange new shape it gives a person. So at first, she had assumed these rumours, so soon after Isla's departure, were simply more of the same uncontrollable shifting of Petro's usual shape. But then, she began to listen, really listen, and what she heard when she went into the market one morning made her hair prickle like fire.

What she heard, from Lott the cheesemaker and Jon the fishmonger and Silse the tailor and so many others was this — Petro was buying food as if he were feeding a family of ten. Last week alone he had bought a total of twenty fish, seven sacks of wheat, five rounds of cheese. Those who worked his land said that his vegetable garden was almost bare. Several others had seen Petro at Dari's eating four full dinners, one after another, so that even Dari in his most affable voice finally said, "Petro, are you certain all is well with you?", to which Petro did not reply but simply threw several coins upon the table and stormed out, leaving Dari to throw up his hands and mutter, "Four dinners! That just isn't right!"

Some islanders with a heightened propensity for the dramatic whispered that Petro must be hiding someone in that declining, arthritic house. Some of these went as far as to imagine they had heard strange voices and shapes shuffling past lit windows long after midnight. Others who did not believe Petro would tolerate anyone living in his house insisted he must have embarked on some new experiment or cataloguing venture, or that the food must be rotting because Petro's frame remained as slender as ever and anyway, no single person could eat all that food.

But the oracle had her own suspicions, and a month later, when Petro started buying vegetables too from town and others confirmed that his garden was indeed ravaged and bare as the rocky cliffs, the oracle looked into his eyes and understood that Petro had finally succumbed to the terrors of the Hungry Ghost.

Then, she had touched his shoulder as he rummaged through a box of over-ripe mangos in town and said quietly, "I know what ails you." But he had not come to her. And so for months she simply watched but could do nothing.

Then, three days ago, Petro himself had stumbled up the dusty path to her home among the silver mangroves, and it was the first time in his life that he had come this way. Out of some unknowable desperation, he had allowed her to coax him into her sunny kitchen where she and the boatman now sat, and without waiting for the formalities of first taking a cup of losa, he had said, "I can't stop eating. You must do something!"

Then he told her of the hunger that haunted him day and night, that pursued him like a great beast of the world, that sunk its claws into his belly and would not release him. There were dreams too, nightmares that rose in his mind's eye even before sleep was upon him. "There is a Being — not a man, a horrid horrible creature with an enormous mouth that stretches so wide. It cries and cries in a dreadful, high-pitched voice. And its head sits upon a long, skinny neck. The neck stretches and stretches, this way and that, with loose skin like a chicken. Its body is emaciated, as if it hasn't eaten for many lifetimes, and it reaches for me as if to devour me and I cannot escape it."

"When did this hunger first come upon you?" The oracle asked him. "And when did you first see such dreams? After Isla left the island?"

Petro nodded, but then he shook his head. "That was the

first time I saw the creature," he said, "but I feel it has been with me for much longer, as if it has only just now taken form in my mind." Petro's eyes darted around the room, as if he expected to see this creature in his waking hours as well, and then he looked directly into the eyes of the oracle and shouted, "You must do something to rid me of this thing!"

To calm his raging mind, the oracle had reached across the table and laid a hand upon his forearm. "It is the Hungry Ghost you see," the oracle had told him. And then she had explained that the Hungry Ghost is a tormented creature because although it has an enormous mouth, only small morsels of food can pass through its long, thin neck and so it is always and forever starving. "It is destined to suffer because what it consumes is never enough to fill it."

"So it can't possibly devour me?" Petro asked, looking calm for the first time since she had watched him wander up the path to her house. "I shouldn't be afraid."

"Petro," the oracle shook her head. "The Hungry Ghost is you. It is your very self."

"How did he take it?" the boatman asked.

"He is still eating," the oracle replied. The oracle stood up from the table and put two more pieces of wood in the stove and the kettle on to boil. It was time for more losa.

"Petro is all but lost to us," the oracle said, and the boatman could hear a sadness in her voice that was the sound of the funeral cries over the sea wind. "But there is another that I am also worried about. There is so much to do, so many moments of pain for these people who live always in the past. One day, my daughter might be able to help them, but there is so little I can do!"

"You are thinking of Lucas, I think," the boatman guessed, and the oracle nodded.

"He is approaching the age that his father passed from this life. He has been quiet, but now there is a restlessness in his mind that will not leave him. He has not yet joined the fray of traders who have set their minds against the Council, but he is under the fear of death, and so there is no telling what he might do."

35

The day Tomas's sea-worn boat finally touched shore on the island the clouds had sunk so low that their mists blew against the sand and held the view close and immediate and made Tomas feel as if he were wrapped in a damp cocoon and held apart from the world. He had hoped for more.

Still far out at sea, his eyes had searched the horizon before him, waiting for the luminous purple hills to rise into sight, waiting for some sign that this return would be for good. Far above him, a gull cried land, but still Tomas could not see the strong salute of his lighthouse, nor feel the welcome that he yearned for in his heart.

Instead, the wind fell and the mist closed in about him and though it was mid-morning, Tomas lost sight of the sun. Taking up his oars, he rowed towards the sound of the beach, and it was only when he had pulled the hull far up the shore that Tomas felt the weariness in his bones and remembered that he had not slept in three days.

The lighthouse was as he had left it — the pots and cups and flat metal plates still resting in the basin where he had washed them and left them to dry. His oyster baskets still hung on their peg by the door. His paintings stood in the corner on cloth stretched over homemade wooden frames.

Nothing had shifted, as he had hoped. The house was still empty, still felt desolate without his father's presence. There was not even the layer of dust one would have expected after so many months away, as if time had not passed here and Tomas had simply returned to the moment he had left behind years ago. Pulling his cot outside, he fell upon it, waiting for the sun, and when at last the sun burned away the clouds and seared into this back, he fled to the shade of the mango tree and slept and slept and did not stir until the sun had returned to the morning sky.

"Tomas has returned home."

The news spread through the town though he slept with ears closed and dreams quieter than the frenzy around him. Fathers who had worried at Tomas's departure as if it were a contagion which their own sons or daughters might contract by some invisible, insidious insect bite sighed with relief. But the mothers and grandmothers of the island exchanged sideways glances, for they remembered that he had left numerous times before. Why should this time be any different than those earlier returns when hopes had been raised and fears settled only to be muddied again with Tomas's departing footsteps? How could they be sure that he would remain with them now when even Tomas himself could not have said such a thing.

When Tomas finally opened his eyes the next morning, he was met by the curious stare of a little boy who stood just out of reach, watching Tomas sleep as if he were waiting for something unexpected to happen. His eyes were wide almond wells of faith, and when Tomas saw him, he started and spoke the boy's name — "Rohnan?" — for it was Lucas's son and Tomas was amazed that he had grown so tall and felt an immediate sense of relief at this proof that time had indeed passed on this solitary island.

"What are you doing?" the little boy asked without taking his eyes off him.

"Well, I was sleeping," Tomas said.

Sitting up, he felt the awkwardness of his bones, and he stretched this way and that while he felt his insides crack unwillingly back into place.

"Do you remember who I am?" Tomas asked the boy, but the boy neither nodded nor shook his head nor shifted on his bare feet but simply stood staring back at Tomas, so Tomas told him again, "I'm your Tomas-da. Your da is my greatest friend since we were your age. I met you when you were first born."

It was impossible to say whether this made any impression on little Rohnan, and for a moment Tomas stared at Rohnan and Rohnan stared at Tomas but only Tomas seemed uncertain what to do.

Finally he rose and collected the blue blanket he had used in the night. "Well, if you are just going to stand there you can help me carry this cot back into the house," Tomas said to him, and he threw the blanket over one shoulder and bent to pick up one side of the cot, and to his astonishment the little boy was already at the other end of the cot, grasping the wooden frame with his small, slender hands.

After the cot was put back in its corner, Tomas wandered around the vegetable garden, taking stock of what had survived, what might return to life, and what was lost, and Rohnan followed him back and forth, watching where he looked, kneeling whenever Tomas himself bent to inspect some plant up close, and after an hour, Tomas noticed he was even holding his hand to his small pointed chin as

Tomas often did when contemplating some piece of a puzzle that lay before him.

"I think your mother will probably be wondering where you are," Tomas said at last when he realised the sun was almost at its peak. "You'd better run home."

"What's that mark on your back?" Rohnan asked instead, and for the first time in many years, Tomas remembered the mark of the sea that crossed his back.

"It's the sign of the sea," Tomas told him. "The oracle gave it to me years ago when I became a man."

"What's the oracle like?" Rohnan asked.

"Ask your ma if you can come back tomorrow to help me with this garden and I'll tell you about the oracle then," Tomas said to him. "Do you think you could help me with this garden?"

"Oh yes," said the boy. "I can help with a lot of things."

Tomas bent down on one knee to look the little boy in the eye. "You'll have to help me pull these weeds, and you'll have to learn about the plants so you know how to care for them."

The boy nodded earnestly. "I can do it."

"Okay then. If your mother agrees, I'll see you tomorrow. Now run home and tell your da that your Tomas-da is well," and as Tomas watched the little boy skip over the rocks and around the wildflowers that grew despite all odds in the thin soil of the path, he touched his hand to his back, tracing the veiled lines of the water he could never see.

It took three days for Tomas to work up the courage to walk the path of the silver mangroves to the oracle's cottage in the cliffside. As he approached the gate, his eyes filled with the memory of his father and of the day his father had brought him to this same gate and turned back, leaving his son alone to face his own future. For a moment, Tomas felt the pull of his heart against the fabric of his chest and wondered if he would ever walk another day of his life without this childish ache of missing his da.

"Come in when you're ready." The oracle's voice glided into his thoughts.

"I hope," Tomas paused, unsure of what he had come all this way to say. "I hope it's okay that I've come," he finished and his voice did not come from his mouth, but somewhere deep in his belly. It sounded awkward and afraid.

"I'm always glad to see you, Tomas. I was wondering when you would finally remember me," the oracle replied, and she smiled so that he could calm his breath and speak again from his heart.

36

The oracle's home was not as Tomas had remembered it. From the days he had come to breathe the fires and become a man, he had imagined the oracle's house as a cave, dark and mysterious. It had been a profound place in his imagination and one not to tread upon without a depth of cause.

Yet as he stepped cautiously into the oracle's kitchen, he found it full not of gnarled roots and suspicious fragrances but simply of jars of herbs he recognised, herbs his own father had used in their nightly meals. A pot of water for losa tea sat rumbling on the stove. There was a table of thick wood with the same soft curved edges as the table at home which Jaro had made with his own hands. In fact, the only unusual thing Tomas could detect was that the light seemed warmer in this yellow room, as if it were truly the womb of the island, forgotten and abandoned due to an anticipated aura of labyrinthine secrets, unwelcome clairvoyances and perhaps even sorcery, which now failed to materialise.

The warmth penetrated his skin beyond the capacity of the sun, and it was this warmth and safety that caused

Tomas to slump down at the table as he would have done at his own home, and when the oracle asked, "How are you, Tomas?" he found himself answering honestly.

"Terrible."

"What's so terrible?" The oracle asked, wrapping her hair into a loose knot at the nape of her neck, seemingly unperturbed by the pitch of Tomas's desperation.

He did not know what else to say. And so Tomas simply told her the truth about the years he had spent away from the island. He told her about Muran and the other women he had used for their raw comforting skin and their eyes that were incapable of judgement. He told her about the wealth of his pearls which had not brought him happiness, about the endless sea that only reflected back to him his own loneliness, about all the days that he missed the island of his heart but how the island itself had abandoned him for every time he returned hoping to find the place he used to call home, he found instead an island which had become a voiceless stranger and refused to welcome him.

"My life has been a disaster," Tomas said.

And then he spoke of the man he might have been, the man he believed his father had seen in him, a man who knew his way through the woods though he could not see beyond the vines and the trees, a man who knew what he wanted from his life, a decisive man who knew what he loved and why, a man who was unafraid.

A man who knew how to be a man.

"But I am not that man," Tomas told the oracle. "I lost everything that had any meaning to me and now I don't know what I want. I used to love this island. I wanted to build my own home here. But it seems the island is trying to drive me away."

Yet even as he spoke these words, words his mind had

been repeating again and again upon the vast oceans where there was only himself to hear — *I loved Isla, but she left and I did nothing to stop her. I lost my father, my home. I have nothing* — a surprising thing began to happen. Tomas himself began to wonder whether this story he kept telling himself about his life was really true.

Before her, the oracle watched this rare wind-blown man melt back into the boy she remembered skipping over the large rocks that had been smoothed by the sea, sitting patiently as the birds hovered close so that he could sketch them in the beauty of mid-flight, and though she could not tell him so, she knew that he was exactly the man his father had believed he could be.

But because she could not speak of Jaro, she said, "I want to tell you a story that has often helped me."

And then she told Tomas the story she had learned when she was young during the early days of her training, of the fisherman who went to sea for two months and failed to catch a single fish. "Such bad luck, the people said, to go for so long without catching a fish! It must be a bad omen. But the fisherman said nothing, Tomas. He simply waited."

"Several days later," the oracle continued, "the fisherman decided to leave the usual fishing areas behind and take to the open sea, and there he caught an enormous fish, so big that he could not fit its body into the boat, but had to tie it to the side and leave it hanging in the water. When he finally reached shore, all the people gathered to see this fish that was the biggest fish ever caught. How lucky, all the people said, to catch such a big fish. It must be a good omen. But the fisherman did not nod his head, Tomas. He simply pulled the fish to shore and brought out a knife."

"That night the fisherman and his wife began to eat the

great fish, and they immediately fell gravely ill. What terrible luck, the people said to each other, to fall ill from the only fish he has caught in two months! It must be a bad omen. But even at this, Tomas, the fisherman did not reply. For days the fisherman and his wife could not leave their beds, and while they were ill the other fishermen continued to row out to sea. One day a storm blew in from the east and many of the fishermen who had gone out that day did not return. How lucky, the people said. You were ill and so you were spared! This must be a good omen. But the fisherman said — we'll see."

"Do you understand?" the oracle asked, and Tomas ran a hand through his thick curly dark hair and looked at her with brown islander eyes. "The man didn't judge his life from the point when he wasn't catching any fish," he said.

"It means that things come and go in our lives, some look bad but are good, and some look good but are bad. And because this is so, one should suspend judgement because things are not always as they appear," the oracle replied.

Tomas rubbed his hands over his face and his warm golden skin attested to the months he had spent at sea under the unrelenting sun. "So you are saying maybe all these things have happened to me for a reason?" he asked.

"I'm not saying there is a Great Reason, Tomas. I'm saying, suspend your judgement of your life, because no one can see all ends. Not even you." She smiled and the seriousness that he had so often remembered of her was nowhere written on her face.

The oracle brought another cup of losa tea to the table. "I'd like to tell you something else, Tomas, that I think you are ready to hear. I told you once that you must come to know yourself, to know what you are and what you are not."

When Tomas nodded, she continued. "You speak to me of the past, of your childhood, when you and the island were one, when there seemed to be little separation between yourself and the birds and rocks and trees and sea winds. Now you are troubled because it appears that you and the island are not one, that this was an illusion of childhood. A chasm has opened up between you, dividing you from the fabric of this old world, cutting you off from the basic flow of this place you used to call home."

"When you were young," the oracle told him, "you were taught that the island was the centre of the world. You believed this just as you also believed the great illusion. You looked out at the world through your own eyes and believed that you were at the centre of this world. Then Isla left and you saw that people are different and that different paths stretch out before them and that you are not, in fact, the centre of all things. You have travelled and so you have also seen that this island is not the centre of the world. And so now you believe this: that there is the island, and there is the rest of the world, and that they are separate and distinct from each other, just as you see that there is You and Others who are not you. You see these things and so you believe that what you see is the truth."

"But you said — know what you are and know what you are not," Tomas said, and he searched the space between them for the map of his life that she seemed to see although he could not. "So I realised that this is who I am — weak, not strong. I am this," he said again, raising his hands. "I dive for pearls and waste the money wandering the sea. Isla always had direction, you know. She always knew what she wanted. That's who she is, and I accept that I am not that person, even if I wish I was."

"Yet you are no longer the same person as the baby who was born on this island, Tomas. Nor are you the same as the boy who came to me for initiation those years ago."

But Tomas simply shrugged. "Everything changes. I understand. What does this have to do with anything?"

In the fading afternoon light, the oracle closed her eyes, searching for a way to explain though she knew there were no words. And for the first time, it seemed to Tomas that she looked tired, as if the island itself sat upon her shoulders, or as if the years of solitude had finally taken their toll. Then, without speaking, the oracle stood and walked over to the kitchen counter where she began to grind spices for the evening meal.

Tomas listened to the thump thumping and the scrape scraping of the stone pestle and mortar and he breathed in the scents the mortar released into the air. For many minutes, Tomas slipped into this space between time, where no thoughts could haunt him and there was only the steady thumping of the stone handle in the stone bowl. He breathed in this space and for a time he did not think of Isla or his failures or his father or the unrelenting loneliness that would not let him sleep. Instead he simply sat, listening to the hypnotic sounds in his ears and when he returned, he noticed slowly and without condemnation that the shadows had shifted and that the tide now rocked against the edge of the cliff below the oracle's house, covering the spidery legs of the mangrove trees.

It wasn't until they both had eaten and Tomas had carried their bowls to the basin that he finally admitted, "I don't understand what you are trying to tell me."

The oracle wiped her hands and put water for losa on to boil. "I know," she replied. "There are no words to tell you the things you need to know. But I will tell you this — our mind is wonderful, but it has its own nature. At times, our thoughts help us solve our problems, create new solutions, dream great dreams. But the mind can also distort the way we see the world, and this can cause us great suffering."

"It is the mind's nature to categorise and distinguish one thing from another," the oracle continued, "and this is very useful when I am out collecting herbs for my medicines, or when you are building or repairing your boat. But another consequence of this great ability of the mind is that it convinces us it can do more than it actually can, and so while it tells us that it sees the truth, in reality it gives us a distorted perception of ourselves. It tells us — I am this, and not that. I am weak, not strong. I am a failure, not a success. Or it can tell us — I am a success, not a failure. And so we believe these things the mind tells us are true because we are accustomed to trusting the mind, since it has shown it can do so many other useful things."

The oracle paused to take the kettle from the stove and fish out the pale losa buds. Then she turned to look at Tomas and said, "But the mind cannot do everything, Tomas, and we must not trust it with the great task of life which is beyond its abilities."

"And what is this great task of life?" Tomas asked, although he already knew.

"To understand what we really are, Tomas. And what we are not."

When Tomas shook his head, the oracle caught her breath, for she had caught a glimpse of Jaro that was as brief as the wind, and her heart jumped because she realised that she still missed him.

"Let me ask you something, Tomas," she said. "Can you swim all the way around the island?"

"Yes," he replied, for he had done so once in a wave of recklessness just after Isla had left the island.

"And can you swim underneath the island?"

"No."

"Why not?"

Tomas's brown eyes narrowed. "You would reach the floor of the sea," he replied, for he had seen it often enough.

"And if you could swim along the floor of the sea, where would it take you?"

"It drops off like a great chasm," Tomas told her. "But if you swam far enough, it rises up again as it approaches land. To the south and west, it rises into more islands like ours, to the east you would come to the Merchant City and then to the plains of Mongru. To the north, if you swam far enough, the floor of the sea would take you to the shore of the mainland."

"True, true," said the oracle nodding. "And what would happen if all the water of our sea were drained away? You could walk over mountains and plains of the sea floor all the way from this island to the mainland or any other island, could you not?"

"Yes," Tomas nodded again, "but I don't see..."

"So you could say," the oracle was watching Tomas closely now, her hand resting lightly on the smooth wooden table between them. "You could say that this island is not, in fact, separate from the rest of the world, and that the water only provides an illusion of our division."

Tomas frowned but he could not think of how he could disagree. And then the oracle told Tomas the second most shocking thing of his life — "if this is true for the island," she said, "that our perception of its distinctiveness from the rest of the world is only an illusion of the waters, then what other illusions of the mind do we also believe and take as truth?"

And then the oracle told Tomas, "Once you let go of such misperceptions and allow yourself a chance to simply be in the world, then the island will return to you and you will no longer feel separated from it as you do now."

37

Isla waited in the uninhibited blaze of the fire. Above her head, the thick wooden beams of the Elixir Coffeehouse spread out like the protective armour of time which might help everyone forget and forgive. Outside, the autumnal winds beat heavily against the windowpanes and the sound mixed with the erratic voices of the people who came and drank and hurried off again.

Tonight, Isla was not in a hurry. It felt strange, after so many years of rushing to just sit. Jackimo would be here soon. He had asked her to meet him at their usual table to speak about the future. Isla looked down and studied the edges of her fingernails. Was she nervous? She couldn't tell. She knew what Jackimo was going to say when he sat before her in his dark black robe and took off his fur-lined hat. They had known each other for years now, much longer than they needed to, perhaps much longer than they ought. But they both had understood each other's vulnerability, for once they were officially married many things would change.

Isla glanced over her right shoulder to the corner where

they had first sat when things hadn't seemed so certain. Above the low table and leather cushions the wooden ceiling beams were carved with images of cats with large wild eyes, mythical winged beasts with threatening claws, images of the three-headed king who was wise and brave and true.

Back then, Isla had stared at these carvings as a foreigner in exile, and she had felt afraid because she still did not feel at home with such signs of the mainland which everyone else seemed to read with ease. Those were the days when Isla still stood uncomfortably in her high wooden-heeled shoes, longing for a fluency of mainland life which she felt might never come. But home, Isla had realised, was a strange thing — a feeling more than a place — and it had crept up on her slowly, without hurry or invitation until it found her on this night so many years later deciding whether to marry a mainlander and create a new family here.

That first night that they were alone together at the coffeehouse, Jackimo had seen her watching the carvings as if they knew life, and he had not laughed at her as another might have done, or waited for her to confess her inexperience so that he could enlighten her with his superior knowledge. Instead, he had said, "This is why we must love the mainland, in spite of all her flaws. All places have their mysteries, their winged beasts and magic fairies, their monsters and heroes. But only the mainland has defeated them all with the light of the Rising Sun, the logic of progress."

Out of all the houses of the coffee district, the Elixir was their favourite. It had stood in this place for three hundred and seventy years, or so they claimed. It had once served coffee in golden bowls to the infamous seven princes who had made a last stand against the contracting landscape of their kingdom. It had been the coffeehouse deemed most worthy by the royal councillors of the fourth age who had written — *neither magnificent spires nor marble floors do we need, for the Elixir contains that which is unseen and thus most powerful.* Most mainlanders believed the councillors spoke of themselves and their wise council which was often debated and brought to life within the walls of the ancient coffeehouse, or simply that the councillors had become intoxicated by the enervating flow of the dark bitter drink. But Isla thought that perhaps the councillors had meant the Elixir itself which, with its dark red walls echoing with firelight at all hours of day or night, was the kind of place that inspired extravagant dreams and the kind of whimsical idealism that might just come true.

Jackimo had been so full of hope in those days. So full of faith in the good intentions of the world and the promises of the future. In this, he had not changed. "We have such little time here on this earth," he had said then. "Such great dreams and such little time." Years ago on that first night, she and Jackimo had both struggled to release themselves from the muddy grounds of their pasts. They had pulled and groaned with each step as their feet had stuck in the treacherous marshes of doubt and guilt and insecurity. But they had had faith. They had put one foot in front of the other in what had seemed then like an endless march.

And now, at last, they had arrived. Jackimo was no longer one of the many faceless junior banking merchants whose white collared robes displayed their inexperience. Now he worked for the Central Bank. At last he could stand on the Avenue and know that he was Someone. That his work mattered to many people. And Isla could also stand, robed with the jewels of the empire in her hair.

Sitting near the stone fireplace, Isla now watched as the fire illuminated the carvings of the same cats' eyes and dragons' wings and the three crowns of the mythic goodly king. Now she saw them with older eyes and knew what they meant and where they had come from. She knew the stories that trailed in their ancient steps. Soon, she would be promoted to the level of senior scribe and would be sent to only the most important of the Lost Regions. The desert was the beginning of her final ascent to the summit. So she could sit in this small coffeehouse and know that she was Someone too.

Isla sat in her seat, sheltered by the shadows of low ceilings and dark corners. She breathed in the warm aromas of coffee that whirled around her. It was strange how so many days and months could fly by without a thought, and then suddenly Isla could find herself again on a precipice of change and it was in these singular moments that the world would fall still around her and she would wonder again if this was really the adventurous life she had expected, if it was enough. And if it was what she wanted.

Isla sipped her coffee and reflected on the unpredictable turns of destiny that had brought an island girl like her to this ancient building in the centre of the mainland city to sip such a dark, startling drink after so many years drinking losa. She looked around her at the myriad of faces that filled this coffeehouse and knew she was not alone.

Coffee-drinking had been an old habit of empire, and some of the coffeehouses that stood on the western side of the administrative district had inhabited that very place for several centuries or more. Yet the habit of drinking that bitter brown liquid by sipping with slow delicacy had intensified in recent years.

Many believed that it was the fever with which the

young mainlanders had consumed the coffee in the early days of innovation that had caused the original outbreak of insomnia on the mainland. The young mainlanders themselves claimed it was a symptom of progress. Either way, these days it was only the elderly, those who had grown up in the quiet days after the final decline of the last kingdom, who were concerned by the red-ringed eyes and trembling hands and obsessive work ethic that came from an overconsumption of the drink. Everyone else on the mainland became fastidious converts, and because the young who were most severely afflicted by the insomnia also spoke the fastest, worked the longest hours and tended to produce the latest novelties and time-saving technologies, the spreading insomnia was assumed to be a blessing, the mark of a new age, an omen of the revival of the kingdom.

It had taken Isla time to accustom herself to drinking liquid so thick and acrid when she had been raised on the clean, soft flavours of losa. For the first year of her life on the mainland, she had searched the various markets for a hint of the familiar purple buds only to be continually disappointed, for while mainlanders loved her losa plant to dye their clothes, no one imported the soft, young buds that could be used for tea. Finally, Isla had given up her search and given in to the startling bitter drink that everyone sipped with the regularity of prayer and that made her heart pound in her throat like a lost lover who had rediscovered hope.

The last great mainland kingdom had made the city a centre of architectural beauty, and the tall buildings and wide avenues of the Central Administration District proclaimed the kingdom's power that spread north as far as the high mountains and west as far as the sea of sand. Then, the buildings had been made with the finest white stone,

stone that would last as long as the infinite expectations of the kingdom and was carved with exquisite artistry. There were fountains too, spread out like stars throughout the city, and the water that flowed from their thousand spouts was scented by the rose petals that fell into the miniature aqueducts that supplied the water to the city. People born in the time of the last great kingdom had been proud, proud of their birthplace, proud to be from the centre of power that they fit into easy as a glove, proud to belong to the place that was the centre of all things. It made them stand tall in their shoes and walk with the grace of those who know they are superior because they were born in glory.

After climbing to such heights, it took many years for the city's inhabitants to accept their kingdom's obvious decline. By then most of the outer regions had been lost — the battle-cries said 'returned' — to local rulers, and the kingdom had contracted as if it had taken one great breath over the course of a thousand years and must naturally and inevitably breathe out again. Still, the inhabitants of the city would not believe it. They had been born into the wondrous order of power and would not countenance such chaos which meant the relinquishing of their birthright. It took more than two hundred years and seven generations for the reality of their fall from grace to set in, but once it did, the people of the mainland city experienced a sense of devastation and loss that far exceeded the extent of their actual fall. They had believed for as long as history could recall that they were special, the chosen few, because they lived at the centre of the world, were acquainted with the gadgets of modernity, knew the latest discoveries of science and astrology and mathematics. Their society was the most advanced in architecture, poetry and music, and not a child roamed the streets who could not write his own name and recite the basic hymns of the seven saints.

But the city began to look grey and as each region surrounding the city was lost to local heroes and unknown warriors, the water supply running into the city was reduced. One-by-one, the fountains were turned off and the rose petal scent soon existed only in the reminiscences of old women, and then fell into myth. The great buildings of the kingdom seemed to shrink as if they were slowly sinking into the quicksands of time and black crows descended on the city, watching like centurions of death from the noble heads of stone statues, waiting for the kingdom to fall to its knees.

It was in these last moments of decline, when people in the mainland city had lost all sense of purpose, all understanding of what their life meant, that the Philosophy of the Rising Sun had emerged as if from the earth itself. The Philosophy of the Rising Sun had revealed to the people of the mainland city that the reason for their kingdom's decline lay in stagnation, a lack of growth, and fundamental misunderstanding about why we were all here on this earth. The answer was simply to get moving again. We are all here to be productive. Create New things. Create More. The New, it was said, would inevitably lead to Growth, to Progress, and a rise to Glory. The More we have, the Rising Sun professed, the better off we will be.

The Sun had risen, and the inhabitants of the city were thirsty for some sort of meaning, something to reconfirm their great standing in the world order. So few bothered with such seeming trivialities as where exactly they were going, what this Progress was headed for. The More we have, the better off we will be, people repeated to each other on the streets. Once everyone has More, once everyone has everything they want, we will all be happy and at peace.

The Philosophy of the Rising Sun and the idolatry of the New spread through the city, and in only a single generation its perspective of the world had taken on the authority of common sense. *Soon,* mainlanders began to say, *we will be a great kingdom once again. Soon,* they told each other in a thousand winks and nods and knowing glances, *soon we will lead the world to happiness and freedom.*

We have found our place, Isla thought to herself. *We know the possibilities of the mainland, perhaps even more clearly than those born in the city itself.* Isla thought of Jackimo and the life they would have together. For a moment she felt something in her break open and tears rose to her eyes like the sea she had trapped inside. And it was as if a sudden cloud from her past had crossed the path of the sun. But then she saw him step through the threshold, his face filled with hope as he searched for her, and she quickly wiped her eyes and brought a smile to her face. He was a good man. He was the right man for the life she had chosen. And when he spoke to her about their future, she knew she would make the right decision.

38

When Isla finally returned to the desert many things had changed. The finances from the Central Bank had been distributed to the desert people and work was already underway to raise the dam wall and expand the water reservoir. With it, the warm browns and ochres and earth oranges of the desert had flushed to a ragged green. Tents which had once rested on rippled carpets of sand now spread their roots into patchy shrubs of grass. Expanding tracts of crops, which would never have blossomed in such a hot and hostile land before the advent of excess water, now grew freely.

She was different too. Isla, once only an island girl, was now a senior mainland scribe overseeing the desert project. And she was now also set to marry a senior banking merchant, a mainlander. *Perhaps now I am a mainlander too*, Isla thought.

As Isla stepped away from the caravan that had marched her two days into the desert, she felt that she was finally in control of her life. All was as it should be. The long years of training and the years before when all she could do was dream and hope for a chance to leave the stagnating island of her birth… it all had led up to this moment. Isla fingered the thin dark cloth of her senior scribe's robe tailored especially to suit the hot desert climate. She felt her heeled shoes sink into the sand beneath the carpet that had been laid for her. Ahead the large scorpion tent shimmered through the radiating heat like a mirage. But it wasn't a mirage, Isla told herself. It was real. It was all real. She had finally been given her chance to make a real difference in the world. A chance to leave her mark… to prove her life meant something more than the mere passage of time.

Isla stepped through the folds of the large tent and felt the change in temperature with a sigh as the cool water snaked through the channels of the tent swallowing the heat into its invisible belly. In the corners of the room, women wound the wheels of the fans round and round, sending wafts of breezes here and there.

As if to confirm the power of her new status, it was the chief himself who greeted Isla, solemnly and without the warmth of trust, but as he had always done to the senior mainland officials on Isla's many previous trips to the desert. He offered her a cup of coffee which she took and drank standing there before his long, serious face. Isla nodded and smiled, although the bowl in her hands made it impossible to clap as she was used to doing. The chief's dark eyes seemed to widen in approval, or perhaps relief, or perhaps something else that Isla could never imagine.

When at last he spoke, his voice was filled like the brimming reservoir with all his proud convictions — "These days, Madame Scribe, others look at us desert people and envy our success. At last they say — if only we could be as those desert people who have all that they desired."

Looking across the heads of his people gathered in the

scorpion tent to meet the mainland senior scribe, it seemed as if he were peering across the rolling expanse of the vast desert, and he spoke again. "People must feel productive," he counselled. "They must be able to see the concrete value of their work. They must be able to measure their contribution and value within society. But the key to success," he said, raising both his dark sun-stained hands, "is never to be satisfied, to always strive for More. We have done this, and now we have become a great people among all the desert tribes. Now our children will have more than we ourselves had, for this is the way the world should be."

That day and the next were filled with meetings, listing the mainland's requirements before the next portion of the loan would be released, checking and rechecking the numbers of the desert project's accounts — How high would the wall stretch? How many stones? How many men working? How many hours? All was measured and accounted for with precision. The accountant from the Central Bank sat to Isla's right at the long, low table that had been set up at the front of her tent, murmuring at the figures on the paper before him, making different calculations that added up to the same results — Bigger. Which was always Better.

In the afternoons, as the sun reached its summit in the sky and everyone fled to the central tent for relief, or to their own homes to sleep the heat away as they had always done before the waters came, Isla wandered to the back room of her tent where a large pool of water had been filled from the reservoir. Unwinding her salty, sweat-soaked robe, Isla eased herself into the tepid water. Holding her breath, she sank below the surface, letting the water capture her dark ringlets and spread them out suspended around her.

Time seemed to shift, her arms, her hair, her head moved slowly through the water, as she once had done.

Then, emerging, she crawled to the flat wooden side of the pool and stretched out, turning the handle of the fan above her and watching the blades slide through the air, round and round overhead. The heat was like a tide, it pulled away from her as the water evaporated from her skin. Then slowly, the tide would roll in again, the heat descending upon her gentle as a death, and Isla would roll off the ledge and into the water again.

Beneath the surface there was only muffled silence, the deep humming water makes in the ear. And then, without warning, Isla remembered the day when she was still a girl on the island, standing at the edge of the pool Tomas had found, wanting to leap in to meet the water as she had done a thousand times. Rolling back onto the wooden ledge, Isla listened to the silence of the afternoon desert and sank into the tangible memory of her past, coarse and uneven in her mind. But not unwelcome.

What had happened? She remembered standing at the edge facing her own reflection, and somehow she had gotten in the water...and Tomas had said something to make it okay. What was it? Lying so many years in her adulthood, Isla strained to see and then gave up. *Where is he at this moment?* Isla wondered to herself. But then she realised that was the wrong question, for he was of course still on the island, as he had always been. *Still, I hope he's well*, she said to herself, alone in the tent in the desert. *I hope he's happy. I wonder if I will ever see him again.*

The question startled her lazy, sun-soaked mind, and a sudden choking sob rose up in her throat before she could bury it. Isla sat up suddenly on the edge of the wooden pool of water, and the sadness in her heart came not from the fear that she would never return to the island, nor the realisation of how much she had changed, how far she had come to even contemplate such a question. It came from somewhere deeper, a cavern that held the secrets of her destiny and forced her to see the unspeakable possibility that Tomas, her Tomas, had not been a part of her future after all.

Why did Eva never write of him? Why did she send news of the true state of her father's health, news of Lucas's marriage, the birth of his children, even news of Marco who had all but disappeared into the bosom of his fishing community, but never news of Tomas. Had he married some foolish island girl who had been satisfied enough to stay behind, have his babies, clean his house? How could he be satisfied with such a life?

Was he different now — after so many years? If she stood before him now, would he still glance sideways at her, his eyes sparkling with his latest secret that no one but Isla would ever hear? And how many years had it been since she had remembered to wonder such things? *Perhaps it is better this way,* Isla thought to herself. *Perhaps it is better to forget it all.*

39

That evening, wrapped again in her official scribal robe, Isla received a new visitor. The older woman stepped forward fearlessly into Isla's tent and stood in the lamplight, hands at her sides, and she did not move even when Isla beckoned her to please come and sit on this rug.

"I hope you will have some losa tea with me, Darrah," Isla asked, finding she was more nervous than usual at this planned meeting. But also more excited.

The woman stepped onto the rug and folded herself up, tucking her legs beneath the folds of cloth that wrapped about her this way and that. She held her hands out to take the bowl of losa tea from Isla, and Isla saw that her hands were thick and muscular and that they contained many lines that Isla knew the wise would have called lifelines, which were carved into the woman's dark skin by the desert.

The older woman sipped her tea slowly, her eyes taking stock of the tent, the papers, the lanterns hanging from metal rods stuck deep in the sand, the dusty layered carpets and the fluttering break in the cloth like an eyelid that led to this mainlander woman's private room at the back of the tent. "It's my job to oversee the dam project," Isla said trying to attract the woman's wandering gaze. "The mainland wants to make sure everyone is well...is taken care of...receiving the benefits of this expansion. I always speak to the men, the chief and his councillors, but I wanted to speak to the women also...to get their thoughts...to listen to their concerns and needs. I was hoping you could help me," she finished, wondering if she sounded too eager, still too inexperienced.

"You won't know how to help us," the woman said, and her eyes did not bother to meet Isla's.

"I'd like to try," Isla said. "I know I'm new to my position, but I have worked on many projects, and I have been assigned to this project for several years as a novice scribe. If you could explain to me how you women see things...what it is you need...I could try to get it for you."

"You don't understand," the woman said. Her voice was suddenly harsh as the sand against the tents during a windstorm, and Isla felt the woman was accusing her of something, only she couldn't see what she had done. "You people have brought a great lie to the desert, and now most of my people believe you. They work and they work for this dam but no, Madame Scribe, they are not well because they can no longer see the lie."

Isla put down her bowl of losa tea. A great wave of foreboding washed over her like the nausea of seasickness, and she longed to close her ears and hide as the desert people did from such dangerous sandstorms that reshaped even the landscape in their path. But duty compelled Isla to ask the woman, "What lie?"

The woman's piercing gaze fell upon her. "The lie of More. The lie you people have brought with this water. The lie that now we are happier and more free than we used to be."

"There have been no lies," Isla protested, clapping her hands with inherited authority. "The mainland has helped your people pursue their dreams and desires. This is the way of progress, Darrah. After all, everyone wants More."

"No."

The word left no room for argument, but Isla continued. *Everyone can be reasoned with,* she thought to herself. *Perhaps she simply hasn't understood the Philosophy of the Rising Sun.* "The dam has brought more water to your village. It makes it possible to grow more crops, more sisilus to sell in mainland markets so that you can buy anything you want. The dam..."

"The dam is a lie," the woman interrupted. "The dam may make my people feel they are pursuing their dreams... but the wise know that you can't get something without giving up something else, and it is a lie to believe that the world has infinitely more to give. All this may seem the way to a good life. To have More," the woman flung her hand dismissively. "But because my people have believed you and this Rising Sun nonsense, they are less satisfied, less happy, less free."

"How can you say your people are less satisfied or less free?" Isla almost shouted. "After all we've done to help you!"

She heard herself telling the woman — "The water in the reservoir irrigates many more fields of crops than the river ever could. The dam means that you people can buy so many new things. It gives you so much. What fool would refuse this for some backwards, idle life!"

Around them, the silence of the desert sat solemn and patient, waiting to be heard, but Isla had forgotten how to listen to things such as deserts or oceans or night skies. Instead, she only heard the sound of her own voice listing all the work she and her mainland colleagues had done to fund the dam project. She told the woman — "The reservoir now helps you hold back water for your own use," even though she knew that the people were not meant to drink the reservoir water, that the desert women still collected water to drink from the tributary rivers, and that the reservoir had been built to irrigate vast new fields of crops. And Isla also knew that it was not food that was grown in the expanding fields, but rather a certain desert succulent that the desert people called sisilus that improved the quality of the skin and was in increasing demand on the mainland.

Yet instead of nodding with some new realisation, as Isla had expected, the old woman got to her feet, gathered the folds of her dress and swung her long yellow shawl around her head and over her left shoulder. "Come. I will show you," she said to Isla, and so Isla had no choice but to follow the woman out onto the warm, sun-soaked sands that held heat even as the sky slipped into darkness.

On padded bare feet the two women followed the path along the river as it soared upward towards the fading horizon. The sands, which had lost the white searing brilliance of afternoon were now a pale orange as the last rays of the sun fled over the dunes, and Isla knew that soon the sands and fields of rugged, green crops would turn grey and dissolve into sky black.

After a time, the old woman cut away from the river path, and they walked towards a high dune that stood at the edge of the irrigated land. From the top of the dune, one could see the whole village, the straight lines that marked the irrigation channels in the fields. *The tents look small,* Isla thought, *like the glowing fireflies we used to chase on the island.*

And then Isla looked past the village, and suddenly she saw the enormous desert, lonely and still, the dunes rolling majestic. The power of the place surrounded Isla because she felt rather than thought that it stood without time.

"When I was young and for as many generations of memory as have been passed down to me, the river has been here, our life source." The woman's voice had changed, and she spoke gently into the sinking air. "I can count back twenty generations, and in that time there have been many years when the river shrank and many years when it grew beyond the place where our tents now stand. But in all that time, the river has never become so low that we did not have enough."

Darrah paused. "There are places in this world that never have enough," she admitted. "Places where people go hungry, where people and their animals die from thirst, where people are at constant war and cannot be free. But that is not this place, daughter of the islands. That has never been our reality, although our life here in this desert has never been easy."

"But things are better now," Isla replied. "With the dam and the water reserves, you have More and so you will never have to be afraid of not having enough. Changes and hardships will not touch you so harshly."

"No," the woman said once again, and the desert silence prickled against Isla's skin.

And then the woman said, "When I was young and for as many generations of memory as have been passed down to me, my people have used the river to grow what we needed. Everyone had enough food, and when there was extra time and water for sisilus, we grew it and traded it for things like losa tea that we drank and savoured until it was gone and there was more to sell. In those days, there was time, and so people learned to play instruments or to sing or to tell stories."

"Families were not perfect." Darrah shook her head. "I am not saying that. People fought, argued. Certain people became bored and left the village, and there were others that migrated from larger places upstream and settled here. But people were wise and knew the difference between their needs and their desires, and because they had enough, they limited their desires and were satisfied and felt at peace in the world. They were not afraid — even during the generations of the mainland raids when people did everything they could to protect themselves, they were not always afraid as they are now...always afraid that they might not get what they want, always afraid they won't have enough or that they will lose what they have acquired."

And the woman told Isla, "We used to be a rich people. Rich in time. Rich in space. We had time to spend with our families, our friends. Time to sit, to play. Time to gaze up at the stars at night and contemplate greater mysteries. But this dam has been the end to that life. Now, I look down at my village and I see a people who are always looking to the future and no longer see what is right in front of them. I see a people who need more and more to feel satisfied, and this need is like a demon that never rests, so they work and work but their work is never enough. I see a people whose worth is now measured only by the money they earn, and now my generous people want to be paid for everything they do, and the opportunistic young sit in the seats which used to be reserved for the wise. Even the chief has surrounded himself with such infantile councillors and the knowledge of experience, true wisdom, has been banished because it cannot buy the silver bracelets and fancy clothes my people have come to desire."

"And still," she continued, "my people must work harder and harder and longer and longer, but what they acquire is never enough and does not satisfy them. The more my people think they need, the more vulnerable they are." The woman's voice faded, slowly, gradually, into the desert night. She sighed and looked across the fields, and the rows of tents that glowed in the dark under the canopy of rising stars. Then she looked at Isla. "I am not wise enough, daughter of the islands. I am not wise enough, and so I do not know why my people believe such fairytales or what I alone could do to protect them. But I know what I see, and what I see is that my people are vulnerable because the demon of desire will never be satisfied and this path they call progress will never lead to happiness. I am not wise, so I cannot say why we are less free than we used to be, but a person feels a freedom stolen deep in their bones."

"But there must be progress," Isla tried to explain gently to the old desert woman. "People should have opportunities to use their efforts to make a better world for themselves."

"This is true," the old woman replied, "but why is it you mainlanders always think there was no progress before you arrived? You think you are the only ones who know how to progress? The only minds who can inspire innovation? The only hands with medicines to heal? Well, this is simply your own blindness. Do not doubt it, daughter of the islands, the mainland is not here to help us."

"Stop calling me a daughter of the islands!" Isla demanded with all the authority she could bring with the clap of her hands. "I am a senior scribe from the mainland, and I am telling you we are here to help!"

"If you don't believe me, you should visit the village downstream," the desert woman replied, "for I shudder to think what this dam has done to the others who also rely on this river."

"Our people have a saying. *Van-le jai-wa-le* — the outer takes the shape of the inner. The outer world can only ever take the form of our internal world. They share a likeness which is not always apparent. But for those of us who still know the old language, who see the stars in our mind, the river in our body, such things are obvious, for it cannot be otherwise. No, the mainland is not here to help us. There is only one reason I can perceive that this great mainland kingdom would involve itself in our insignificant desert affairs, and that is the mainland's desire for power, and its desire to have more than it can create for itself."

"Why are you telling me this?" Isla asked the woman. She could feel her heart racing against the rising fear in her mind.

At this the woman reached out her rough, sand-worn hands and took Isla's thin, warm fingers between her palms. "Because, daughter of the islands, I remember that once you cried over a bowl of losa, and so I know that you have a memory of life beyond what is the mainland's only way. Your heart can understand what I am telling you because there is some part of you that can still remember another kind of life."

40

In the evenings, Lucas listened to his uncle Cassius recount again and again the arguments of the Losa Council. Most evenings, his uncle sided with the other traders, dreaming of a wealth he had never possessed, speaking of worldly gadgets he had never seen, claiming that the losa growers who stood against increasing the cultivation of losa would be the source of the island's demise.

"Mark my words and a bag of losa," he would say as he repeated to Lucas and Aimen the arguments they themselves had made to each other in the languid days after their return from harvest trading.

"The growers have always been greedy, thinking they are better than us," Cassius's voice boomed across the table where his family gathered to eat each evening. "Take that Sylvia Prenai, always her long, bragging speeches, year upon year, wearing jewels as if she were queen. But tell me, what man willingly ties himself in chains? Why should we chain ourselves while these growers wear their jewels?"

"Remember what the desert man told us," he would say when he perceived that his nephews, whom he considered his sons, had begun to daydream, gazing beyond his wide, sagging face to the rustling sunlight outside. "Remember the desert man," he would say as if he had met this man himself. "If losa is what we grow best, then it is nature's law that we should grow as much losa as possible. This is our advantage and we should use it."

Yet on other days, and for the sake of what Cassius perceived as his deep wisdom and just application of reason, he would argue the other side, praising the wisdom of the Losa Charter and the generations of growers and traders that had come before this corruptible generation. "You see," he would say on these evenings as the sun sank low, and he would rub his round belly as he spoke, "we shouldn't be too quick to ignore the laws of the Charter. We cannot be too hasty, Lucas, and just throw away these rules that were written by great men and have lasted many generations." "We must respect the traditions of the island, Aimen, and step carefully in our affairs."

Through each tirade, Lucas sat at the long wooden table, his wife Rosa and two children Rohnan and Ria to his right, his brother Aimen and Aimen's wife swollen with pregnancy across from them, his mother watching them as she sipped her soup with eyes veiled by lowered lashes.

Cassius always sat at the head of the table, his chair pushed as close as his large belly would allow, and he spoke to the family, as he did most evenings that Lucas could remember, in a monologue of broken thoughts while the mosquitoes and crickets warmed the air with the comforting sounds of their humming. In the past, these evening talks had usually focused on topics such as the state of the trading business (although until now, little had ever changed), the likelihood of storms, the varying successes of his friends and their sons, the quality of the mangoes from his own sons' trees or the virtues of long afternoon naps.

Now armed with a new topic of conversation, Cassius's stamina seemed endless. But Lucas had grown used to these heavy evenings, as he had to his uncle's endless chatter, and he and Rosa had begun their own mutiny stirred up from the depths of their boredom by encouraging side conversations with their children who were the only ones at the table who were never reprimanded for speaking at the same time as Cassius.

It wasn't until one evening several weeks after the mutinous Council meeting that Lucas overheard his brother Aimen call their uncle "Da", and he awoke with such a start from his dozing place at the table that his mother's eyes flared up in their fading light and Rosa clutched his hand beneath the table for him to keep his silence. For several moments, a shock resonated in his bones, and Lucas simply looked dumbly from one face to another as if he didn't recognise the members of his own family. Gradually hearing returned, and Lucas heard Cassius, who was entirely unaware of the tension rumbling beneath his table, repeating the same arguments he had made against the losa growers on many evenings before.

Or perhaps it was not the shock that Aimen had called Cassius "da" that tore Lucas from his usual evening stupor, for this had been common practice since Aimen had turned five and had forgotten his own father as if he had never existed. Rather, it was as much the shock of actually having *heard* anything at all at this stagnating table, as it was the sudden and profound imprint of his father's face before him that shook Lucas out of his false sleep.

For the first time in his waking hours, Lucas remembered the dreams he had of his father, which had begun to seep so slowly into his mind over so many years that he could never place them in time, nor remember which nights they had come upon him. He knew only that more and more often his night time thoughts dwelt upon the memory of his father and these dreams always revealed his father's true face, which he had only been able to sense but never recall in his waking hours — until now.

With his father's face before him, Lucas looked at his uncle. How different this sweltering man felt from the man's tall, quiet brother who had been Lucas's father. Lucas remembered his father in brief images now — for instance, racing up the hill behind their house where his own family still lived. His father had always run ahead, laughing, at the start, but had inevitably fallen behind his young son just before the finish line and Lucas smiled now, thinking how foolish he had been not to have realised his father had always let him win.

In Lucas's mind, his father had become many things, and Lucas could not say for certain that all of these things were true, only that he felt they must be true, as he felt the sea must end somewhere although he had never seen such a place but knew it by the solidity with which it dwelt in his imagination. His father must have been clever beyond the requirements of his trade, for in most of the images Lucas held of him, he was reading. On certain nights, Lucas remembered, he had emerged from the pages of a book with eyes wistful and flickering and would gather his son and his wife, and later little Aimen and baby Caira, and read aloud to them tales of adventure and magic.

So often, Lucas had sat at this table, watching this slovenly body of his father's older brother sitting before him, feeling his mouth fill with bitter words. He knew that his uncle was not a cruel man, though at times Lucas resented him as if it had been Cassius himself who had caused his father's sudden death.

No, Cassius was not cruel. Nor had he ever neglected his responsibilities to Lucas's mother or any of her children. After the death of Cassius's wife during childbirth, Cassius had returned to the family home and had taken up residence in his old childhood bedroom, and had never moved since. Yet despite such infantile behaviour, Cassius did not hesitate after the sudden death of his younger brother to rescue the broken pieces of Lucas's mourning family and take them as his own.

As a child of eight, Lucas had been too frightened by his mother's midnight pacing to feel anything but gratitude when his uncle Cassius had arrived one evening and, putting a hand upon Lucas's small warm head, told him not to worry, that there would be a man in the house again. Yet as he grew older and became more and more frustrated with his uncle's boorish ways that seemed so different to his laughing, carefree father, Lucas had begun to wonder what possible desperation his mother had felt that she had exchanged the beautiful memories of her dead husband for the current reality of this brother. For a time, Lucas had cursed his mother for her weakness that had brought them into his uncle's home and his mother into his uncle's bed. But then he had begun his life as a trader, and working in the family business as a man had forced Lucas to abandon childhood rage.

Now, with his father's face before him, Lucas looked at his uncle and understood that it was not his uncle who had pushed his father's memory from their lives. Rather, it seemed to him that this must be the way of the world, a world which shifted recklessly under foot and tore people indiscriminately from its foundations.

It was in this moment that Lucas realised what felt like a great truth — that the only people whose memory survived their deaths were the people of great fame. People like Manel Prenai. Their names lived on forever. Manel Prenai with his stick and his wise words and his unfailing strength in the face of the devious mainlanders. Manel Prenai's memory had survived among the islanders, and it seemed to Lucas as if, through the very persistence of memory, Manel Prenai had survived his own death.

I must make a name for myself, Lucas thought, as he stared out unseeing across this eternal dining table. *I will establish my reputation among the people of this island, so that my name will always live on. Forever. Even when I am no longer on this earth. I will become even more famous than Manel Prenai.*

Then Lucas spoke to his uncle, and neither Cassius nor Lucas's wife Rosa, nor Lucas's mother could have understood what had made this sullen man transform his typical tone of disregard into a ferocious passion.

"You are right, uncle." Lucas said. "If the Council can give no reasons to explain why there are limitations on the losa grown on the island, nor why the growers should profit above others, then the Council must yield to our request. Tomorrow I will speak to some of the harvesters, for we must ally ourselves with them if we are to gain a majority in the Council."

41

The Council was sluggish and hung with fools. This Lucas knew, but whether it was backwards, archaic, a sign of withering times, he was not so certain. He thought back to the mainland traders, the vast, worry-free wealth they had promised and the kind of life their visions foretold.

Yet there was a piece of his mind that could not quite imagine life without the Council. It was an institution without a face on the island; it had no building, no physical presence. And still it was woven so finely into the fabric of islanders' imaginations that it seemed impossible to dissolve. So when Lucas met a small group of harvesters under the wide banyan tree far from town, he began by saying, "The Council should stay as it is. We are only asking for a change to the Charter which will benefit us all."

The harvester men and women looked each other in the eye, and it seemed to Lucas as if they spoke many words with such looks, but all remained silent. A few slapped rambling mosquitoes from their arms and several men wiped their foreheads with twisted white cloths in the fierce heat. "What do you want from us?" one harvester asked.

"I'm asking for your support," Lucas began again. "You harvesters work long, hard days..."

"What you're asking," one of the women interrupted, "is for us to stand against the grower families we've been working with since we could stand tall enough to reach the new buds, families our parents worked with to save the harvests from storms and disease and every kind of unexpected thing. These are people who come into the fields with us, work side-by-side with us most days, and we've never been late with a harvest so long as I've been alive."

"Don't think I don't know we're all islanders, Mila," Lucas said. "We traders have always had good relations with the grower families. But what I'm saying is this — things should be fair. And can you honestly say it's fair that you work through every season and still life feels like a struggle? I've seen traders from other places, a desert man who had more than most of us could ever dream. Is that fair? I've seen things in the markets of Joon that would make life easier for us. Things that would give us a bit of peace. Things we could all afford if the island grew more losa. In this case, should we just be satisfied with the very basic needs for our families' survival? Is it so wrong for us to want a little more?"

The harvester women touched the thin cloth of the skirts that wrapped around their bodies like cocoons. Fingers lingered over threadbare patches, holes that had been mended twice before this hot day. One woman called Josai thought of the man that she watched always out of the corner of her eye, thought that with such fine, new things, he might look towards her and discover love. The man standing next to her also looked deep into Lucas's face, thinking that perhaps if he could get new tools from these markets, things would be easier. And if he could earn a bit more, he could afford a new bed, maybe a new house a bit farther along the coast.

And so it began among the harvest workers who from that day forth spent more and more time dreaming of wealth and the ease of their lives to come. Lucas now spent his days walking between his shop in town and the homes of the harvesters, where he leaned back into family-crafted rocking chairs, sipped sweetened losa tea on breezy front porches, listened to the pernicious fears of the harvester people and gently nurtured the fragile alliance between these people and his trading community.

He admired them for their caution, for their loyalty to the grower families that stretched and strained under the unexpected conditions of these times but refused to break. And he admired them for the lazy, familial way they lived among each other without argument and without examination. So he spent more and more afternoons sitting with the men under the fragrant airy tides of the mango trees, listening to the women's concerns over the security of their work, debating with the harvesters' sons about the future security of their families. Lucas had known these men and women from childhood, had sat next to Mila's daughter and Josai's sister at school, remembered recruiting Nara and Palo to ball games in the evenings before time and routine and responsibility had descended upon them all.

He had known them. And yet he had known nothing about them, for he could honestly say he had never entered a harvester's home before his work had compelled him up the hill and along the coastline to their collection of houses that seemed to multiply and expand across the island plateau like runner-blades of grass. Roofs rose and swooned under the seasonal rains, were patched and sagged again over a web of covered walkways.

One-room bungalows had been built up and extended until they crowded and merged with the flourishing homes of other harvester families. New kitchens were built at random and marriages were finalised only after the couple had finished construction on a new branch of the husband's home (which was often shouting distance from the wife's). Occasionally a harvester's daughter would fall in love with a fisherman's son and leave the protected web of the community. Or a harvester's son with long ties to a grower's family would reveal his secret romance with that grower's daughter which would inspire a wealth of gossip and dramatic overtures but never shock or final condemnation. But for most intents and purposes, the harvester families did not encourage intimacies with the traders.

So although Lucas had spent his small island life among the pathways of these people known by their harvesting trade, it took him almost an entire harvest cycle before he was able to call each person by name. Yet from that moment at his uncle's dinner table when he had suddenly divined both the true image of his father's face and the new meaning and purpose of his life, Lucas was tireless in his dedication to winning over the harvest workers to his cause. He left his own home quickly after a breakfast of eggs and fruit, and he did not come home until the evening sky had grown dim and the heat had faded from the streets.

His wife, Rosa, believing his new commitment to work would end with the final decision of the Council, did not complain about his lengthening absences from the home. But then the decision to review the Charter was postponed again at the Council meeting.

That night, after Rohnan and Ria were asleep, Rosa poured two thin glasses of the spicy dark liquor she and Lucas had once sipped every evening after they were first married and had relied on like the cover of darkness to loosen their timid tongues and open their bodies to one another. She carried the glasses out to Lucas who sat brooding on the front porch in the swelling darkness and rolling a polished stone back and forth between the palms of his hands.

"Lucas," she said, putting her hand softly across his shifting fingers, and she handed him the glass. Then, sitting next to him on the step she asked, "What's troubling you darling?" not because she didn't know but because she suspected that he himself did not.

"I'm thinking of what to do next," Lucas said without turning towards her. He swallowed a large gulp of his drink, coughed and then stared at the remaining dark liquid swirling in the glass. "This decision by the Council to postpone again is a big blow to us."

"You'll try again next time," Rosa replied.

Sipping the drink, she tried to weave her fingers into Lucas's hand but he gripped his glass with one hand and the smooth, hard stone with the other and his grip held fast. "Harvest will come again sooner than we think, Rosa. If the harvesters decide not to trust me and take this risk, they will all go to work in the fields and everything will fall apart."

Lucas did not speak aloud his other fear — that the growers themselves might catch wind of the shifting loyalties of the harvesters and start to think of new possibilities for themselves — grow more losa on their own land, perhaps give the harvesters a larger share, cut the traders out completely and allow mainlanders to come directly to the island. They might think — no matter what the traders do, they aren't growers, they don't know losa, nor own enough land. They are nothing without us.

Rosa heard the warning in her husband's voice that

trembled like the high branches of the trees before the onset of rain, and so she said nothing. After many moments, when she sensed the safety of the spreading darkness, Rosa told him what she had come to say. "Rohnan misses you these days, Lucas. He often asks for you before bed. He wants to tell you about his work, how he helps Tomas. He wants to know why you don't sing to him and tell him your stories like you used to."

At this Lucas softened and he put a warm, heavy arm around his wife. "I know," he said. "I'm trying my best, Rosa. I'm trying to make a name for our family, secure a better life for us." He finished the last gulp of his drink and stood. "One day Rohnan will understand that I am doing all of this so that he will have a better life. His father will be a great man, someone he can be proud of…"

In the cover of darkness, Rosa sat, holding her glass unfinished in the palm of her hand. She tried to move, but it seemed as if some unspoken trepidation held her frozen in her body, and so she waited silently for the feeling to pass, watching the stars and thinking things she could not say aloud.

42

Across that same wide expanse of darkness, permeated with the smells of smoking wood fires and spicy stewed meat and resounding with the fatal creaking of cicadas, Petro leaned back in his familiar wicker chair and thought of his wife.

Would Myrium, who had remained so young and unburdened by the weight of time, even recognise the flawed, decrepit man that he had become? Would she be disappointed in him? Petro felt he knew the answer and hid his bones further in the cocoon of an old blanket he now wore almost constantly even in the heat of day. He felt heavy, as if he finally sensed the physical burden of his decades spent in mourning. *I was so different then, when we first met!* He thought to himself. *A strong, young man with land to his name and bigger dreams than anyone else knew. And light, light as air.*

He had seen her the very day she arrived on the island with the traders returning from Joon, her long hair curling like currents of water and silver eyes marking her as his future wife in a way he never could explain. Yes, she had been his from the moment he saw her standing on the dusty island path, untethered in the world in a way he had always imagined he himself might be one day. He had seen himself standing this way in his dreams, on the street of some foreign place, far from any remnants of home. In these daydreams, he had always imagined himself so confident — a man in exotic skin. A man who had broken through the expectations of his life. So when he saw this silver-eyed woman standing at the dusty crossroads of two paths, he had expected her to radiate this illusory sense of adventure which he had always coveted for himself.

Instead, he found her shaken from the long days at sea and staring down these two roads as if one was the right path that would lead her to happiness while the other was the wrong path that would lead to certain despair and she had no way of knowing which path was which.

"That path leads into town and this path goes along the hills to the homes of some of the losa growers and the Palm Losa," he had said. "Where are you headed?"

In the heavy shadows of the expanding night, Petro smiled as he remembered how his wife had looked at him in that first moment as he had imagined people might look at him on one of those foreign streets, as a man of strength and courage and adventure, and he had felt foolish at the pride that had surged in his belly at how clever he was to know the island of his birth.

If I had told her about my maps, Petro thought to himself, *it would have broken her heart.* The idea of leaving the island that she had chosen as her new home would have been too much. Better to have kept her laughing as she had at almost everything — the way he pulled at the corners of his moustache when he was thinking, the way he sipped his tea, even the way he counted the harvest crop against his fingers.

And so he forgot, didn't he? He made himself forget...an effort made easier once they had married and Myrium had moved into his bed. She had laughed there too, with unexpected grace, and he had loved her and been happy.

Petro's hands trembled as he stuffed dried leaves into his pipe and lit it with a coal he had brought from the stove. The shrivelled leaves smouldered and danced in their bowl. There was nothing but memories now. Memories of a past that could never be resurrected. The child she had borne him, a child made in her own image, had grown into a selfish woman and had forgotten him.

Now, decades downstream, Petro allowed himself to feel again the pain of his loss, to wander without time or urgency over the moments of that past life when he still held his beloved wife. In the fading chambers of his mind, Petro grasped at the memories of this elusive woman, features of his wife's face which now were distinguished from those of his daughter only in the way the blood raced in his veins.

When such sudden fits overtook him, Petro would force himself back into the empyrean lands by imagining the smell of his wife's skin — white wakes of gardenias in her footsteps, the occasional green glimpse of wild thyme. But these thoughts rarely rescued Petro from despair because the scent of Myrium eluded him, lingered in the realms of his mind and refused to invade his nostrils as they had once done, and he was forced to concede the declining potency of her memory.

The hunger that the oracle had called a Ghost had finally left him, left him empty as this family home that echoed and creaked and drowned in afternoon silences, and though he would never have dared let anyone know, he had begun sleeping in Isla's small bed because it was the only room in that house that could see him through the void of each night.

Where was she? Why had his only child left him? Petro never tried to answer these questions, only asked them again and again like a mantra he used to mark the undetectable passage of time. Where was Isla? Who would take care of him now that his bones creaked and even the taste of losa tea no longer comforted him. Had it been so awful to live in this home with him? Had it been so intolerable? He had loved her, hadn't he? He had only wanted the best for her — but she had always resisted, always been ungrateful. How had she, such a small infuriating girl, dared to leave the shelter of her island home and wander the world unprotected and alone? How had she dared to leave him? How had she dared to leave when he had not?

He had begun to dream. That was another problem. And the dreams of his waking hours were of the last remaining pathway, the last threshold still waiting for him. His own death.

Sitting on the porch of his forgotten house and the edge of his waning days, Petro suddenly looked into his hands as if they were something foreign, objects of impossible loathing. Was it day or night? Evening or morning? Had he been sitting here long? The whole night? The constant ache of his body gave no clues. Should he eat? Perhaps he would go for a walk in his fields. He was a landowner after all, a landowner with responsibilities. Under the dim light of the moon, Petro inched down the porch steps and out into the indeterminate night.

43

There were no quiet moments, and for the many months that followed Isla's trip to the desert, life seemed to race towards some imagined finish line that was always just around the corner, after some project deadline, then just beyond the stack of reports that had covered her worktable while she was away.

Still, things were exciting, weren't they? The desert people from her project village had More, and despite the old desert woman who whispered warnings steadily in Isla's mind, Isla felt certain she was doing what was right. The old woman simply hadn't understood the Philosophy of the Rising Sun. "How can they complain when they have More?" Isla said to assuage her doubts. "She is just an old woman who doesn't want things to change."

For how could Isla doubt that this was the life she had always dreamed of? She had reached a position in the Mainland Administration that she had scarcely dared imagine possible. She was working with the most progressive minds in the mainland city at the centre of the developed world, and there could be no doubt her work was making a mark.

Then Jackimo's father fell ill and talks which had been of marriage and celebrations were postponed with the new urgency of how Jackimo would move his parents down from their village to the mainland city. So Isla began to spend her evenings making arrangements, rearranging Jackimo's house — which would one day be her house too, she reminded herself again and again — to make room for his parents' furniture, and to find another housekeeper who could act as a nurse for Jackimo's father and an extra pair of hands to cook and clean and run the errands that two extra people would require.

Yet there were moments amid this frantic activity when Isla found that she had paused in the middle of some crucial activity and her mind had become lost from time. In these unforeseen, cavernous moments, Isla stared unseeing into the great void that follows all wayward beings, and this place was filled with a single question that, if it had taken shape, would have sounded something like the abyssal drone of the deep, impenetrable sea. *Why isn't this enough?* Or perhaps it would have been, *Why don't I feel happy?*

But these moments were as fleeting as the evening sun, and then Isla would blink and find she had returned to the dark solid wood floors and bright lanterns and high white ceilings and spring smells of Jackimo's house. From the window, the painted dragon would raise its regal head, and through the pale paper screens, Isla would perceive the scent of the yellow roses growing gloriously outside and she would remember the task at hand.

"Everything is happening so fast," Isla confided to Neha one evening. "I am making all these decisions, and half of the time I'm not even sure if they are what's best, or even if they are what I want. It's as if my life has taken on a momentum of its own and I can't stop it. I can't even stop for a moment and think!"

"Don't worry," Neha reassured her, clapping her hands with conviction. "Everything is going well. You have your work. You have Jackimo. As soon as all this drama with his parents settles down, things will get back to the marriage preparations. You have the perfect life, Isla. It is the life everyone dreams of."

And because she could not disagree, Isla smiled at her friend. "I know you're right, Neha. I'm just so busy, I must not be thinking clearly."

"It's good to busy," Neha reminded her, picking up her bowl of coffee again. "Being busy is how we know we're alive, how we know we're going somewhere. Just consider the other possibility." And Isla nodded because she knew boredom and remembered days that stretched out with nothing to fill them, and so she knew that what Neha said was true.

Three weeks later Isla found herself standing in a new pair of silk shoes, her shoulders pressing against the vague, empty space where Jackimo had been standing before the doors of his parents' coach had opened and he had rushed over to greet them. She watched Jackimo as he ushered his parents into his proud, urban home, answering a thousand questions at once and speaking in a voice Isla had never heard before — his voice from the mountains. She clasped her hands in front of her, as if praying for some unlikely miracle that his parents would like her, though Isla did not believe in the gods any longer, and the more violently the earthquake shook in her bones, the more rigid and still she became, so that as Jackimo's mother approached her, what Isla was sure she saw was a faint, frozen statue of a woman with a foreign smell and a thousand flaws.

And then, something entirely unexpected happened that made the earthquake tremors fall still and her eyes flood with unsummoned tears. Jackimo's mother took Isla's soft, uncertain face in the palms of her hands and, kissing both her cheeks, proclaimed in a voice that was strong and certain as the high peaks must be when they speak to the sky, "You are like our own daughter now, Isla-che."

As she spoke, the scent of thyme filled Isla's nostrils, surrounding her like a cloud descended from the high hills, and in that moment, Isla imagined she had finally come home and so she laughed with a joy she had hidden since childhood and did not speak of the tears that fell against her pillow in the empty silences of her midnight bedroom at Madame Rohal's, for how can anyone speak of the things they do not want to understand.

Still, why am I not sleeping? Isla wondered.

"It's all the excitement, dear," Madame Rohal pronounced, nodding with her pointed chin as she always did when giving advice.

"It's because of all your success, Isla," Jackimo concluded, sitting next to Neha at the coffeehouse down the street from their home. "Big ideas don't leave us to sleep, trust me. It's a good sign that your work is becoming even more significant."

At this, Neha only nodded, but when Jackimo had left the two women alone, she whispered — "It's just pre-marriage nerves, Isla. Remember what I was like last year!"

The constant stream of advice and the sheer lack of time to think sustained Isla for a time. This was everything she had always wanted, she told herself. This was her dream life, and now that it was finally real she was determined that it would make her happy.

And then there was Jackimo's mother, whose presence in

their habitually hectic mainland life was as thick as gravity and reminded Isla of those dawn days of her childhood when her father had swung her round and round through the air so that she merged with the rushing, blurring, living world while he had seemed to stand still and smiling at the centre of all things. Such memories came to her without the joy that so often accompanies nostalgia because Isla did not long to return to such happy times when her father had seemed full of paternal devotion. Instead she felt bitter that this love had been unfairly stolen from her when she was still too young to understand how much she had needed it.

Yet despite her carefully cultivated habit of running away from her own father, Isla found that she did not have to learn how to accept a mother's love or a father's loyalty. From the day they arrived, Jackimo's mother and father inhabited a welcomed place at the very centre of Isla and Jackimo's frenetic love and evening discussions over thick warm meals of soup that Jackimo's mother never allowed the servants to cook, turned again to marriage plans and Isla's own imminent move to this warm family home.

One evening, Isla arrived at Jackimo's house to find only Jackimo's mother at home. Who knows whether it was her devotion to the desert people with their stories of midnight raids and the lost children of their past, or whether it was simply the random shifting sands of her own mind that made Isla recall this untold history of the mainland kingdom.

"Is it true?" Isla asked Jackimo's mother, as she picked up a knife and a handful of chillies to chop, "...that the mainland used to take children from the outer regions to be slaves?"

Jackimo's mother looked up at Isla then, and it seemed to Isla that this woman's large blue-grey eyes which travelled across her face were more solid than the stone cliffs of her mountain home and had never been afraid.

"Of course, you are from the islands, Isla, so perhaps this evil did not reach your shores, but everyone from the outer regions knows the stories of the Lost Ones."

And the way Jackimo's mother's eyes continued to survey Isla's face made her voice fail, for she felt certain that this mountain woman had already seen — had seen from the moment they had met — something in Isla's visage that had long been hidden even from Isla herself.

Isla blinked quickly against the fiery fragrance of chillies but her silver eyes continued to burn.

44

The letter came on the first day of the new week. It was not from the desert chief, who would never have called upon the mainland for help himself, but was written and signed by his son and looked as if it had been drafted in secret under the unsteady light of a lantern or beneath the wide, black desert sky.

Many people have become ill, Isla read. *The water in the reservoir has become increasingly covered by a thick layer of red algae. The sisilus crop has not been affected and will reach the mainland markets as usual, but it is feared people in the village can no longer drink the water from the reservoir as they had begun to do, nor use it to bathe or cool their tents.*

For the next four days, Isla did nothing but work. She wrote reports to every senior scribe in her department and met with many of the most senior officials she had worked with in her years as a novice scribe. There was nothing she could do, they all assured her. No one could have predicted the spread of disease in the reservoir, and anyway, the extra water was meant for the precious sisilus crop, so coveted by mainland markets, and not for the desert people.

No, they all repeated, the mainland could not send more assistance to help those who had fallen ill from the stagnant waters. "Your projects are all great success stories," they told her. "They weren't meant to drink the water or use it to bathe or cool their tents. This was their mistake — they still do not understand the message of the Philosophy of the Rising Sun or their role in the revival of the kingdom."

"Perhaps the dam should not have been raised higher," Isla replied. "Perhaps the reservoir of water was big enough."

"Don't let a small setback shake your confidence in this work." Her colleagues told her. "You have given those people more than they have ever had. You are helping them to join the mainland. This is of utmost importance. You are changing the face of the world."

And so Isla tried to put her mind at rest. Still, the image of the old desert woman Darrah floated constantly before Isla's mind, and the platitudes and empty responses she received from her colleagues and superiors only spurred her to work harder.

Yet things continued to get worse. More letters from the village said the chief's son had fallen ill and that many of the older members of the tribe had not been strong enough to survive the disease, though none of the letters listed these elders by name.

It was then that the mainland decided to intervene, for how could the desert people contribute to mainland progress if they were all too sick to work? A medical team was despatched to the desert village with a sudden urgency, and Isla began to receive reports via the mainland messengers that crisscrossed the outer regions. The reports described the crisis in the desert in predictable terms — Isla, as the senior scribe of the region, was informed of how many were sick, how many had already succumbed to the algae poisoning, how many would be able to recover.

The reports listed how much water must be drained from the stagnant reservoir and how long it would be until the water in the reservoir was restored to its maximum capacity. Later, reports marked the decline in productivity due to the sudden labour shortage — which was not bad enough to alarm anyone in the Central Administration — and reiterated the desert chief's requests for further growth as soon as the sickness was under control.

The reports spared Isla the sight of the dead, carried to their shallow desiccating graves on biers hung with coloured strings, but she could imagine well enough the sons and brothers and fathers marching on wide, silent feet through the ageless sands while the women filled the scorpion tent with wails that rose above the wind. At night, her dreams were filled with the sight of a wall that was the edifice of the Rising Sun and also the side of the desert reservoir. In these dreams, the wall grew and grew, higher and higher, and the water expanded out and out and out to the desert horizon, and even in this shadowy dream world, Isla understood that this enormous beast would never stop growing, would never be satiated.

Isla wished she could go to the desert herself, but she had so much work to do in the city she could not to be spared. This was the mainland's reasoning.

Finally, against all dictums of the Central Administration and against the wisdom of her years of training, Isla sent a message to the desert chief. "Water will continue to flow from the river and it will be enough. Please do not raise the wall of the reservoir, for increasing the size of the dam seems only to bring greater suffering to your people." It was with trepidation that Isla sealed the letter and handed it to the mainland messenger who stood in her doorway, and after he had gone, Isla sat at her desk waiting for her hands to stop trembling.

What am I doing? Isla asked herself again and again. *What business did I have in the desert?*

The letter she received in return several weeks later — the first written by the desert chief himself — should have put her mind at rest. *The river was enough for our ancestors, Madame Scribe*, the chief had written, *but our needs have grown and it is no longer enough for us. The heightening of the dam and the enlargement of the reservoir will continue as planned.*

There was no doubt in the direct tone of the desert chief, and Isla remembered that once, it had been said that this chief had never felt fear. And, looking at the letter in her hand that smelled of turmeric and dry heat, Isla tried to remember that the dam was not a beast, and that it was only natural for things to continue to grow. She remembered that it was the Philosophy of the Rising Sun which had taught mainlanders (who had then taught the desert people) how to progress, how to use their time wisely, how to dream of an age of infinite wealth and happiness for all. *After all,* Isla thought to herself, *how can I blame the desert people? This wanting More is in our very nature.*

And yet, despite these assurances, something in Isla's mind had awoken — an old seeker whose questions may have been dressed up in new words but were essentially the same. And so against her will, Isla began to wonder about her own work. *Am I helping?* She found herself asking as she walked down the Grand Avenue of the Administrative District. *Why is it so important for these places to join the mainland? Why is it so important for everyone to be the same?*

She passed the Great Fountain where the goddesses

blew their watery wishes in the four directions of the kingdom a voice in her mind called out to her. *No one can have More without giving something else up*, and she wondered whether there wasn't something to this old island saying after all. She stood in Neha's studio among the artwork she had always perceived as the most innovative. *Is doing something different, just to be different, enough? Does Newness actually give something meaning?*

And because her mind could not answer these questions as quickly and confidently as it used to, Isla took her questions to the people she trusted most.

45

The coffeehouse where she met Neha, Abé and Jackimo was the oldest in the district — at least that was its claim. Its ceiling sagged into the reliable support of thick dark beams painted with the sign of the dragon, the mark of the rose and other symbols too ancient for the living to recognise.

The weather had turned cold, and Isla peeled her hands from the soft gloves and cradled the bowl of coffee gratefully between her palms. The coffeehouse was busy — more so because the outside seating had been abandoned to the falling leaves that spread according to the whims of the autumnal winds. Around her, the coffee district beat with the same sacred pulse of the city's heart, groups of banking merchants sat, pulling the smoke from their water pipes and nodding towards Jackimo as they parted company.

In the corner, a group of novice scribes sat huddling over their coffees, speaking of the frantic day. They had glanced at Isla as she stepped in, shaking the cold from her robe, and Isla saw in their eyes the unmistakable words she had so often repeated to herself back in those days — *if only I were a senior scribe* — and the longing of these words fell on her like a memory she wished she could now live up to.

Isla sat at the low table on a pile of ochre cushions that held the same scent of racing thoughts and unrestrained energy that pulsed in the air of the place. She sat next to Jackimo, holding her coffee and leaning against the steady wooden frame of the wall, waiting for Neha and Abé to arrive. They were late as usual, and arrived in a gust of wind from the open door that swept the candle flames on their table.

The light leapt up onto Jackimo's face and for a moment, Isla was distracted from her shadowy thoughts and noticed how handsome this man was with his clear, earnest eyes, his clean dark hair. And for no reason at all, she remembered again how Jackimo had been the first one to recognise that her ancestors had come from the mountains. He had seen another side of her — the face of her mother. He had always known, she thought with satisfaction, that she was never supposed to be on a small island isolated by the solitary sea.

It wasn't until Neha and Abé held two steaming bowls of coffee in their hands that Isla spoke the words that had haunted her sleep — "I've lost my purpose," she told them. "I've forgotten why I am doing all of this."

They listened as Isla told of the stagnation of the desert dam, of the algae that had caused the illness that had led to the death of the desert chief's son and the majority of the elders in the village. She did not speak of the old desert woman, since she did not know for certain whether she had fallen victim to this mercurial plague, but always the woman's face wavered like a phantom before her silver eyes.

"We're working for More, Isla." They seemed to speak with one voice. "We work for more power to make the decisions we think are best, more money so we can buy the things we need. More, so that one day we won't have to worry about the future. So we can be free and happy."

They said these things with confidence, as if they were the most obvious things in the world.

"I just keep thinking," Isla found herself saying, "we are supposed to be progressing, moving forward. That's what the Rising Sun proclaims. The More we have, the better off we will be. Innovation and hard work will take us there. But what if people aren't better off? What if, after all my work, after all the mainland's efforts, people in that village are actually worse off than they were before?"

"That's absurd, Isla." It was Jackimo's hand on her shoulder, trying to find words of comfort, words that would bring her back to the mainlander woman he knew. "Think of how much you've helped these people! With all these extra crops to sell, they have entered the mainland kingdom. They have been given a chance to make More of their lives — just like you always say you wanted on the island!"

"It's opportunity you've given them, Isla," Neha added. "Freedom to move forward. After all, who wouldn't want the life we have?"

"Yes," Jackimo agreed. "The Philosophy of the Rising Sun brings us all great freedom — freedom to live where we want to live, to buy whatever we want...to have the best of everything. We have the freedom to live without limitations. The freedom to live out our dreams."

He had pulled her to him then, against the warm, steady side of his body, and this gentleness made Isla close her mind against the doubts that had spawned an army there. She sighed and smiled over at Neha and Abé. They sat across from her in their dark, evening robes, Abé's collar rimmed with a single line of gold thread, Neha's earrings sparkling against the candlelight.

They looked so happy, so confident and at ease, and Isla remembered that it had not always been so easy for them. *And yet here we are,* Isla thought to herself. She remembered that she had sat in this same coffeehouse one evening many years ago when Neha had been distraught after Abé had ended their relationship and she had been convinced her life was falling apart.

And they had met here again, a year later, when Neha had announced that Abé had returned and had asked her to marry him.

The four friends had sat together across so many tables, over so many bowls of coffee and water pipes and worries about their futures. They had celebrated Abé's promotion to senior historian at the Institute of Higher Learning, and Jackimo's successes as he moved up the ranks of the Central Bank.

They had mourned the loss of Neha's mother, and then Abé's father. They had discussed the details of Jackimo's parents' move to the mainland and had encouraged Neha when sales of her artwork were down...and then cheered when sales rose again.

Most of all, they had made Isla feel like she was no longer a stranger in a hostile foreign world. They had made the mainland her home and because she trusted these people with her life, Isla listened to the warning in the air that was the sneaking dread of change, and she did not speak the force of her doubts that she felt sure would divide her from these people she loved so greatly. Things would be okay in the end. *After all,* she said to herself, *who wouldn't want the opportunities we have? Who wouldn't want the life we lead on the mainland?*

Isla was thinking these very thoughts on her way back from the coffeehouse that night, when she rounded the corner of Sahel Street and saw a man with curly dark hair standing in the unpredictable winds of the season. The air tossed his long coat against his legs and his glances flew here and there. He was holding a single piece of paper, which he gripped in both his hands that were bare even at this time of year. He looked up the street, where the cobbled lane whispered its secrets and gave up its fallen leaves to dance in the air. And then he looked towards her and Isla stopped still in her shoes and her own gloved hands flew to her mouth.

For a moment that was long and short and without time they stared at each other, and what passed between them was all the years of words that could never be spoken. And then, something in Tomas changed, a welling in his eyes, or a sinking in the familiar folds of his face, and it reminded Isla of the way he had looked at her once before, on the day he had carried his father's bier upon his shoulder and she had walked beside him in white, watching him from the corner of her eye.

At once, Isla let out a strangled cry of despair that should have belonged to the island but which she had to release instead onto the lonely foreign lanes of the mainland — because this was her Tomas who had come all the way from the island to find her, and she knew this truth with a certainty that had no name and from the infinite things Tomas said with his eyes. Her father was dead.

PART 3: THE ISLAND

46

The island hadn't changed. And yet everything felt different. Isla walked the paths of her childhood as if in a dream, nostalgia driving her down old forgotten walkways, around the wide banyan trees she had once viewed as friends, along sea coasts where she had whispered her naïve dreams to the sea, hidden her hopes in the unreliable pockets of salty wind. She marvelled at each cliff, each mountainous tree, not quite believing it was still there, right where she had left it, when she had changed so much.

Isla was surprised at how good it felt to be home, to wave at Jon the fishmonger who came out from behind his shop table with deeper creases around the eyes and hair gone completely white but who spoke in the same voice when he called her by name and shook her shoulders, "It is you, Isla. It is you!" To call out from the steps of Dari's Café — "Do you have any sweet cakes today, Dari?" — and watch as a heavier, sun-browned Dari stepped into the front of the café, disbelief written across the thick wild eyebrows that framed his dark eyes.

Dari had not spoken a word, but he had taken Isla into

his chest and had held her so tight that Isla remembered at last what it meant to be home, and when he finally released her and they looked each other in the eye, they realised they were both crying. But where others had hugged Isla even while chiding her that... "It's been too long, girl, too long that you were away...", Dari had simply smiled and said, "Welcome home, Isla-ja. We've missed you." And then, as she stepped off the front steps and out into the sunshine, he had called after her, "Come by tomorrow, girl, and you will have your sweet cakes!" Yes, Isla was glad to be home, to know there was this place, her island, that would always be here waiting to embrace her whenever she wanted to return.

And yet there were moments that sprung up like riptides, yanking her below the placid flow of the day, and she would suddenly feel like a stranger, lost in her homeland. The day after her arrival she began talking to a group of women on the market street, and Isla had clapped her hands with enthusiasm, and Lott had looked at her with a strange, suspicious eye and asked — "Why are you clapping like a fool, Isla? Just listen to what I'm telling you," before she proceeded relaying her gossip. Later, Isla had asked about the Co-operative's view of this year's losa crop, knowing that few islanders could resist discussing the details of the approaching losa harvest. But the crowd had grown quiet and moved away and someone had whispered, "There is hardly a Co-operative to speak of these days since the divide between the traders and growers. Haven't you heard?" And Isla had shook her head, feeling lost and out of place among the local news she no longer knew anything about.

And then there was Tomas.

He had spoken solidly enough on the boat when she had asked him specific questions, but Isla had been nervous at seeing him again after all these years. She had felt so confused as she looked at his face, so familiar and yet so foreign. And so she had wrapped herself in the memory of her father and had kept back the words she longed to speak to him.

For his part, Tomas had not asked her anything at all — not of her mainland life, nor the years that had passed between them. The first morning at sea he had said, "Your hair is different," without taking his eyes from the horizon, and Isla had touched her straightened, oiled hair and remembered when it had been wild and had flown in her face with the winds.

They were strangers to each other, and the distance became more painful, or perhaps simply more obvious, once they reached the island that was their home. As the boat glided to dock, Tomas had tied the bow and secured the vessel to the side of the wall. Then, as if he had sailed every day of his life, he had jumped to the dock and stretched his arms up into the blinding sun and yawned. "Ahhh, good to be home."

"Yes it is," Isla had replied, but Tomas had looked at her with surprise, and Isla had understood that he had not been talking about her. What was this place? What was this island without Tomas by her side? Isla had never considered that they might never recover from that night in the underwater cave, that they may never understand each other again.

The day after her arrival, Isla spent the afternoon sitting on the front porch of her forgotten house with Eva, sipping cup after cup of losa tea. "You don't know how much I've missed this," Isla said.

Eva smiled, patting her sleeping baby against her chest. In the losa terraces before them, her two oldest boys chased each other screaming and laughing easily. "The funeral was nice, Isla. Everyone was there," Eva said, watching her friend. "We tried to wait for you. Tomas left the night we heard. He wanted you to be there, to be able to say goodbye, give your da your old bands and light his fire, but there just wasn't time..."

"It's okay," Isla said. "I know the mainland is far away. It's okay. I didn't need to say goodbye."

Eva looked at her, and Isla remembered what it was like to live among people who knew you so well you could not feign even courage before them. "It is nice to have you back for awhile," Eva said, looking at Isla over the crown of her baby's head, and Isla thought how different Eva looked now, her eyes calm like the wide sky, so much older, so much an island woman.

For the first time in their relationship, Isla was the one having the adventures. She was no longer the awkward, wild girl watching from the sidelines as the beautiful, confident Eva ran beneath willow trees with boys, snuck out of her bedroom window at night, shared smoke and spiced liquor at the heart of midnight and recounted the tales of adventure to Isla the next day. Now, Isla was the one with the adventures to tell, the exotic life away from island monotony. Yet as Isla sat in the wicker chair, thinking these disloyal thoughts, all she could dredge up was a strange awkwardness, a silence about the life she was leading which suddenly didn't feel as important as she had expected.

They talked about Eva's growing family, about Isla's father's funeral, about Isla's plans to sell the house where she had been born and the weeks of work it was going to take to clear it. They talked while the sun sank towards the surface of the sea, falling on the porch at a harsh slant that made the women squint and shield their eyes. They talked as Eva fed her daughter and the boys ate the snacks Isla brought from the kitchen.

"It's so nice to be home," Isla sighed into the thick afternoon air. "So nice to come back and know this place will always be the same..." Over her shoulder at the edge of her porch, the hibiscus tree had grown wild and Isla pulled one of the large red blossoms from its branches and twirled the stem between her fingers.

"A lot has changed while you've been away, Isla," Eva said, eyeing her quietly.

"I know, I know. There has been some squabble in the Co-op. And everyone is older...Eva you have to catch me up on all the gossip. I feel like a fool not knowing what's going on!" Isla said, laughing. "What about the boatman, for instance? Is he still coming every year as usual?"

"He was coming several times a year," Eva nodded, "but he hasn't been back since Madame Prenai died last year."

"Madame Prenai died!" Isla couldn't believe it. "What has happened to the Palm Losa?"

"Nothing. It's just sitting there, empty." Eva shrugged. "No one has thought too much about the house and, anyway, the land is still in dispute because of what's happening in the Council."

Isla tried to press Eva for information on the dispute in the Council, but Eva just laughed and shook her head. "You know me, Isla. I don't understand these things. Never cared to. You should talk to Lucas — he's right in the thick of it... tried to drag Tomas in too. But you know Tomas, he's far too gentle for all that fighting."

"What would Tomas have to do with an argument between traders and growers?" Isla asked.

At this, Eva's eyes darted out to her boys who were scrambling up the mango tree not far away. "Not too high boys," she called. "Rafa, help your brother." Then, she turned back to Isla with a strength in her eyes.

"Lucas thinks Tomas was doing trading work when he was away from the island. He was away for many years, you know Isla, after you left. It's only in the last few years that he's settled back down here."

"Away? What do you mean away?"

At this, Eva simply shrugged. "I don't know where. I let him tell me what he wants. You'll have to ask him yourself."

Isla's eyes fell on the bright petals of the hibiscus she still held in her hands so that Eva would not see the sudden tears that had blurred her vision. Who could say how, but in that moment, Isla understood that loyalties had shifted and things that had once seemed so unchangeable, so unquestionable, had changed after all.

47

Isla woke in her bed the next morning and for a brief moment, saw her room without memory. Sunlight careened from the window across her bare legs where she had kicked the quilt away. On the shelves next to the door, an old doll slumped in its dusty blue dress against the line of books. A small wooden table stood in its usual place in the corner of the room, although it was missing the chair.

Isla closed her eyes and breathed in the familiar humid air of the island morning and a thought came to her as if it had waited for just the right moment to approach — *everything is okay*. Isla could only think of one word that could name this feeling and her lips moved, whispering into the air this feeling. Peace. And when the word was spoken she knew she had not felt such a thing in a long, long time.

But such certainties do not last, and before Isla could grasp what this might mean, the feeling was gone, and memory returned her to the bedroom she had slept in every night of her childhood, listening to the sounds of her father shuffling in the evening lamplight, waiting for the faint puffing sounds of her father lighting his pipe. And with this memory, Isla collapsed back into her responsibilities, and she sighed and swung her legs off the side of the bed, because she was no longer a child and she had work to do.

She began in the living room, opening languid, dust-sealed windows to the living sea breezes, flooding the room with the strong, encouraging morning light that held off the shivering images Isla's mind could conjure even in mid-day, of her father old and sick and alone in this house.

Isla had just finished sweeping under the long table and wiping a cloth over its dusty surface when the island women began to arrive. They came in twos and threes, carrying plates of food, cakes and vegetable soups from the bounty of their gardens.

No one mentioned the devastation of Isla's father's garden, and Isla did not ask although she was sure they all knew what had happened in her home even if she did not. Instead, the women entered the house without knocking, knowing that no man lived there to take offence, and each pair of feet that stepped over the threshold brought hands that busied at cleaning and straightening and reheating the growing mountain of food and boiling pot after pot of losa tea.

The women came and went in waves so regular that Isla thought it impossible that all this happened without some hidden coordination, but she stopped trying to resist when one woman who had worked the losa rows with her father since Isla had been a small child told her in an uncompromising tone that, "look girl, do you think you're the only one who knows death?"

The next day was the same. While Isla scrubbed the wooden floorboards and sorted through the collection of rusting pots and pans, several women had tackled her father's bedroom, so that by the time Isla looked up, the bed had been stripped and all of her father's clothes tied into sacs to be washed and redistributed. Curtains were pulled from windows and scrubbed and wrung out to dry over the side railings of the porch. Old sheets that Petro had crumpled and torn and heaped in the last years of his self-imposed confinement were taken from the faded house balanced on the confident heads of women who returned the next day with these same sheets in mended stacks smelling clean and new.

In the evenings, after the children were asleep, Eva would wander down to the house and sit on the floor holding a cup of losa tea while Isla sorted through piles of her father's old insect collections and thick files of family records going back to the early days of losa growing on their land. So, Eva was also there when Isla found a small box of her mother's things — things her father had kept and held during desperate days when he found himself alone with a small daughter and the future had still seemed so uncertain.

In the box, Isla found a white night gown which looked so small in the quiet lamp light as she held it up between her hands. There was also a thick notebook whose pages were blank except for one sheet which held a sketch of her mother that Jayan had done and signed just after she and Petro had married.

"She looks so much like you!" Eva said, and Isla found herself staring at the image of that face that was her mother and remembering suddenly that Jackimo had recognised the mountains in her eyes, and remembering also the way his mother had looked at her when she had spoken of the Lost Ones.

In the close light of the lamp, Isla held this picture of her mother's face and began in an unsteady voice to tell Eva about the mountain people who looked like her and like her mother. "I meant to ask father about it," she said, "when I came back."

She paused and listened to the crickets sing in their high rusty voices that echoed like a wall of sound, and she heard herself say, "Now I've lost them both, so I suppose I will never know..."

After Eva had gone, Isla hovered over the plates of food on the table, wiping invisible crumbs, collecting bowls of soup and filling the empty house with the comforting sounds of normal life. Then she brought a cup of losa tea out onto the porch and sat in the rising stillness that was so unlike the high energy of the day. It wasn't often that Isla simply sat without the buzzing of work and worries to distract her. In fact, Isla couldn't recall the last time her mind had emptied in this strange way. With nothing to do, no reports to write or work to complete, she felt at loose ends, adrift in the sea of the world.

And though there was fear and uncertainty, Isla felt something open up and suddenly she found that there was space to breathe. In that moment, between doubt and loneliness, a small thought came to Isla — *what if things are not as I have taken them to be?*

She listened to this thought as the breeze gently shook the leaves above her head, and she watched the sanguine light of the moon as it rested against the ground that was her land now — her responsibility — and she remembered what Tomas had said to her about his own responsibility to the lighthouse in the days after his own father had passed to the sea. She listened to the insects creaking in their hidden places and the birds that called in indecipherable melodies between the trees.

For a moment, as brief and delicate as starlight, Isla saw the house and the land without the eyes of her childhood, and she glimpsed the beauty of it and wondered why she had been so desperate to leave the warm peace of this home.

And then, as if to answer, Isla remembered the last time she had seen her father. The memory pinched her awake with its cruel memory — her father desperate, her own face red with fury and tears. He would have said anything to keep her from leaving the island, she knew, but back then she hadn't understood why. She was only leaving for a year, she had told him. She just wanted to see the world.

Isla understood so many more things now — things that he must have foreseen then — that she may never come back. That once you set off on a new path, that path changes you. That the current of life has a force of its own. She remembered the look of him as he stared at her with his red eyes. She remembered the look of the room, the heat of her cheeks, the sound of her feet pacing against the wooden floor. She had looked at him and cried, "All I want is for someone to show me the way...I need someone who can tell me what I should do with my life. But how can I ask you? You don't know any more than I do!"

She had been desperate then too. But now, looking back across the waters of so many years, she no longer felt the white, trembling anger nor the weight of injustice that had chased her off this island that was her home.

Isla breathed in the fading scent of nocturnal smoke and felt only a spreading silence that rippled far out into the darkness and could not be destroyed. She wondered now if perhaps there were no answers to such questions, no sharp clarity to find in still waters, no right path or wrong path to take. In these shadowy moments there seemed only her own riotous thoughts rolling over and over themselves in the constantly shifting tides.

48

Tomas awoke for several mornings with a sinking premonition that he had imagined Isla's return — as he had done in his mind for so many years. Had it been a dream, all those long days on the liminal sea, his fumbling awkwardness amongst the sophisticated crowds of the mainland streets, Isla's look of shock and then despair when she had finally found him standing at her doorstep so many years too late?

Had there been love in her eyes, sudden like the lightning he had longed for? But then, Tomas thought, what was love after so many years? A tepid nostalgia for what was long past, long forgotten. He was no longer such a fool as to think otherwise.

So for the first few days after Isla's return, Tomas found himself lying on his bed under the soft morning blankets that had come from his life in the Merchant City, his mind replaying over and over the events of his recent voyage. She had looked smaller than he had remembered her, as if the bustle of mainland life had drained her of the powerful, charging confidence of her youth. This is what Tomas thought of most — how his strong, wild-haired Isla had been replaced by the small, sleek-haired woman standing on the grey cobbles of the mainland street, and he had realised in his heart the sadness of the truth — he did not know her.

You did your duty, he told himself during these morning battles. *You tried to bring her back in time, but how could you control the whipping winds that harnessed that damn boat to the same point underneath the night sky for three days on your way to the mainland? How could you have changed the heat of the island? Islanders are always sent to sea the morning after their death? Isla must have known she would never see her father again. It was her own choice to stay away.*

Tomas told himself all of these things, and for the first time he felt grateful he had been witness to his own father's passing, that he had held his father's hand, carried his father's bier and now he would never have to look back. Tomas had felt his life begin to flow in time with the island again after so many years away.

But then Petro had died, and Tomas had found himself thrown back into the murky waters of responsibility to his past. He had expected, then, for things to change. He had returned the woman of his constant dreams to the island in the hull of his boat, that same predictable vessel he had worked so hard to build for the very purpose of fleeing her memory. As the island rose into sight, the morning clouds had cleared and Tomas had seen the true colours of his home. He had stepped onto the dock, held his hand out for Isla who had climbed ashore on uncertain legs. But things had not changed as he had expected.

Instead Tomas went back to his steady life, rising at dawn to extinguish the lighthouse flame, dozing again as the birds and monkeys woke and called to each other from the trees. In the mornings and evenings he worked in his garden. Sometimes he wandered into town to buy fish and talk with friends. On certain afternoons when the sky was clear and sun at its strongest, he would glide out with his small canoe and dive for oysters since it never hurt to have a box of pearls hidden — just in case.

Rohnan usually visited him in the afternoons, and after they spent time talking about school, Tomas continued teaching Lucas's son to train gulls as his own father had once taught him. And on evenings when the moon was bright, Tomas walked the coastal path along the ridge, as he had become accustomed to doing, until he came to the house above the silver mangroves, knowing that the oracle would be waiting for him with a cooked meal and easy conversation. It was not as it had once been between them, so awkward and Tomas full of fear. Instead Tomas and the oracle found that age and time had softened them both, and Tomas began to feel that, if he had lost his father, then at least there was the oracle to offer advice and teach him how to live.

The first afternoon of his return, Rohnan had come to proudly confirm that he had "visited the gulls and lit the lighthouse flame every day while you were away Tomas-da." And he had smiled and put his arm around the boy's bony shoulders, knowing that he would get on with his life.

On the first evening of his return, Eva had wandered up to his house. He had seen her from the garden and had called to her, "I'm here Eva," his knees stained with earth as he stood.

"So you brought Isla back!" Eva had said. "Does she seem well? Will she stay long?" And Tomas had surprised himself by saying, "She's a different person, Eva. I don't know that woman anymore." Then he had added, "I'm sure she will not stay long. She is a mainlander now."

"Isla will never be a mainlander," Eva had scolded him, swinging her daughter onto her other hip. She had paused for a moment, watching Tomas return to the row of tomato plants that were coming into bloom, and when she realised he had spoken all that he would say, she said, "Well, I'm off then," but she had touched his shoulder as she passed and she had let her fingers linger to speak the words she could not say, and Tomas had understood.

And yet after Eva had wandered back down the path, Tomas found himself blinded by memories of Isla. And most tantalising of them, the day he had woken up with her in his arms. It came to him unbidden, as memories of her had always done, creeping upon him when he wasn't standing guard or following him into his dreams. It was the day after they had put his da to sea, the day they had spent lying hidden in the grasses staring up at the clouds and feeling happy simply to feel the touch of each other's skin.

At some point he had felt Isla sigh and something very deep inside of him had trembled with a joy he felt could not belong to him, a joy that was almost fear, and his longing for her in that moment was so fierce that as the ripples of sound settled he lay without breathing lest it overpower his better judgement. For now, he knew, he must be satisfied to lay quietly with her under the wide wide sky. After a time he felt her breathing shift, and he knew she had fallen asleep, and still he had lingered in that borderland of awareness unwilling to abandon the feel of her body against his to the oblivion of sleep. And then he too had slept for a time and had awoken to the sensation of her moving away from him. He had cracked one eye, reached out to feel the rumpled sticky cotton of her dress against her waist. "I'd better go," she had said, but he had pulled her back to him and had been surprised when she came so willingly. "I know, but father will be looking for me soon."

Her words had brought back to Tomas, like a wave crashing down on him, the image of his own empty home, and he had shut his eyes and rubbed his hands across his face. "Oh Tomas!" she had said, because she knew him. "I hate the thought of you going back to your place alone! I wish I didn't have to go back... I wish..." her words had hung in the air, and an awkwardness had risen like a sudden heat for they both knew it was too soon to speak the next words aloud.

"It's okay, Isla," Tomas had said quietly at last. "That's how it is now. I'll be okay." But still she had lingered, not believing him.

He had helped her up from the grass then, because he knew he must. Helped her tame her wild streaming hair into a knot at the nape of her neck. He had felt his confidence draining from him, and so he had not tried to kiss her goodbye but had merely squeezed her hand and then set off down the road towards the lighthouse that had become his. But after a moment he had heard the miraculous sound of her footsteps coming after him like an echo of his own wild hopes, and he had turned to find his beautiful Isla fling her arms around his neck and press her warm mouth against his. Then she had held his face in both hands, staring at him with her bright silver eyes. "I see you, Tomas-ja," she had said, and he wondered still what she had meant and what she had seen.

In the tepid heat of his garden, Tomas squeezed his eyes shut tight and groaned. Why did he torment himself with these memories? Why did his mind remind him again and again of things that were not meant to be. These memories of her, of them, of the short days when they were happy — before they began to fight and before she left him — they were like treasures, pearls stored in a tiny box in the cave of his mind that he took out and rolled like rare delicacies across his tongue.

That evening, like all the others of that remarkable year, Tomas climbed the lighthouse stairs and sat on its roof-like ledge, breathing in the cool sea air and watching his mind cartwheel and spin and slowly, slowly settle like a bird on the water until it was calm and clear as the clearest, calmest day at sea. He listened to the crash of the sea, the wind of the world as it entered and left his body, the silence that penetrated sound. And when his mind became still, Tomas looked into himself as eyes peer into the depths of water, and he searched for the mystery of his life. It was an uncommon stillness he found that evening, for often his mind would not settle and his heart would race with the sensations of the world, but sometimes, sometimes, as this night, Tomas would see a glimmer of peace, a stillness beyond himself and his island.

In these rare moments that stood out like pearls in his life of frustration and sadness, Tomas would see that there was space behind and above and beneath his thoughts. And it stretched out and out and out... *Know who you are, Tomas, and who you are not*, the oracle had said, and in these rare moments Tomas knew that he was not the person he thought he was. These thoughts, these feelings of sadness, anger, regret, did not belong to him. They stood apart like ships sailing past the lighthouse, like the waves that rose and fell but could never express the depths of the sea. In these rare moments, Tomas felt the space that surrounded him and he sank out into its depths and sighed with strange relief as the Tomas he thought he was fell away and he was finally only himself.

For several mornings after his return, Tomas awoke with a sinking premonition that he had imagined Isla's return. Yet there was a second woman who had returned to the island of her birth, although she had arrived with less fanfare, and that too amid the dawning shadows that had always marked her existence. She was the oracle's daughter, and she had returned to the ambivalent island of her birth after a decade and more of training to assume the responsibilities of the position to which she had been born.

By coincidence, or perhaps by fate, the first islander to detect her presence even before the hull of her boat found the sandy shore of the island was Tomas. As was his habit, Tomas had risen before dawn and climbed the long wrapping stairs of the lighthouse to the flame that was still glowing in the morning darkness. As the first light broke the sky, he extinguished the flame and had been about to descend the precarious steps when a figure in white caught his eye. Close at sea in a small flat boat, a woman glided through the calm waters.

Even from this distance, Tomas felt certain that he knew this woman, and yet he was equally sure he had never seen her before. Her hair was knotted at the nape of her neck in the island way, yet her skin was pale unlike all islanders who lived their waking hours under the tempestuous sun. The feeling that rose in his heart as he watched this woman was so powerful that Tomas was sure the woman would turn her head and look towards him as he stood atop the lighthouse. But the boat passed beyond the mangroves and around the corner of the land, and she did not look back.

49

The oracle was not a saviour, nor was she an embodiment of some goddess sent to the island to enlighten its inhabitants. She was not a prophet, for she had nothing particular to foretell. The oracle was a healer. Many islanders came to the oracle to heal their physical pain, and because she came from a long line of women who had lived on the island all of their lives, the oracle gave them seeds that drove out parasites, juices that cooled raw burns, oils that eased digestive fires and all manner of island herbs that would calm fevers, anxieties, midnight fears and prolonged lethargy.

But this was not the oracle's true calling. The oracle was a healer of suffering. Her true purpose was to understand the nature of suffering, which spread its roots in the mind, to know the possibility of its cessation, and to prescribe a program of healing which was called *the path*.

For as many generations as any islander could recall, the island had been home to an oracle who always had one daughter — though islanders never spoke of how but looked suspiciously at their men whenever an oracle became pregnant or announced her new birth. The oracle raised her daughter, always naming her Althea, and when her daughter had reached the age of maturity and wisdom, the transition was made and, it was said, the ageing oracle disappeared into the folds of spaces and time.

There were many stories of the oracle-line, myths that few islanders now heard spoken. Stories of powerful women who raised still-born infants from the dead. Stories of illicit love between the oracle and certain island men. But these stories stretched back into the dark ages beyond the sight of generations and anyway, no one on the island would have associated the quiet older women who lived against a cliff by the groves of silver mangroves, who came to town for fish and losa tea twice a month and spoke in a natural human voice, with such wild, magical stories.

The oracle had faded on the island, faded from the people she was meant to heal, distanced by time and insufficient training from the spiritual truths she was meant to nurture and keep alive. As a girl, the oracle had seen the islanders moving away from her mother. She had watched as the growth and cultivation of losa had consumed all of the islanders' attention, seen as her mother had struggled to remind them of the inner world that was of life and the spirit and the true source of happiness.

But she had also seen what her mother had not — that the skills of the oracle had declined over the generations. There were so many questions that her oracle mother could not answer, so many experiences she herself had had during their nightly meditations that her oracle mother could not explain.

"What training could she have given me?" the oracle found herself saying to her own daughter many years later. "All I know are the things that I learnt from her and the days

I have spent on this earth with myself. I cannot teach all that you will need to know. You will renew the island, Althea. You will bring the deep truths back again from the mountains to this island so that people will know again the path to happiness and the way to their true selves."

"I don't want to go, mother." Althea — which had once been her own name — had looked at her with large dark eyes. "I'm afraid." And the oracle had forced the sadness from her mouth and said to her daughter, "I know you are afraid. Be afraid, but go anyway."

Many years had passed between mother and daughter. Many many years of moons.

And then one morning, the oracle heard the creaking of a door and in the kitchen of their small house stood Althea bathed in the white light of the oracle, and the old mother stood still in her nightgown in a flood of tears, teetering between a great joy and a sudden embarrassment that she had not felt her daughter's coming.

"I'm home mother," the young oracle said, and seeing the paralysis of her ageing mother's voice, she ran to her across the room and buried her face against her mother's neck and held her as tight as the wind that blasted over the cliffs while her mother stroked her dark hair.

They had tea that morning in the wide, generous sunshine of the front garden. The young oracle was famished from her long, frugal days at sea and ate her mother's flatbread as if she were making up for all the years away from home spent eating foreign foods and yearning for warm sandy soil and the high fragrances of losa in bloom.

For lunch, they ate fish cooked in soft oil and sour herbs and the old mother looked up from her worn kitchen pans to feel her daughter's warmth next to her, chopping vegetables and crushing herbs for the meal. How she had missed this beautiful girl. She was the same, even in the mantle of the oracle — still wrinkling her nose as she crushed the herbs against the sides of the wooden mortar bowl. Still that dark freckle under the corner of her right eye that she had always told her daughter was a beauty mark — "A star fell from the sky one evening when you were very little and it landed right against your cheek while you lay sleeping and made that mark there, Althea" — and she had almost believed it herself.

In the garden, the two women sat eating their fish. "Were you okay?" the mother asked. "Just tell me, was I right to send you away?"

The young oracle looked at her mother, and for the first time, saw that her mother had not always known the right thing to do. Even as the oracle, there had been doubt. The mother she had known as a young girl had always seemed so strong, never cried, never expressed that all was not well.

Yet here she was, an old woman now with all the worries and fears and sadness at being separated from her only daughter flooding like the rising tide to her face. What could she do but take her mother's hands in hers and look into her warm eyes with all the conviction an oracle could feel and say, "I'm okay, mother. I missed you, but I was always okay."

"There is so much I need to tell you," her mother said. "News from the island — so much has happened while you were away, and it is up to you now to try to guide things right." She paused and her gaze trailed out to the sea.

And then the mother looked into her daughter's dark eyes that were so much like the girl's father's and said, "Tell your old mother, then, what you have learned at the foot of the mountains. You must teach me all that you know, for I have felt a great yearning my whole life for the things my own mother could not teach me."

So under the canopy of whistling birds and the buzzing insects, and as she tore bread and tasted its familiar sweetness, the young oracle began her story.

50

Tomas would forever remember that day for the yellow dress she wore and the way her hair fell wildly about her shoulders like the untamed vines of the jungle. It was the way he always pictured her.

Now she came towards him, dress hiked up to reveal her slender legs and bony knees as she marched through the underbrush on what had once been a well-worn path between her house and his. Small branches that had looked soft and pliable from a distance tore at her legs, making her journey much more arduous and painful than she had planned, and so when Isla finally reached the clearing where Tomas stood between his garden and the lighthouse, her words came with the fire of these thousand tiny scratches. "Why haven't you come to see me? You think I'm a stranger now because I've been away? That I have nothing to do with you anymore? Were you never going to tell me that you'd left the island too?!"

The words hung in the air like a thread that could unravel the cloth, and Tomas turned to the small, dark haired boy who had leapt up at the sudden sound of Isla's voice. "Rohnan, this is Isla," he told the boy. "We're going to have a talk, so why don't you go on home for today and come back tomorrow."

"But what about the gulls?" the boy's face fell. "You said you would help me teach them some new tricks."

"We'll have to do that tomorrow instead," Tomas said, and then he kneeled to face the boy and whispered something in his ear which Isla couldn't hear but which must have satisfied the boy's disappointment for he smiled and began to step carefully between the beds of earth until he was safely out of the garden. Brushing his earthy hands together he turned to go. Then, looking towards Isla, he scowled and said with an uncompromising sternness he had acquired from his father, "Don't you yell at my Tomas-da, lady!" and thrilled by his own audacity, he tore off down the hill.

Tomas couldn't help but laugh at this small attempt at bravery, but when he turned he saw Isla's face had split like the broken glass he had seen in the Merchant City, split in a thousand different directions.

"That's Lucas's boy, Rohnan," Tomas said, eyeing her as he would an animal in the wild who might dart away or leap upon him and without warning. She was more herself now, with her island dress and her voice coming at him straight from her heart. Or rather, more as he remembered her. Tomas didn't know who she was now. Only that he had so recently seen her small and straight in her mainland robe with her hands clapping instinctively as she spoke words that were carefully chosen.

"Why is he here?" Isla asked, her voice hesitating, transforming back into her more reserved, mainlander self.

"Lucas is busy these days. He's been busy for awhile. So

Rohnan comes down and helps me in the garden. I'm teaching him to train the gulls."

"Just like your father taught you," Isla remarked and something in her face softened and for a brief instant he knew her again.

"Do you want a drink, Isla?"

Everything moved so slowly, slower than any dream. He had built up such a wall in his mind over so many years that now it seemed impossible that Isla was actually here, stepping carefully through the rows of his garden, stepping through the open doorway of his home. It had been different out at sea, both of them strangers in a strange untethered place. That had felt like a dream and Tomas had known that in three days, and then two, and then one, he would wake up. Now Isla stood in the round room of the lighthouse, in the home they had played in together so often, and it seemed to Tomas as if she had become real. And he could not believe it.

He reached to fill a glass of water but when he turned to hand it to her, she was not looking at him for her gaze was running over the familiar room, and Tomas knew, over the many memories of the past. What he would have given, years ago, for this moment which he would have called 'a second chance'.

He did not think like this now. Instead Tomas felt resentment coil like a snake in his heart. Why was she here, intruding on his tranquil island life? What could she want from him after all these years?

"Here..." he handed the water to her and tried to keep his face even and still, but when her fingers brushed against his hand, Tomas felt something inside of him surge forward like a great wave of the sea. And something else rose up too to lock that thing away. *I will not got back to that place*, a voice inside him spoke, low and cold like a monster from the sea depths, and hearing it, Tomas pulled into himself until his heart felt like a rock, heavy and solid and unbreakable in his chest.

They walked together out into the white sun, across the flat, grassy stretch to the acacia tree which stretched its wizened trunk up from the cliff and stretched a wide canopy of leaves overhead like an umbrella. There Isla folded down into the shaded earth, her dress taking the shape of the woman he remembered. Above her the tree swooned and rose according to the habits of the wind, climbing through forces greater than gravity or time to its summit above the cliff. Below, the sun shone white against the sea, and for once he noticed Isla was not compelled to gaze out across it. She no longer needed to imagine what was beyond the sea.

Shielding her eyes against the sharp glare, Tomas saw Isla look up at him as he stood guarded and staring stiffly towards her. For an infinite moment they stared at each other, waiting for the other to speak. Or perhaps trying to discern what they might possibly say.

"Just tell me, Tomas," Isla said at last. "Why haven't you come to see me? Will you never forgive me for leaving?"

There were so many things Tomas wanted to say. His tongue burned with the fire of all that had gone unsaid in his life. "Why haven't you come here if you wanted to see me?" he replied suddenly, hoping to hurt her. "I went all the way to the mainland to get you — what more do you want from me, Isla!"

The words came out with an anger he had never shown her, and he looked at her quickly, but her face was covered in shadow and she did not speak.

"You've chosen a different life," he began again, trying to steady his voice. "And I don't blame you for it. But I've made a life here...a good life. And you can't come back and expect everything to be the same as it always was, as if we were all just waiting for you to return. Things have changed, Isla. The island isn't the same as it used to be."

"And neither am I." He added, taking a breath.

"I know things have changed, Tomas!" Isla's voice was soft like the shade that hid the subtle changes in her face. "Of course, I know things have changed. My father is dead. The Losa Council is disintegrating. You left the island and no one seems to know where you went...and I do have a life somewhere else."

She paused and Tomas could hear his heart thumping against his chest.

"I guess I just wanted to come home, you know? To a place in the world where I'm not a stranger. But I suppose my father was right after all. Things change. And sometimes you can't come back." She sighed with a great sorrow that touched him deep in his soul, and in that moment Tomas found himself stepping towards her, reaching out for her hand so that he might bridge the great distance between them. But then tension shot through his arms as if he were held back by some invisible chain, and he knew it was of his own making and that he had made it to keep himself safe.

Isla stood up, unsteady under the heavy shade of the tree and the harsh tone of Tomas's voice, and after a moment she raised her hands to him, folded before her in the island way. "I'm sorry to have bothered you, Tomas... I should go..."

"Isla, I didn't mean..." Tomas searched for something he might say that was honest and true and somehow kind. *Her da has just died*, he berated himself. *Why are you speaking to her like this?* But his mouth felt dry and empty and he could not find the words.

"No, no," Isla shook her head, her gaze heavy on the earth at his feet. "I've expected too much from you, Tomas. I'm sorry... I guess..." She paused and bit her lower lip. And then she forced herself to look at him with her wide, silver eyes. "Perhaps I always expected too much..."

She brushed her hands across her face. "Thank you for coming to find me. I'll always be grateful." And while the war raged in the pit of his stomach over whether to speak or simply let her go, he found that Isla had already hurried out onto the longer road that traced the coastline, leaving behind the irretrievable path through the overgrown shrubs like a memory from the past.

51

That night the yellow moon hung low in the sky, and Tomas walked the familiar path past the large banyan tree with the trunk that twisted like a face and always wrenched his imagination, trailing him like a spectre, until he could see the comforting glow of the oracle's open windows, glowing with candlelight.

Even at the gate, Tomas could smell the orange spices hanging like a thin veil in the air, and for an instant he felt hope return to him, hope that perhaps he could indeed resume to his normal life — his new life where Isla was a distant memory and peace had returned to him.

He would not think of Isla, he decided, as his hand fell on the smooth wood of the gate. He would not think of the sadness he had seen in her today — the vulnerability he had forgotten in his memory of her always bold and strong as she dug her way to the centre of the earth, as she swung up into the highest branches of the banyan trees, as she had walked towards the dock and away from her island.

He would not over-think things this time. He would not think of her at all. She was a part of his past. Soon she would leave again and would be nothing to work out between them.

Instead, Tomas vowed, he would remember the presence he had perceived out at sea that was clear and luminous and stretched out and out. He would remember the things he had learned from the oracle. He would remember the story of the fisherman who had withheld judgement and refused to name things as good luck or bad.

He would also remember, Tomas told himself sternly, that it had been his own exalted expectations, his own resistance to change, his own skewed perceptions and especially his own stubborn inability to let go of the pain of his past which had caused most of his misery. None of the things that had happened to him nor the suffering he had endured was Isla's fault. He had become a man, at last and in spite of himself, and he knew now that he must hold these things in his own hands.

The door was open and Tomas stepped across the threshold easily and without inhibitions, knocking absently against the wooden frame to signal his arrival and calling out a greeting in his own voice.

Then, Tomas stood still, as if arrested by an unexpected turn in his usual path, for there she was, standing barefoot in front of the kitchen counter, her dark hair falling like water down towards her slender waist. It was the woman he had seen gliding on the sea, and as he stood before her, he now realised that she wore the loose, unmistakable white cloth of the oracle.

A hand fell on his shoulder. "This is my daughter, Tomas. She has returned from the great mountains to take her place as the oracle of the island."

Tomas did not turn to look at the old woman, his oracle. "Welcome home," he said quickly, and he clasped his hands before him so that these strange women would not see how they shook.

The young oracle smiled at him from across the room. "It's nice to meet you again, Tomas. It has been a long time since we were children." She spoke clearly and with the confidence of one who is certain of their place, of one who is at home, and so Tomas did not say he did not remember her from those days. Yet looking upon her, the peace Tomas had clawed back as he had stood at the gate fled him again, and he understood without reason that this woman was about to change the course of his life.

52

Nostalgia is a fickle thing, descending at the least likely moment in a place you thought you hated, doing a thing you battled against in nightmares. But when something becomes 'the last time', suddenly it takes on a quality of love born of the labour of the years, and it becomes something else entirely. This is what Isla thought as she stood in the hills of losa on the first day of her last harvest on the island.

Work was steady in the losa fields, and Isla was able to busy herself among these people, walking slowly along the rows that glowed purple like the pale evening sky, talking with the harvesters about which buds were ready, which rows were lagging behind, which had come to high quality and which could not be sent off to the trading island for sale. It had been many years, but Isla had not forgotten the talk of losa, the look of the iridescent purple buds, the colour of the leaves that would be best for dye.

As she walked back and forth along the rows, Isla felt her feet filling with a heavy weight, thick as wet earth. Her movements slowed to a crawl and her mind wandered even as her hands ran softly over the purple cloud of her rows. She had been on the island for three weeks — maybe longer, it was so difficult to say. She should be getting back to the mainland soon — back to her life, her work, back to Jackimo. He would be wondering what was keeping her. Things on the mainland happened so fast, so efficiently. But the island seemed to suck away her will to race through each day. It forced her to linger, somehow holding her, a willing captive, in its embrace. *Why did I tell him I'd only be away a few weeks?* Isla shook her head. There was still so much to do, so many decisions she had been left to make alone. *I need more time. How did I forget — the island is not like the mainland.*

"Isla, we need our tea," a woman called over her shoulder. Isla jumped — she had forgotten the tea. "I'll just get it now," she called back, turning towards the house that loomed high above her in the shadows of the trees.

"Why can't I remember even the simplest thing!" she cursed herself again. "I am never this forgetful on the mainland!"

The truth was, Isla was tired. She was not sleeping well — her dreams fitful images of her father's face, his look of disappointment that she had never returned to take care of him, his look of loneliness when everyone had abandoned him. *Why couldn't I have come back — every once in awhile? Just to check on him, help at the house. Was it really so hard?* But then she knew the answer.

The tea boiled quickly in the warm air, and Isla poured it into a large pot, anxious to get back outside, into the breeze and light. "She should have been here," Isla heard herself whisper in the empty room. "It shouldn't have been left up to me." But the words did nothing to absolve her of the guilt she felt in this room where the walls echoed all the things they had witnessed in the eclipsed years she had been away.

Quickly Isla stepped back outside, balancing the large pot of tea in one hand and the basket filled with cups across her other arm. Down the terraces of the hill, down the carefully tended rows, the first of the losa blossoms and pale green leaves flew through the air. They were caught, just as one thought they might hit the ground, by women carrying soft grass-woven baskets and by young girls in the spontaneous hammocks they made with their dresses. The wind was calm, the sun shone with the pacific heat of mid-morning.

Isla watched as the air filled with shades of indigo, imagining that the boundary between earth and sky had blurred and that at any moment she too might begin to float on the optimistic breeze. Slipping back into an old pair of work sandals, Isla waded through the sea of purple towards a group of women who had just begun to fill their baskets. Each nodded to Isla when she joined them, pausing in their work to fill their cups while children ran between their legs and insects leapt up from what had seemed until that moment a tranquil leafy home.

After awhile one of the women began to murmur in a soft voice that sounded at first like a sentimental sigh but grew instead into the seductive call of a familiar harvest song. Isla listened to the voices swell like a canopy above them, and she wished she could sing with them, sing as if she had never left this land or these people, as if she wasn't a stranger here.

The second round of the chorus began and her fingers worked to pull the buds whole and intact from their stalks. She could see Mila next to her pulling the losa with unhurried hands. Mila stopped to swat at a child who had run too close to the basket of losa and then, rather than returning to work, gazed up through the web of leaves towards the pale blue sky. Isla watched her. A minute passed, then two. Finally, Isla asked, "Is something wrong, Mila?"

"Just looking..." Mila answered, and her gaze floated easily as a feather on the breeze back to the task before her.

"If we hurry and work efficiently, we can finish this whole row today," Isla suggested, but Mila smiled at her and replied, "Well girl, I guess the losa will be here tomorrow if we don't," and she went back to singing as she threw deep purple clusters of losa high into the air.

Isla knew that these songs coursed through Mila's veins as sea water did in the fishermen's, that she had been singing these same words year after year since her first losa harvest as a child, and that she would continue to sing from this same meagre repertoire of songs until the day she died. Isla did not envy Mila her narrow life full of things that were always the same. And she knew that it was one thing to enjoy the harvest after so many years away, and quite another thing to do it year after year after year.

And yet, as Isla watched Mila's head nod to the predictable rhythm while her hands danced among the tender branches of the losa rows, she noticed something she had not, or perhaps could not have seen before, and that was the tantalising shade of happiness. And then, Isla realised something even more startling, something that would have been unwelcome had it not hit her with the heavenly and most burdensome weight of truth. She felt happy too.

It was a feeling both illuminating and calamitous in its implications, for how could she be happy doing work that had no great purpose? How could she be happy here? Isla pulled three more buds from the bush in front of her while she contemplated this mundane mystery, and it occurred to her as she did so that this island of her birth was filled with at least one thing the mainland lacked. And that was time.

Isla couldn't remember a period in her years on the mainland when she had felt so filled with time. Like silence, it stretched out around her as an invisible wave, connecting and protecting her from all things. *I am always so busy on the mainland. Everyone is always so busy. No one has any time. What is the cost of that?*

In the indeterminate stretch of afternoon torpor, the sun seemed to halt in its journey across the sky and everyone joined in that singular sigh of weariness and could feel nothing but the droplets of sweat caressing their goose-pimpled skin. Clouds of purple and the scent of losa surrounded her, and time began to lose its tight hold on her mind.

And then, for no reason at all, Isla remembered the fairies. *Fairies love our losa, Isla, because they love all the beautiful things of the world and our losa is the most beautiful of all.* Who was this voice in her head? Isla searched the pathways of her mind but there was only this single thought and no footprints to trace it.

"Is there some story about fairies on the island?" Isla asked Mila.

Mila looked at her surprised, and then she smiled as if Isla were still the young, wild girl she remembered running along the paths between the bushes, throwing losa into her hair where it caught and trailed in thick wind-blown knots behind her.

"Well," she said, "fairies love losa because it is so beautiful...they like to make their dresses with it — these are things we tell our children."

"And fairies are afraid of birds..." Isla murmured. "And

they tease the monkeys by tugging on their ears... How do I know these things. Where did I hear these stories?"

"Your mother told you." Mila said this as if it were the most obvious thing in the world.

Isla was silent after this, but her mind considered this revelation. She thought about her mother, who had once worked beside these women, her hands coated in island earth, her lips tracing the rhythm of these ageless songs. All the stories she had ever heard about her mother attested to her deep contentment on the island, but Isla had always felt suspicious of these tales for islanders loved to believe that their island was the best of all places and that no one could help but be happy on their island that sat at the centre of the world. Yet her mother had stayed here, hadn't she? She had willingly traded a life on the mainland for one on this island. It didn't make sense.

As Isla moved down the row, fingering new leaves and ignoring the ache in her arms, her mind worked over her life on the mainland. For many years, through the interminable period of her training at the Central Institute and then as a novice scribe, her mind had stopped its incessant questioning because she had believed that she had found her answer. The source of her future happiness lay in achieving her goals, which she called her dreams. If only she could become a mainland scribe — then she would know she had lived a good life. And then if she could be promoted to senior scribe, certainly then she could rest assured that she had done something important.

Yet none of these achievements had brought the satisfaction she had expected. As soon as she reached one goal, she would find herself in a new race with a new goal that promised the same prize as the last — Happiness, Satisfaction.

But where was this happiness? Where was the promised satisfaction that would linger rather than dissolving into air like a mirage? *Shouldn't I be happy by now?* Isla thought to herself. *I have seen the world, like I always dreamed. I have become a senior mainland scribe. I have become the woman I used to dream about. So if this isn't enough to make me happy, what will be?*

"Slow down, Isla. You're crushing the losa." Mila laid a hand on her forearm and Isla realised her hands had sped up with the pace of her thoughts.

Then, suddenly, Isla began to laugh. Slow down? It seemed so absurd. The irony of it all shook her, and Isla laughed and laughed until she could no longer stand. She laughed until she had buckled at the waist and dropped the branch of losa she was holding to the ground. And though they did not know the reason, all the women began to laugh with her, until the hills echoed with a cacophony that scattered the flock of green parrots and inspired the monkeys to chide the women from the safety of the trees.

53

At another time, in another age, Isla's return to the island might have been the event of the year. Certainly under normal circumstances, it should have satisfied the thread of island gossip for many months with debates over Isla's changed appearance, her likely intentions to stay or leave the island again, the fate of Petro's family home and land that held coveted losa-growing rights.

But these were not normal times.

No, times were perilous and few islanders could escape the constrictive tension that had grown between the losa growers and the traders. The harvesters, whose vote on the Council could sway the tide, had suddenly become the power brokers of the island, thanks to the unfailing efforts of Lucas, and it was said that more and more harvesters were selling their allegiance to the highest bidder, although the harvesters themselves denied this as vicious rumour.

With only a week to go until the Council took a final vote on the matter of expanding losa production, and with this act potentially nullifying the Losa Charter, the island could talk of little but the conflict. Would there be enough harvesters siding with Lucas and the traders to sway the three harvesters who sat as members of the Council? Had the growers, sensing their peril, already formed an outside alliance with mainland traders who could bring in foreign workers to replace any traitorous island harvesters who failed to remain loyal to their grower families? Rumours inundated the island like a flood, but no one knew anything for sure.

Lucas watched the changes that had come to the island as one who stands at the eye of the storm. *No*, Lucas thought, clenching his fists as he walked. *The mainland traders must not be allowed onto the island. It would devastate island life.* He remembered the stories of Manel Prenai. The voice of the great man rang in his ears. *Say, you mainlanders...* a command from the wise to the weak minded. He would be that kind of man. He too would speak in a devastating tone that would shake the mainlanders in their high heeled shoes...if it came to that. Then he remembered where he had first heard the true story of the great Manel Prenai, and he turned and began to walk in the opposite direction towards the lost hills for he knew just the person he needed to speak to.

"Isla."

Isla blinked and saw Lucas dressed in a dusty cotton shirt, his brown eyes red with a weariness that did not match the energy of his stride. "Hi!" Isla started from her chair. "Sorry, I didn't see you."

After Isla had heated water for fresh losa tea and both she and Lucas had taken their places in the creaking wicker seats of their fathers, Isla spoke. "You've come to ask me about the land."

"Yes."

"You want to know what I'm going to do with it. Who will get the losa rights?"

"Actually, I wanted your advice, Isla." Lucas let out a sigh that was filled with the exhaustion of one who has lost his way.

"Lucas, what has happened with the Council?"

"It's impossible that you haven't heard."

"I have heard. I've heard about ten different stories. So I'm asking you."

Lucas looked up at her from between his hands. His elbows dug further into his knees and it seemed to Isla as if he were actually sinking through the mouldy wooden floor.

"Perhaps..." Isla rose from her seat and disappeared into the haunted shadows of the house. When she returned, she held a bottle of spiced liquor in one hand. Picking up her cup, she tossed the remaining losa tea over the porch railing and replaced it with the pungent dark liquor.

Lucas smiled. "Remember when I stole those bottles from my uncle and you got so drunk you threw up all over Tomas's feet." He laughed, but the sound was not beautiful as it should have been. And then he swallowed a mouthful of liquor and looked his friend directly in the eye.

"I want to do something important, Isla" he said all at once. "I want to do something so people will remember me...so I won't disappear."

Seeing Isla nod, Lucas felt confidence return to him and so he decided he would tell Isla, who had lived among the wonders of the wider world, the simple truth. "Us traders, we met a man while we were on Joon last year. There are always so many things in the Joon markets, so many amazing things, Isla. But the past few years there have been even more than usual — and we traders are only human. We wanted to have those things for ourselves.

And to take home to our families. But we couldn't afford them."

Isla nodded and her eyes were without judgement, so Lucas continued. "And then we met a man — not a mainlander, Isla — he was a desert man with thick coloured bands in his hair. And he had so much. He told us that if we grew more losa, like the desert people had done with their sisilus crop, we could earn more money. And then we would also be able to afford all those things for ourselves."

As Lucas listed the luxuries he had seen, cloth and food and shoes and jewels and so much more, so much More, Isla felt as if she had been pulled out of time, for she was also a mainlander now and for many years these things that Lucas called 'luxuries' had been part of her daily life.

"What did this desert man tell you, Lucas?" Isla spoke carefully, weaving her way around the fierce foreboding in her heart.

"He said the mainland kingdom wants to help regions like ours advance, that if we take a loan from the mainland we can hire the latest tools and extra labourers and convert all available land on the island to grow losa. He said if we grow more losa, we will be able to have More than we have now, that our children will be better off than we have been."

"So you see, Isla," Lucas finished, "I have to convince the Council to burn the old charter that limits the amount of losa grown on the island. If I can do that, if I can free islanders to grow as much losa as possible, we will all have more and I will have done something, something big, something that people on the island will always remember."

"Hmmm..." Isla said, and she looked out to the mango trees where two large iguanas were inching out on a thin limb towards the ripened fruit. Then she raised the glass of spiced liquor to her lips, remembering that day long ago after the Binding Celebrations, her first time really getting drunk on this fiery amber liquor.

"Tomas never told me I threw up on him…"

"He wouldn't have, would he?" Lucas shrugged as if this were obvious.

Shaking her head, Isla looked at Lucas and saw the light in his eyes that was the burning desire for More. She knew it well. She knew exactly how it felt.

The search for More gives rise to insatiable craving. The desire for more wealth, more power, creates a world where nothing is ever enough. This idea had slowly begun to infiltrate Isla's heart, though she had not yet put such thoughts into words. What Isla did know as she sat in her father's favourite wicker chair on the melancholy porch looking into her friend's face was first, that she had done everything she knew to do, and second, that none of it had been enough.

"I used to dream," Isla said, "of a place where all things were possible, where people had more than we have here and were so much happier. I have lived on the mainland for a long time, Lucas. And I gave up a lot to be there, my friends, my home, my relationship with my father — even if he was a miserable man." She laughed a twisted sound.

"And Tomas." Lucas said.

"And Tomas," Isla nodded. "But I thought I was pursuing my dreams. I thought I was getting close to happiness… close to giving my life some great meaning."

"For the past four years," she continued, "I have worked with the desert people you speak of who used to live a small life in an infinite sea of sand under a vast scorching sky. Then they heard about the Philosophy of the Rising Sun — that having More is better. That having More leads to a better life. Mainlanders believe this with their whole being. They believe in the potential of infinite growth — that we can always have More because if you work hard there is always More to have."

"But Lucas," Isla said, looking her friend in the eye. "I have had More — I have had all the things you speak of and more things than that — and I don't think I'm happier for it, though I wish I could say that I was."

"But the desert man was happy, Isla," Lucas protested. "I saw him with my own eyes. He said his people were progressing... that they *were* better off..."

"Lucas, I worked with the desert people. The man you met... his whole tribe has fallen ill. The water the mainland helped them store in the great dam they built grew stagnant and so a poison spread and killed many of the desert people. Yes, it is true that now they can buy many luxuries from the mainland — rose syrup to drink and silk heeled shoes to wear and water pipes to smoke and beautiful cloth and gold bands. But they also have to work all the time to maintain the purity of their reservoir, and the water that used to flow freely in their river is no longer theirs but is prioritised to feed the sisilus crop they grow for mainland markets, so they must buy much of their food from the mainland too."

"I'm carrying this now," Isla felt her face tighten and her eyes squint as she peered into the depths of her own culpability. "Because I was part of the mainland party who brought this story to the desert. That More is Better, and New is Best. And maybe I'm wrong. Maybe they are indeed more free and happy because they can buy whatever they want. But so much is no longer their own. Even their time is not their own like it is for us islanders. And they are not free to enjoy their music or teach their children the tales of their tribe. What they have had to sacrifice has also been great." Isla's voice faltered as she heard the words of the old desert woman leave her own lips as if she had finally understood their meaning.

Around them the smell of damp and rotting wood seeped up like a rising tide of decay, and no revitalising winds blew across Isla's motionless face as they should have done on some idyllic island which was a place far from here. Instead, mosquitoes whined in her ears, and the evening of that hot, exhausting day was heavy with a morbid humidity and the smell of the slow decomposition of her childhood home.

Then, in that moment which was lost from time, a voice also rang out in Lucas's mind that pierced through his vague clamouring thoughts and unmanifested fears. *More comes with sacrifices of its own, Lucas. Never forget. In order to get more of something, you always have to give something else up.* It was a voice which had spoken to him on this very porch many years before. *Never forget*, it had said. But Lucas had forgotten. Until now.

For the first time in the many long months of his work with the harvesters, Lucas remembered the stories Petro had told him of Manel Prenai. He realised that it had not been Manel Prenai's walking stick or his booming voice that had challenged the mainlanders and had made him famous. Manel Prenai was revered as a great man on the island because he, unlike all the others, had foreseen the implications of the mainlanders' call to grow more losa. He had understood that no one gets More without giving something else up.

Lucas gripped the arm of his own sagging wicker chair and shook his head. Why hadn't he remembered this before? Lucas thought of the mainland treasures he had seen in Joon market, and for a moment, he allowed his heart to long for these beautiful things. But, no matter how much he craved such wealth, he believed the look in Isla's eyes when she had said these treasures had not brought her happiness. He could see it for himself.

"But is it right for things to always stay the same?" Lucas asked Isla. "If working for More isn't the answer, then what is?"

"I don't know," Isla said at last. She shook her head but she did not clap as she would have done. Instead her eyes searched the tree for the two iguanas. Had they reached the mango? Had one pushed the other off the branch? In the fading impenetrable light of dusk, Isla squinted but she could not see where the two iguanas had gone.

54

"At last," the boatman said as he glimpsed again the shimmering iridescent shores rise up on the horizon like an oasis of good hope. It had been many months of moons since the boatman had set foot on the island. Perhaps it had been years. But as he had stood on the dock of the mainland city port several days before, the boatman had noted a weariness in his mind, and what had begun as a sliver of intuition grew into a deep aching in his soul for the quiet shores of the indigo island and the protection of the silver mangroves.

The boatman had looked out then, across the tin roofs raised against the mercurial sea winds like forlorn flags of the poor surrendering to their inevitable fates, remembering the feeling that had first driven him from this city and out onto the wide sea. It was there again, creeping into the depths of him and he knew he must leave this sordid city for a sweeter forgotten place.

Just then, as the morning fog rolled across his sandalled feet and a cough sent tremors through his lungs reminding him of the creeping, unpredictable passage of time, the boatman heard a voice calling out. "Messenger. Messenger to sail to the indigo island." Peering through the fog, the boatman could see two old sailors, wayward folk with beards far wilder and longer than his own, pointing the young boy in his direction. He was the only one who ever went to such a small island.

"I hear you are the one who goes to the indigo island," the boy said when he had finally reached the boatman and gathered courage enough to speak.

"I am," the boatman replied.

"I have a letter. It must reach the island as soon as possible. The sender is willing to pay a high price in advance to the one who agrees to deliver it safely."

"You are right on time," the boatman told the boy with a mysterious grin. "I was just about to raise the sails."

The seas had been calm and the skies bright this time of year, and so the boatman had made good speed and was able to relax into the wide silence of the water. For three days his gaze rested on the horizon. Then on the morning of the fourth day, he glimpsed the floating purple cloud of the island rise up before him and knew he had arrived at last.

Where would he stay now that Madame Prenai was gone? What would the island be without the impractical hospitality of that ostentatious, graceful woman? These were not questions which concerned the boatman, for rarely did he perceive land and know what lodgings awaited him that night. And so he did not wonder, as he stared at the rising hills, what had happened to the Palm Losa, nor did his thoughts dwell upon the final fate of the Losa Co-operative that had occupied the oracle when they had last sat sipping her pale losa tea in the late island afternoon. It would remain standing, or it would dissolve, and it was not for the boatman to say which outcome would ultimately benefit the island.

What he did think, as he sailed through the timeless hours and ethereal light of that early morning was that he would miss Sylvia Prenai. He would miss the way she had always asked him "So, what is the program for the day?" as if he was a busy man or the island the sort of place where people marked the time. Sylvia Prenai had never surrendered to the circulating suspicions that the boatman was a scoundrel — it had always suited her to believe he was a man of clandestine wealth and enigmatic eminence. Yes, he would miss these minor rituals that had flavoured his life so distinctly on the island. *Things will be different now,* he thought to himself. *But then, they always are.*

By her own count, although one could never be sure, Isla had been on the island for over a month when the boatman delivered Jackimo's letter to her door. She was not surprised to receive it. She had perceived the quiet sifting of time, like sand through a sieve and sensed she had been gone too long. Certainly longer than she had intended.

For an instant, instinct urged her to lay the letter down on the table, as she had so often done with letters from her father. But then she remembered that things had changed, that this was a new kind of letter and that her father was dead.

The letter from Jackimo was three pages long, full of the poetry of remembrances and requests for her to return. "Your life is here," the letter said, and Isla knew that it was true. The life she knew was on the mainland. Her life with Jackimo. It was the life she recognised.

That is me, she thought to herself. *That is who I am now.*

But a moth cannot return to the cocoon once it has broken free and taken to the air, and not even the wise women of the world can reverse what has already been transformed.

She could not go back to her old life. Isla knew this even before the words formed in her mind. She had seen a different truth in the losa fields — that the mainland was an enthralling, spectacular place, a place of plenty, a place of productivity, a place of all that was new. But it was also a place that caused great suffering, for it asked that its people work and work but never pause for thought. It asked for a stream of innovation so constant that its people could never rest for a moment to look around and notice where they stood. It offered only a promise of More when its people wanted to find that spectacular and precious feeling that was Enough.

She had seen too that her work as a mainland scribe was exciting and made her feel important in the world. But she had also seen a different truth in the faces of the desert people that continued to haunt her. She saw now that her work in the outer regions was not part of the mainland's desire to help people, to promote the progress of humanity by providing the opportunity for everyone to have More. She, Isla, mainland scribe, daughter of the island, was playing a role in a much larger game, and that was the Game of Power, and it was as ugly and vulgar as the desire of one person to dominate and control another.

Isla thought of the faces of the desert people she had worked with as a mainland scribe and the faces of her own islanders also blended there. She could not let her own island fall to this fate.

No, she could not return to that life as it was.

And yet, she also knew she could not remain on the island. As much as she loved her people and as much as she had been welcomed back as any daughter of the island, she had become a stranger here. Perhaps she had always been a stranger.

I will write to Jackimo, Isla told herself. *I will explain all of this to him. I will sell the house and the land as soon as harvest is finished.*

For the first time in many years, Isla had found time to think. To step back and contemplate her life. What she had realised, slowly and over the many empty hours of each evening when she gazed across her silent hills after the harvesters had all gone home was this — the Philosophy of the Rising Sun was not the truth she had once taken it to be.

It speaks of progress and advancement, Isla thought to herself, searching for the words she would use when she wrote to Jackimo. *It tells us that in order to progress we must continually work for More and pursue innovation in every circumstance. It says, 'More is better, New is best'. But Jackimo, it never says where we are going. And shouldn't we ask where this kind of progress is leading us? It tells us we should work and that the products of our work are the testament to our value. But should we not also consider what this work does to us, what the demands of mainland life do to its people?*

Isla thought about the boatman. *Many years ago,* she thought, *a man told me that all people desire happiness and that the questions we ask in the quiet moments about the ultimate meaning of our lives can be answered. I have worked on the mainland for ten years and it is only now that I realise, I have found neither happiness nor true meaning. I have had moments of happiness, moments of joy and pleasure and peace, but none of them have ever lasted.* And Isla realised she needed to understand the meaning of her life more than she needed a big house or a prestigious job or fancy clothes. She needed to feel Fulfilled more than she needed More.

I will return to you soon, she would write in her letter to the mainland man she would soon marry. Perhaps they could discern a way to change the mainland. Together.

55

Isla was kneeling before the great wooden cabinet of her childhood demons, surrounded by the air of apprehension that she had always felt by the warped squeaking of its forbidden wooden doors, when her father's oldest friend, Jayan knocked against the hollow frame of the open door.

Peering in, Jayan found Petro's grown daughter looking lost in the cavernous spaces of her own home. Her hair was different, sleek like the black cat that used to wind its way around the thin ancient ankles of Sylvia Prenai before it had died on a late afternoon in its sleep and sent its owner reeling into the fateful realms of her last decline. Jayan wasn't sure what this sudden comparison might imply, whether it was some portent forewarning of things to come, or whether it was simply that he was so unaccustomed to seeing a grown woman's hair flowing loose without regard for the sea winds.

Then, he saw the map that spread before her with its brittle edges and brown places that reminded him of the sun-stained skin of a fisherman's hands, and he understood that the premonition that had startled him at the threshold of Petro's house had nothing to do with Isla but had come to him from the unexcavated depths of this map that had stored all of Petro's forgotten dreams.

Jayan had to call Isla's name three times before she looked up from the place she had retreated to in her mind, and when she finally met his gaze, Jayan breathed a sigh of relief for he saw in the woman's full silver eyes that it was Isla after all.

"I see you found his map then," Jayan said to comfort her, and he did not bother to go to the stove for a cup of tea, but simply pulled up a stool and waited for the questions he knew were now his responsibility to face, because he was the only one left who knew their answers.

"I remember seeing this once as a child," Isla said, running her fingers across the delicate paper as if expecting the coloured contours of its mountains and seas to press back against her fingertips.

"That was what the world looked like to your father." Jayan removed his pipe from the pocket of his shirt and tapped it absently against his knee, moving as people do when they are enacting habits as old as their bones. "Me and Fazza never had much interest in the rest of the world. We were busy trying to cajole all the girls we were...well... and keep up with the lies we told our parents when we were out late gambling in the caves on the ridge."

Jayan laughed and wondered whether Isla would believe that once upon a time he had darted on alternating nights between the beds of three island girls and that none of them had been his future wife. "But Petro was always staring out to sea. He didn't say it, but we knew what he was thinking. Only once, when he was quite drunk and losing at cards did he ever let it slip... called us bastards and said he was going to leave the island, go on some fool adventure..."

"Adventure? My father?" Isla shook her head and there was anger, or maybe it was a daughter's resentment in the words she spoke even in these precarious days after his death.

"I don't believe it," she told him, but Jayan nodded.

"He had such ideas in those days, Isla, before your mother. Who knows whether he would have ever gone through with it. It was a long running bet between Fazza and I. In fact," Jayan added, gesturing at her with his pipe that hadn't held smoke for many decades, "I believe I still owe Fazza two silver pieces over that." He chuckled to himself. "Yes, yes. I always thought he might go. I'll give him those pieces tomorrow," Jayan finished and then glanced quickly at Isla and felt relieved to see she hadn't taken offence.

"Anyway," he sputtered, "your mother arrived on the island with the traders after one of their trips to Joon, and after that, well, everything changed. She was set on making her home here, you see. Loved the island more than most islanders, Myrium did. After that, your father didn't talk about leaving anymore."

"He used to get this old thing out at night," Jayan said, pointing at the map as if accusing it of some crime Isla could not imagine. "Thought we didn't know. But you could always tell he'd been looking at that map at night from his mood the next day. Foul and violent as a storm. I guess that's the way it is with dreams. They don't leave you alone just because you decide not to follow them."

Jayan waited for her questions, but Isla was silent and did not ask the things he was sure were in her heart. *I have said my piece,* he thought to himself. *I have told her the truth about Petro, and that is all I came here to do.* When Jayan got up, he only patted Isla's shoulder and did not speak aloud the words that were in his mind, because telling people they would be okay at times like these was as useless as whispering over an easterly wind.

It was only after he had gone and the afternoon light fell through the open doorway that Isla looked back at the map and noticed a tiny mark in the farthest corner and a winding line carved in foreign ink that had not belonged to the original map.

It was a path, a journey that led into the wild places of the world, the adventure of her father's dreams. And a small hole opened up in Isla's heart at the instinctual sense that she had just lost the only part of her mother she had known, for she had always believed that her own longing for adventure had come from the silver-eyed woman she had loved so greatly and had hardly known.

Isla stared at this ink pathway for a long time. She thought of all the things she had done in her life, all the directions she had taken, all the decisions she had made based on this distorted view of her parents. Would she have responded differently to her father if she had known this truth about his past? She hoped so, although it was impossible to say such things for sure. But maybe, just maybe, her words would have been softer. Perhaps she would have stripped some of the anger of those early years from her letters. Maybe she could have loved him without the restraint of a thousand bridled horses who long to run but are not free. Maybe. If only she had seen this hidden thread that had stretched out to her from her father and had been his true legacy to her — a sense of adventure.

When she looked up, the house around her had changed, and she saw that it was not the prison she had always believed it to be, but was simply a house with rooms that had watched a man grow up and grow old and lose his way.

With sudden nostalgia, Isla folded the map, but then thought better of it, and instead of hiding it away in the unkind recesses of the cabinet, she walked over to her father's study that still smelled of his smoke, and after she had cleared several piles of old books from the low shelves, she took four pins and spread the map out wide upon the wall.

Although she hardly realised it herself, this was the moment Isla decided to keep the house which was her small place on the island, for she suddenly understood that after all these years and all she thought she knew — of her father, her mother, this house, the island and even herself — she had seen nothing clearly.

"I thought I saw things as they were," Isla said, and her voice blew through the stale empty house like the wind from the sea, "but perhaps I saw nothing but my own blind expectations."

56

"The Losa Council was founded by great men of this island." The Council meeting had begun, and Lucas had waited long enough through the droning voices of old men to say his piece.

"The Losa Council was founded by great men," he began. "It was founded on great principles. But these great principles have been forgotten, for those who remember them no longer walk among us."

The day of the epic Council meeting was swelteringly hot. It was the kind of day islanders hid indoors, fanning themselves with languid hands and drifting in and out of consciousness on their grass-woven cots. It was the kind of day when even the soles of the feet beaded with sweat. But despite these obvious deterrents, the islanders had dragged themselves out of their habitual afternoon stupor and gathered at the bonfire circle near the centre of town, as much to glean the gossip of this open warfare as to hear the final vote of the Council.

Lucas looked out over the faces of the islanders. He saw Isla standing in a group of other grower families, speaking with a soft smile upon her face and folding her hands as several grower families wandered up. When he had left her sitting on her porch several days ago he had still not known what he would say to this Council, for he had spent months arguing one side and now found himself transported unexpectedly to an entirely different position.

Then he had met the young oracle, a woman a few years younger than himself but with a look of the ancient about her. "You look deep in thought," she had said, breaking through the chaos of his mind, and because she was not simply a woman or an islander, but the oracle and the embodiment of wisdom, he had simply said,

"I'm trying to think, what is wrong with wanting More?"

"Ahhh, a difficult question," the oracle had replied.

"You have travelled in the world," Lucas said, folding his hands to her, "so you must also know what wonderful things the world has to offer. Why should we not take as much as we can? Why should we not try to grow and progress as much as possible?"

"You can do those things if you wish," the young oracle had said to him. "But I always like to look at the world in cases like these, and what I have noticed is this — a gull does not continue to grow no matter how many fish it eats. It grows to its ideal size and then stops. A mango tree never grows as tall as a banyan tree no matter how much the sun shines and the rain waters its roots. It grows to its ideal height and stops. Nature seems to find a balance between what the world can provide and how far to grow. Perhaps there is some wisdom in this." Then the woman raised her hand. "I must be off."

When she was gone, Lucas had looked out at the sea and understood at last — It is the mainland philosophy that is wrong. Infinite growth isn't possible because the world is limited and there will not always be more to take. And then he had known not only what side he was on, but what he would say.

Now, standing before the great gathering of islanders on the flat-cut edge of a wide tree trunk, sweat dripping mercilessly from his forehead, Lucas raised his voice above the crowd. "Those who remember the great principles of our Losa Co-operative no longer walk among us. So we have forgotten them. And I had also forgotten."

"As you have heard, the Joon markets are now filled with treasures. And we traders are only human. When we saw these treasures we wanted them for ourselves and for our island. We thought — we islanders should also progress with the times, we too should enjoy the advantages of this new age. And we thought — if we could grow more losa on the island to sell at the markets at Joon, we could all become wealthy people."

At this many traders and a few harvesters cheered.

"But then, I remembered something a wise man once told me. " Lucas said, raising his hand and searching for Jayan's face. Lucas found him standing next to Isla

"I remember," Lucas nodded towards this man who had always been kind to him. "He said — *In order to get more of something, you have to give something else up.* He said — *more comes with sacrifices of its own.*"

At this, some of the older women nodded their heads and murmured to each other, "That's true, it is," and others murmured back, "True as true."

"It is not human nature to want More. It is only our nature to look at the possibilities the world offers and decide which things are important, are of most value to us, and then to pursue these things. For mainlanders, wealth is the most important, and they believe their wealth will continue to grow and grow forever. But we islanders know the riches of the world go far beyond wealth, and so we should hold tight to the things we value."

"The mainlanders," Lucas proclaimed from his pedestal, "are addicted to this search for More, and they may work themselves into the ground to get it. But as Manel Prenai once said — the losa grown on this island is purified by the sea air. It is nourished by the slant of the sun against our hills. It is imbued with the qualities of the island soil. And now, I say — The people on this island are raised on the sea air and easy flow of time. We are nurtured by our families, our friends, our neighbours. We are enriched by the beauty of our land. And so we must protect these things that we hold sacred and most valuable. We have our own values on this island, and we know the value of having Enough."

At this the losa growers raised their fists in triumph, but Lucas was not finished.

"That said, it is not right that things should always stay the same. We should keep limits on losa growth, but we should also reform the charter to bring justice to the Cooperative, for many feel the growers profit more than the rest from the sale of losa. Therefore I propose, firstly, that the Council should include the voices of the tillers, for despite appearances, losa growing and its results impact everyone. The members of the Council must also rotate to reflect the concerns of all who are growing, harvesting and trading losa. Finally, it should be the Council that determines the percentage of profits given to harvesters and traders, not the individual grower families."

None cheered when Lucas finished his speech, but instead the traders huddled together, the harvesters wandered to a patch of shade, and the losa growers grumbled resentfully to each other. Men of the Council fingered their carved voting sticks as members of their own community spoke across one another, arguing one side, then another.

Lucas sat down on the tree trunk to watch the spectacle, which would decide not only the fate of the island but also his own destiny. Would he be the great man of his generation? The man who had brought reform to the island. The man who had preserved that which was most precious?

Or would he fail? Would his speech be lost in the slippery fog of memory? Would he remain just another islander — like his father, destined to be forgotten. Years later, Lucas would remember these hours under the sweltering sun as a single moment of fear and doubt. But in truth, the time stretched on and on as Lucas watched the crowds, trying to guess the direction of the tide, and it seemed to him an eternity.

This state of affairs lasted most of the afternoon, but finally, as the sun began to sink and stomachs began to growl, the islanders gathered together again at the fire circle and the members of the Council stepped to the centre of the circle.

As the men laid down their carved voting sticks, one-by-one, Lucas felt his ears grow cold, and a knot formed in his throat like a pearl of hope, for here was his destiny being laid out before him like the lines that criss-crossed the palm of the hand.

He looked across the circle at Isla who stood with the other grower families and he knew, as Samuel, Jobe and Fazzar laid down their grower sticks, that she had been his ally. One-by-one the traders stepped forward into the circle and laid down their sticks. One-by-one the harvesters. And when the last vote was laid, Lucas heard a huge cheer swell around him until it filled his mind. He could feel men patting his back. He could feel Rosa next to him squeezing his hand, but he could see none of them for he was blinded by the image of his father's face.

"At last," he thought to himself. "At last, I have done something great, and I will never be forgotten."

57

Lucas climbed the path away from his house, and when he reached the top of the hill, he saw that the land had lost its final purple ribbons and bows to the wind and that harvest had finally come to an end. He imagined, as he stood still in his dusty sandalled feet, that he could still feel the profound fragrance of losa enveloping him in a cocoon of that single moment, the moment of his triumph.

Yet when he sucked the air into his nostrils what he smelled instead was the scent of fish rising off the sea and the stench of rotten fruit stirred up by the flies that buzzed beneath the mango tree. The island was the island, just as it had always been.

Lucas paused for a moment, wishing he had decided to go with the trading party that had left that morning for Joon. Then he shook his head to clear it and told himself sternly not to be so weak. *The islanders will not forget what I have done. I must be patient and keep working with the Council and allow things to change in time. Surely Manel Prenai did not become Great in a single day.*

And yet the days passed, one after another, and change

did not come. Rohnan pouted at dinner because Lucas had still not made time to see his gulls. Ria whined each evening when the crickets set about their grating lullaby which signalled her time for bed, and Rosa's eyes looked strained, as if the thin mantle of trust that she wore as his wife, had worn too thin for the rising chill of this new season. There seemed no way out. No escape. No grand finale at the unveiling of the man he had become.

One-by-one the new members of the Losa Council were chosen. From the harvesters, there was Tellos, Mila and Freson who all worked for different losa-growing families. From among the losa growers, Joal, Nessus and Joseph who owned the land next to Isla's and had promised to make her a generous offer on any part of her father's land she was prepared to sell. And from the traders, two men joined Lucas as three and what could be said about all of them was that they were young sons of reliable trading stock and everyone hoped they would follow in their forefather's measured footsteps. In addition to these, three new men from among the tillers — those landholders who grew food-crops rather than losa — joined the Council's reinvigorated ranks.

These chosen ones — apart from Mila, the only woman on the Council, who steered clear of inflated talk and such obvious self-aggrandisement — met at Dari's most afternoons to discuss their new roles and responsibilities, and to sit and drink their losa tea before the eyes of the islanders wandering through the main town. To outsiders, nothing much seemed to happen on these afternoons, but to Lucas, these were important Council meetings and he found himself waiting impatiently for the sun to round the pinnacle of the sky and the late afternoon to come. And always the question hovering in his mind — *have I done enough? Will I be remembered?*

Late one afternoon, just as he felt his face turning green with restlessness and pent-up fury, Lucas looked up from the torturous thoughts of his mind and saw Tomas walking down the hill path towards his house.

"Hello!" Lucas waved with relief from his porch chair and saw Tomas raise a wide hand.

Tomas and Lucas had been friends since before their memories began, and they were not men who chewed their words and were silent and nodded their heads meaningfully, but were the kind of men who smoked and talked late into the night. They were nocturnal friends, friends whose voices were strengthened and whose thoughts were clarified by the illuminating darkness and the timeless hours after midnight. So they were already on slightly unfamiliar ground when Tomas sat down next to Lucas on the porch in the sluggish afternoon heat and accepted a cup of losa tea from Rosa rather than a rolled leaf from Lucas.

It could have been these deviations from what had become a powerful ritual between these friends. Or it could have been Lucas's expectations, vague and formless as they were, that Tomas had come to speak of his success with the Council. Whatever the cause, as soon as Tomas took his first sip of tea, Lucas felt a strange sensation in his bones, as if he were sitting imperceptibly on a slope. He stood up to move his chair but the feeling persisted, subtle but maddeningly irritating. He could not find his balance and so he sat, half convinced his chair would begin to slide slowly away from Tomas towards the edge of the porch and down the hill to the sea.

"So, Rohnan came to visit me yesterday," Tomas said, eyeing Lucas as he shifted this way and that in his chair.

'Mmmm,' Lucas mumbled. He was not interested in talking about Rohnan or his gulls. They could talk of these trivialities any time. What Lucas wanted was for Tomas to ask about his work, to comment on his great success. What he wanted was for Tomas to act differently towards him — to acknowledge that he had achieved something great and had become a new person, better than the old.

"I thought maybe after the Council vote, I wouldn't see as much of him," Tomas continued, "but he still comes every day."

"Fine." Lucas decided that he needed a smoke after all, even if it was only mid-afternoon. He pulled a bag from his pocket and began to pinch the dried leaves to separate them.

"Lucas," Tomas said. "I'm trying to talk to you about your son."

"I can see that," Lucas said without looking up. "What is your point about Rohnan? He comes to see you. I know."

"He comes to see me because he doesn't have you, Lucas. It's come to my mind many times, and I've let it go on for too long without saying anything. Rohnan misses you. He's too young to say it, but I'm your oldest friend and so I will tell you. A boy needs his father."

At this, Lucas looked up, his face filled with fire. "You don't need to tell me how a boy needs his father," he said, his hands tense and still. "I am here. I am working for him and for our family."

Tomas was quiet while Lucas finished rolling his leaf. He took a long drink of his tea while he listened to Lucas puff to light the leaf and then take a long drag. He listened to all the things Lucas was saying without words and, as the blue smoke mixed with the humid heat on the porch, Tomas was suddenly struck in his heart by a deep sadness and longing for the way things used to be when they were all young and their friendships were as strong as the hanging ropes of the banyan trees and as clear as a full moon night at sea.

What had happened that things had become so complicated between them? How could it be that Isla was on the island and he wasn't speaking to her? That here was Lucas, sitting before him smoking and sipping losa tea, and still Tomas could not reach him?

Lucas inhaled again with the rolled leaf gripped between his lips and then sighed. "Look, I know you think you are doing the right thing here," Lucas said at last to his friend. "But you don't know anything about having a family. There is a lot of pressure. Pressure to be somebody. Pressure to make a name for yourself because time is passing you by. You have to do something great to be remembered, Tomas. Something big, you know?"

"Did your father have to do something big for you to remember him?" Tomas asked.

"I'm the only one who remembers him, Tomas." Lucas replied in a voice as cold as stone. "The only one! I remember the day we put my father in the sea. My mother gave back his band and then forgot him and so has everyone else. So don't come here and lecture me about the importance of a father."

There was a long silence in the afternoon, and finally Lucas said, "We all do the best we can, Tomas. Have you even spoken to Isla since she's been back? Have you told her what happened with you after she left?"

"She knows I left the island," Tomas replied flatly.

"Because Eva told her," Lucas returned.

Tomas was silent for a long time. At last he reached for the rolled leaf in Lucas's outstretched hand. "You're right. We all do the best we can."

58

During the days of harvest, Isla pulled the losa buds with the other harvesters and watched mountains the colour of indigo rise before her eyes like clouds moving in from the sea. But in the early evenings, when everyone had abandoned the terraced hills for the warm, friendly comforts of their homes, Isla found herself standing in the fields alone, thinking of Tomas.

Once, many years ago they had felt like one person. The same. Only their small sun-browned bodies had divided them, and this had seemed so insignificant a thing. Once they had craved the same sweet island foods, raced towards the same banyan tree, waited until dusk at the top of the lighthouse, peering out into the blinding sea, straining to perceive some passing ship, some sea monster, the first star on the horizon.

Once, all these things had seemed enough for them to feel the same. Two arms of a body that was the island. Tomas, her best friend, who shared her secrets, who knew the blue shaded places on the island that she used to hide from her father, who was always able to distinguish her true smile from the one she used when she was sad. Tomas, who was now a man, and now a stranger. Tomas, who didn't want to know her.

Isla stood alone in the losa fields she had never wanted to inherit, and as she stood flushed by the heat that fell like a thick cloud around her and paled by the deep purple flowers of blooming losa that hovered just a few feet above the earth like a thousand butterflies of destiny, she remembered a time when she had not felt alone. *Perhaps it is inevitable,* Isla thought, *and we must all come to such solitude. Perhaps the years of childhood are only an illusion. We came from different families, had different bodies, dreamed different dreams. So we were never really the same, no matter how fiercely we believed.*

On these melancholy evenings, loneliness drove Isla away from the echoing silence of her home, but pride kept her away from the paths that led directly to the lighthouse. And so often she spent her evenings wandering along the outlying paths of the island coastline, feeling her hair whip scandalously in the wind and keeping one eye fixed on the vast, changeable sea that comforted her with its timelessness while the other scanned the path ahead, hoping always to find Tomas up ahead, hoping Tomas would find her here on this lonely forgotten path.

In all her weeks on the island since their fight, she had only seen Tomas twice. Once, he had stood among a group of men at Dari's, his broad shoulders shaking with laughter at something one of the men had said, some piece of island talk that was inaccessible and off-limits to an outsider like Isla. She had watched him, awed by the easy way he moved among these men who were strangers to her now after so many years away. She watched as he drew a rolled leaf from his pocket and lit it on a candle from one of Dari's small front tables and blew the smoke up over the heads of the crowd like a man she did not know. And then, he brought one wide hand and ran it through his wild mass of curly dark hair, just as he had done as a boy when he had begun to think about something separate and apart from the conversation before him, and Isla had been forced to turn away by the fiery tears that had sprung to her eyes at this familiar sight.

The second time she had seen Tomas was an evening gathering at the fire circle. She had searched for his face while the crowd had sung old island tunes and shouted and murmured to each other during the long interludes. And then, the cheese-maker Lott had shifted her weight, and Isla had seen him, standing apart from the chaotic crowd — but not alone. The woman who stood next to him was tall, and though her hair was bound in the traditional island way, and her golden face was smooth and set with the almond eyes of an islander, she wore a special robe that enveloped her body in a soft white. As soon as she saw them, Isla's eyes darted away, and she tried with all the determination she possessed to listen to the music while a banshee clawed at her throat until she could hardly breathe.

She could have gone to Eva's for the evening meal, or joined Lucas's expansive family at his uncle's home, and she had gone as often as her heart would allow, but though these friends helped her pass the evenings, they were no cure for the loneliness that followed her even into the fragrant kitchens and to the centre of these riotous family dinners and made her feel an outsider even among her own friends.

So instead Isla walked, searching for the friend she had lost, searching for the answer to her life she had thought she had already found. She wished she could tell Tomas about her father — about how it had been her father who had always dreamed of seeing the world and how her mother, a Lost One, had fled the mainland and had found peace on this island of her daughter's birth.

She wished she could tell him that her father had been a weak and selfish man who had still loved her, though she hadn't been able to see it, and that her mother was not the adventurous heroine of her dreams but had simply been a woman who had been lost, most likely born on the mainland streets to a mother who had been stolen from her home and family, and that that lost woman had finally found love.

She wished she could tell Tomas she had been wrong, that she had built a world on assumptions that had turned out to be anything but true. She wished she could say — *I'm sorry, I'm sure I also did this to you.* But all the evenings that she walked, carrying these thoughts like a weight in her belly, carrying them trapped inside a throat which had sealed itself tight and could not cry out, she did not meet Tomas. He was not out walking, looking for her, and she could not bring herself to go to him, as if crawling, as if begging for redemption.

And then one evening, Isla followed a sloping path that carried her with the force of fate close to the water's edge, and she found herself among a green cluster of silver mangroves. Such trees seemed old even when they were young, and they reached gnarled bony fingers into the brackish sea waters, nurturing all colonies of nascent life before they grew large enough and wise enough to face the open seas. And from the deepest shade of this grove, a figure emerged, balancing carefully on the web-like roots and ducking under the mass of branches overhead. Over one arm she carried a small basket that held any number of mysterious sea things, and as she drew closer, Isla could see the woman wore a white robe that held her body like a cocoon, and she had strange tattoos that wove spirals like permanent island bands around her wrists.

Seeing Isla, the woman raised a hand and smiled. Then, without hesitating, she jumped into the shallow water and waded over to where Isla stood on the sandy shore. "I'm so glad you've come," the woman said. "I'm so glad you've come at last."

Had the oracle been expecting Isla? Was it fate that had guided Isla to this woman who lived among the silver mangroves and would be responsible for changing the course of her destiny? These are things impossible to say. All Isla knew for sure was that there was something quiet and deep in the young oracle's eyes that allowed Isla to skip the superficial introductions usually made between strangers, and compelled her to speak the truth.

"I'm looking for someone who knows things," Isla told her. "I'm looking for someone who can help me."

"What do you want to know?" The oracle asked. "Start from the beginning."

So Isla began to tell the young oracle the story of her life as she told it to herself. She told of her father, of her longing to know the world beyond this small island, and of her journey to the mainland so many years ago. She told of her life on the mainland, full of energy and activity and purpose. A life that, for a long time, had felt meaningful. It had not been easy, Isla assured the woman, who sat on the sand listening to her story with calm, open eyes. It had not been easy. But there had been goals, clear goals to pursue, things to achieve, ways to get better, improve, climb to the top.

"I thought this was my destiny. If I could only become a

mainland scribe, I could make my mark on the world. And then, finally I would feel my life had been worthwhile. I would feel I had done something important."

"But..." the oracle looked at her, and Isla was uncertain whether the oracle was asking a question or making an observation at the inevitable end to such a path.

"But there was always something else, a new thing I had to do." Isla paused. How could she explain? "You see, the mainland..."

"I know the mainland well," the oracle replied, and Isla could not disguise the surprise that flew to her eyes.

"You've been to the mainland?"

"I've seen more places than you might guess, Isla." The oracle smiled. "So I do understand what you speak of, this yearning to accomplish great things. It is a common desire. But this life on the mainland has also not brought you the things you are looking for," the oracle noted.

Isla looked at the oracle with a face in pain and eyes that did not shine silver but were instead a dull grey like a flat, heavy sky. To the young oracle, she looked like a drowning thing, inundated by all the truths that had come to her uninvited and at great cost — that the happiness she knew was always fleeting and that life was full of things that were dissatisfying and painful and unjust.

"You are looking for something," the young oracle spoke and her voice sounded older than her years, "but you have forgotten what it is. You believe you are looking for some Thing — a job, a role, an activity or accomplishment that will give you a sense of meaning. But these things are merely means to an end. What you are really looking for is the same thing all of us are seeking — happiness, fulfilment, satisfaction, peace. They are all names for the same feeling. In its pure form, it is like light that lifts you from the usual weight of your body and lifts the invisible veil of the mundane world around you to reveal the splendour of the universe. It is a state of Being beyond thought, beyond the contingencies of your life — and this sense of happiness *can* last, if you find its true source."

"Are you saying that's possible? To be happy all of the time?"

"The happiness I am speaking of is not the same as pleasure," the oracle shook her head. "It is quieter. It is a feeling of fulfilment, a feeling of peace within oneself. This happiness is the birthright of all beings on this earth. It is part of our very nature."

The oracle paused and shifted her basket onto her other arm. "But we are easily confused in life, Isla," she continued, "and so many people will not find this feeling of peace or joy apart from the briefest moments because they are looking for it in all the wrong places. They look for happiness in wealth, believing that if they could only have a bit more, they would be happy. They look for it in their accomplishments, believing that if they could only achieve 'this' or 'that', then they would be satisfied. They look for it in their status in society, believing that if they could only become an important person, they would feel safe and confident and valuable."

"But the world is a transient place," the oracle said gravely, "and things of this world will always be vulnerable because they are built on a foundation of sand. Everything in the world is impermanent, Isla — our wealth, our work, our successes, the other people in our lives — even our very Selves. They are all impermanent and will not last forever. This is the one great truth. Everything changes. Nothing lasts forever. And so it is fool's mission to look in such a place for lasting happiness, for a sense of fulfilment or a peace that endures. Lasting happiness can never be based on impermanent things."

"So what do I do?" Isla asked. "Where can any of us look if not here in the world?"

"The only place that is left," the oracle replied. "We must look within ourselves. We must listen to the part of ourselves that is connected to the greater universe. Sit long enough and it will come to you. Sit until the mind falls quiet and you will begin to understand many things."

The oracle stood and dusted the sand from the smooth palms of her hands. Then, she looked down at Isla and, finding the young woman's face still encaged by a thousand worries, she laughed. "Don't worry, Isla. This happiness is our very nature. It is already deep within us. And if we are still, we cannot help but find it!"

59

If Isla could have seen what the oracle saw, that she walked close to the razor's edge of truth, perhaps she too would have returned home that night and eaten a warm, spicy meal and settled into the quiet of the evening. But Isla had not been trained by the wise seers of the world and did not know what future lay before her. All she could feel was the chaos of her mind. The doubts. The fears that tracked her footsteps like a hunter and her a wild thing. And so while she wandered slowly back along the coastal path, darkness fell and the new moon failed to rise in the sky.

Twice, Isla stumbled and her heart raced with visions of her tumbling over the edge of the invisible sea cliff. Blackness was before her and all around her. Isla's pace slowed to a crawl as she stuck one foot out in front of the other, feeling tentatively for the reassuring sensation of solid ground.

I'm not getting anywhere like this, Isla thought to herself. For a moment she stood, uncertain what to do next. But because there was nothing to do and no where to go, she surrendered to the darkness and sat down at last on the dusty invisible path.

Above her, she could barely make out the shadows of clouds as they travelled across the starless sky, but when she lowered her gaze she could not see the path before her or behind her, nor the vast, outstretching body of the infinite sea.

In the middle of this darkness, Isla thought of Tomas. She remembered the feeling of seeing him with the young oracle at the fire circle. What did he have to do with her? Why had they come together? It was as if Isla were reliving this moment. She felt the banshee grip her throat and it seemed to her, sitting alone in the dark night as if she were choking.

This isn't happening now, Isla whispered to herself, straining to see through the dark veil of the night, fighting against the heat that had risen to her face and the desperate pounding of her heart. *This has already happened days ago. It's over. Why am I so upset?*

She tried to reason with herself, but her mind was like a wild animal that had grown bold in the presence of its captive host, and there was no stopping it. The night was never-ending as Isla relived her journey with Tomas on the boat back to the island, then, the fight with him by the lighthouse. *What more do you want from me, Isla?* She heard his voice again and again in her mind, and the anger of his words lashed at her like a whip.

Her mind began to dredge up these images, and they swam before her eyes bringing with them the residual emotions of experience. Her heart raced, then fell, her face flushed with the heat of anger, then was washed with the tears of grief and regret. So many memories from her past came like ghosts to torture her.

More thoughts. This time of the mainland, of the woman she had seen in the reflection of glass at Neha's art exhibition the night she had first met Jackimo. She had looked at herself standing tall in mainland heels and scribal robe, her hair oiled and combed into long bands that hung down her back. Was this woman really her? Was that who she wanted to be? In her mind, the reflection of this woman stared back at the windblown Isla of the island, and she felt divided from herself.

And then, another wave of thoughts. Her future. A fearful, uncertain place. And Isla thought — *What am I going to do? Is my life with Jackimo what I really want? What if it is and I can't make it work? And what if it isn't — then where will I go?*

More voices came to her mind. Her father telling her she was ungrateful, that she was making a grave mistake. *Ubash* she heard the unidentifiable voices accuse her. Voices in her mind that had begun to doubt the course of her mainland life. Voices that told her she had no place in the wide world.

Who can say how long Isla listened to the torturous twisting of her mind before she heard a voice in her head that was not her own and was not a voice she had ever heard speak aloud in the open world.

Be Still, it said.

Who had said this to her? Who had thought this thought? Such questions are unanswerable, unfathomable to those who do not understand the power and wisdom of the universe. This thought came to Isla, and she heard it — she heard it with a part of herself that she had never noticed before. She heard it with the self that listened to her thoughts but sat apart from them, the one who watched her heart flood with anger and fear and sorrow, but was not touched by them.

I will wait, Isla thought. *For once, I will just sit and be still and see what happens. After all, it is too dark to go on, so what else can I do?* So Isla sat again with herself on the sandy, winding earth path that she could not see, before a sea that she could only hear, under a sky she could only guess was still above her, and waited to see what would happen.

And what happened was this — she sat and sat, and her mind spun stories before her. Some of these stories were true, things that had happened to her in the past, and some were imagined, scenes of things she might do or things she should have done. But after a time her attention began to return to the present, and Isla began to listen more and more often to the soft, steady sound of the waves rolling upon the shore below. For long moments that stretched outward like water, Isla surrendered to the path she knew lay beneath her, and she listened to the waves of the sea. Then, suddenly and without warning, her mind would drag her off again on some trail of thought, and it would be a long time before she remembered that she was sitting alone on a path by the sea. And yet in those moments, her mind would become quiet, and Isla began to sense a presence beneath the layers of her mind, a part of herself that was also greater than herself.

These were not radical realisations which Isla made in the illuminating darkness of that night, and they did not flood her with the sensation of sudden insight that makes one want to jump and leap and speak in tongues. Yet the longer Isla sat watching her mind, the more obvious and simple it all seemed. Her mind did not do that many different things. It replayed memories. It planned for various imagined futures. It created fictive experiences and played them before her as if they were real. And it tried to solve the remaining problems that were left to her — how much Iosa was left to harvest? Who would buy her father's house? How would she try to change her work on the mainland?

These were the things her mind could do. But there seemed a great many things her mind never did. It was never still, never rested anywhere for long, even on pleasant thoughts that seemed wonderful and full of the possibility of happiness.

And it never seemed any closer to answering the questions that laboured in Isla's heart — what am I doing here on this earth? What is the meaning of my life?

There was something else as well that came to Isla in the timeless hours of darkness — a presence behind her thoughts, behind the mind, so still you hardly even knew it was there. And when Isla sank back into this part of her self, she felt its radiance and was filled with a joy and peace she had not yet known in her long life, though it had been with her all this time.

When dawn came to the skies and the island was illuminated by the purple hues of losa in bloom, Isla opened her eyes and felt once again whole. All at once she remembered something the oracle had said the day before. Or had it been the boatman many years ago? *Certain kinds of knowledge can be learned and passed down through the generations, but true wisdom cannot be taught or passed down. It can only be discovered by each person as they walk their own path.*

Like a true adventurer, Isla stood and, dusting off her crumpled skirts, she turned her back on the path she had been following towards her father's empty house and set off to walk the island and find herself.

60

In the evenings, the young oracle would often find Tomas sitting patiently on the wooden railing of the fence soaking in the warm island sunset. When he heard her footsteps, he would always turn a brown contented face and smile, and then he would jump lightly from his seat and ask, "do you feel like a walk this evening?" And she would nod, a wrap for her shoulders already clasped in her hand.

The young oracle looked forward to Tomas's evening company in a life where she had often been alone. After all, she was young and beautiful despite the weight of wisdom in her eyes and the years of solitude she knew awaited her in this life where she might walk with a man beside the sea but may never call him her own nor wake each morning to the warm comfort of his presence in her bed. But she wouldn't think of these things, she decided. She would just walk and talk and enjoy his company and not ask anything of him that she herself was not able to give.

So they talked of magical things as they walked the winding path on the cliffs above the sea. They spoke of the life force that breathes through the body and weaves its way through all things. They spoke of the way it felt when they were in its presence, the way it sounded like the sea. That this force was both magical and utterly mundane, that at times it felt wonderful and surprising as an exotic land with scents unrecognisable and languages that were indecipherable and sounded like music, and that at other times, it felt old and familiar as the island and just as simple and unexciting.

They spoke of the foundations of peace, of the life such a peace required, of what they had seen when stillness had descended upon them and they had seen into themselves. And they spoke of the untouchable wonder of looking into another's eyes and seeing not simply their face but deep down to the great Seer in them that looked like the great night sky and felt like the universe.

Other evenings they spoke of island things, of the growing seasons and tides and daily concerns. Tomas spoke often of Rohnan, who was such a beautiful little boy with a soul older than the years of his life, but who had to be coaxed into confidence and given space as wide as the sea before he would speak his thoughts aloud. And he told her many stories of his father, of how Jaro had first taught him to train the gulls, and of the day Jaro had given him his first cup of spiced liquor, and the nightmare he had seen in the oracle's cave of his father's death that had eventually come true.

"And what about your mother?" the young oracle had asked him one evening.

"I never had a mother," Tomas had told her. "She left the island just after I was born. But I never felt like I missed her. Father rarely spoke of her, but when he did, he was never sad. He never let on that he longed for her, although I imagine he must have missed her a great deal. But then, Isla never had a mother either, so I suppose it never seemed a strange thing, not to have a mother." He said these things without hesitation or any trace of nostalgia. Was this the truth — that he had never missed his mother? Was it a lie? Even as a man grown, Tomas could not be sure of such things.

"And Isla?" the young oracle asked. "You speak so often of your father and Rohnan and Lucas and Dari and even Marco, but you've never mentioned Isla until now."

Tomas looked at the young oracle, her dark hair tied back and wrapped in the island way, the dark mark under the corner of her right eye that rose and twinkled when she smiled.

"There is nothing left to say," Tomas told her and his voice was low like the deep forested valleys, full of nocturnal creatures and hidden things, and so she did not tell him she had spoken with Isla herself only a few days before.

Instead she said, "It must have been very different for Isla than it was for you."

"What do you mean?"

"Well, from what I've heard, Petro was hardly the kind of father Jaro was to you. And Isla is also a woman, Tomas. It's hardly surprising she felt she needed to know the place her mother came from."

Tomas stepped off the path and put both hands in his pockets and stared out to sea, looking for something solid, something he could rely on to see him through this moment when his heart beat erratically against his chest. He couldn't be sure whether it was this new perspective on Isla's departure that felt like an excavation of an old story he had told himself so many times he had taken it as truth, the story that Isla had left him. Or whether it was that this possibility came from this new woman's lips and made him feel as he had often felt looking at his island from out at sea where it seemed he did not know his own home.

"You should make peace, Tomas," the young oracle's gentle voice found him out at sea and pulled him back to the present and into her company again.

Tomas watched the oracle's face, so young and open, and yet she held a quality of stillness that does not accompany age but rather comes by soaking the skin in silence as he had done out at sea.

"Yes," he nodded because he knew she was right. Tomas knew the island's oracle never married — that it was this woman's destiny to live alone in the house beside the ridge, to be protected only by the expanse of silver mangroves that filled the bay below. But there was something in her eyes that felt familiar, as if he belonged with her. And so, without knowing why and without wondering at the consequences as he might have done in earlier days, he allowed himself to be drawn to her, and it was most days now that he found himself walking along the coastal path and speaking of things he had been unable to say for many years.

Then, one night after their walk, Tomas and the young oracle returned to find the oracle's mother waiting in the garden. She raised her hand to Tomas, but in her mind she thought, *this has gone on long enough. It is only my own weakness that I have not spoken sooner. Jaro would be disappointed in me — after all these years as the oracle to have become simply a mother again...*

"What is it?" the young oracle asked when Tomas had gone, for she saw an old courage in her mother's warm brown eyes that she remembered well. The woman who was a mother but was also the oracle gestured to her daughter.

"Sit," she said. "There is more to say and time is running out."

And then she told her daughter the secret of the oracle. "You are the island's oracle now, Althea. And one day you must have a daughter to carry on the line of the oracle," she said more firmly than necessary, "and daughter, there is only one way to conceive a child."

The mother watched, but the young oracle's eyes did not widen when she told her daughter that she must lie with a man and how it must be done.

"You must choose someone kind, daughter, a good man," she told her. "One that is not yet married and one that understands the unalterable fate of the oracle." And then she told her daughter how to care for herself during pregnancy, and all the complicated methods of keeping one's pregnancy and later, the child's parentage, secret from the islanders.

"He must never come to you once your daughter is born," she stared firmly into her daughter's eyes, as firmly as her own mother once had done, but inside her heart was breaking because she knew, even if her daughter did not, that this law was the most painful burden the oracle had to bear.

"Faith in the oracle rests on the unbroken line," she explained, hoping to give her daughter enough strength to resist the temptation that would come one day as surely as the next wave upon the shore. "It is not the oracle's destiny to have a family, for a family turns one's thoughts and creates an insular mind. And the oracle is for the island. She is its caretaker, its wise seer, the healer of suffering, the holder of the knowledge of the path to freedom."

"I understand, mother," the young oracle said quietly as the first fireflies began to flicker around her. "I will know the right man, and I will raise the daughter he gives me, and I will teach her to be the oracle of this island. I know it will not be easy, I can see in your face, but please don't worry. I have been through many years of training, and I will know what to do with my daughter."

"And you must also know what to do if you have a son."

The space between the two women fell silent, but it was not still, for even the air reverberated with the waves of this mother's unexpected words.

"If I have a son?" The thought had never crossed the young oracle's mind. The young oracle was not naïve. She had long suspected what she might have to do with a man, though for the years of her training she had put such thoughts from her mind. But to have a son? The oracle only ever had a daughter!

"If your first born child is a girl, you must give her the name Althea, the name of the next oracle, and you must never again lie with a man, or if you must, there is an herb I will show you that will protect you from any consequences. But daughter, I must tell you, because my own mother did not — if you have a son, the father must raise it and you must forget that he was ever yours."

In the waning light, a shadow had fallen across the mother's face, and it seemed to the young oracle that in that single moment her mother had aged a hundred moons and half a lifetime.

"Your mother never told you..." the young oracle began.

"I was her first born," the mother replied, "as she was of her mother."

"But you needed to know..."

"I needed to know," the mother said simply.

And then, unable to hold back the flood waters of this secret kept so long beneath the earth, she clasped her daughter's hands. "I had to give him away, Althea," she said softly, firmly. "I had to. It is the way. The oracle cannot raise a son. So I gave him to the man who was his father, to the man who was also your father…"

"You gave him to Jaro," the young oracle finished.

"I gave him to Jaro," she replied.

61

Isla sat down on her bed with a sigh and pressed the small string of pearls to her forehead, and her mind fled back over the years to the day Tomas had given them to her. Then she shook her head in her hands. Nothing about her return to the island had turned out like she had expected.

Even with her eyes closed, Isla could sense the presence of the wooden crates that stood in the main room like attendants awaiting her return to the mainland. The weight of these crates pressed down on her, but her mind was so tired from its constant vacillations.

I should return to my position.
I should change the role of the mainland scribe.
I should quit my post.
I should convince Jackimo to move from the mainland city.
I should sell my father's house.
I should keep my father's house.
I will return to the island.
I will probably never return to the island...

It was finished. Whatever the right or wrong of it now,

Isla had resigned herself to returning to her mainland life. *There is no easy path, and there is no right decision*, she thought, *but I must see things through.*

The boatman had agreed to take her back across the water to the mainland. Tomorrow, she would accept the offer on her father's land, leaving out the house and gardens. She was an islander, but she was also a mainlander now, and she understood without regret that it was her destiny to live between worlds.

Isla remembered the night they had first met, and Jackimo had seen past her island voice to her eyes and had known from that first moment that she came also from the mountains. He had seen something in her that no one else had seen before. An acknowledgement of her mother's heritage, an inheritance beyond that bestowed by the island. She thought about the fact that, in all the moments she had doubted her abilities — as a scribe or as a mainlander — Jackimo's faith in her had never wavered. And she remembered how he had been the only one who had understood why she had never returned home. He hadn't criticised her or demanded any moral justifications. No, Jackimo had absolved her of her guilt and had said logically, "Isla, it is possible that your father loves you and that he only cares about himself." *When I get home to Jackimo*, she thought, *maybe things will seem clearer.*

But then, as if these words had tempted fate, Tomas's face flashed in her mind, his dark brown eyes watching her, just watching, as if he saw down into her, beyond her mainland self or her island self, down to the presence she had perceived that dark night on the lonely path. And so, as it always was, she thought of Tomas.

Yet for all the memories she had with him throughout

the long days of their childhood, memories which far exceeded the number of days she had spent with Jackimo, this time she did not think of particular words he had spoken or any of the reckless things they had done. Instead, she only saw his face, his warm brown eyes framed by his unruly dark hair. And slowly she realised that the face she saw was his face that day he had showed her the underwater cave — during those hours when they were still too young to fear what struggles lay before them, and she was still too young to realise that he already loved her.

In her mind, she remembered his brown, sun-burnt skin and the way his eyes had watched her as he floated in the cave just above the water line. She remembered the deep purple light that had surrounded them that afternoon like the beautiful veil of losa in bloom. And in her mind, time passed and she watched as his face changed, grew, aged, acquired an angular shape and a quiet determined look.

She recalled the smile he wore when he had guessed her secret, the way his eyes looked through her as he did when he was thinking about things he could not put into words. She remembered his look of seriousness and awe as he tried to draw the gulls in mid-flight. And she remembered the way he had looked at her with a haggard despair the night that his father had been put to sea.

A thousand faces of him, which she knew so well despite the years that had separated them. And in all these changing faces, Isla looked back into his eyes and saw into the depths of him, and she could not say why her heart leapt or why her eyes filled with tears at what she saw there.

Slowly, Isla stood and wandered, as if for the last time, through the empty caverns of the house, from her room, into the main room, through the doorway of her father's study, back into her father's bedroom. It felt like a dead thing, this house, a carcase that lay still and sad and without that magic breath which gives life to all things.

"I'm sorry," she whispered, although she wasn't quite certain whether she was sorry for the way she had neglected this house, or for the fact that she would not really miss it when she was gone.

Out on the porch, the afternoon sunlight slanted through the trees like ribbons of light, and she paused for a moment to take in the peacefulness and simple joy of this place that was so different from the wild, wonderful energy of the mainland city.

Two places, separated by a sea. Two homes, so different from one another — and neither of them the places she had hoped they would be. On the one hand, Isla saw that the mainland was like the brave hero charging off into a future bright with the lights of progress, confident in the righteousness of its purpose. A city of heroes, forcing the world to surrender to its greater vision. But against her will, the mainland had also taken on another face, and Isla saw also that the mainland was like a maze through which people raced and raced and never found what they were really searching for. She saw that the mainland was a place where everyone liked to believe they were advancing from one generation to the next, over the decades and centuries when the truth was that most people still concerned themselves with the same things — food and drink and comforts, family, friends, lovers, their reputation, their own grand accomplishments that were suddenly dwarfed when they stared up at the night sky, and all the little things that make up the small world people inhabit.

Then there was the island. For Isla knew better than

anyone that the island was no paradise. That it was familiar and predictable and still filled with people whose eyes were focused only on this small plot of land in the wide earth, determined to believe that this island was all there was or would ever be. And yet, since she had returned, the island had also taken on another face, for the oracle had shown her that the answers she had abandoned the island to seek were actually hidden much closer to home. And it had been on the island, not the mainland of her great expectations, that she had seen through the muddy undulating waters of her mind and down down down to the presence beneath where things felt whole and complete and magical again.

As much as Isla wanted to deny it, the truth was that while the plumage of her external body — the way she clapped her hands or brought a soft lilt to her voice or straightened her hair with scented oils or let it fly wild and curly in the sea winds — had changed over time and with the seasons and the company she kept, there was some deep part of her that had not changed as much as one might have expected.

Looking up, Isla gazed across the peaceful view of her hills. It was the same as it had been every morning of her life on the island, but the simplicity of the trees and bare earth and rows of losa had been transformed from the cocoon of this thought. It was as if Isla were looking at her land for the first time and what she saw was that each thing pulsed with the life force of the universe. The leaves of the mango trees and the long wild grass and the losa that was the lifeblood of this land shimmered as sunlight reflects ephemeral and untouchable and real on the surface of water.

Sitting down on the porch step, Isla realised that her eyes had filled with tears at the sight of this magical world that lay beneath the surface of things. This was what she was looking for — this magical, wonderful world, and herself a part of it all. Why hadn't she seen it before? Why did she have to see it here, on this island that she was leaving behind?

62

Any other island man in his position would have nodded his head, tapped his forefinger against his brow and thanked the Isa for his great luck in life, for by island standards, Lucas was a rich man. His wife was still beautiful with her almond-shaped eyes and sensible smile, and she had blessed him with a lovely daughter and a bright-eyed son who still idolised him. The house he lived in had been the house of his father, and this was a valued marker on an island, distinguishing him as the favourite son among his notoriously large family.

But Lucas held the weighted memory of his father's premature death, and the immense fear he associated with the idea of death was matched only by his determination to avoid a similar fate. So there had been his trading work, his chaotic politicking amongst the harvesters and traders during the crisis of the Losa Council. And despite his successes, his worries of death and his fears of disappearing into the folds of time would not leave him.

Over the days that followed the big council meeting, Lucas fell into a profound melancholy, which no amount of smoking or spiced liquor could make him forget. He sank deeper and deeper into the well of his sorrow until he forgot altogether what it felt like to be happy. He had forgotten the balmy days when his great triumph had been stealing a bottle of his uncle's spiced liquor to drink with his friends by the rebellious circle of the fire. He had forgotten the mango-sweetened days when he had fallen in love and lay naked against Rosa's golden skin and cared for nothing but her and the taste of her untameable lips. He had forgotten the nights he and Tomas had smoked and talked about their dreams for the future, nights when it had felt as if they should only keep following the path they were walking, straight and steady, and in time their dreams would inevitably appear on the horizon before them.

Before his mind's eye the image of his father wavered unsteadily, taunting him with his youthful look and reminding him that Lucas was now older than his father had been when he had passed to the sea. So this was why Lucas did not notice the creeping streaks of black that began to weave their way across the sky one afternoon with the early warnings of a great storm.

Slowly, the clouds gathered until they stood like levitating mountains, looming above the island, threatening to collapse with their great weight and crush the centre of the world to oblivion. And it was only when his brother Aimen called to him from the top of the hill and strode at a pace towards the house, that Lucas looked up from the fog of his mind and noticed the black stain spreading across the sky.

"There's going to be a storm," Aimen told him with a grave look in his eye. "The fishermen say it'll be a bad one."

"Looks like it," Lucas nodded. "Bad enough to head underground?"

"Think so," Aimen replied. "We're headed to da's as soon as we can secure the house."

"You mean to uncle Cassius's," Lucas said, bristling at his brother's common slip of the tongue.

"For Tali's sake, Lucas! When will you let that go?"

"When you remember where you come from!" Lucas stood abruptly from his chair.

Aimen shook his head. "Now's not the time. I'm headed home." Turning, he stepped lightly down the steps of the house, and Lucas heard him call, "I'd secure the house and get Rosa and the children to Cassius's cellar soon," though Aimen did not look back.

Lucas had enough time to secure the house before the wind began to pick up. Boards covered all the open windows, the furniture from the porch had been moved inside, and heavy tables and wooden chests of clothes had been shifted to hold the back door and to provide extra support for the bedroom windows. *Although*, Lucas thought, *it will all be for naught if the roof doesn't hold.*

Rosa had packed their food, various articles of clothing, and certain sentimental items into cloth sacks, and the children had each chosen their favourite toy to take with them to the underground shelter of their grandparents' cellar. They did not say goodbye to the house, for how could they have believed what destruction lay ahead? Simply, Rosa took her daughter Ria's hand while Lucas pulled the thick dining table as close to the door as he could manage, and then he slipped through the small space of the threshold, hoisted the largest sack over his left shoulder and the family set out through the rising wind and under the malevolent sky that had turned an unnatural shade of brown.

When they reached Cassius's house, Lucas's mother was waiting for them at the door. She did not say, "What took you so long!" as she might have done in the days before Lucas's strange fever, but rather kissed them each in turn and ushered them down the hall and through the hatch in the floor that led to the dark cellar. Behind them, Lucas heard his uncle pushing their own wooden chest against the front door.

The cellar was cool and smelled damp as a bog. In the blinding darkness, he felt someone hand him a blanket and he stumbled with the members of his family over piles of food and large tubs of water to a clear space in the corner of the cellar. Lucas's mother placed the single candle on the floor in the middle of the room and, as his eyes slowly adjusted to the shadows, it seemed to Lucas that the candle cast a strange light across the faces of his family, revealing their true thoughts, so that his son looked up at him not in adoration as Lucas had often perceived, but in doubt that this father could really protect him, his brother watched him not with envy at his new position on the Council but with the sympathy of one who watches a fish writhing helplessly upon the shore only inches from the life-breath of water.

His mother too seemed to have changed, for as Lucas watched her pat his uncle Cassius's hand, he saw that she looked at him not with the love he had always feared had replaced the memory of his real father, but with tolerance and acceptance and a compassion that sprang from knowing certain things the rest of the world does not.

And Rosa, his beloved Rosa. The flickering of the candle made Lucas mistrust his sight, but what he saw through the shadows was a sadness in Rosa's face that he had failed to perceive in these anxious, hurried days. But there it was, clear in the dim light, the sadness she wore deep in her heart, and she seemed to him as a woman trying to stand through an earthquake, as a woman trying to stand when everything she had come to trust had gone and even the very land beneath her feet had betrayed her, though she hid this sadness behind reassuring smiles that comforted her children.

Within the hour, they could hear the rain beating against the roof and the wind screaming against the sides of the house. "Da?" Lucas heard Rohnan whisper, and he pulled Rohnan's face into his chest.

"Don't be afraid," he said, feeling an old warmth return at these words spoken to comfort his child. "Don't be afraid. I'm right here."

Through the darkness, Lucas heard his mother begin to sing. It was an old island song.

He went away, shilay, shilay,
Through the mists of the dawning sea.
I saw him go, shilo, shilo,
Though it pained my heart to be
Here on the shores of island sand
Here on the shores of this indigo land
Without him I cannot be free.

A song about a woman and a man. A song about love. A song about loss. It was always the same with these island songs, and yet for the first time, it felt to Lucas as if he were hearing the words from his mother's lips, and he suddenly understood as he had not before that perhaps island women sang these songs from a deeper awareness than he knew. They sang from experience. They sang about their fathers and husbands, their brothers and friends. They sang about themselves. And so he listened,

...shilay shilay
As the sea rose up to meet him
I saw him go, shilo shilo

And nothing I did could keep him
Here on the shores of island sand
Here on the shores of this indigo land
One day at sea I will meet him.

Above them, the house shook with the voice of the storm, crying like a forgotten banshee, rattling in its old bones, and booming with the threats of war and universal destruction. Gradually the candle in the middle of the small underground room fell dim until Lucas could not make out the faces of his family gathered in heaps of homemade quilts surrounded by the necessities of life when all else had been stripped away.

At times the noises from above grew so loud that Lucas was certain the roof had gone, that even the waves of the sea far below had risen up to crush them in their human frailty. But as the storm wore on, hour after hour, his nerves wore so thin that an unlikely peace descended upon him, as a lone soldier that surrenders after a long, blood-stained battle, and he simply sat wondering, but not fearing, if this would be his end.

It had been a great age since Lucas had been capable of sitting still, feeling the heat of his son's cheek on his lap, knowing rather than wishing for contentment. Here he was, grown from a young reckless boy into a man that had lived and worked and had, whether through habit or luck or fate, surpassed the lifespan of his father.

And yet, he was entirely incapable of gratitude, so consumed were his thoughts of death. He lived close to it, as if the only thing that separated him from death were a paper-thin sheath. Time. And how quickly it went! For whether he lived to thirty or eighty, death would come to him, as it does to us all, and if he simply ceased to exist and was forgotten from the records of humanity, it would be as if he had never existed at all.

If this was to be his fate, he wondered, if this was the only fate left to anyone, what meaning was there in life? If death was the only destination, what did any of it matter — his good deeds, his missteps, his love, his hate, his work? It had been many months, perhaps years, for who could say such things, that Lucas had sat without feeling this wide truth of the universe before him and he was exhausted from the feeling of his own impotency, the inconsequential nature of his life.

Lucas had spent so many months of days before this day of the great storm working to establish his reputation, his status — for the only comfort he could find was in the possibility that he would be remembered long after his death, that his life would be remembered forever. This was not possible for every individual in the vast sea of humanity. It was a privilege reserved for great men alone. So, he too would be a great man. And his reward, he thought, would be the immortality of his name. He might die, but his name should live on forever.

The peace of the dark cellar had given him space to consider these thoughts, to mull over the events of the past year with a detachment he had not felt in the tepid heat of his home. In the cool darkness, Lucas's mind drifted over these thoughts like a bird on a morning breeze, calm and full of hope for the coming day.

And then suddenly and for no reason at all, a different thought came to him through the silence. Lucas heard this voice in his head that came from no one but himself, and it said, *All things that are born, also pass away*. And then it said, *Everyone is forgotten in the end, Lucas, even the greatest of men. Eventually everyone is forgotten*. This had always been his greatest fear. And yet when he heard the truth of these words that had come from himself, Lucas suddenly felt a great burden lift from his shoulders as if a yoke that had chained him to a particular life had been broken. And he was free!

Lucas gazed over the faces of his family and for the first time, rejoiced in the smallness of his own life, for he saw the possibility of freedom hidden in this truth — he could live whatever life he wanted, because nothing he did would ever change the currents of the ocean or the presence of the island or the course of the universe. One day, he would be forgotten, but the island would still be here, and the sea would still flow with the currents that made up its nature. And perhaps one day the island would no longer rise out of the sea, but the universe would continue to change and flow and manifest new forms of life.

In the darkness of the storm, Lucas reached out and brought his arm around his wife. He could feel the beating of his own heart against her cool body. "I'm back," he whispered in her ear. "Please forgive me darling. Forgive me. I'm back now," and he felt the depth of her love when she leaned into his body and wrapped her arms around his neck and said, "okay."

63

The clouds had begun to gather by the time Isla set out for Tomas's lighthouse, filling the sky with the deep azure blues of evening, though it had just passed mid-day. For a moment, Isla paused, wondering if it was wise to journey across the island when heavy rains were certainly on their way, but this was her last chance to see Tomas. Isla was determined to make amends, and perhaps also to confirm the indisputable logic of her return to the mainland by speaking this news aloud to Tomas. No matter how many doubts continued to plague her, Isla felt her return to her mainland life as an inevitable reality. She had made her choice. She had made it years ago, and putting one foot in front of another was the only thing she knew to do.

Yet when she reached the lighthouse, the wind had grown cold as a foreboding whisper. Tomas was already shifting his gardening tools and hammock and woven cot into the shed, and he did not pause when he saw her approaching.

"What are you doing here, Isla, a storm is coming!"

Hoisting the cot over his head, he headed towards the open shed door.

"I needed to see you. I'm leaving tomorrow."

Tomas emerged from the dark recesses of the threshold. "You are," he said, and Isla couldn't tell whether he was surprised or whether he had been expecting her to leave for weeks. Then he strode back towards the garden and continued collecting baskets of green tomatoes and beans he had picked that morning. "Well, give me a hand then. It looks like it's going to be a bad one."

They had only been working for several minutes when Amos came running towards them calling from the road. "Tomas! Hey Tomas! It's going to be a bad easterly!" he shouted as he ran. "The fishermen come in from the sea this morning said maybe the worst we've seen!"

"Bad enough to board the windows?" Tomas called back as Amos drew nearer.

"I should think so. The fisher-folk are all in a frenzy preparing their houses and storing fresh water, and that can't be a good sign."

"Okay Amos," Tomas nodded, clapping him on the back. "Thanks for coming out here. You'd better get back home and help Sera and the girls. Where are you bunking down?"

"Our pantry's stone and hasn't got windows," Amos replied. "We've always been alright there."

They shook hands and bade each other well as men who have known each other all their lives, and then Amos turned and began to jog back down the path under the deepening sky.

Tomas took flat boards to the windows of the lighthouse while Isla began to pump fresh drinking water into every available bucket, bowl, and cup she could find. She filled the bathing tub, searched for the extra store of candles, and carried loads of firewood from the shed, which was sure to be soaked, into the lower floor of the stone lighthouse.

They worked for what seemed only minutes but could have been hours, calling directions to each other in voices that felt familiar and comforting in the midst of the rising winds. In the shed, Tomas tied down what he could with thick rope and dragged several large dead tree limbs into the shed so they would not be thrown about in the storm.

And then the rains came, sudden like a scream from the skies, pelting the crown of Isla's head and driving through the thin blue shirt that covered Tomas's shoulders.

"Come on," Tomas yelled, grabbing Isla's hand and running for the lighthouse.

"Wait, there are still…"

"Isla," Tomas said, pulling at her wrist, "it's over. We've done all we can. We have to get inside."

Inside the lighthouse, Tomas and Isla sat in the candle-light listening to the groaning and screaming of the wind. The rain beat against the sides of the stone lighthouse from all directions, and there was a wildness to it that Isla did not recognise from memory.

Tomas handed Isla a towel and she wiped her face as he lit the candles on the dining table. With the windows covered by boards, the main room of the lighthouse was full of darkness and as the frantic activity of the past hour subsided, Isla felt a shyness return to her and she hid gratefully in the shadows of the room.

"Do you want a cup?" Tomas was at the stove pouring himself a cup of losa. "It's cold, but we'll melt if I light the stove with the windows boarded up like this."

"Sure," Isla nodded and stepped towards him to accept the cup he offered.

"I'm glad you're here," Tomas said, and Isla wasn't sure if

it was simply her imagination but it seemed as if his voice softened around the edges. "Your da's house isn't a good place to be in a storm like this."

They sat down at the table, the room filling with *drune* around them. To chase away the awkwardness they felt at the humming sensation of their skin, they made obvious observations about the storm and speculated on where their friends would have found shelter. Lucas's family would be with his mother and Cassius in their cellar, Tomas knew. Eva's husband had built an underground bothy where he distilled his own spiced liquor, and Isla guessed this would be where their family would ride out the storm.

Yet, there were many on the island, Dari, Lott, the boatman… that neither Tomas nor Isla could be sure would be safe through this kind of storm, and they spoke of these friends in trembling voices, the nascent fear of the storm still pulsing strongly through their blood.

64

Time stretched on and the only measure was the candle that dripped and shrank and then had to be replaced. And then replaced again. Still the winds screamed with incalculable wrath and the boards on the windows warped and shuttered under the pressure of the storm.

And then without thinking, Isla heard her own voice break through the awkward stillness that had spread out between them. "The storm is going to take the house!" And these words, which had left her mouth before she had realised the truth of them, shocked her.

Tomas reach out and put a wide hand on top of her cool fingers, and she said again into the darkness, "Oh Tomas, this storm is going to take the house," and she didn't know whether this thought made her feel happy or sad.

He waited for her to continue, such was the weight of her words, but Isla simply ran her fingers into hair that had yielded to the wild of the island winds, just as a carefully constructed house must yield over time to vines and flowers and the web of growing things that advance with the natural tenacity of the jungle. In the candlelight, her skin burned a golden colour and her eyes held flecks of silver as they had once done when she had felt young and full of the early sparks of inspiration.

Tomas shifted on the bench and leaned his back against the wall. "I'm sorry I got angry with you when you came here before," he said. He paused for a long time. But then to Isla's surprise he continued, "You know, I never really thought what it must have been like for you in that house. I've been thinking a lot. So many memories have come to me since you've been back." He sighed and Isla wondered what he had remembered and whether these memories had brought him joy or simply more anger.

"I didn't think of it then, but I remember how often you were here at the lighthouse. How we hardly ever played at your house. And I was thinking about your da. He was so harsh with you sometimes, Isla. He never really saw you. And I didn't really think about what that was like for you..."

"We were young," Isla told him, shrugging in the way she so often did when islanders spoke of her father.

"We weren't that young," Tomas replied. "It's not an excuse. But I always had Jaro and you always seemed..." He paused again and his warm eyes caught the light of the candle and held a certain faraway look that Isla knew. Then he smiled and his gaze fell upon her. "You were always a tough, wild girl. You never let anything stop you. You know, I used to watch you climb up the banyan sometimes, and I'd see how high you were and I used to be scared to death because I knew I'd have to climb at least that high too!" He laughed to himself.

"You didn't have to follow me," Isla felt her mouth twitch with a smile.

"You think I'd have let you beat me climbing! Not a chance!" Tomas almost laughed, but then his face shifted and for a moment Isla saw him watch the flicker of the shadows dance on the wall and she knew his thoughts had raced out in another direction. "It didn't occur to me how hard it was for you to grow up without your mother and with Petro as a father," he tried again, "but it should have."

"Well, it's all past now," Isla shook her head.

She let him refill her cup. Looking out into the dark shadows of the room, Isla thought about her own house, the crumbling, old, decrepit house that she had hated and loved and that was all she had left to remember her mother and father. What was happening to it? Right now, as she sat here, safe in the stone fortress of the lighthouse? Would the roof hold? Would the rain that was surely pouring through the wooden slatted window shades flood the house? Would the water reach her crates that stood neatly packed and waiting for her in the centre of the room? Would everything be destroyed?

For a brief instant, Isla thought of her mother's white nightgown that she had held against her face and then gently packed away with the other things she would bring back to the mainland, and in her mind she saw the muddy waters of the storm swallow it whole and drag it out of the house and down the hill and out into the wild sea. Lost in thought, Isla felt a warm hand against her arm, and then a wide palm like a blanket against her cheek.

Without speaking, Tomas stood and walked out of the gentle sphere of candlelight. A few paces away, he searched for his box of leaves and smoking weed and was just about to return to the table when there was an enormous roar, an ear-splitting crack, and the board that had protected one of the windows split.

Immediately the candlelit room plunged into darkness. The wind screamed through the tiny opening in the stone wall, and Isla and Tomas could hear things being thrown from their shelves and ripped off the walls.

Isla stumbled towards the shape that was Tomas, and they yelled at each other over the voice of the wind to hold this in place, stand here, watch out, hold on tight. Isla pushed her weight against the board while Tomas put nail after nail into the wooden frame. The wind was a wild thing, and it beat with each unpredictable gust against the board, threatening to fling it mercilessly into Isla's face.

"Stay here!" Tomas yelled in her ear. "I'm going to reinforce it from the outside."

Isla wanted to grab his arm, tell him not to go. She wanted to cry out "don't leave me!" but she needed both hands to hold the board in place and before she could bring the words to her lips, she saw Tomas opening the door to the deafening violence of the storm and then he was gone and an eerie quiet came over the room that sat apart from the pounding rain and roaring wind outside.

That wind! Isla thought. *That wind could rip a banyan from its roots. It could send a fallen branch soaring through the air and crashing into anything in its path.*

Outside Tomas gripped the sides of the stone wall with his fingers and inched through the driving rain to the window. The sea was an evil black, as if it had been turned by the temper of the storm, and Tomas did not recognise in it that beautiful still place where he had once heard true silence for the first time and felt its peace.

Using the force of the wind itself, Tomas shifted the piece of wood he was carrying up the wall until it slammed into the alcove of the window. It took only a few nails on this side before Tomas felt certain it would hold. Breathing slowly to calm the rush in his head, Tomas moved back along the base of the lighthouse until at last he felt the alcove, then the door and he pulled himself inside.

"You can let go now," he said to Isla through the sea of darkness, but he could hear that Isla did not move.

"You can let go now, Isla," he said again, feeling his way around a fallen chair, the edge of a table, over the debris that covered the floor.

"Isla?"

He could feel her breathing next to him, feel the warmth of her body, the beads of rain that still clung to her arms as he touched her. But the room was pitch black without the candlelight, and Tomas couldn't find her face in the darkness.

"Isla?"

And then he realised she was crying. In the black sea he found her, his hands brushing against the sea tears that fell from her eyes.

For a moment, he longed to hold her. But Tomas remembered this feeling from other times, so many other times, and so he fought against it and held himself very still.

And then, in that quiet that had fallen over them like a veil, Tomas felt the weight of her forehead fall against his chest and her hand reach up to clutch his shirt and without hesitation he wrapped his arms around her shoulders that felt so small as they shook, and his wide hands, still damp with rain, entangle themselves in her wild hair.

"Did something hit you?" He felt Isla shake her head, but still she did not speak.

This is too hard, Tomas heard a voice in his mind whisper to him. Tomas felt himself sinking back into the familiar feeling of drowning which was both pain and bliss and had no name.

Perhaps just for this moment, he told the voice. *I'm not a child anymore. I know who I am. Perhaps I can love her for this moment and accept that nothing lasts forever.*

"You're alright Isla-ja," he said, stroking her head as it lay bowed beneath his chin, wondering how it could be that she wasn't his.

Isla-ja. Isla-love. The word cut through all the dark confusion of her mind, all the years of swallowing her fears and putting one foot in front of the other because she believed it was her destiny and she didn't know what else to do but see it through. It pierced through the logic of her life to a pearl buried deep within her and wrenched her heart open until she could no longer hold the pain of it herself and the soft choking sound that tore from her throat was a sound Tomas had never heard.

"Isla!"

"I'm lost, Tomas," was all she could think of to say. "I'm lost. I'm lost in the dark."

"Isla, what..." Tomas felt the world shrink around him until there was only the sound of his breath and hers, of his body and hers, surrounded by a vast darkness and a storm that raged on and on.

"I had to leave..." her voice finally came again, broken and almost imperceptible among the ragged sounds of the storm that still crashed around them.

"I had to... I needed to see things. I needed to know..." Her words came in gasps, as if she herself were clutching at some truth she did not fully understand.

"But that doesn't mean I wanted to lose everything here... you and Eva and father and my home. And now things haven't turned out like I thought. I'm not... And now... I'm alone in the dark..."

Tomas knew nothing that had happened to her over the past ten years. He knew nothing about her mainland life.

And yet before he could think his hands passed over her face, tilting her chin until he felt that they were looking at each other through the blinding darkness, and he felt the energy of her presence burning into him.

"I see you, Isla-ja." He said this to her quietly so that she would hear him truly and know what he felt in his heart.

There was silence in the room as the eye of the storm brought the world to the most profound stillness that is only possible after the brutal destruction of its winds and rains.

"Do you see that I still love you?" she whispered at last through that quiet black sea.

In truth perhaps he had seen it. Perhaps he had seen it in her eyes when she had caught sight of him on the streets of the mainland, or in the way she had looked at him on those days on the liminal sea, for when she spoke these words into the darkness they did not make his heart jump with surprise but instead felt as obvious as the cry of the gulls in the skies, as inevitable as the crash of the waves against the shore. The words fell across his face soft and true.

Yet even now I feel afraid, Tomas thought to himself. And then he thought, *but I am tired of this fear. It is not love but fear that has worn me down and made me lose my way. But I know what I am and what I am not. I am great and wide as the sea. I cannot know all things, and I cannot predict the winds of the world, but I can love this woman still.*

And then he kissed her and it felt the only truth of her life. Isla surrendered to the sound of her destiny changing course and knew that at last she had found her way home.

They did not move from the place where they stood, at first because Isla still shook from the storm within herself, and later because the darkness and dissolution of time had wrapped them in a cocoon so safe and true that they could only stand holding each other amidst the destruction of the world they had known.

Finally Tomas felt Isla's grip on his arm relax and he slowly moved to find a candle. The light burned a hole in the black room and made them squint. Tomas placed the light on the table and looked back to the dim place where Isla stood. Then he saw something that made him smile in that crooked way she knew so well, and he said, "You look just as you did the day we tried to dig a hole through the centre of the world."

Isla stood to her full height and stepped towards him into the light. "No," she said, "I must look quite different. I think this time I've found the way through."

It was these words, among all the others, that convinced Tomas that she had finally come back to him. And he brought her into his arms and kissed her again and again and felt the sea well up in his own eyes as he realised he never had to stop.

"I don't know what this means, Tomas." Isla whispered against his face. "I don't know if I can stay here forever…"

"Then we will go somewhere else," Tomas replied. "The world is wide, Isla-ja. And so are we."

65

Our greatest fear is our fear of death. We are born knowing that one day death will come, and from that moment our lives are filled with a profound dread of annihilation. So we vacillate, throughout our lives, between our desperate attempts to forget our mortality and our unrelenting search to find a greater meaning to our lives.

The boatman knew such things, as he knew the old language that flowed beneath the current of people's daily talk. He knew that, young and old, fishermen, growers, harvesters and traders, islanders and mainlanders, men and women — all people felt the unique quality of their individual lives. All people felt they were destined for great things.

Like an army they descended on the world, scrounging among the riches of the earth, struggling to make their unparalleled mark, fighting for recognition and fame, wandering like lost souls unwilling to face themselves. Like hungry ghosts, they devoured anything that might fill the emptiness that consumed them, and they looked in madness at those uncommon few who did not horde what they had and scramble for more. Like dying men, they strove to create an image of themselves that would last beyond their weak and mortal bodies — an immortal piece of themselves. Something of themselves that would last.

The language of men was so complicated, so convoluted, so filled with twists and turns and webs of meaning. But beneath it, the boatman knew, flowed the old language that was the language of the world, and this language was so simple that it was almost indecipherable, and thus it took many more years to understand.

The boatman had felt the coming of the storm to the island like a wind foretelling change. He had set out to check his boat under comfortingly clear skies, but the island fishermen he found at the docks were already ill at ease for the shoals of fish they knew had left for deeper waters and that was an ill omen, they murmured, an ill omen indeed. In this wary state, the fishermen needed no more encouragement than a few gathering clouds, and the boatman watched as seven strong men began to hoist the boats from the water and carry them up the steep, cobbled hill to higher land.

All morning and into the afternoon the boatman worked with these men, while houses were secured and the word was spread throughout the island that a great easterly was coming. He laboured until an unnatural earthy brown colour began to work its way across the sky, and on its tails an evil black, like a sneer, that hinted of worse things to come. Then, with a surprising lightness in his heart, he bid the men farewell and good wishes, and though they insisted he should ride the storm with them, for their homes were solidly built and stacked together for protection, the boatman shook his head and headed out on the path that crossed the island towards the cove of silver mangroves.

The storm had come then, like an army from the east, a storm that had already flattened villages, screamed across islands, sent boats capsizing, and kept traders, sailors, adventurers and travellers of all kinds stranded in time. For time stands still during storms such as these, and all who witness their destruction and mighty power must bow their heads in surrender and wait.

And when, at last, the end had passed and the sky had cleared, the boatman left the refuge of the oracle's cavern and looked upon the island with his imperturbable eyes. What he saw was that all the finery and flair that had dressed the island of the past, all its layers of personality, its great adorations and the things that it had shunned, the look of its face — all of it had gone. The island stood bare and in ruins. But it also stood true. It had survived.

The boatman looked off to the left, and in the distance, he saw that the lighthouse still stood with its white-washed walls like a shining pearl and that its light had been lit that morning as a beacon of hope to them all. And so he, like all islanders, walked towards this light, walked across the land where all paths had been erased, walked with the proud brown-eyed woman that had once been the oracle, walked with the daughter who had taken her place.

The boatman raised a hand to islanders as they all trudged across the forsaken land, climbing over broken tree limbs and skirting around pieces of wood that had once been roofs and walls and gates and fence posts and now looked like none of these things. He walked towards the growing crowd of islanders that had transformed the uprooted trees on the land near the base of the lighthouse into benches and spoke with each other of fear and survival and the sound of the wind. Eva and Lucas were there, standing amongst groups of children who ran in packs, giddy with the force of change and a newness that did not hold the consequences that it held for their parents.

Suddenly, the boatman noticed that he was walking alone, and he looked from the crowd of islanders back to where the old dark-haired woman stood with her daughter. Then, with a gentle smile in his eyes, he turned back.

"That place is not for us," the old woman said to him, her gaze meeting his in the clear morning air. And when she saw him nod, the woman who had once been the oracle said, "It is time for us to go."

For many years, the young oracle who had once been called Althea had been preparing herself for this moment. There is only a place for one oracle on the island, her mother had often told her, and she had always known she would not have her mother to comfort her and keep her throughout her adult life, nor would she see her mother grown old and frail and nurse her until she passed from this life to the sea.

And yet the truth of her mother's sudden departure fell upon the young oracle like the unreality of the storm itself, and she stared and stared from her mother to the boatman and back again and could not speak. She had simply assumed the previous afternoon when this wild-haired man had appeared at their doorstep with the storm at his back, that he sought shelter with the oracle and nothing more. For how could this woman, young and beautiful and still in the dawn of her voyage, have known the power of ageing love? She had been absent from her mother's life for so many long years, and it had not occurred to her until this moment that there were many things in her mother's life and in her mother's heart that she did not know.

As the mother and her daughter waited by the shores of the silver mangroves for the boatman's craft to appear around the cove, the mother took up her daughter's hands and held them between her palms. She did not have to say, *I have lost my purpose here, Althea*, for the young oracle knew that her mother was a wise woman with the power of foresight and the wisdom to heal suffering and was not bred to be a sentimental creature. She did not have to say, *There is a place for only one oracle on the island Althea*, for the young oracle knew this truth like the lines drawn on the palms of her hands. And as the red-haired adventurer pulled his boat up to the shore and lifted his hand to the only woman he had profoundly loved, the young oracle understood that there was a new life waiting for her mother. And that was enough.

Later, the oracle and the boatman gazed at the island from a distance, across the undulating waters to the place where the land rose unexpectedly and without reason out of the sea. Across time, they watched it as it rose up from the watery depths, stood for a time among the forms of the world, and slowly dissolved back into the great sea. And then the boatman raised the sails and the wind carried them over the horizon.

GET THREE DAYS ON THE LIMINAL SEA FOR FREE!

Read a missing scene from *The Boatman* for FREE.

Three Days on the Liminal Sea is the story of Isla and Tomas's journey back from the mainland to the island:

When Tomas finds Isla on the streets of the mainland after so many years apart, he carries with him tragic news from the island of their birth. Isla must return to the island to face not only her father's death but the larger questions of life that *continue to elude her and the love of the man she left behind. It takes three days to cross that liminal sea between the mainland and the island, and during the journey, Isla questions everything she thought she believed in and everyone she thought she loved.*

Now you can read this novella for FREE. Simply sign up to my author newsletter and I'll send you the ebook. Building a relationship with my readers is one of the very best things about writing, and I occasionally send out newsletters with details on special offers, new releases and updates on my creative journey. Don't worry, I won't inundate your inbox and you can unsubscribe at any time. That said, I hope you love getting these fun tidbits from the island of my imagination and remember...I LOVE hearing from you too!)

To get your FREE eBOOK, simply head to http://eepurl.com/c4JgIj or you can email me Sarah@sarahbhunt.com

A SNEAK PEAK FROM BOOK 2...

The Colour of Losa
Chapter 1

From the deep fog of sleep, Alsi awoke. For the briefest moment she still believed everything was as it should be. She believed this waking would be like every other, and she would find herself in her blue woollen blankets with the mountains by her side. It often took only a single breath for Alsi to wake, but this time it was many breaths, many thick labouring breaths. And that was how Alsi knew something was terribly wrong.

A splinter pierced her mind with an ache she had never known, and Alsi slowly became aware that the breath that was coming and going did not feel like the cold pure mountain air she knew, but as if she was breathing heavy fog because the air itself was thick. Thick with sweat and something else that smelled foreign and sour. Claustrophobic and still.

Slowly the terrible truth spread through her mind. Slowly, not because what had happened was unclear, but because her mind rebelled against the truth of it and she tasted her opposition to the truth as its own bitter poison.

She had been taken.

She had been taken in the night. As she slept in her beautiful woollen blankets that had been made for her at the time of her birth and woven with the markings of the bear, the snow leopard, the bell, the seven snows, and the eternal knot in the hopes that she would find her destiny, they had come for her. Mainland raiders. She was not the first of her mountain people to be taken, and she knew all too well where she was headed.

Now that she too was a Lost One.

And then another thought came to her and made Alsi struggle to open her eyes though they felt like rocks in her head. Did she still have it? Was it with her? The Unseen Map she had been entrusted with as she began this journey into the deepest of places and into the heart of the mountains.

"The Lodestone..." her lips moved without a sound.

To the nescient eyes of her mainlander captors, Alsi looked only like a young mountain girl. Her small body, her exotic voice and her silver eyes would make her a treasure to some rich mainlander family who would pay a handsome bride price. *They do not know me*, Alsi thought as she struggled to sit up. *They do not know who I am or where I am going. I must get out of here. I must find the lodestone. I must get back to the mountain pass where I will be safe.*

The cart jerked, throwing Alsi onto her side and she felt the lurching movement of the horses as they pulled against their harnesses and the bumping of the wheels over the rough winding road.

This was not the direction she was meant to be travelling. She was Alsi, born under the sign of the Great Star and destined long before her birth to walk the Way. Everyone of the mountains knew the stories of the secret wisdom path. Each morning as the sunlight stretched over the snow-covered peaks, the women and men of the mountains would rise and touch their foreheads, acknowledging many things. The power of the sun to bring them another day. The power of the earth to give them life. The power of the mountains to protect the wisdom of their people.

Even as a child Alsi had known her destiny as a carrier of the Lodestone. There were many who studied the old ways, who knew the depths of the mind and the profound mysteries of the universe. But only a few in each generation of the mountain dwellers were given the sacred lodestone and shown the way to the secret stone archway where they would follow the Unseen Map through the labyrinth of the mountains to the place of pure liberation.

This isn't supposed to happen! Alsi could feel hot tears filling her silver eyes even before they had fully opened. *I haven't even begun!*

Alsi had said goodbye to her family many days ago. "You will feel our love for you in the heart of the mountains," her mother had said, looking deep into her eyes. She would never say with words "I will miss you, daughter of my life," but she had allowed her eyes to say it. Just for a moment. Just so Alsi knew. And then her mother's eyes had widened again with that deeper knowing and she had looked to the mountains. "Go well, daughter. May you find what you seek and return to us with this wisdom. May the seven snows protect you."

"And the Unseen Map guide your footsteps," her father had nodded, laying a hand upon the crown of her head. She could feel the warmth of his touch in her memory. Even now, when she breathed this heavy air that could not belong to her life. Alsi struggled again to sit up, grunting with effort. Her whole body felt heavy, as if it did not belong to her.

Suddenly a flash of light cut across her vision and she heard a man's voice. "One of them is awake. Shall I put her under again?"

More light flooded the covered cart.

"No leave her." Another voice. A harsh clapping of hands.

Alsi pulled her knees to her chest, trying to make herself very small. Around her she saw the arms and legs of other girls and she heard their laboured breathing that did not resemble sleep. For a brief moment she struggled against the rope that bound her wrists, but when she saw they would not yield she relaxed again.

I must use my mind, she thought. *I must use my mind to find some way out.*

Alsi twisted her wrist, trying to reach the inside of her arm where the Lodestone was always bound while she slept. Had they taken it already? Would they know what it was when they saw its rough hewn shape, the markings that distinguished it from any ordinary stone.

Next to her two other girls began to shift and moan, pulling themselves against all their best intentions into consciousness, and into this new despair. One sat up suddenly, gripping Alsi's leg with her fear. "Where are we?" The voice asked, though they all knew the answer. Alsi did not speak, but her silver eyes met the gaze of the frightened girl and they held each other in their mutual terror. Alsi tried again to twist her arms and reach up to feel her inner arm, but it was no use. The ropes held fast and she could not tell whether the lodestone was still with her, and whether she had any hope...

Another flash of light shot through the dark wagon and

this time it did not recede. "Get them up." She heard the voice of a mainlander and though it came to her ears with a gentle lilting tone, to Alsi it sounded threatening and full of malice. "Get them all up." And without a word, Alsi felt hands upon her again, pulling her up and tearing her away from her destiny.

Chapter 2

Isla looked out across the island, her silver eyes searching for the land she recognised in that morning after the storm. What she saw instead was a great devastation, the battlefield of violence that had been waged between the earth and the sky. The land that sloped downward from the lighthouse was strewn with tree limbs and the great tree that had always stood at the edge of the cliff lay on its side, its roots rising unnaturally into the air.

The storm had come upon them the day before like a fury from the sea, and although islanders were used to such tempests, none had seen wind with such power in their lifetime nor knew of such things from their fathers. This storm had robbed the island of its calm familiar face where the same roads of childhood led to the same destinations and the same trees and rocks and houses marked the way. It had swept the island into an ageless chaos of broken tree limbs and boards of wood that had once had a place as part of a wall to a house or a support to a roof or a post of a fence — all of it now lay strewn across the land at awkward angles, assaulting the islanders' sight with visions of a foreign land.

It was as if the very life of the land had collapsed in on itself. So many of the trees that had tried to stand strong and true, had been cracked apart, torn from their roots and left like carcasses of what they once were. Forests of pine and groves of mango and citrus trees and all the beautiful flowering trees, the hibiscus and frangipani and magnolia, so many of them had been brought down by the storm. Some of the palms and the great banyans had faired better, though even these looked battered, the palms rising like tall sticks without their fronds, the banyans stripped of many of their leaves and smaller branches.

Standing on the cliff with the lighthouse at her back, Isla reached for Tomas's hand, and for a moment they stood together in the clear morning light at the end and the beginning of the world. Gazing out out across the broken land of her childhood, Isla felt small. The morning sun shone out without a trace of malice, and Isla felt the humid heat of the island rise up all around her. And yet the clear blue sky and the return of the song of the island that was a harmony of creaking crickets and crying gulls and soft crashing waves did not comfort her.

Tomas squeezed her hand. "I will raise the light," he said, glancing up to the top of the lighthouse. His voice was like an anchor amidst the winds and waves that still echoed in Isla's mind, and when she turned to look into Tomas's face, she saw not her childhood friend looking back at her but the man Tomas had become, and in that brief moment something inside her also remembered her own strength.

She took a deep breath, and with it, grew back into her self — the self she had become when she had left this island of her birth all those years ago to seek adventure and to find her own way in the world. The self she had become through her struggle in the mainland city and, then through her work as a senior scribe leading teams of mainland administration officials into the outer realms of the Lost Regions.

In that moment and with that breath, she also grew back

into the self she had become when she had returned to the island only a few months before to face her father's death and the shadow beasts of her past. And the self she had become the night before, in the midst of the worst storm the island had ever seen, when she had finally found the strength to hold true to herself and to her heart.

Tomas's face was lit by the sun and he looked unshakeable standing beside her, as if he had weathered so many storms already he could now survive anything. But then he turned into her and wove his wide hands through the tangled curls of her wild dark hair. Pulling her into him, Tomas let out a long deep breath that shuttered as it left his body, and when she heard it Isla felt all the grief that this man held for his island which had always been the deepest part of who he was. For that short moment, she let him hold her, let his body tell her all the things that he could not.

Then his grip relaxed, and he looked down into her face. "We have a lot of work to do, Isla-ja," he said.

(*The Colour of Losa* is out now! Get your copy today to continue the journey.)

DID YOU ENJOY THE BOATMAN? YOU CAN MAKE A BIG DIFFERENCE

Honest reviews of my books help bring them to the attention of other readers and help spread the word about my book. As an independent author, readers like you make a massive difference to my creative journey and help me continue to do what I love — write more books!

If you've enjoyed this book, I would be very grateful if you could spend a few minutes leaving a review (as short as you like) on the book's Amazon page.

Thank you so very much! I know this takes time and I really appreciate it. This really does make a difference.

Sarah

ABOUT THE AUTHOR

Hi, great to meet you! I'm Sarah, an independent author and one of those who wanted to be a writer since I was a kid. I grew up in the tropics of south Florida and somehow life has brought me to the UK where I write, teach yoga and live with my Scottish husband and my two beautifully wild boys.

I make my online home at www.sarahbhunt.com, you can connect with me at:

- facebook.com/SarahBethHuntwriter
- twitter.com/sarahbhunt
- instagram.com/sarahbhunt

Printed in Poland
by Amazon Fulfillment
Poland Sp. z o.o., Wrocław